CHINA RUN

A NOVEL

DAVID BALL

SIMON & SCHUSTER

NEW YORK   LONDON   TORONTO

SYDNEY   SINGAPORE

SIMON & SCHUSTER
Rockefeller Center
1230 Avenue of the Americas
New York, NY 10020

SIMON & SCHUSTER and colophon are registered trade-
marks of Simon & Schuster, Inc.

For information about special discounts for bulk purchases,
please contact Simon & Schuster Special Sales:
1-800-456-6798 or business@simonandschuster.com.

Book design by Ellen R. Sasahara
Manufactured in the United States of America

10 9 8 7 6 5 4 3 2 1

Library of Congress Cataloging-in-Publication Data

ISBN 0-7432-2743-3

ACKNOWLEDGMENTS

TO COME

DEDICATION TO COME

PROLOGUE

SHAO LIN was haunted by the memory of the bitter winter when she had dug a shallow grave for the baby. A rare cold front had descended from Mongolia and turned the sky that day as cold and leaden as her soul. She'd scratched through the snow and pawed at the frozen earth until her fingers bled. Hot tears mingled with her blood. The hole was soon big enough, because the bundle was so small.

A girl, it was. Xiao Xi. A small happiness.

But there was no happiness at all. With permission for only one child, the child must not be a girl. A woman came into the world to bear sons, not daughters. Sons to carry on the family name. Sons to inherit the family's possessions. Sons to support parents in old age and then to sweep their graves. Daughters married away, worthless. For a hundred generations it had been so.

"So you are your mother's daughter after all," her husband raged when she called out to him that his firstborn was a girl. "You are cursed!" It was true. Her mother had borne four girls and no boys. Her mother's mother had six children—all girls. He had worried the affliction ran in her family.

The face of her mother-in-law was grim as she took the baby. "I will do it," she told Shao Lin. But she had not had to do a thing. The baby made it easy. There was something in her throat, something in the way—mucus, perhaps—and she wasn't breathing right. She was choking and needed a slap. The mother-in-law set her down and turned away. The baby went blue and stopped struggling.

Afterward Shao Lin trudged through frozen fields to the hilltop where her husband's great-grandfather was buried beneath a rubble of stone. It was no longer permitted to bury the dead in the ground. Land was too valuable. She should have set the body in the Yangtze, where it would slip away to the sea. But

9

she didn't care about that. She'd done enough that day for her family. She'd done enough that day for China. She'd done enough that day for a lifetime.

There was another memory. Another permission from the government, long awaited, when for a time they stopped tracking her periods on the chalkboard in the village. Another baby was being allowed into the district.

Their baby.

This time her husband wanted to know. They took savings from the box beneath the bed. She traveled all the way to Jiangyin on the back of a cart to see the doctor. He had an ultrasound machine. Everyone used them now, said the old women of the village. Ultrasounds could find girl babies before they were born, and then the easy thing could be done. They made her drink water until she was near bursting and then helped her onto a cold steel table. The doctor rubbed her belly with jelly and pressed a cup to her skin. She strained to see the gray mass moving about on the little black-and-white screen. After a time the doctor nodded and pointed at something.

Shao Lin saw only a smudge. The doctor said the smudge was a girl.

She had an abortion while her husband waited in the hallway outside. She closed her eyes to the cold steel and the doctor's rough hands and told herself it was the best thing.

But the ultrasound fooled the doctor. The dead child was a boy.

Her husband went crazy with grief and anger. He left without her, left her alone on the table. For a whole week her mother-in-law wouldn't let her into the house, so she slept in the straw near the sun-warmed mud walls outside, next to the goats and the sheep.

The next time she left home, to have the baby alone. The child was born in an orange grove beneath a bright sun and cried loudly through strong lungs. When Shao Lin saw it was another girl, she thought about killing herself with the knife she'd used for the cord. It seemed the only way. She couldn't let the child destroy their family, their lives. She couldn't keep it and she couldn't kill it. If she abandoned it, she might spend years in prison.

Shao Lin thought of her cousin, in Suzhou. She was shunned by the family, rumored to be a woman who knew the night streets. To Shao Lin it didn't matter. She needed help and there was nowhere else to turn.

She wrapped the child in warm blankets and walked down the path to the big road, where a farmer gave her a ride on the back of his wagon. He smiled broadly at the child. "A blessing," he said. As they bounced along country roads, the baby fed at her breast and then slept. Shao Lin saw she was beautiful but tried not to look at her face because it was too difficult to look away again. She covered the child and stared dully out at the passing cabbage fields. She spent the night at Shengang town and caught a bus the next morning.

Suzhou was crowded, everything fast and frightening. She had an address. She hunched over as she wandered the streets, trying to hide her baby—her crime—from view. Whenever she saw a policeman she turned away, terrified that somehow he might see into her heart and know her intentions. But no one stopped her. No one challenged her. Finally a shopkeeper pointed the way.

Her cousin was a weary, kind woman who was surprised and pleased to see her. If she was a whore, Shao Lin saw no sign of it. The woman listened sympathetically as Shao Lin unburdened herself. "I do know a man," she said.

He arrived that afternoon. His face was fleshy and pockmarked. He wore a baggy Western suit and smelled of fish. Shao Lin disliked him instinctively. When he stripped the child naked, to examine her, Shao Lin's resolve nearly collapsed. She reached for the child, but her cousin restrained her. "There is no choice better than this one," she whispered.

The man looked up. "I'll go if you want," he said. "But if you leave her on the steps of the hospital, we'll get her anyway. This way there's something in it for you."

"What will happen to her?"

"She'll live," he said simply.

Satisfied with the child, the man wrapped her once again in blankets. He did it quickly, without tenderness. He took a wad of bills from his pocket and peeled off a few. He thrust them at Shao Lin. Without thinking she started to reach for them, then faltered, horrified and ashamed. He tossed the bills onto the floor at her feet. He grunted a good-bye to Shao Lin's cousin. As he opened the door a lusty wail erupted from the blanket. He paid no attention. The door closed behind him. Sobbing uncontrollably, Shao Lin slumped to the floor. Her cousin picked up the bills and put them in a drawer.

Shao Lin sat on the floor until dusk. Several times she retched, needing to throw up, but nothing would come. She declined her cousin's offer for a meal and a night's rest.

When she was strong enough, she stood up. She fled from the house and into the night.

*   *   *

That night a phone rang at a walled compound outside Suzhou.

"Wei?"

"I have another one," said the man with the pockmarked face. "Off the books."

"Yes?"

"This one is perfect. Only two days old. Healthy and well formed. Her mother was exquisite."

"Very good."

"I . . . I want more for this one."

There was a long silence on the line. "We shall see. Bring her to me."

Shao Lin lied to her husband and to the population control officer, saying the baby died in childbirth. Her husband returned to his fields. The population control officer asked no questions because she didn't care about the answers.

No baby meant the quotas were safe.

CHAPTER 1

SUZHOU
Jiangsu Province
The People's Republic of China
May 1996

I T BEGAN the way it always had in her nightmare, the very same way it had begun once before. There was a knock at the door.

Allison Turk barely stirred in her bed. Even five days after arriving in China, she was jet-lagged. Her body was completely mixed up, and now she was lost in the deep sleep of exhaustion. Then the baby gave a little cry and Allison startled awake instantly. She blinked and tried to clear her head. Had she heard something before Wen Li's cry? The room was dark, the curtains drawn.

It had been a difficult night. She'd tried to cut the baby's fingernails and clipped a bit of skin right off her finger. Wen Li bled, but it was Allison who cried, feeling stupid and clumsy and despairing of ever being a good mother. And then as they sat on the bathroom floor while Allison tried to bandage the wound, which wasn't much but seemed awful to her fearful eyes, Wen Li had toppled off her lap and banged her head on the tub, and then they were both hurt and crying. To top it off, Wen Li had then developed a fever and rash and spent a restless few hours. The fever had broken quickly, but even so Allison had been up every twenty minutes to make sure she was still all right, still breathing. It was three o'clock before she drifted off to a fitful sleep.

The knock came again. More quickly now. Insistent.

Allison threw back her covers and sat up. The blanket in the crib was bunched up and she could see just a tuft of dark hair and a tiny bare arm

13

wrapped around Pooh. Wen Li hadn't let loose of the bear since they'd met. Allison watched until the blanket moved, almost imperceptibly. In the other twin bed Tyler slept the sleep of the dead in the way only a nine-year-old could. It would take more of an earthquake than a knock at the door to wake him before ten.

She put on her bathrobe and crossed the room, reaching for the knob just as the knocking began again. She opened the door and pulled her bathrobe tighter. It was Nash Cameron, another of the parents in her group who had come to adopt a baby. He was abrupt and pushy. He treated his wife, Claire, with coldness and even his new daugther, Katie, with seeming indifference. He offered no greeting and didn't wait for her to say anything.

"There's a problem. It could be bad. We're meeting in my room."

Allison blinked, trying to wake up. "What? What do you mean? Meeting? What kind of—"

But he cut her off, turning abruptly and darting back down the hall, calling over his shoulder, urgency in his voice, "Hurry up!" He moved quickly in the dim hallway. He stopped at Ruth Pollard's room and knocked again. Ruth was another of the new adoptive parents. Her baby was beautiful, tiny and frail. Her name was Tai. Ruth called her the Wee Duck.

Allison closed the door and felt the first stirrings of dread. From the beginning she had worried something would go wrong. So many things could happen, just as they had before . . . She forced the thought away. She hurriedly pulled on her jogging clothes, wondering whether to wake Tyler and Wen Li and bring them along. She'd never left them alone. She glanced at her watch: just past seven. The Camerons' room was next door. She decided to let the children sleep. She wrote a quick note for Tyler, telling him where she'd be, and propped it on the little writing desk.

At the sink she washed the sleep out of her eyes and brushed her hair. She regarded herself in the mirror. Dark circles under her eyes showed the strain of travel. Her face was puffy. She looked awful. Too many jets, too many bus rides, too much stress. She shrugged. There was nothing she could do about it. She could regain herself when she got back to Denver, when Marshall would be there to help.

She closed the door softly behind her, pocketing the plastic card that was the electronic room key. The Chinese had surprised her with their modern hotels. She'd expected something more like skeleton keys. There was much about China that surprised her.

The door to the Camerons' room was ajar. Allison knocked lightly and walked in. The little room was full to overflowing with the five other American families who had come to adopt Chinese children. They had traveled together for much of the trip from the States, visiting the same orphanage to pick up their babies. Through a numbing blur of endless days they had shared airlines and cramped bus seats and diapers and teething stories and tips about Chinese microbes. Most were not friends but forced fellow travelers, making the best of their company and now counting the days until they could return to the States and begin their own private lives with their babies.

Claire Cameron sat on a chair next to the crib where her new daughter, Katie, slept. She was a quiet woman, dominated completely by her husband. When she spoke it was to complain about the hotel, the streets, the markets, and the fact that so few Chinese had the good manners to speak English. She'd been crying. Ruth Pollard sat on the bed holding her daughter, Tai, who was still asleep. Ruth was a single mother who had made the trip to China alone, just as she intended to raise Tai alone. It took guts and stamina and a certain lunacy to do that, and Allison liked her. Next to Ruth sat Wally and Ruthann Jackson. Allison knew them as Bible thumpers from Montana, harmless enough but annoying with their constant preaching, especially when they tried it on the Chinese, who responded with strained politeness. Barry and Ceil Levin were Amway distributors from Minnesota who said little and kept to themselves. Roger and Cindy Lawton were ranchers from East Texas. He was a bigot and a bore whose venom never ran dry.

The tension in the room was palpable, its occupants tired and fearful at the abrupt summons. Nash closed the door behind Allison, then faced the group.

"Yi Ling called me twenty minutes ago and asked that I get us all together," he said. Yi Ling was their Chinese interpreter and guide. She'd been with them every step of the way, first meeting them at the airport, then translating and negotiating and helping them in a country where they couldn't find a bathroom without assistance. She'd been superb. "The director of the orphanage called her late last night. He was meeting with an official from the province. I didn't understand who the official was, exactly. Someone from the Ministry of Civil Affairs, I think. Anyway, he told her a mistake had been made with our babies."

The room erupted, everyone talking at once. "What do you mean a mistake? *Another* damned screwup? What kind of mistake this time?"

asked Roger Lawton. Nash waved his hand impatiently, dismissing questions for which he had no answers.

"I'm not certain. Something to do with special-needs families getting healthy babies."

Allison caught her breath at that. It was true, one of the regulations of the Chinese government. She had expected a child with some sort of handicap—a heart murmur, a hernia, or simply an older child, a toddler—something besides a healthy infant. Under Chinese law adoptive parents had to be at least thirty-five and have no other children in order to qualify for healthy babies. Otherwise they qualified only for the special-needs children. But the rule was loose and so many babies needed adoption that somehow everyone in their group had gotten a healthy infant. Of course, no one questioned it and the issue hadn't arisen during their trip.

The Chinese had sent Wen Li's medical report to Allison and Marshall six weeks earlier, along with a tiny snapshot of a bewildered-looking infant. It was all Allison had to go on then, all she had to know her new baby. She and Marshall had had to make their decision to adopt on the basis of just the photo and the one-page typewritten report. Allison had made dozens of blowups of the photograph and shipped them excitedly to everyone she knew. She read the report a hundred times: *Height: 60 cm. Weight: 5.9 kg. Eyes, ears, throat: normal Teeth: none. Lip and palate: normal. Heart, lung, kidney and spleen.*

On it went in dry style, ticking off the particulars of a thirteen-pound Chinese mystery. The report was five months old, but she read it in bed at night with Marshall, trying to paint flesh and blood and character onto the dispassionate report with the brush of her imagination. She showed it to her pediatrician, who pronounced everything fine "on the surface," he said. Then she worried about what the Chinese doctor had missed. She'd heard the exams were so superficial that the baby might be retarded or deaf and they wouldn't notice.

It was a crap shoot, adopting a baby made from someone else's genes, and it worried her sick. "It's a crap shoot giving birth to a baby made from your own genes," Marshall reminded her. She fretted and paced and dreamed and hoped.

She looked at the photograph for hours. She talked to it, sharing family secrets. She stared at it at night, where it was propped by her alarm. She smiled at it in the morning, at the baby peeking from her perch beneath the refrigerator magnet. She hummed to it from the shower, where she could see the child looking innocently back from her niche on the bathroom mirror. From each angle Allison saw something new in her features. At night the child looked pensive. In the morning she looked afraid. There was charm and personality in her face and quick wit in her eyes. She imagined the baby's history a hundred ways. Had she been loved or abused? At an orphanage or with a foster family? Was she from a farm or a city? What was her mother like? Had her ankles been branded so that her birth mother might identify her someday, as she heard was so common?

A thousand questions raced in her mind, questions for which there would never be answers. A thousand doubts crowded in as well. She worried that she wouldn't love the baby or that the baby wouldn't love her. She worried that she wouldn't be a good mother, that the baby might need something and she wouldn't realize it and the child would go on wanting, deprived, saddled with a mother who couldn't read the signs of need because she wasn't of her own flesh and blood. Crazy worries, irrational worries, stubborn worries that wouldn't let go. She worried too about Tyler, about how a nine-year-old would react to losing center stage, and she worried about Marshall. Was this *her* dream more than his? Was it *her* need, more than his, to adopt? Was she selfish to want a child? Upsetting a wonderful family in order to do it?

Over the weeks she fell in love with the child in the photograph but never framed it, because somehow a frame was permanent, and until it was all settled she knew nothing was permanent. She'd made that mistake before, decorating a nursery for an expected baby, then suffering the empty room when the baby died. She'd made the same mistake a second time, thinking a baby was hers before it really was and then losing her, too. A frame was the same thing.

Then had come the long trip to China and the anxious ride to the orphanage, and the electric moment when the auntie held up the little bundle. Trembling, Allison pulled back the blankets. Wen Li had dark hair, thick and wild as if it had been freeze-dried in some bizarre poked-out pincushion fashion. Combing didn't help; the hair was short and popped back up, spring-loaded. She had great dark oval eyes, so soft and liquid that Allison felt she could go swimming in them, eyes that were alive and curious and held all the intelligence and spirit she had prayed for.

Then came the careful count of fingers, and at the very first possible moment, with Tyler helping her in their hotel room, Allison had stripped her down for a bath. She was shaking in excitement, nervous and full of wonder and hope and dread at the squirming child. Everything was normal and pink and *there,* as she'd so desperately hoped it would be. The knees and elbows all worked, and while Wen Li was being poked and prodded she peed all over Allison and flashed a wicked grin. Tyler laughed and Allison's heart melted instantly: she had a healthy nine-month-old with a sense of humor and without so much as a cold. She blessed her luck and held her child and felt a fool for worrying.

While waiting for papers they'd spent four wonderful days together in the hotel. Allison began to learn to read those little eyes that flashed want or showed need, eyes that laughed or demanded, eyes that could be angry or content, hurt or just sleepy. Every so often Wen Li would do her hooker blink, a slow, sexy, luxuriant blink, as if she'd been taught to do it in some high-end brothel and it was the most natural thing in the world, and it made Allison laugh out loud.

On the third day Tyler propped her up between pillows, announcing he was going to teach her to sit up. He gave her careful instructions in English and then let go. Wen Li gamely held her position for an instant, then crumpled like a sock. After a few tries she got too close to the edge of the bed and tumbled off. Allison caught her in midair, swooping her up just in time. Wen Li shrieked in wild delight through her five and a half teeth. Their eyes met and their souls touched somewhere, and in that instant they knew it was perfect.

Marshall was a fly fisherman, and usually he threw everything back. Sometimes, though, he'd hook one that he couldn't give up, a fish he just had to bring home. *A keeper,* he'd call it.

Allison knew that's what she had, too: an undersize, wild-haired, can't-sit-up keeper.

The orphanage had named her Wen Li. Allison and Marshall liked it and added Maria. Wen Li Maria Turk. Onetime orphan of China, future American citizen.

Yes, perfect.

Only now perfection was a problem.

Nash looked at his watch for the fifth time in less than two minutes. "Ms. Yi said she'd be here by now."

Ceil Levin stood up. "I'll make some coffee," she said.

She busied herself with the thermos of hot water and the glasses and the bitter bags of instant Nescafé that were all they could get. As she was handing them out, Ms. Yi arrived. She was a small woman even by Chinese standards. She was in her mid-thirties, her hair jet black and her skin so perfect that it seemed to glow. She doted on the babies. She spent every spare moment with the different families, helping with their adjustment as if she'd been a mother a dozen times, even though she had no children. She was a magician, able to find medicine in the middle of the night or special formula or arrange an impromptu tour of the lovely gardens and canals of Suzhou. She was their unflappable escort, able to deal with the pains of group travel and government bureaucracy with grace and ease.

That was the Yi Ling they knew, but now they could all see something had shaken her composure. She looked haggard and worried. Allison thought she'd been crying. She gave a polite little bow, looking around the room and smiling at each of them.

"I am so sorry to have disturb you so early," she began. Her English was halting but clear. "This is most distressing, I'm afraid. I do not know how to explain, exactly." It was clear she was struggling. It was not polite to be so blunt, to state the point so directly, but Yi Ling had no choice: there was no time for normal manners. "There is some—some controversy in the local government, I think. Between the Ministry of Civil Affairs and the Ministry of Justice." Both departments were jockeying for influence in the foreign adoption process in China. Their fights had led to delays and conflicting regulations. The wrangling had become painfully familiar to foreign adoptive families during the previous few months. "An official of the Civil Affairs has reviewed each file in the province. He inform Director Lin of the Suzhou orphanage that this group has the"— she groped for the right word—"the incorrect babies."

"What the hell do you mean—" began Roger Lawton, but Nash cut him off:

"Let her finish."

Yi Ling nodded. "He say only babies with problem or older babies should come with this group. Not healthy babies. He say you give babies back. He say"—she waited a moment, until the gasps and cries had subsided—"he say you get other babies, Monday morning. Good babies, he promise."

Allison felt the blood rushing in her head. For a moment she thought she hadn't heard correctly. Then her knees went weak and she half collapsed, half sat on the bed.

Oh, dear God, not again. Please, not again.

Ruth Pollard was suddenly holding Tai much closer. The baby stirred and gave a soft cry. Ruthann Jackson mumbled a prayer. There was silence then as the shock of Yi Ling's words settled over the room.

"Jesus Christ," breathed Roger Lawton at last. "I knew this would get screwed up somehow."

Yi Ling looked at the carpet and said nothing.

"I don't want a different baby," Claire Cameron said plaintively to no one in particular. She reached over the rail of the crib, her hand on Katie's hair. "They can't do this. Can they?"

"This is a god-awful joke." Barry Levin's face was red and his hands were shaking visibly. His wife, Ceil, let her coffee cup slip from her grasp. It fell to the carpet and she began to cry.

Yi Ling was mortally embarrassed but steeled herself to her duty. "Of course I would never joke about such a thing," she said earnestly. "I am so sorry. Director Lin is bringing a van to collect the babies. They will be here at eight. We must be ready then, in the lobby."

Suddenly everyone was talking at once. Eight o'clock! Less than an hour. A time on a clock made it all suddenly real.

"What can we do?"

"Nothing, I think, until Monday. Then perhaps we can talk with the ministry and make it right. We will call Beijing, of course." Yi Ling tried to hide her discouragement, to sound hopeful. She'd already been up most of the night trying to fix it and felt defeated.

"Is this legal? Can they do this, Nash?" asked Claire Cameron.

"Who knows? I suppose they can do whatever they want, and then make it legal afterward." He stared out the window. "It's their law, their country. And we have no papers yet making the adoptions final." They had been waiting for the notaries, the Chinese lawyers, to complete the certificates of abandonment and adoption, the papers that would allow them to obtain Chinese passports for the babies and then American visas. The papers should have been completed two days earlier. No one understood the delay, but no one was particularly concerned. Their travel schedules allowed time for unforeseen delays. "Expect the unexpected," the adoption agency told them repeatedly.

Nash paced, restless and thinking. "Until the notaries are done, nothing is official. Not under anyone's law—Chinese or American."

"But *they* told us which babies! *They* sent us pictures and medical reports! *They* told us everything was ready!" It was Cindy Lawton. Like the rest of them, she'd had six weeks to stare at the two papers announcing the identity and health of her baby.

"Well, *they* fucked up," growled Roger Lawton. "Or lied." He glared at his wife. He lowered his voice somewhat, but the others still heard. "I told you we should have gone to Russia to do this. We could have gotten a white baby, too. You should have listened." His wife flushed at his words. She started to say something but then closed her eyes and rocked back and forth.

"Shut up, Roger," Allison flared.

Barry Levin shook his head. "How did someone like you ever get past a social worker?"

"Social workers are as stupid as—" Lawton began.

"Be quiet!" snapped Nash. "And think! What are we going to do?"

"What *can* we do?" Levin asked. "Hold the Chinese authorities back at the door? We have no rights here. We're in the country at their invitation. You said yourself we have no papers. Nothing is legal yet. The babies don't belong to us. There's no decision to make. We have to give them back, as they ask." He paced, thinking. "Look, I know Jack Fentress in the consular section at the embassy in Beijing. We were roommates in school. I haven't talked to him in a few years, but I'm pretty sure he's still there. I'll call him Monday. He'll help us get this mess sorted out."

"And if he doesn't?" asked Nash.

"He will. This is just some royal bureaucratic screwup. Even a third world government can't be this crazy."

"Like hell they can't. This one's been crazy for a very long time."

"They said they'd give us other babies, right?" Levin asked Ms. Yi, grasping for the only hopeful thing in what she'd said.

Yi Ling nodded. "There are many children. Good children."

"Well, that's not the end of the world, then, is it?" Levin said, trying to lift his wife's spirits. "These are wonderful babies we have. We've all gotten attached to them, but they aren't ours and there are others who need us, others just as deserving. We'll get attached to them, too, and love them just as much."

"Why can't we keep these babies until Monday, until we can be sure that this is what must happen?" Ceil asked. "Then we can see about it all."

"This I have already tried," said Ms. Yi. "It is why I was late arriving. I was asking the officials for delay. No one would listen to me. Even Director Lin. In such matters he have no choice. He must follow ministry order. He say the longer we wait, the more difficult the task. He say we must do it this way."

"*Difficult!*" Claire Cameron laughed bitterly. "How can they be so cruel? God, I hate this place."

"Is not the same people," said Ms. Yi, knowing that her words were meaningless, that the distinction didn't really matter. "Director Lin was in discussion for much of the night with the ministry. He is as upset as you at this directive." In fact Yi Ling had thought Director Lin surprisingly cold and unmoved as he delivered the startling edict, but she was too polite to say so.

"*Upset?*" Ceil Levin said derisively. "*He's* upset? These aren't *his* children."

"They aren't ours, either." Barry Levin's voice carried the gentle reproof of reality. Already resigned to the unfathomable ruling, he put his hand on his wife's. "We've no choice, Ceil. We have to give her back. We'll try to work it out Monday. Even if we can't, at the very least we'll get another baby. It'll be all right, you'll see." Ceil nodded as she wiped away the tears welling in her eyes. There was nothing else to do, of course. She squeezed his hand.

For a while no one said anything. In the silence Tai woke up and began to cry. She coughed raggedly and Ruth turned her over and patted her on the back, trying to clear her rattling airways. Ruth was in her late forties, short and a bit heavyset, her hair thick like graying steel wool. Everyone liked her. She was the toughest of them all, everybody's favorite aunt. She'd been up long nights with her baby, giving her the medicine the doctors had prescribed for her upper-respiratory infection, trying at the same time to get her over a case of prickly heat, a severe diaper rash, and an ear infection. Ruth had stamina befitting a mother half her age and showed none of the strain she had to be feeling. She was simply determined to get Tai through it: fatigue had no place. They'd all taken turns helping. Even Yi Ling had stayed up all one night with Tai, mixing formula and medicine and drawing soothing baths of oatmeal for the prickly heat. Tai was a fighter, but she was frail. Just when one problem seemed under control, another one arose. Ruth had been counting the days until she could get her back to the United States.

"Surely they can't mean me," Ruth said. "Not Tai, I mean—she's sick, you know? She's not—"

"I am sorry," Yi Ling said. "I asked that, too. They say Tai qualifies as healthy. Her problems only temporary."

Ruth's eyes clouded and she whispered something so softly that only Allison heard. "I can't give her back," she said. "She'll die if I give her back. I know she will." Tai stopped coughing and Ruth turned her over again, sitting her up on her lap. Tai smiled and reached up, trying to pull the glasses off Ruth's nose, her tiny hand waving wildly. Ruth found a bottle of juice in her bag and Tai settled for that instead.

"I just can't do it," Ruth repeated, this time loudly enough for the others to hear. Allison saw her hands were trembling.

"Well, I can," said Roger Lawton. He pulled one of the little airline bottles of Scotch off the glass shelf above the room refrigerator and twisted off the cap. He downed it quickly and reached for another. "We're not waiting for another baby. We're going to give her back and then we're leaving," he told his wife. "Screw the bastards. Screw them all."

"She has a name, Roger," his wife said softly, defeated. "She's Annie. Call her that, will you?"

"Well, you'd best forget it before you get more attached. Annie's an American name, and she's not American and she's never going to be American. She's going back in half an hour and she can goddamn well get her old name back, whatever it was."

"This is God's will, Ruthann," said Wally Jackson, trying to comfort his wife, who was still praying and holding their baby. "He has a plan for us."

"I know it," she nodded, sniffling. "His will be—"

Allison couldn't take any more. Her temples were throbbing. They weren't accomplishing anything here. She needed to get back to her room, to Wen Li and Tyler, to think, to make some phone calls. She willed herself to get up. She crossed to the door on uncertain feet, stepping over legs and around chairs. "They can't take her," she mumbled, shaking her head. "They just can't." Nash Cameron watched her intently. She closed the door hard behind her and ran down the hallway. She fumbled with the plastic card. Finally the light winked green and the clock clicked and she was inside. The children were still sleeping. She closed her eyes and stood with her back to the door, leaning against it for support. Her heart was racing. She was nauseated with fear.

Oh, dear God not again. Please, not again, not three times. I'll die if it happens a third time.

She had to do something. Quickly.

There's no time.

Call Marshall.

She flew to the desk and pulled open her bag, flipping through the plastic envelopes as she hunted the credit card. Damn it! Why couldn't she ever find it? Then she had it and picked up the phone, punching in the endless string of numbers for international access. Her hand shook as she dialed, and she knew she was losing the fight against the panic rising inside. Her breath was shallow, her insides in turmoil. With everything else, Wen Li was beginning to wake up.

The syrupy singsong recording was maddeningly slow. "Thank you for using AT&T," it said. "Please dial the area code and number you wish, followed by your ten-digit access number and your PIN . . ." Drone, drone, drone. Hastily she began to dial, then had to start over when she realized she'd hit a wrong key.

"Damn!" she muttered, and as she began again Wen Li started to cry. Allison closed her eyes, set the phone in its cradle, and went quickly to the crib. Wen Li saw her and smiled. Allison felt the wave of overpowering tenderness she experienced every time she saw the baby. She lifted her gently and held her close. "Wen Li," she whispered, closing her eyes. "Mama's here. It's all right."

But it wasn't all right. Nothing was right, nothing at all.

There wasn't even a bottle ready. There hadn't been time to make one. Allison went back to the desk, holding Wen Li with one arm while she propped the phone receiver on her shoulder and tried to finish dialing. For a moment she wasn't sure where she'd left off. She closed her eyes and willed her heart to slow down. *Calm down, calm down.* She kept dialing, praying she'd hit the right keys.

There was a delay, and then a hollow sound on the wire, and she knew she had it. After more long seconds the phone began to ring.

Wen Li started to fuss. She was hungry. "There there . . ." She slipped Wen Li down onto her knee and propped her there, bouncing her lightly up and down, trying to entertain her.

No answer. *Come on, Marshall. Answer the phone.* Wen Li grabbed at the cord and nearly yanked it from Allison's grip. She could be so strong for such a little thing. Allison strained to stand up, shifting Wen Li onto her hip and trying gently to get the cord away.

At the other end she heard the phone pick up. "Marshall?" she blurted, and then she realized it was the recording.

"You've reached the Turks," her own voice said to her from seven thousand miles away. "We can't come to the phone just now. If you'll leave your name and number . . ."

In despair she waited for the recording to finish. She never knew machines could take so long. *Marshall, please be there. Please.* After the beep she started talking. "Marshall, are you home? . . . Marshall, pick up! Please! . . . Marshall, pick up the phone!" But she knew it was in vain. Marshall wasn't there. He wasn't here with her and he wasn't there, either. He wasn't going to pick up the phone. Her mind raced. "Marshall, I need you, there's trouble. If you get this message in the next half hour"—she looked at her watch and did the time conversion, fifteen hours minus—"if you get this by five your time, call me at the hotel. We're still in Suzhou. Marshall, please, quickly!"

She wondered if she should tell him what was happening, to give him an idea, a head start. Marshall was an attorney, accustomed to crises, to thinking quickly, dealing quickly. He would have been in the room with her right now, taking charge, but a severe ear infection and fever had kept him home at the last moment. She decided there was nothing to be gained from it. Just as she decided, her silence triggered the automatic switch on the other end anyway. The machine hung up on her. At that instant she realized she should have told him Tyler was all right. God, she'd probably give him a heart attack, her voice all panic and no details. She started to dial him back, but her eyes fell on the alarm clock by her bed.

Seven-forty. *Twenty minutes.*

Marshall would have to wait.

Still holding Wen Li, she ran to her big suitcase on its stand near the desk. She threw aside the clothes, looking for the little packet of adoption papers. She found it and struggled to open it with one hand. Wen Li was getting louder now, more impatient. Allison needed help. She turned to other bed. "Tyler! Tyler, wake up!" she called, desperate. She shook him on the shoulder. "Tyler, I need you to take Wen Li for a minute. Can you make her a bottle? . . . Tyler, wake up!" Tyler stirred, but that was all.

She bounced Wen Li a little more, trying to entertain her. She spilled the papers out onto the desk and pushed them around until she found the one she was looking for. At the bottom was the number of the American consulate in Guangzhou. As she sat down at the phone she realized she didn't know how to make a call inside China. She opened the desk drawer and pulled out the hotel's welcome booklet, flipping through until she found the right page. "Local calls charged to the room . . . long-distance domestic calls charged to the room, please dial eight, then . . ."

Again she punched at the numbers, forcing herself to go more slowly so that she wouldn't make a mistake.

The phone was silent for a moment, and then there was a fast beeping. The circuits were busy. In frustration she slammed down the phone. She thought for a moment, then picked it up and dialed O. After three rings the hotel operator picked up.

"Ni hao," came the friendly voice. "Hello."

"Yes," Allison said. "I need a telephone number, please, for the American embassy in Beijing. Can you get it for me?"

"Ni hao," the operator repeated helpfully, adding a string of Chinese.

"Do you understand me? I need help with a number."

"Nummer?" came the tentative reply. "Room service?"

"A telephone number," Allison said slowly, drawing a deep breath and forcing herself to be patient. Some of the operators spoke excellent English, and some of them . . . well, some of them spoke excellent Chinese. "I need you to find me a telephone number," she repeated as clearly as she could.

"Plenty, please," replied the operator. "Moment." Allison waited, assuming the operator was asking a supervisor for help. Moments passed and nothing happened. Her anxiety mounted, and then suddenly she heard a dial tone. The line was dead.

Angrily she slammed down the receiver. Wen Li was squirming and miserable. Allison wanted to shut everything off, to cover her head, to start the day over. She couldn't believe this was happening.

"Tyler! Wake up!"

She picked up the phone again and dialed the consulate in Guangzhou. There was a silence again, and finally she heard the phone ringing. At the same instant there was a knock at the door.

"Tyler! Can you get the door?" She stretched with the cord and nudged at him with her foot.

"Hunh?" Tyler stirred again.

"Get the door, please!" Tyler sat up and rubbed his eyes. He looked confused and grumpy. "Get the door!" she said again.

The phone picked up. "Thank you for calling the consulate of the United States of America," said the recording. "Our office hours are from eight to five, Monday through Friday. If you know the extension you are dialing and you have a touch-tone phone, you may dial that extension now. If you are a Chinese national and want visa information, dial 225. If you are an American businessman and need assistance from the consul's office, dial 221. If you are an American citizen and this is an emergency, please call . . ." She reached for a pen and scribbled down the number, her heart sinking. She was running out of time.

Damn all machines, she thought.

Tyler opened the door at last and Nash Cameron stepped in. His expression told her to get off the phone. Allison finished copying the number and hung up.

"They're going to be here in fifteen minutes," Nash said. "The others are going to meet downstairs. Are you coming or what?"

All she wanted to do was panic, or cry. Instead she looked at Tyler. "Tyler, make a bottle for your sister," she said.

"She isn't my sister," Tyler said. He hadn't wanted a baby sister from the moment the subject had arisen in Denver, and he hadn't showed signs of softening in Wen Li's presence. Every day was a challenge for Allison, trying to get him to accept Wen Li, trying to get him even to accept Allison herself. She was only his stepmother. He was Marshall's son by his first wife, and Tyler was a long way from being comfortable with her. "You said I wouldn't have to do anything for her," he reminded her, a tone of bitter accusation in his voice.

"I know I did, Tyler. But please. I need your help. I need to talk to Mr. Cameron."

"*Dad* wouldn't make me do it."

"Well, he isn't here right now. *Please.*"

Tyler grumped and muttered something under his breath, but he picked up the thermos of water the hotel kept hot and went into the bathroom, where the formula and bottles were kept. She heard him making the formula.

"What are you going to do?" Nash repeated. "We haven't much time."

At that moment the awful reality of it all swept over her as she felt Wen Li squirming on her shoulder. *They want to take her away. Take her away in a van, back to the orphanage, to exchange her for another child.* It was all too horrible, too sudden, too fast.

"I don't know," she said truthfully, knowing how weak she must sound. She swept the hair out of her eyes and shook her head. "I just don't know." She'd never felt such helplessness, such confusion and uncertainty.

She needed time—time to think, time to figure out what to do. She looked again at the clock.

Fifteen minutes.

She heard something fall in the bathroom and a splash. "Dang it!" Tyler cursed. He'd dropped the bottle and made it Wen Li's fault. "I *hate* her!" Allison tried not to listen.

"I'm not going to do it," said Nash.

"What do you mean?"

"Just that. I'm not giving in so easily. We've got to get out of here. We can go to Shanghai. There's a consulate there. It'll be open Monday. They'll help us."

"I was just trying to call the consulate in Guangzhou. They're closed, but I got the number for the duty officer."

Nash grunted. "You're wasting your time. All you'll get on a weekend is some junior clerk. Even if you can reach him, he won't be of any use. He'll fill out a form and promise to notify somebody important. He'll tell you to do what the authorities say to do. What else *can* he say? He sure isn't going to tell you to flip off the Chinese. Besides, before you can even half explain the situation, the orphanage people are going to be knocking on this door," Nash said. He tapped his watch. "Allison! It's Saturday morning. Thirteen minutes until eight. They haven't left us enough time to do anything except what they want. Don't you think they knew that? They're pushing us around, just like they do everyone. We don't have to let them, Allison."

She fought back her panic. It seemed hopeless. Nash paused and looked at Wen Li. "If you give her up now, you'll never see her again. We have to take the babies, Allison. We have to leave."

The notion stunned Allison. It was too much, too fast. "Jesus, Nash," she breathed at last. "This is *China*."

He shrugged, as if the thought were of no concern. "We're only going to Shanghai," he said. "It's eighty miles! How big a deal can that be? How much trouble can we get in just going to see our own government? And what choice have they left us?"

Allison's agony raged between disbelief and hope. Something inside her refused to believe what Nash was saying. There had to be another way, a different plan. Yet the more she thought about it, the more she hoped he might be right. "Claire agrees?"

"Claire does what I say. She's packing. Look, I'm not going to beg you or argue with you. You can come along or you can go downstairs with the others. I don't really care. I think our position will be stronger in Shanghai if there are more of us, but the others have already caved in. God and the white race and the law and all that," he said sarcastically, referring to the Jacksons and the Lawtons and the Levins. "Anyway, I'll be at the stairway in five minutes. I thought I'd extend the invitation. It's up to you." He turned and left, pulling the door closed behind him.

"I'm not cleaning up this mess," Tyler announced from the bathroom. He emerged a moment later carrying Wen Li's bottle. Formula powder covered his arms and smudged his cheeks.

"It's all right," Allison said, taking it from him. "Thanks." Wen Li settled on her lap and began drinking eagerly. For the first time since Allison's rude awakening that morning, she clung to a moment of peace. She brushed the hair back out of her face and smiled down at the tiny being in her lap. A grin blossomed on the little face as the dark almond eyes caught her own. Allison felt her warm body and smelled her baby smell and felt overwhelmed once again as Wen Li looked up at her. It was a physical feeling, strong and glorious, a feeling of wonder and beauty and extraordinary joy. She had worked so hard for this, waited so long.

She thought about what Nash had said. His idea was as extraordinary as everything else that had happened that morning. The thought of defying the authorities in the People's Republic of China shook her to the very quick of her being. It was unthinkable, absurd. Maybe dangerous. No, she was overreacting. He was probably right—how much trouble could they actually get in simply leaving for Shanghai? It wasn't far. And what would they do to an American citizen, anyway? To a woman fighting for a baby she'd been promised, at that? Could it get worse than losing Wen Li? At the moment, she couldn't imagine anything worse than that.

She knew she would probably be breaking some law. There was Tyler to consider, and Marshall, who didn't even know what was going on. She had no one to advise her, no one to talk with about what to do. She was an engineer whose world was straight lines and neat calculations and the orderly precision of physics. She was accustomed to the careful analysis of problems, turning them over and over until they yielded to logic. In this there was no order. If there was a law at work inside her, it was one of nature, not of physics or math.

A stroke of Chinese lightning had flashed and set her world on fire. She had to make a decision, and she had to make it *now*, with nothing but instinct to guide her way. Wen Li sucked hungrily at the bottle, and Allison stroked her hair. She was no longer the wallet-size, two-dimensional orphan of the photograph or a clinical subject whose brief life was summed up in a one-page medical report. Allison held her in her arms and felt her warmth and her need. She thought of the Chinese whim that had brought them together, and of the Chinese whim that now threatened to rip them apart. There came a flash of anger, of defiance, a moment that would change their lives forever. This child was not just some chattel to be exchanged with another at the pleasure of some faceless official.

Wen Li's picture belonged in a frame. Her frame.

And Allison Turk knew with sudden certainty that she would not be meeting the van from the orphanage.

"Tyler, we need to pack."

CHAPTER 2

AT FIVE MINUTES to eight two identical black Liberation vans turned off the Shiquan Jie Road into the long hotel driveway. They were waved past the guard post the hotel manned to keep street peddlers away from hotel guests, then threaded their way through impeccably tailored gardens lining the road to the front door. Before the engines had stopped, Director Lin of the Number Three Children's Welfare Institute stepped from the lead vehicle, his face set with grim purpose. Three aunties from the orphanage waited in the second van while their driver came to open their door from the outside. They chattered nervously, peering out the darkened windows of the vehicle.

Director Lin, a stern bureaucrat with an air of absolute authority, waved impatiently for the drivers and nannies to hurry. He went ahead into the hotel. Near a bank of elevators in the center of the lobby was a large lounge area with easy chairs and coffee tables. He spotted three of the foreigner families there, waiting with their children. Director Lin was distressed not to see Yi Ling, who should be handling these delicate matters with *lao wai*. Well, no matter, he thought. His English was passable. He would do it himself.

He bowed slightly as he reached the group. His countenance had grown a pleasant smile, a hasty addition that said nothing at all was the matter in the world. *"Ni hao,"* he said with forced cheerfulness. "Good morning." Barry Levin nodded, but everyone else maintained a stony silence. Roger Lawton brooded alone on a couch. His wife wept quietly while Annie sucked hungrily at a bottle. Ceil Levin stood numbly, waiting. The Jacksons' heads were bowed in prayer over their baby.

"I am so sorry for this trouble," Director Lin said.

"Just get it over with, will you?" Roger Lawton said.

Director Lin's expression tightened, but he kept a polite exterior. "Please know that I quite understand your distress, but you must realize Chinese law must be followed. I assure you all will be made well Monday morning. You will be delighted with your new babies. And now, please, where is Ms. Yi?" He directed the question to Barry Levin, who seemed the most collected and civil of the group.

Levin shrugged. "She was here a while ago. I think she went back upstairs." For a few moments the group stood awkwardly, waiting for Ms. Yi and the missing families to appear. No one said a word. The director lit a new cigarette from his old one, his face lost in clouds of smoke.

"I can't stand this anymore." Ceil Levin broke the silence. "I don't know what we're waiting for." She hugged her child, approached one of the aunties, and handed the baby over. The child started to wail. For a long agonized moment Ceil hesitated. Fighting for control, her lip quivering, she turned at last and took her husband's hand. Together they hurried away, toward the elevators. A great sob erupted from her as she went.

The auntie tried to hush the baby, cooing and smiling and bouncing it up and down. The baby howled. The Lawton's baby started up then, and the noise prompted Cindy to move. Gently she handed her over to the second auntie. "Her name is Annie," she said. "Ann-nee." She said it slowly, singsong. "She likes it when you call her that." The auntie didn't understand but smiled broadly. The baby was still crying. Cindy pulled a toy from her bag. "Give her this," she said, holding it up where Annie could see. She pressed a button that started a melody. Annie stopped crying and listened, distracted. "See? She likes it." The auntie held the toy above Annie's upturned face, cooing and soothing the baby. The peace lasted only an instant; Annie started up once more. Three days earlier the reverse had happened: she had screamed relentlessly the first time Cindy held her. Annie was particular and liked routine. Cindy managed a brave smile and fought back the instinct to help quiet her. The auntie was gentle and experienced and clearly loved babies. Annie would quiet down soon.

Cindy turned and looked for Roger, to return with him to their room, but he was already moving off in another direction, searching for an open bar. Her shoulders sagged a little. She walked alone to the elevator.

The third auntie was waiting. Ruthann Jackson whispered something to her baby, who had managed to sleep through the racket. She gave the child to the auntie, along with a plastic bag she'd packed with extra diapers, formula, and a miniature Bible she hoped someone would read to the child someday. After she'd let go, she and Wally drifted slowly across the lobby, looking back now and again, finally passing through the revolving door to go for a walk outside.

Director Lin let out a quiet sigh, hugely relieved that the scene had not been more difficult than it was. It was terrible *die fen,* his loss of face, but not nearly so horrible as what would happen if his deception were discovered.

He hadn't slept in the two days since learning what the fool clerk at the ministry had done during his absence. The resulting stress had caused his back and legs to erupt in angry boils. It was agony to sit in a chair or ride in a car. Yet boils would have been the least of his troubles had he not caught it. Now, luckily, the foreigners were doing exactly as ordered. He had had the patience to wait until today, Saturday, when he knew their embassy would be closed. Already he had three of the babies back. Three to go. By Monday new babies would be in place. The whole affair could be buried and, with good fortune, quickly forgotten.

Now he wanted only to finish it quickly. Impatiently he watched the elevators, checking his watch and smoking incessantly. His patience lasted two cigarettes. "Wait here," he said to one of the aunties. "I will see what's keeping them."

He crossed to one of the marble desks in the lobby and spoke sharply to the assistant manager. "Dial the room of a *lao wai* for me." He couldn't remember the foreigners' strange names and consulted a small notebook. "Turk Allison," he read. The assistant manager picked up the house phone and called the hotel operator. A moment later he was connected to the room.

Allison flung clothes into her suitcase in a mad race with the clock. Tyler was barely moving, little help in the rush. He carried his own backpack and was putting his things inside, but at a glacial pace. He kept getting sidetracked, stopping to flip through a *Game Gear* magazine or fiddle with the buttons of his electronic game.

"Tyler, hurry, please."

"How come? Why are we in such a hurry, anyway? All we've done so far is sit."

"We have to go to Shanghai. They're waiting for us. It was . . . it's a sudden trip."

He seemed to take that all right. He'd explored every inch of the hotel, from its four restaurants to the bowling alley on the sixth floor to the janitor's closet he wasn't supposed to get into. He hated the hotel. The fitness room trainer wouldn't let him work out with the weights, saying he was too small and would get hurt. "Look who's calling *me* short," he'd grumped of the little man. Another staffer wouldn't let him get in the hot tub, saying he had to be fourteen. The only place he was allowed to go was the swimming pool, and it was too cold. He was ready to be rid of the place.

Allison carried Wen Li in a Snugli that kept her tight against her body so she could work. Wen Li babbled contentedly, Pooh in one hand and her bottle in the other, while Allison whipped through their things, determined to pack only what little they absolutely needed. Ordinarily she traveled light, never realizing how much baggage came with a baby. She had to get rid of two of the suitcases, not wanting to lug them along.

An air of unreality gripped her as she worked. *I'm abandoning my things,* she thought. She dumped everything out of one suitcase and began sorting through the pile, separating out the things she needed. Jeans, yes. Sweater, no. It was hot, hellish hot, and she'd overpacked. Dress, no. T-shirts, yes. Diapers, wipes, bottles, formula, comb, sleepers for Wen Li—she flung them all in. She ran to the bathroom for the first-aid bag and jammed it in. She scooped the adoption papers off the desk into a manila envelope. She patted her money belt to check the familiar bulges of cash and traveler's checks and the passports for Tyler and herself. All there.

She looked at the suitcase and realized she was out of room. She had to sit on the lid to get it closed, then snapped it shut and pulled it off the bed. It clunked to the floor. It was heavier than she wanted, but there was no time to get rid of anything else.

The room was a mess. Allison's existence was orderly, her things always neat. She felt a twinge of pity for the maid who would have to clean up after her, then realized guiltily that she'd be skipping out on her bill. The thought appalled her until she remembered they had her credit card imprint at the front desk. She'd pay all right, probably double for the mess. She threw a hundred-yuan note on the bed for the maid and felt better.

She hung the camera around her neck. It was Marshall's Leica, the one he'd owned since before they were married. It banged against Wen Li, and the strap was choking. She took it off and set it on the table. Marshall would be furious. Well, it was only a camera. She'd get him another one.

"You're going to leave all this stuff?" Tyler asked in amazement as they started for the door. "What about Dad's camera?"

"We'll come back for it," she said. She wondered if it was true. She looked at her watch. Less than ten minutes since Nash had left the room, although it seemed much longer. Heart racing, she opened the door and pulled her suitcase behind her into the hall. Just as the door slipped shut, the phone inside the room began to ring. *Maybe it's Marshall,* she thought, fumbling for her key. With a groan she remembered she'd left it on the dresser. "Tyler, do you still have your key?" He shrugged and started to search his pockets.

"Never mind," she said. The phone would have to ring. She picked up the heavy case and started down the hall.

As she turned she gave a little gasp, startled. Yi Ling had approached unnoticed and now stood watching her with a puzzled look. Yi Ling's gaze took in Allison's suitcase and Tyler's pack. Allison felt a surge of panic and knew her face was flushing.

She'd taken too long. She'd blown it. Caught before she'd begun.

Instinctively she held Wen Li more tightly to her breast.

Yi Ling had never passed a more difficult night. There had been no sleep, no peace, since she'd learned of the extraordinary order to return the babies. That the decision had not been hers didn't matter. She had lost all face just the same, in front of clients she cared about. She was ashamed. Humiliated. The caprice of the ministry was shocking. Her first reaction was disbelief, then fury, but quiet fury: in China one's furies stayed tucked neatly beneath the surface, simmering but never boiling over.

At first she had argued calmly with Director Lin, appealing to his sense of justice and fair play. He seemed strangely unmoved, almost surly, resigned to accepting the edict without a whimper. She offered to call the ministry, to argue. He refused to let her. "I've already done that," he snapped. She did not know him well and assumed him to be a man who would not defy authority, a man clinging to a position he intended to keep until he retired—something, she knew, that would not happen if he took exception to every arbitrary order that came along.

"There is nothing to be done," he said. "We have our orders. And besides," he had reminded her, "this is only a temporary situation. The families will receive other babies. They will be all right. In a month everyone will have forgotten. Time erases all."

Yi Ling lost her temper at that, appealing to his sense of compassion, of concern for the babies. It did nothing but raise his ire. He lectured the guide as a father might rebuke an impetuous child. "I remind you, Ms. Yi, that you are a guide for the agency, not a civil official. I have tried to be courteous, to listen to you with patience. But this does not concern you or your agency. Remember your duty and leave such affairs in the hands of others." She started to object, and his eyes clouded and his tone sharpened. "Now I am grown tired of this discussion. Your continued arguments will leave me no choice but to report your lack of cooperation to your superiors. I have no wish to see you replaced, but press me a moment more and I shall."

For Yi Ling it would be the easy thing to let go, to give in, to push this decision, like so many others in her memory, into the easy forgetfulness of time. Accept fate humbly, letting it all drift into a murky subconscious where it could atrophy until it shriveled away and troubled her no more. She had done that all her life. There seemed to be less pain that way.

As long as she could remember she had been taught never to make trouble, never to stand out, never to object too loudly, never to challenge authority, never to think for herself, never to say what she wanted. To live properly was to please others—her father, her teacher, her boss, her husband, her mother-in-law.

The one matters less than the many. Follow the forms. It was the litany of her life.

Then two years ago the population control officer told her to have an abortion. She obeyed but things went wrong and along with the baby she lost her ovaries and then her husband, who wanted a child and abandoned his newly barren wife.

It's all for the best, you'll see, they whispered as she lay in her hospital bed. *All things for China. All things for the forms.* She told herself it was true, because if it wasn't, it was too awful to endure. Yet it was all a delicately wrapped deception, pretty on the outside and ugly within. She was young and adaptable and excelled at the lie. During her lifetime God had changed from Mao to materialism, but the devotions were still the same. *Mask your feelings, hide your anger. Do as you're told.*

She became numb, as so many of her friends were numb. She passed her days without thought, trying to find in her career what she had lost in her husband. She worked for the China International Travel Service. The CITS was the ultimate government bureaucracy. While others were losing their jobs in a changing economy, hers was guaranteed because the country had opened its doors and tourism was thriving. She spoke English passably and had a knack for working through obstacles and surly clerks and client squeamishness over having to squat over one of China's notorious hole-in-the-floor toilets. She made more in tips than salary, and her clients kept coming back.

She made money for the CITS, and her job was secure. And even then a veneer of lies covered everything she did. She was schooled in what to say—and what not to say—to foreigners. She attended classes to learn the proper masks to wear, the correct tongues to use. "We can always fool a foreigner," her instructors said with a wink, and it was true—she could. A military base could become a police barracks, a mental hospital a convalescent home, the Xinsheng Works a glove factory instead of a women's forced-labor camp. The *lao wai* didn't know the difference. They couldn't read the signs or see behind the masks.

She told herself there was no harm in little lies. Everyone in China told them, in one form or another. Everyone in China believed them, in one way or another. They were white lies, Chinese lies, lies so carefully threaded through reality that soon one couldn't tell them apart, and this seemed to suit everyone. The government encouraged the lies even when they seemed pointless, and it never occurred to her to challenge them.

For work she memorized the government line about human rights and the one-child policy and the lack of freedoms and the progress of reform and the other indelicate questions tourists always asked, and she did her best to repeat it when the subjects came up. She discovered there was a way to lie that suited the government, suited the tourists, and suited herself as well. She was good at it. The way she said things ended up being truth in a way, even if it was truth all bleached out.

Her conscience slept in the soft bed of little lies, a bed in which sleep was possible, if never serene. For two years she kept it up.

Until the order came to change the babies. That night Yi Ling felt the burden of lies more heavily than ever before in her life. It was stupid, a sad, senseless struggle for influence between petty officials who battled constantly for position, for money, for control, with weapons of *guanxi*, greed and gall. Yes, the ruling was arbitrary, but arbitrary orders were the norm. Who in China did not know that? One learned to live with the arbitrary. Today's order from the Ministry of Civil Affairs might be reversed by tomorrow's order from the Ministry of Justice; both might then be overturned by the Ministry of Public Security. Such was *rén zhi:* individuals ruled, not law. She knew that the babies' birth mothers had been coerced into giving them up, and now the foreigners who wanted them so desperately were being denied. She hurt inside in a way she hadn't hurt since losing her ovaries. She cried into her pillow and pounded it with her fists.

Despite her anguish, she felt herself slipping into the old familiar place: perhaps, she heard herself saying, perhaps Director Lin was right. Soon this awful order would be behind them. There would be other babies, other families to help.

Go along, Yi Ling. Go along, in the way of the ages. She hated herself for the thought.

When dawn came she summoned the courage to make a phone call to the governor of the province. She couldn't get through. The automaton inside her propelled her to the hotel, where, fatigued, bleary-eyed, and beaten, she buried the troublesome little voice of objection in its familiar grave of oblivion. There was work to be done. There was duty to answer.

After the meeting in the Camerons' room, she accompanied the three families who were ready to the hotel lobby to await the arrival of the orphanage staff, then went back up the elevator to help the others. The elevator door slid open silently and she was greeted by the floor attendant, an efficient young woman who stood behind a desk and saw to the security and needs of the hotel's guests on that floor. As Yi Ling stepped off the elevator, she glanced at her wristwatch. It was getting late. She hurried down the long dark corridor toward Allison Turk's room. Duty had to hurry. It was impolite to keep Director Lin waiting.

Then she came upon Allison and Tyler, their luggage in hand. She couldn't read Western faces very well, but she recognized in Allison's a look of panic, of guilt, of—she didn't know what, exactly, because for the first time in her life, and without understanding it, Yi Ling stood face-to-face with her own conscience.

"Mrs. Turk?" Yi Ling asked uncertainly. "Are you—do you need . . . ?
" She wasn't sure of her question, and she didn't know how to finish it.

"I—we can't do it," Allison stammered, not knowing what to say.

"Excuse me, please? I do not understand. What is it that you cannot do?"

"Give her up. We're leaving. Please don't try to stop us."

Yi Ling stared blankly—first at Allison, then at Tyler, who was looking at Allison with a question on his own face, then back at Allison again.

Allison seemed to set her mind and picked up the heavy suitcase. She started down the hall without saying more. Yi Ling followed along behind, completely confused. Allison wasn't walking toward the elevator. She was headed for the stairs.

"Leaving?" Yi Ling repeated, feeling stupid. She was tired, her brain not functioning. "Please stop. Please explain."

"You can't stop us." Nash Cameron stood just inside the door to his room, directly across from the stairway. Claire was behind him, holding Katie. Nash inserted himself between Allison and Yi Ling, taking charge. He was unfriendly and abrupt.

"Pardon? Stop you from what?"

"We have no intention of letting your government take these children. We're going to see the embassy in Beijing," he lied. "You can tell the authorities if you must, but if you really want to help, then turn around and go back down the hallway and pretend you never saw us."

"Beijing?" Tyler said to Allison. "You said we were going to Shanghai." Allison stopped him with her strongest "not now" look.

Yi Ling had no response. Beijing, Shanghai: she was dumbstruck. The notion was too overwhelming to comprehend, and it took a moment for the reality to set in. She looked behind Nash and had another surprise. Ruth Pollard stood with a suitcase in one hand, diaper bag in another, and tiny Tai supported in a makeshift sling that nestled on her chest. Ruth was sweating from the effort, but her face was set in grim determination. A flicker of fear crossed her expression when she saw Yi Ling. They'd planned to avoid her altogether while Nash went to the street to find a cab. Now everything was in jeopardy.

An eternity of strained silence passed in the hallway as the Americans and their Chinese guide regarded one another, each uncertain of the next move.

From her station near the elevators, the floor attendant was watching the curious gathering, just as she quietly watched everything that happened on her floor. She started down the hall. Ruth Pollard saw her coming and knew they had to hurry. She hadn't heard the first part of the conversation, but she knew instinctively that a critical moment was at hand. Ruth was the closest of all the Americans to Yi Ling, through their common bond of helping Tai get well. Ruth liked Yi Ling immensely but knew she worked for the government—or at least some government agency—and that they were putting her in an impossible position.

"Please, Yi Ling," she implored the guide, her voice but a whisper. "I know you care. Don't let this happen. Tai needs a chance. Let her go with me. Let us all go." Her eyes welled up and she held Tai closely.

At that moment Yi Ling made her own fateful decision. Her heart was torn between disbelief and delight, between dread and hope. She thought of the three families she'd left standing in the lobby and of the three families standing before her now. One group represented order and obedience, the constant of her life. The other represented—she didn't know what, exactly. But she looked at the babies, and into her own heart, and for the first time in her life she made a decision from heart instead of duty. At that moment her job didn't matter, the forms didn't matter, the consequences—well, she could lie, couldn't she? She did that so well, after all. She could plead ignorance or confusion. It just didn't matter. The more she thought about it, the more certain she became. She didn't care what they'd do. Not this time. The words came before she even knew what she was saying.

"But you cannot make such a trip without help," she said. "You will not make it outside Suzhou. There are authorities. Police. They will—"

"We *will* do it, with or without help," Nash said firmly. "Now please move out of our way. We're going now." He reached to push the handle on the door to the stairwell.

"Wait—*I* will help you."

Nash shook her off. "I don't mean tomorrow, after we've given the babies back," he snapped. "Tomorrow's too late. We won't do that. We won't give them up. Not without a fight first."

"Yes, yes, I know. I understand. I will help you," Yi Ling repeated. "I will help you today. I will help you now."

Director Lin punched impatiently at the elevator button. His anger was mounting, his stomach churning, his boils on fire. He did not like to be kept waiting, not by dull-witted and rude *lao wai,* not by anyone. They hadn't answered the phone, and they hadn't come downstairs. He had no idea where Yi Ling might be. She had acted most uncooperatively the night before. She had flayed his nerves with her impertinence. He would have to speak to her superiors. Perhaps she was off sulking. But no, they'd said she was here. If so, it made no sense. What was keeping them?

The elevator arrived with a ding and he stepped in, repeatedly pressing the DOOR CLOSE button. As in all elevators, that particular button seemed to be disconnected; the more he pushed it, the more it didn't work. He waited impatiently until some mystical force gave its blessing. The door slid shut and he started up to the fourth floor.

Yi Ling thought quickly, her instincts taking charge. She herded everyone into the stairwell and turned to meet the approaching floor attendant.

"*Láojià,*" the attendant said with a courteous smile. "Excuse me, but these guests are leaving?"

"*Bù.* No. Taking a tour."

"By the stairs? Wouldn't they be more comfortable on the elevators?"

"They're fine," Yi Ling said, her gaze firm. "They like to exercise."

"They have always taken the elevators before," the attendant observed uneasily. Yi Ling looked at her watch in a display of impatience. She looked over the shoulder of the attendant, expecting to see Director Lin any moment. If he appeared, they were finished. She beckoned to Allison and Tyler to move into the stairwell, ever the guide in control, nodding and smiling, nothing at all wrong.

"Excuse me, please," the attendant pressed stubbornly, "but why do they carry their baggage?" She didn't like what was happening. She didn't want to pay for stolen whiskey or beer or candy.

"They were too cramped in their rooms." The lies came easily, as always. Yi Ling's manner grew stern. She needed the girl to leave. "They are storing them with the concierge, if it's any of your concern."

"I only wish to help. Please, may I call for a porter? Esteemed guests should not struggle with such heavy bags."

"*Xièxie, bú yào.* There is no need. Now please forgive me, but we must go." Yi Ling gave her a sharp glance of dismissal and stepped into the stairwell, pulling the door closed behind her. She let out a sigh. Her stomach was in knots. This was not going to be easy. Everything was too orderly in China, too well planned, too public. Even a simple floor attendant could upset everything. She half expected the girl to push open the door, but then heard her padding softly back down the hall. *Probably to alert the front desk,* Yi Ling thought.

"Hurry, please," she said, ever polite, and they descended awkwardly down the concrete stairwell, bags bumping the walls, babies held tightly, everyone struggling to manage the passage quietly and quickly.

She stopped them on a dimly lit landing at the second floor. The first floor would be too busy with hotel staff. "Wait here for me. I will get a van and come back for you. It is important to be quiet. The director of the orphanage is in the hotel. Already he look for you, I think." She turned and quickly descended the rest of the stairs, pushing through one fire door and then another that led to the lobby. She hurried out the front door, straight to the vans, where the drivers were talking and smoking. She knew the chauffeur of the rear van, a bone-skinny middle-aged man named Wang whose van belonged to his rich uncle. He was often hired by the CITS as a freelance driver, although this morning he was in the service of the orphanage. He nodded politely.

She opened the passenger door and got in. "Please come now," she said, forcing herself to be calm in spite of her nerves.

Driver Wang gave her a puzzled look. "I was told to wait for Director Lin, to return to the orphanage."

Yi Ling used her most authoritative voice. "Those arrangements have changed. We must pick up the *lao wai*. Director Lin will meet us later."

Driver Wang hesitated. "I must report to him," he said dutifully.

"I have already done so," Yi Ling snapped. "Come now. My clients are waiting."

Driver Wang fidgeted uncomfortably. It was most irregular. He followed orders meticulously. Yet the agency of Yi Ling was a valued client of his uncle's. He did not relish making decisions on his own and ultimately decided to do the safest thing. He would obey the last voice of authority he heard—hers.

Director Lin knocked loudly at the door of Allison's room. There was no answer. He consulted his notebook and went down the hall to the Camerons' room. Again he knocked; again there was silence. Just then the floor attendant emerged from Ruth Pollard's room, a maid from housekeeping in tow. The floor attendant was more relaxed now. No costly bottles of whiskey were missing, and there was still luggage in the woman's room. She would check the others to be sure, but it appeared her earlier fears were ungrounded. She saw the director at the Camerons' door and hurried to meet him.

"*Ni hao*," she greeted him politely. "You are looking for the *lao wai*?"

"*Shì.*"

She indicated the stairway just across the hall. "They left just a few moments ago," she said helpfully.

He grunted in surprise. "They used the stairs?"

She nodded. *Lao wai* were always doing odd things. "Their guide was with them."

Director Lin shook his head. The foreigners were foolish indeed, using stairs when there was an elevator in the building. Anyway, his boils chafed and he smoked too much to use the stairs. He walked back down the hallway, fuming at the rude *lao wai* who couldn't read a clock or follow instructions. His impatience with Yi Ling was growing. He was getting angry.

Downstairs, as he crossed the lobby to where the aunties were waiting, his frown grew to a scowl. Still only three babies; no foreigners in sight.

"Where are the others?" he asked sharply.

One of the aunties shook her head. "We thought they would be with you. They have not come here."

Director Lin glanced around the lobby, looking for the door to the stairway. They'd had more than enough time to arrive, even walking. He lit a cigarette. He saw an "EXIT" sign above and behind the glass partition of the lobby restaurant and started toward it. He pushed through the door. An empty corridor stretched away toward the service entrance. Off to one side was the stairwell, blocked by a fire door. He opened it and looked up, listening. Nothing.

"Yi Ling!" he called. Silence. "Yi Ling!" he called again, knowing as he heard his voice echoing up the concrete stairwell that something—he didn't know what—*something* was wrong.

He let the stairwell door slam shut and hurried down the corridor. There was a service area near the rear entrance. Doors led off to the kitchens and laundry. A cook wearing a bloodstained apron stood beneath a no smoking sign, smoking a cigarette.

"*Ni hao,*" Director Lin said. The cook nodded a silent greeting. "I am looking for some *lao wai.*"

The cook spat on the floor. "Then you will find them for sure. There are *lao wai* everywhere in this hotel." Director Lin winced at his own stupid question. The cook grinned wickedly, delighted to upstage any stuffy *zhi shí fèn zi* in a starched Western suit.

"*Tā mā de!*" the director cursed. "Don't be impertinent. Five *lao wai,* carrying babies. There's a Chinese with them."

The cook hocked and spat again. This time he pointed to the door. "They just left."

The director banged through the door and onto a loading dock crawling with porters and carts. He was just in time to see the tail end of what he thought was his hired black van, disappearing around the corner. Flipping away his cigarette, he raced down the ramp and through the parking lot, panting heavily before he'd even reached the corner. The agony of each step made him want to cry out, but his fear was stronger than his pain, and he kept going. At the front side of the hotel, where the road bisected, he saw the van turning into traffic. He refused to believe his own eyes and ran toward the front of the hotel, sweat now pouring from his brow. As he rounded the corner, his heart skipped a beat. Only one black van stood waiting, its driver standing nearby. The other van was gone. He called out to the driver, firing questions across the distance, snapping back in outrage at the answers.

At last Director Lin believed the unbelievable. He stood gasping for breath. He felt a shooting pain in his left arm. He feared he was having a heart attack. He almost hoped for it.

He had to call someone.

Tong Gangzi?

No, never! You know what they'll do to you if they find out. You know what they'll do to your family.

He raced for the lobby, to find a phone. He had to trust the police to do their job. He had to hope they could do it quickly. And when they caught Yi Ling—if he lived long enough to see it—he'd carve her delicate golden ass like a pig on a platter.

CHAPTER 3

CHINA

The word kept turning over in Allison's mind as the van made its way through the cobbled streets of Suzhou. Wen Li nestled comfortably on her lap, teething on a book with thick cardboard pages. Allison was lost in reverie, staring out the window, eyes focusing on a winged roof or a cypress tree, then glazing again as the world outside the window became a blur, everything a blur as she considered what she'd done—no, what she was *doing*.

China. The word itself was as exotic to her as the land it named. The Himalayas and the Wall; the enchanted hills of Guilin; the junks on Lake Taihu, their square sails set against the wind; pagodas rising from the morning mists; the ceramic armies of Xi'an; the real armies of Tiananmen. Dragons and tigers; Marco Polo and Genghis Khan, eels and dogs for dinner. A different world, so much more than just foreign. She had felt it the first time leaving Hong Kong, when she and Tyler had pressed their noses against the window of the jet taking them to the mainland. The British colony slipped away beneath the clouds and she'd felt an excitement tinged with vague dread. She couldn't deny her fright, born of a lifetime of stories about the cryptic land that passed beneath the belly of their plane, a sad and secret and tragic land. *The People's Republic. Red China. The land of fear and Mao, land of beauty and mystery and suffering.*

She knew it was irrational, but it still made her uneasy, and she wasn't certain why. She scoffed at her own thoughts. That was all old, outdated. Cold war bullshit. China had changed since those days, hadn't it? The country had thrown off the yoke of ideology and opened its doors to the world. Her own journey was proof of that. Yet she had come to get a child in a delicate process of adoption in which anything could go wrong—*had* gone wrong for her once, in the United States no less, horribly wrong. Everyone said adoption was safer in China, easier, that the mothers never came looking for their children, never asked for them back. Yet she had never shaken her unease. No matter what anyone said, the fear always simmered inside—until that morning, when it finally boiled over.

China. The van passed over creeks and then along the Grand Canal, crowded with low-slung cargo boats making their way to Hangzhou or Beijing on the ancient imperial waterway. From the water of the canals rose centuries-old stone walls, hiding behind them a way of life she could never understand. A jumble of images and feelings and profound impressions, and it frightened her all the more because she grasped so little of it. She was an engineer. She needed to understand things from the inside out, but China was impossible. She'd read the guidebooks and looked at the films, but nothing had really prepared her. It wasn't just the new sights. The noises, even the smells, were like nothing she'd experienced before. The food was alive. Eels shimmered in buckets; chickens dangled upside down from hooks outside the stails, their blood dripping to the street. She couldn't read a newspaper or a street sign or a menu. She felt stupid pawing through her guidebook, pointing at what she wanted to eat, unable to say anything but the simplest things, then saying those wrong as her mouth refused to make the sounds. And more than once she confused symbols, starting for the men's room. Even Tyler knew better. She knew nothing of the law, few of the customs, little of the music.

She was like a child here, helpless, hopeless, and naive, adrift in a foreign sea.

China. A land of stark contrasts. A nation that could produce the delicate beauty of Suzhou's Garden of the Master of the Nets, a little paradise of poetry, paintings and ponds where the feng shui soothed all who entered, where even Tyler had paused in awe. Lotus flowers drifting on glassy ponds, graceful pavilions rich with calligraphy and exquisite paintings, stone statues and craggy rock caves. So serene, so filled with peace. Yet outside its gates, a nation that could be harsh and ugly, a nation that made its own women abandon their children in the name of the common good. That disturbed her, yet she was thankful for it: but for that ugly side of China she wouldn't be here, would never have a baby. She pushed away her thoughts of reproach, fearful they might be unlucky. The baby in her arms mattered more than politics, more than a nation's morality. She could do nothing about China, but she could do much for this child.

China. Stone bridges arched gracefully over the water. She admired their lines and absently calculated loads and watched tough women struggling with heavy buckets slung from poles they balanced on their shoulders. She looked into their faces, wondering. *Is that her mother? Her aunt? Is that what she'll look like? What would her life have been if the fates hadn't brought us together? What will it be like now? Will I ever know? Can we stay together?* A vendor struggled with a great overloaded cart of wheat; another with a barrow on which a plump pig rode trussed on the way to slaughter. Buses were piled high with passengers and chickens and boxes of fruit.

They passed over the outer moat of the city, and she watched a dragon boat passing lazily beneath the bridge, making its way to the festival races, where it would come alive in a timeless ritual of color and speed.

The van stopped in a crush of traffic. Two policemen on a motorcycle pulled up next to her window. The older one, riding in the sidecar, stared straight at her, a sour expression on his face. She looked away quickly, pulling Wen Li closer. Traffic eased and the police moved on, uninterested, but her heart was pounding just the same. She'd never done an illegal thing in her life, never broken the law or the rules. She returned library books on time and drove the speed limit. If a store clerk gave her too much change, she gave it back. She reported every nickel on her taxes and never even butted in line.

Even so, her pulse quickened around police. In Colorado when a cop fell in behind her on the road, she felt her throat tighten, dreading the lights that never came, the siren that never sounded. Something inside her instinctively feared authority. In China it was worse because of her private fears, her ignorance, because of China's history, and because they were everywhere: uniforms, different colors, a star here, a stripe there, all representing the iron hand of the government.

Yes, she knew, she was afraid of the police. All police.

And now, for the first time in her life, she had a reason to be.

China. She knew nothing about the country except that she'd broken its laws and taken one of its children. She looked from Wen Li to Tyler, and the doubts flooded in.

She was afraid.

She wished she were stronger, more certain of herself, more certain of anything at all.

How can I know if what I'm doing is right, when I don't know what I'm doing at all?

*   *   *

They were sitting in the rear of the big van, Allison staring out a window, Tyler near the aisle, a *Game Gear* on his lap. Yi Ling sat in front, next to the driver. Behind her, Nash, Claire, and Katie shared one of the big seats. Ruth Pollard was in the middle, tending to Tai.

Allison felt Wen Li's diaper. It was wet, so she began to change her. Tyler studied the process with distaste. "All she does is eat and poop and sleep," he said.

Allison smiled. "That's all you did when you were her age."

He flared at that. "I did not! You didn't know me then!" It was his usual technique, to remind her that she was not his mother. She let it pass.

"Well, babies are all pretty much alike."

"Not me." He went back to playing his video game. "How come you lied to me?" he asked without looking up.

"Did I lie?"

"In the room you told me we were going to Shanghai."

"That wasn't a lie. That's where we're going."

"In the hallway Nash said we're going to Beijing. I heard him tell Yi Ling."

"Well, we're not. We're going to Shanghai, to the consulate."

"So *he's* a liar?"

"I guess we weren't really sure what we were doing. It's complicated, Tyler."

"I'm not a baby. I can understand things."

"I know it." He understood so many things, so well.

"Besides, Shanghai wasn't the lie I meant, anyway. It was that you didn't tell me we were stealing the babies."

Allison glanced at the front of the van. No one seemed to be listening. Sometimes she wondered how Tyler figured things out so quickly. And "stealing the babies." He took all the soft edges off things, that was for sure. It was impossible to hide behind. "It's something only grown-ups understand" with Tyler.

"We're not 'stealing' the babies. What makes you say that?"

"I'm not stupid. You don't hide in a stairway in a hotel and then sneak out the back if you're just going to go look at some dumb tourist stuff. We never did that before. Besides, I heard Ruth talking to Claire. They were whispering and thought I couldn't hear, but I did." His eyes were dark with knowledge. He was angry. *"That's* the lie I meant, that you didn't tell me. You always say that lies are something you don't say just as much as something you do say." He enjoyed his little triumph: he knew he had her on that one.

She busied herself finishing up the diaper while she thought about different ways to answer. She didn't think she could fool him for long—she hadn't fooled him at all, anyway—and besides, whether she liked it or not, he was involved, too. He was old enough to know more of what was going on.

Allison looked into his beautiful blue eyes that so often held her in anger or contempt, longing to somehow win him over. It was never easy, and this wasn't helping. She'd hoped on this trip to spend time with him, but the baby had taken all the time there was, and if anything, Tyler had felt more left out than ever. Marshall was to have been there with them, to share the load, but he'd been felled by illness. She put Wen Li on her shoulder and tried to get her to sleep. Wen Li was having none of it and squirmed all over, working her way back down into Allison's lap.

"We're having an argument with some Chinese officials," she said. "They want us to give Wen Li back, and the other babies. We don't want to do it."

"How come you didn't ask me? We should have done it. We should have given her back. I don't want her anyway."

"Don't say that, Tyler, please. You don't mean it."

"Yes, I do! I'm supposed to tell the truth, and that's the truth. I don't want her. I don't *want* a sister. I never did, but you and my dad never asked. You just did it."

She felt her own anger rise at that, and her voice was sharp. "There are some things a nine-year-old doesn't get to decide, young man. Having a baby sister is one of them."

"Well, that sucks." He knew the word infuriated her. Before she could say anything he turned toward the other window and buried himself in his video game.

"I remind you, Guide Yi, that I was told to take the babies to the Children's Welfare Institute. Instead you are leading us to the Hunting." Driver Wang was agitated. The guide was leading him onto the new highway connecting Nanjing and Shanghai.

Yi Ling nodded. "*Shì.* We are going to Shanghai for the day. The *lao wai* wish to see the Bund. Tonight we will return to Suzhou."

"Shanghai! I cannot. This was not my instruction."

"I am giving you a different instruction," Yi Ling said imperiously. "I tire of your insolence and your questions. Do you wish to cease driving for the CITS? Is this how you serve your client?"

"I must call my uncle," Wang said miserably.

"I have already done so, I tell you. Just drive!"

Nash Cameron leaned forward in his seat, listening intently to the exchange, his athlete's body tense as he strained to understand what was going on. He understood nothing of the language, but it was clear the driver was arguing.

"What is it?" Nash asked Yi Ling.

"He not wish to go to Shanghai. It is against orders he received earlier today. He is suspicious."

"He works for you. Order him."

"I have already, but today he work for the orphanage. He wants to call them."

As she spoke, the driver abruptly pulled over to the side of the road near a large intersection. Other drivers honked angrily, but he ignored them. He pulled a cellular telephone from its case and punched in some numbers.

Yi Ling put her hand on the driver's shoulder. "*Deng deng!*" she snapped.

Nash read the look on Yi Ling's face. He'd seen enough. He leaned forward and grabbed the driver's shoulder. "Put it down," he said, his voice strong and threatening. The driver stared dumbly at the big-nose foreigner. He understood no English, but he understood Nash. Resolutely he shook his head and spoke urgently into the phone.

"*Shushu,* there is trouble. . . ."

Nash sprang forward, knocking the phone away. It tumbled to the floor and bounced under the passenger seat. Stunned, the driver cursed and reached down to pick it up. Nash cuffed him viciously on the ear. "No!" cried Yi Ling. "Stop!" But Nash wasn't listening. The driver panicked; he looked toward the traffic circle ahead, for the police booth that would be there. He spotted it and threw the car into gear. The van lurched forward, then stopped abruptly as the engine died.

At the sudden motion, Allison's head banged the rear window. She clutched Wen Li tighter and threw her arm around Tyler, trying to steady him in his seat. Tyler's video game crashed to the floor and slid away beneath the seats. Ruth yelped and nearly lost her grip on Tai. Claire's bag turned over, spilling diapers and bottles, but she held on to Katie firmly.

"What is it?" Allison cried. The driver got the engine started and threw the van into gear. As it jerked forward once more, Nash lunged again and Allison realized, horrified, that he was attacking the driver. She saw the reflection of the driver's bloody ear in the rearview mirror. "Nash! Stop it!" she yelled, but Nash slammed the driver against the door. His head hit the window so hard that the glass cracked. The van jerked to a stop. Nash worked his way into the seat, holding the wheel and pinning the driver to the door. He yanked on the handle and the door sprang open. Wang tumbled out to the ground. Horns blared and angry shouts followed as taxis and pedicabs and bicyclists passing nearby had to swerve to miss the sprawling driver. Wang lay still for a moment, then rose slowly on unsteady feet. He put his hand to his head and tried to gather his wits. Then he started bellowing for the police.

In the middle of the traffic circle, a traffic warden stood on a raised platform, orchestrating traffic. When he saw the driver tumbling from the vehicle, he blew his whistle to get the attention of a second officer sitting in a control booth. The second officer started running toward the van.

The passengers inside the van were stunned and trying to hold on. Yi Ling had her hand over her mouth; the sudden attack had caught her completely off guard. She'd never witnessed violence, and the sound of the driver's head hitting the window left her in shock.

"Are you crazy?" Allison yelled. "What did you do that for?"

"Be quiet! Yi Ling, where do I go?" Nash snapped. His legs were crammed high under the dash because the seat was too close. He fumbled for the lever to move it back. The policeman was nearly upon them, Driver Wang yelling frantically and pointing at the van. Nash gave up on the seat and pulled away from the curb, swerving to miss the policeman, who had to jump out of the way. The van shot forward through the intersection, weaving madly through traffic.

"Yi Ling!" Nash shouted again. "Where do I go?"

Yi Ling gathered herself and glanced outside to get her bearings. She recognized the intersection and gestured. "There," she said. They had to navigate the roundabout and drive directly past the traffic platform in order to get onto the correct road. Nash jammed the pedal to the floor and roared past the policeman, who stared in disbelief.

Nash allowed himself a tight smile as he watched them growing smaller in the rearview mirror. He was enjoying himself. The chase was on.

"Brash Gnash," they'd called him in school. He was big and handsome, hotheaded and impulsive, a gifted athlete with a savage streak inside. In his first junior high school football game, he made an important discovery. He hit another player late, snapping the boy's collarbone. He was ejected from the game, but he noticed that his teammates treated him with increased respect. Making others afraid was easy, because he himself was fearless. Violence gave him power. Football, soccer, hockey, women— he lettered in them all, and in each he was coiled and brutal and sometimes ruthless. Women flocked to him.

He was driven to prove himself. He solo-climbed the nose route of El Cap in the winter and camped in the snowfields of the Rockies above timberline in summer. He soared in his hang glider, not stopping even when his best friend, flying alongside him, was hurled by a downdraft into the side of a mountain. He stripped his BMW motorcycle and drove it offroad at breakneck speeds. And breakneck he was: his body was an ongoing work of steel pins and suture lines. He lived his life in a mad race with death, Nash always the winner, Nash always ahead.

He had no close friends but never cared. Brilliant in school, he trained to become a surgeon. He liked the power the knife gave him and the fact that bedside manner didn't matter for a surgeon. His work was done on unconscious people. He cut them open and performed miracles on their insides, like God, and was gone before they woke up. Surgery, like violence, gave him power.

Claire was a sales representative for a drug company, several years older than Nash. She was very successful but had discovered she didn't much care for the world of business. She supported him through medical school, then quit her job as soon as he started a practice. She took up other pursuits. They bought a house, a rambling old Victorian. She wallpapered and painted and learned how to fix plumbing. She loved it but felt unsettled. Her friends were having babies, and she realized it was something she wanted, too. While Nash was happy with their lifestyle and felt no particular desire for children, the thought of a Nash junior pleased him.

They tried for two years without success. Her doctor ran some tests and said she was fine: "Be patient," he said. She looked for ways to occupy her time, but after another year of it she was brooding and moody. The doctor suggested they check Nash, to see whether his sperm count was all right. Nash refused in a shocking flash of belligerence, humiliated and angry at her challenge to his manhood. There were no tests.

When friends had children she resented them and couldn't bring herself to attend their showers. Every time she passed a toy store she wanted to cry. Thermometers and charts governed their sex life, and they both hated it. When she called him at work to come home and perform, he always did, but there was no fire in it. It was an act, for business. They tried to laugh about it, but the laughter was strained. Rutting season was no fun.

Six months later there was still nothing, not even any false alarms. She wept and kept after him, until finally he agreed to a test. Afterward the doctor sat them both down. "Your sperm count is too low. Dr. Cameron. I'm afraid you're infertile."

The words took Nash's breath away. He lashed out at the doctor, accusing him of mistakes, of inaccurate measurements, of incompetence, of confusing his sperm with another man's. The doctor was unruffled. Men often reacted that way. "I don't think so," he said, "but if you have doubts, why don't we retest?"

They did. The results didn't change. Nash sulked for weeks. When Claire suggested artificial insemination using a sperm bank, he exploded in rage. "How dare you!" he raged. "Another man's sperm inside you?"

"But it's all done in a lab," she pleaded. "They'd mix other sperm with yours, and we'd never know, not really, who was the father. Your own sperm might work. And it would still be our child."

"Yours, not mine. Not ours." He couldn't think of it. His ego would never allow it. It was out of the question.

Claire drifted, desperate and forlorn. When a friend suggested adoption, she knew instantly it was right. By then Nash was sick of the whole subject. He'd gotten past the idea of a child. But the thought of adoption wasn't as repugnant to him as the idea of another man impregnating his wife. After months of her pleadings he relented, with two conditions. First, she could never reveal to anyone that they weren't able to conceive on their own. Second, he didn't want a domestic adoption. If she wanted a child, it would have to be foreign—Chinese or Korean or Japanese. He didn't tell her why, that he didn't want a child who could ever be confused as his own, in case the child was somehow imperfect. A foreign child left no doubt that Nash and Claire Cameron were adoptive parents, not biological ones. Imperfections could thus be explained away.

During the year before they were matched with a baby in China, Nash was detached. He didn't help pick a name. Claire went alone to buy clothes and a crib. The only part of the process in which he showed any interest was in writing his autobiography for the adoption application. They needed four pages; he wrote eight. Beyond that he let Claire do it all. The baby was for her. She pretended not to notice his indifference. She told herself things would get better when they brought the baby home.

CHAPTER 4

OFFICER DAI JIN sat behind the massive steel desk in the front hall of the Public Security Bureau at 7 Dashitou Xiang. His attention was riveted on the small television tuned to the quarterfinals of the soccer matches from Beijing. He had twenty yuan on the red team from Jiangsu. Eight other officers crowded into the hall, watching with him.

The phone jangled just as the yellow team from Beijing missed an easy shot. "Aiyo!" one of the officers cursed loudly as cheers rose around him.

"Your team is pigshit," Dai Jin chortled at him, ignoring the phone. Red was on the attack once more, swarming near the yellow goal. The phone rang again and again. Dai Jin answered impatiently. "Wei? Gong an ju. What is the matter?" He had to cover his other ear to hear over the shouts of his fellow officers. "What?" Dai Jin said. He straightened in his seat, the soccer match forgotten.

"The driver said they were going to Shanghai? How many people in the van? . . . Who is driving? . . . What color is the van? . . . The registration number?" He made a new entry in the log book, scribbling down details as the traffic officer at the other end repeated his questions for the driver.

Red scored again, the wizards of Jiangsu now hammering the yellow dogs of Beijing. A cheer went up among the other officers in the room, but Dai Jin heard none of it. The unthinkable had happened, on his watch: Americans with babies they weren't supposed to have. Assault on a driver. Theft of a motor vehicle. An official guide for the CITS apparently involved. All confirmed by a traffic officer. Worst of all, a few moments earlier he himself had dismissed a call from Director Lin as lunacy, when the truth was he hadn't wanted any distractions from the soccer matches.

The sweat of error poured down Dai Jin's brow as the crimes piled up in his log.

He hung up and swung swiftly into action. First he called the radio operator on the second floor, telling him to broadcast the description of the van and the people inside and a statement of the offenses for which they were wanted. The message would be out to all police in Suzhou within sixty seconds. Then he personally called the officer in charge of the toll booth on the Suzhou-Shanghai toll road, to make certain he alerted his officers who manned the toll booths and the highway police who monitored traffic there on their motorcycles. That officer dutifully took down the information and promised that his personnel would have it immediately.

Next Dai Jin made the call he'd been dreading most, to the captain of the PSB, who should have been at the station but was at home, watching the soccer matches. Carefully Dai Jin spelled out what had happened. He left out his dismissal of Director Lin, hoping that somehow the uncomfortable facts might somehow pass unnoticed. But the captain wasn't interested in that, at least not yet, and he peppered Dai Jin with questions.

"You've alerted the radio room?"

"Yes, and the control booth at the Shanghai freeway. The Americans are said to be going to their consulate there."

"Call Shanghai. Tell them to get some patrols onto the freeway this side of the toll plaza at their end. Get the same message to the post at Kunshan."

"Yes, sir."

The captain hung up and dressed quickly. He wondered briefly whether to call the *wài shì ke,* the foreign affairs branch of the PSB that dealt with crimes involving *lao wai.* There were risks involved in not calling them. But the wheels of the police machinery were already beginning to turn, and in Suzhou, at least, he knew they were effective. Fugitives in China had no chance at all. *Lao wai* fugitives in Suzhou had even less. They would be in custody within the hour, and then he could call anyone he wanted, having apprehended the criminals himself.

"Stop here!" Yi Ling said.

Nash pulled the van to the side of the road and left the engine idling.

They were near the entrance to the Huning Expressway toll plaza. They stopped on the next street over, separated from the plaza by a wide, grassy median. An administration building stood next to the plaza, where clerks sat in at least a dozen toll booths, collecting money from traffic entering the freeway.

Yi Ling didn't like it. Four motorcycle police sat in the shade of the administration building, watching the passing traffic and smoking. Uniformed officers walked up and down between booths. Cameras were mounted on poles between each booth, extensions of unseen eyes watching each passing car.

"I think it too dangerous to go Shanghai this way," she said. "Driver Wang knew where we were going. Certainly he inform the police."

"God, I can't believe you hit him, Nash," Claire said. She'd been crying from the stress, and her eyes were red.

"Well, believe it," Nash said. "If I hadn't, we'd already be in the police station. It doesn't matter now, anyway. It's done."

"Please," Yi Ling said, thinking. "Not time for talk now. We must turn around."

"Can we take a back road to Shanghai?" Ruth asked.

Yi Ling shook her head. "The Gong An Ju will be searching all the roads. Better now we go to Nanjing."

"Nanjing! That's the other way, isn't it?" Ruth fumbled in her handbag, looking for her map.

"Yes, but no worry. From there we can take a boat to Shanghai. There are many boats, every day. Not far. The police not look there. Also I have an uncle in Nanjing. He will help us. We can be in Shanghai tomorrow."

There was an awkward silence as they considered what she was saying. They had no way to know what was the right thing to do. They had to trust Yi Ling. Ruth found Nanjing on the map and started to say something, but Nash broke in. "I think it's a good idea," he said, and without waiting to hear what Ruth was going to say, he began swinging the van around. As he did he nearly hit a man pedaling a huge bicycle cart. The man swerved and hit the curb and fell off his bike. He raised a fist and shook it at the van. "Tā mā de!" he screamed.

Across the median at the toll plaza, one of the motorcycle cops noticed the incident between the black van and the cart. He watched for a moment, eyes narrowed, dragging at his cigarette. No one hurt. Just an argument. He turned his attention back to his companions.

"I think I must drive now," Yi Ling said.

"I'm fine," Nash snapped. "I just didn't see him."

"No, it is not that. I'm sorry. In China it is most unusual for a foreigner to drive. Only Chinese. If police see you driving, they will stop us."

Nash thought about that. He was clearly unhappy to turn the wheel over to Yi Ling, but there was no choice. He shrugged. "All right."

Once again he pulled over to the curb. He and Yi Ling exchanged places. She fumbled for the lever to move the seat but couldn't find it. Finally Nash worked the lever for her. Yi Ling scooted the seat forward, her feet barely touching the pedals. She seemed satisfied. She started the engine smoothly but let the clutch out too quickly. The van lurched forward and stalled. She started the engine again and the same thing happened.

"Do you know how to drive?" Nash asked her.

"No license," Yi Ling admitted. "It would be easier with automatic motorcar. But not worry. I can do it." The third time she got going, but in second gear. The engine pinged and strained, but they picked up speed. She mangled the gears trying to make third, her small frame straining against the protesting shift lever. Just as she got it she had to swerve sharply to avoid a bus. The engine nearly stalled, but she kept going, jerking forward straight across two lanes of traffic, miraculously missing everything in her path. Horns blared and tires screeched. All the adults in the van held their breath, expecting the worst. Tyler's eyes went wide, but he wasn't afraid, and he even managed a grin. "Wow!"

A proud smile blossomed on Yi Ling's face when she'd cleared the danger. "See? Driving not so difficult."

The police radios crackled to life in the toll plaza, broadcasting the bulletin about the *lao wai*. One of the patrol officers there knew he'd seen a black Liberation all right, although it had been too far away to see anyone inside. He pulled on his helmet, flipped up his kickstand, and rammed down the starter. The engine roared into life. He punched into gear and turned around, accelerating smoothly into traffic.

Ten minutes later he spotted the van in the distance, turning off the divided highway onto a dirt road that ran past a long outdoor market. The Liberation left a billowing trail of dust in its wake as it sped along the road. The officer cranked up his throttle, the van's speed no match for his powerful Suzuki. The dust was choking as he closed the distance. Twice he had to swerve sharply to miss farmers crossing the road with their carts. Once he had to stop completely, his way blocked by a string of cattle that ignored his horn. He cursed and left the road, crossing a small ditch and bouncing through a cabbage field before getting back on the road.

With nothing left to slow it, the motorcycle again closed the gap. Drawing near the van, the officer couldn't make out anything inside because of the dark windows. The license plate was obscured with mud. He drew up alongside. Pulling close enough to touch the window, the officer looked into the startled eyes of a woman staring at him from behind the wheel. With a sharp motion he waved her over. The van slowed to a stop in front of a line of woodworking shops, the motorcycle staying just beside and a little behind it. As the officer dismounted, nearby vendors stopped what they were doing to watch.

The officer walked around to the front of the van. The driver's side window rolled down. *"Zěn mè le?"* the driver questioned him with her nervous eyes. He stepped closer to the van and peered inside, his eyes adjusting to the dim light.

From the back of the van, eight sets of eyes stared back.

As far as the officer was concerned, they might as well have belonged to the fugitive *lao wai.* Unfortunately, they belonged instead to eight trussed pigs, making their way to market.

They drove through the heat of the afternoon, staying on small country roads that ran forever between fields of cabbage and rice, the road crowded with tractors and bicycles and intercity buses. Everyone in the van was tired, their nerves shot. The sun bore down on them oppressively, superheating the interior. Tai's skin erupted in a rash, and she wailed without pause.

Allison noticed the driver's cell phone had slid along under the seats and had come to rest near her foot. She picked it up and looked at it.

"Maybe I ought to try the consulate in Shanghai," she said.

"Good idea," Ruth said.

"Suit yourself." Nash shrugged. "I told you what you'll get today."

She lost the connection twice but finally got through. At first the consulate operator told her to call back the next morning, then relented after she insisted. She was connected to the duty officer, a junior staffer named

Dooley. At first he listened to her story, bored. She could almost see him yawning over the phone, doodling on a pad. But as she neared the conclusion of her story, he got excited.

"*You've done what?*" he said, making her repeat herself. He listened again.

"You *ran?*"

"They gave me a baby—gave us babies—and then told us we couldn't keep them! What did you expect us to do?" Allison couldn't understand why he didn't share her outrage at the notion.

"Good God, Mrs. Turk, to do what you were told, of course. Instead you've kidnapped a Chinese national. Are you out of your mind?"

"She's my daughter."

"I thought you said the papers weren't completed yet."

"That's right, but they were just about—"

"Then she's *not* your daughter. Not yet, anyway. She's Chinese. She's theirs, not yours."

"You talk like she's a loaf of bread. These are children we're discussing, Mr. Dooley."

"Of course they are. I know that. But they're *Chinese* children. I know you're frightened. But you've kidnapped her. That's all I can deal with right now."

"You're not being helpful, Mr. Dooley. We need ideas."

"I don't have any ideas when it comes to breaking Chinese law. I'm going to need all of your names and passport numbers."

Something told Allison not to give him that. She needed someone more cooperative. "I don't think that's such a good idea just now," she said to Dooley.

"If you're not going to cooperate with me, I don't know why you called, Mrs. Turk." He was angry.

Ruth scribbled a note and handed it to Allison: "How about asylum?"

"Look, what if we request asylum?"

"You can't do that. Asylum doesn't work that way. There are other factors. There has to be persecution."

"Wen Li was abandoned. They were all abandoned. Stuck in an orphanage for the rest of their lives. That's persecution of a sort, isn't it?" *I need Marshall!*

"Not in a legal sense, Mrs. Turk. And you have no legal standing, anyway—you can't even make a request on the child's behalf, because you're not her legal guardian. The law doesn't provide for this."

"Stop talking about the law! Help me! For the love of God, do something! They want to take her away. Don't you understand anything?"

"I'm trying to be patient. I'm on your side here. But staying out is only going to make it worse. You can't possibly hope to evade the authorities. This is China. It's a police state, Mrs. Turk. They may not be visible to you, but they're everywhere. They'll catch you within hours, and then it will get really bad for you. What little chance you have to keep—what's her name? Wendy?—"

"Wen Li," Allison whispered.

"What? Oh yes, whatever. That chance will be destroyed. They'll deport you. Hell, they may even throw you in prison. They're not squeamish about that sort of thing, Mrs. Turk. They're not sentimental, either. Break their laws and they'll make you pay. Turn yourself in, before there's any more trouble. Go to a police station right now. Tell them what you've told me. Tell them it was all a mistake. We'll try to get this resolved through normal channels. The Chinese can be an odd lot sometimes, but in the end—"

"To hell with your channels! I need guarantees, not channels! I'm not taking chances with her. They said they were going to take her away! They took the others already. I'm not giving her up."

"Look, Mrs. Turk. I still don't understand this. How long did you say you've had her?"

"Four days."

"Well, how attached can you get to someone in four days? I minored in psych in college. It takes longer than that to bond with someone. This is simple, Mrs. Turk. Why don't you just do what they asked? Give her back and let them give you another baby?"

"How attached—?" Allison didn't know what to say to that. "*Bonding?* That's the most stupid thing I ever heard."

Nash reached for the phone. "You're being too emotional," he said. "Let me have it." Allison nearly gave it to him. She didn't feel she was accomplishing much.

"She's doing fine," Ruth said. "Let her handle it." Nash shrugged and dropped his hand.

"You don't need to insult me, Mrs. Turk," Dooley said. "That won't get us anywhere."

"Well, so far you're not getting us anywhere at all. Why don't you just accept the fact that we've done this and figure out some way to help us?"

"I told you. I can't help you. The government of the United States can't help you. If you come here, the Chinese will arrest you. If you do manage to get into the consulate, we can't protect you. If the Chinese ask for you—*when* they ask for you—we'll have no choice but to turn you over to them."

"You would do that?" Her voice sank as she asked it. "You would turn us over to the Chinese?"

"I have no choice!"

Allison's heart sank. Nash was right. She'd found a small-minded bureaucrat whose veins ran with regulations, not blood. "You're a big help, Mr. Dooley. I'm glad I had someone like you to call." She couldn't keep the sarcasm out of her voice.

"Look, Mrs. Turk, I want to help. Really I do." Dooley softened a little. He thought for a moment. He lowered his voice conspiratorially, as if sharing some state secret with her, and said: "If you say I told you this, I'll deny it. Shanghai is the wrong place for your problem. We're an economic consulate more than anything else. We do trade fairs. Business things. We don't do adoptions out of this office. They do that in Beijing. And Guangzhou. You'd be better going there."

"To Beijing?"

"Yes. No! Not Beijing. Guangzhou. In the south, in Guangdong province near Hong Kong. They used to call it Canton. They're easier to deal with there—the Chinese, I mean. And that consulate does lots of adoptions. Hundreds. Maybe someone there can help you."

"But how will I get there? That's got to be five hundred miles from here."

"More like eight hundred. I don't know. That's your problem. I can't help you with that, or with any of this." Dooley knew he'd strayed far enough from the line and found his official voice again. "I want to repeat, Mrs. Turk, so you hear me clearly: I'm advising you, all of you, to turn yourselves in. Right now. That's what I'm putting in the log."

"I heard you, Mr. Dooley. Write it in your log."

Allison was angry, frustrated, and afraid. She'd knocked on the door of a supposedly friendly house. She hadn't known exactly what to expect, but it wasn't to have the door slammed in her face. She repeated the side of the conversation the others hadn't heard.

Tyler was listening intently to her, trying to understand what was going on. "He said the police would be chasing us?" he asked, his expression lit with interest. Allison nodded.

"Cool." It was the first entertaining thing he'd heard.

"Guangzhou," Nash mused. "He might be right at that. We were going there anyway to get visas for the babies, before all this happened." They were scheduled to fly from Shanghai to Guangzhou, then on to Hong Kong for the return trip to the United States.

"We can't use our plane tickets to get there. They'd be looking for us," Allison said.

"What about a train?" Ruth asked.

"I hate trains," Claire sniffed. "They're too noisy. I can't sleep on them."

"No, not a train, either," Nash said. "Too public. The police will be looking there. We'd have to find some other way. Overland somehow." The thought of running across south China lit his expression with an old, familiar fire.

"My uncle travel to Guangzhou quite often," Yi Ling said. "I am certain he can help us."

"We're getting ahead of ourselves," Allison said, shaking her head. "I'm not ready to give up on getting help so easily. Ruth, didn't you say something about your brother being a congressman?"

Ruth nodded. "Yeah, but he's a wacko. He and I have never agreed on anything in our lives."

"Is that Fred Pollard? Foreign Affairs?" Nash asked.

"The one and only," Ruth said, grimacing. "The only out-of-the-closet Neanderthal in our family. New Jersey sent him to Congress so he could be among his own kind."

"Whether the two of you agree or not, surely he'd help now," Allison said.

"I don't know, but it doesn't matter. He's off on a junket someplace," Ruth said. "South Africa, I think, or Botswana. He was going to take some time off when he was done and hunt kudus with a machine gun or a tank or something. Real macho stuff. I don't know for sure when he's getting back."

"I'll try to call Marshall again," Allison said. "Maybe he can help us get this overturned before we have to go anywhere. He'll have an idea. He always does."

Nash shrugged, unconvinced. "So call him, then."

Allison punched in the numbers on the cell phone, but instead of the usual long-distance echo on the wire she heard a rapid-fire recording in Chinese. She handed the phone to Yi Ling, who listened to the recording.

"This telephone not use to dial overseas number," she said. "Driver not have international access. Not worry. We will call from my uncle's house."

Night came and they arrived at last in the ancient capital of Nanjing, the Stone City of Sun Quan. It was a city, where Suzhou had been a town. Its crowds and the bright lights and neon signs of its boulevards jolted their senses after the endless flat fields and paddies of Jiangsu. There were hills and thick groves of sycamore and poplar trees. They passed over a river lined with pagodas bathed in bright lights, their reflection shimmering on the water.

Yi Ling turned off the main road and threaded her way through the *hutong,* a twisting labyrinth of crooked streets in which the *lao wai* hopelessly lost their bearings. Finally she stopped the van on a street that disappeared into blackness. "We walk now," she said, and they climbed stiffly from the van, thankful for the chance to stretch their legs. All three babies were fast asleep.

Yi Ling led them through more passageways, too narrow for the van to pass, turning this way and that in a maze of whitewashed walls. The night air was alive with the singsong chatter of the streams of people who materialized from doorways and alleys. Music blared, horns honked, and dogs barked. Bicyclists weaved through streams of pedestrians, bells tinkling impatiently, and the *lao wai* and their guide had to press themselves close to the masonry walls to avoid being hit. One cyclist nearly fell off his bike in astonishment, scraping his front tire against the wall before regaining his balance, then wobbling off as he stared back over his shoulder. *Lao wai* did not often make their way into the back streets of Nanjing.

"We're a frigging walking billboard," Nash grumbled, uncomfortable at being on such public display. "A thousand people will have seen us tonight." They all tried to keep their heads low, to blend into the passing pedestrian traffic, but it was hopeless. From Nash's height to Tyler's youth to the babies in their arms, they stood out even in the dim light.

"It smells awful here," Claire said quietly. "It's so dirty." All China smelled awful to Claire.

"I have to pee," Tyler said. Yi Ling pointed and Tyler disappeared into the shadows by a wall.

Yi Ling turned into an alcove that dead-ended in a high wooden door. She knocked and called out. A small light winked on beside the door, illuminating bright red calligraphy above and on the sides of the doorway. "It is family name," she said, answering Allison's unspoken question while they waited. "Sign say good luck and prosperity for those who enter."

An old woman opened the door and clapped in delight upon seeing Yi Ling. It was Yi Ling's grandmother, who chirped and laughed and ushered them into a courtyard. Presently an old man, white-haired and stooped, appeared from one of the rooms inside. Nodding and chuckling, he greeted Yi Ling, who introduced him as Grandpa Yang. He shook hands all around, bowing slightly to each. He led them into one of the small rooms off the courtyard that served as bedroom, living room, and den and bade them all sit down. All told, a dozen people lived in the house, and in twos and threes they appeared, greeting Yi Ling, cooing over the babies, and tending to the guests. A very young girl brought tea, oranges, and a bag of cookies.

Nash looked dubiously at their host. "This is who's going to help us?"

"No," Yi Ling said. "He is my grandfather. Master of this house. Uncle Yang Boda his son. It is Yang Boda we seek."

Yi Ling talked earnestly for a few moments with Grandpa Yang, whose face grew serious as she talked. He asked some questions, nodding at her answers. Then he called to his wife and issued sharp instructions. A bedroom was quickly vacated for use by the guests. "You put babies in there," Yi Ling said.

"We don't want to trouble your grandparents," Allison said.

"Not trouble," Yi Ling replied. "Honor."

Too tired to argue, the guests settled the babies for the night. Claire and Ruth stayed with them, leaving Allison to call Marshall. Nash left with Yi Ling to look for Yang Boda.

"*Allison?* Are you all right? What on earth is going on? My God, I've been sitting here with nothing but the message you left on the machine. I called the hotel four times and they couldn't reach you. I've been worried sick. Is Tyler with you? Is he okay?"

It was so wonderful to hear his voice, his strong voice, the voice she needed now, and she wanted to cry. She held the phone tightly, cradling it on her shoulder, feeling him through the distance. She explained everything, her words pouring forth in a rush. In her mind she could see him listening, his lawyer's head cocked as he took it all in, weighing, calculating, planning. He said nothing as she plowed through, his silence somehow reassuring. She knew Marshall would make everything all right.

She expected almost any reaction except the one she got. His voice was not warm with understanding, but cold with fury.

"I can't believe what I'm hearing. How could you, Allison? What the hell—just what in the hell are you thinking?"

"I thought you'd understand, Marshall. Especially after Mary—"

"God*damn* it, don't bring her into this." She flinched at the force of his venom. "Don't you use that on me, not now. This isn't about Mary. This has nothing to do with that."

"All right, I'm sorry, Marshall, I didn't mean anything by it—just that I couldn't give her up."

"What about Tyler? Are you giving him up?"

"He's safe, Marshall. He's with me."

"Safe? How can he be safe with you while you're running from the Chinese authorities? Hiding in Nanjing, waiting to sneak off in a boat when it's dark? That's *safe*, Allison? Did I miss something here?"

Her silence answered his question. "I understand why you might do this alone, but how could you do it with Tyler? He's my son. He's only a child. Christ, Allison, if I didn't know you better, I'd swear you'd gone mad."

"He's my son, too," she said desperately. Her world was collapsing if Marshall wasn't with her now. "And I'm your wife, and I need you now. I need you so much. I need your understanding and your help, Marshall, not your anger. Oh, please. This is all wrong, it's gotten off all wrong. I don't want to argue, not now."

"It's a bit late for all that. You could have waited to talk to me first."

"There wasn't time. They were going to take her!"

She could imagine him pacing in his study, staring through the French doors to the trellis, where the roses would just be showing their first buds. Theirs was a peaceful yard, almost like one of the Chinese gardens. Too peaceful, she realized: he was insulated there, safe and away from it all. How could she expect him to understand when he wasn't with her?

"I just don't see how you could jeopardize yourself and Tyler for a baby we don't even know."

"*I* know her. She isn't a shirt that didn't fit, Marshall. She isn't something I can just throw away or exchange. She's a baby. My baby—*our* baby.

I love her and you will, too. I know you will, as soon as you can meet her. Don't you understand? I can't give her up, any more than I could give up Tyler."

There was a silence then, long and painful. Allison felt her lip trembling, and she wiped back a tear. Everything she was trying to hold on to was slipping away, and she felt helpless to stop the slide. Marshall was supposed to fix everything. Marshall was supposed to have ideas, plans, strategies. Just like always. Only now he sounded like a stranger.

"If only you were here," she whispered, fighting back her tears. "You'd understand. You'd have done the same thing, I know it. Please, Marshall." She'd never felt so alone.

"Is Tyler there with you now?"

"Yes, of course."

"Let me talk to him."

She handed the phone to Tyler.

"Hi, Dad." He listened for a moment. "Yeah, I'm okay."

He kicked at the floor with the toe of his sneaker. "Uh-huh." He looked away. "Yeah, it's all right, I guess," he said again. Having a phone conversation with Tyler was never easy, even for his father. He volunteered little and had to be drawn out.

"Hunh-unh." He glanced at Allison, then looked away. "I wish we could give her back, Dad."

Allison fought the impulse to take the phone away from him. She bit her lip, hard enough this time to bring blood. Her eyes misted and she thought of Wen Li. *They'll want you,* she thought. *They just don't understand. I've got to make them understand. I've got to give them time.*

"Yeah, okay, Dad. I will. . . . Me too. Bye."

He handed the phone back to Allison, still avoiding her gaze.

"Marshall?" Her voice sounded weak to her. It *was* weak. "He'll get there, Marshall, I know he will. He just needs time to adjust to a little sis—"

"That's not the problem now. I don't know what to tell you, Allison. I'm thinking, really I am. I'm trying to help. But this is all wrong. It won't work. There's no law on your side. Nothing I can think of from here, not now. I don't know much about the legal system there, except that they have a lot more order than law. But even in this country I'd tell you it was time to see the police, to end it, to turn yourself in."

He was pacing, quiet. He knew how to put sting into even a silence, when he wanted to. She'd heard him do it to other attorneys, to clients. He was doing it to her, now.

"I'm worried sick, Allison. I can't stand the thought of anything happening to Tyler, or to you. And I'm trying to understand, God knows I am, but I keep thinking of the women here who steal babies out of hospitals. Sick women. They always get caught. I don't want you in that situation."

She caught her breath at that. "Are you calling me sick, Marshall? Is that what you think? That I stole her, that I'm sick?"

"No, but China—my God, Allison, you need to stop this. Right now, before it gets any more dangerous. You have no right—*no right*—to try this while you have Tyler with you. Listen to me. You're not thinking straight. You need to turn yourself in. Give her back, do what they say. I'll fly in. I'll leave first thing in the morning. We'll fight them together. But that's the only way. Right now you're putting everyone in an impossible position. You're closing off your options. It may be too late already. I don't know how much damage has been done."

Allison twisted the phone cord in her fingers. "She's such a sweet baby, Marshall. She needs me. She needs *us*. One mother gave up on her already. A whole country gave up on her. I can't do that to her again. She doesn't deserve that. I can't turn my back on her. If I give her up, I'll never see her again. I can't let her spend the next fifteen years in an orphanage, or die there. Don't you see that?" Her voice was breaking now. "I just can't do it." She brushed a tear from her eye, hating her weakness.

"You can't do what you're doing, either. Not with Tyler. Where will you go? Who's going to help you?"

"I don't know."

There was another long pause after that.

"Neither do I, Allison." The pain in his voice echoed in the distance between them. "Neither do I."

The captain of the PSB drained the last of his tea from his thermos. He picked a tea leaf off the top and stirred the weak brew with the end of his pencil, then sucked noisily at the glass. He listened impassively as Officer Dai Jin made his report. It wasn't encouraging.

"Shen has just returned from the Huning Expressway toll booths, Captain. He reviewed every film from the cameras, as you ordered." The officer had sat in an uncomfortable chair in a hot, cramped room, reviewing the tapes, fast-forwarding as streams of traffic passed through the tolls. They were certain the dolts manning the booths had missed the van and its cargo of babies and *lao wai*. "He watched every tape made between eight-thirty this morning and five this evening. There were eight Liberation vans in all, but none the right one. The *lao wai* did not enter the expressway. They must have gone some other way."

A radio officer stepped in. "The bureaus in Changshu and Qingpu have reported, *Dui Zhang.* They have seen nothing."

The captain frowned. That made eight bureaus reporting. Eight bureaus across the breadth of the province toward the sea, and no trace. It was puzzling. Ever the good fisherman, he had cast a wide net, not only on the expressway, but on every highway and road between Suzhou and Shanghai, even expanding the search a hundred kilometers to the north and south of the direct line. There wasn't that much traffic or that many Liberations on the road. The train station was swarming with agents within thirty minutes of the first report, during which time no trains had left the station. A hundred pairs of eyes were watching the long-distance and local bus terminals. The *lao wai* couldn't have slipped through. And yet . . .

He knew he'd have to make some unpleasant calls very soon. One to the provincial director of the PSB, the other to the *wài shì ke,* the foreign affairs branch. He had not caught his quarry as quickly as he had expected. The delays in reporting would not look good. The situation was getting more serious by the hour.

He snapped at the radio officer, "They have not disappeared into nothingness! Call each station again. Be certain they know the van they are seeking."

"I have done that already."

"Do it again!"

"Of course." The officer hurried from the room. The captain continued with Officer Dai.

"You've checked again with the orphanage?"

"In fact it is they who have been checking with us. Director Lin has been calling every fifteen minutes. He's heard nothing. He's very highstrung, near hysterics. He's making threats about what he'll do if we don't make arrests soon. Says if we have nothing to report in another hour, he's calling the ministry in Beijing."

"Remind him it is not we who report to him. He will make no such call without my order." The captain slurped at his tea. Things were beginning to unravel beyond his ability to control them. "What of the hotel?"

"The *lao wai* have not been seen since this morning. The floor attendant reports they were carrying bags. They did not check out. They left luggage in their rooms as if they intended to return."

"You have spoken with the other foreigners, the companions of those who left?"

"Not I, but an officer whose English is good. He spoke with each separately and reports they profess ignorance of the matter. They all say the same thing, that they agreed to meet in the lobby of the hotel as directed by the guide."

The captain grimaced. "Ah yes, the guide. And what of Yi Ling?"

"There is no one at her residence. I posted two men there in case she turns up. The neighborhood committee director has seen nothing, and our informants there report no *lao wai*."

"*Hao.*" The captain nodded. "And what of her *dàng àn*?" He referred to Yi Ling's dossier, the file of her life, the thick file maintained on every citizen in China. It followed a person from birth to death, detailing education, employment, children, marriages, divorces, disciplinary actions by work units, observations about politics, and work habits and attitude. The files were equal parts rumor and reality. Bosses and party cadres and police spent much time with them. The captain hoped Yi Ling's would teach him something of his quarry, give him some clue about what she might be thinking, where she might be going.

"Her *dàng àn* is at the provincial office in Nanjing," Dai said. "I will have it first thing in the morning. I will bring it to you myself."

"Morning is too late," the captain said flatly. "We require it tonight."

"But it is the middle—"

"Tonight," barked the captain.

"Of course, tonight is fine," Dai agreed hastily. "But even without the *dàng àn* we have learned something of Yi Ling," he said. "She does not have a large family. Her mother is dead. Her father lives in Beijing."

"That is of no help to me."

"There is something else, Captain. An uncle she visits in Nanjing." He consulted his notes. "His name is Yang Boda. The director didn't know his exact address, but said he lives near Shengzhou Lu."

The captain sucked at his tea leaf.

Nanjing. It was possible. Unless they'd sprouted wings, they certainly hadn't gone toward Shanghai. Perhaps Yi Ling was more clever than he thought. Perhaps he'd been looking in the wrong direction.

"Call the *gong an ju* in Nanjing. See what they know of this Yang Boda. Tell them to visit his home tonight."

Allison paced the room, seeing nothing, somehow avoiding the furniture. She didn't know what time it was, but the house was very still. She'd never felt so discouraged or alone. She was sick to her stomach and numb with uncertainty. Everything was wrong, everything gone to hell: adopting Wen Li, getting Tyler to accept her, even her belief in her marriage. In the blackest part of the night, all her dreams seemed fool's dreams.

Ruth emerged from the bedroom and shut the door quietly. Allison's eyes answered her question about the phone call. "I see it didn't go well," Ruth said. She crossed the room and they hugged.

Allison clung to the little woman. "It was awful," she said. "No one's with me. Marshall wants me to give up. Tyler hates Wen Li and wants to give her back. He hates me, too. And the consulate . . . They're all saying the same thing. Marshall told me I was a fool. Irresponsible and selfish. A crazy woman." She wiped her eyes with the back of her hand. "Maybe I am crazy. God, I feel crazy."

"Allison, go into that bedroom and look at that child, like I just did. She's lying on her back, passed out and happy, sucking those two middle fingers. She's got a full belly and someone to love her. If that means you're crazy, then she *needs* crazy. The *world* needs crazy. And she needs a mother. No matter what they say, you're the closest thing she's had to one for most of her life."

"I know, but I'm not her mother. Not yet, anyway, and it doesn't look like I'm going to get there, either."

"The hell you aren't! And what am I to Tai, if not her mother? I did a mountain of paperwork and spent thousands of dollars to get a referral, which took me two years. I've had her picture six weeks. I've been with her less than a week now, but already it seems like we've never been apart. I've scooped a ton of poop and haven't slept ten minutes for her fevers and her hives. I've never been through labor, but it can't be any worse than what I've gone through, what we've all gone through. So I missed the episiotomy. Big deal. I'm getting hemorrhoids from lifting her all the time, and my back is killing me. Whether I've got the papers or not, I've earned my keep. I don't care what anyone says. I *know* I'm the Wee Duck's mom."

Allison smiled. "I know it, and I don't mean to be so self-centered. It's just . . . well, I'm afraid, that's all. In Suzhou when we decided to leave I thought we were just buying some time. It seemed innocent enough to go to Shanghai. Then Nash did that to the driver, and since then everything seems like it's on such a larger scale. Instead of an easy trip and help from the consulate, we're hiding and we're in trouble. We were supposed to be on our way home by now. Suddenly everything's all complicated and mixed up, and I don't know if I have the courage to see it through."

"I'm a coward by nature, Allison. And I don't think anyone knows how much courage they have, until they need it."

They sat on the stone floor and Allison drew her legs up underneath her. It felt blessedly cool after the heat of the day. "I've never told anyone this before, not even Marshall. It's not that I did anything horrible, it's just that I'm . . . ashamed. I was out running one night, on a parkway near our house. I had a big heavy steel flashlight with six batteries in it that I carry when I run alone. It was like a club. While I was running, I heard a noise. A woman's cry, so faint I almost missed it. There were a few street-lights, but mostly dark places. I stopped and looked around with my light. Finally, I saw a man on top of a woman, right in front of me. I almost ran over them. God, it was horrible. He was raping her, in the bushes. I saw his back. I saw blood. From her, I think. I saw what he was doing to her. It was brutal, violent beyond words. He saw my light and turned around. I know he was blinded by the light, but he didn't show it. He stared right at me, right into my eyes. I might as well have been another shadow. My presence didn't seem to bother him. He turned around and kept doing what he was doing. His pants were down around his ankles and his back was to me. I knew I had the advantage. I was only a step away. I could have hit him, could have stopped him. With that light I'd have probably killed him."

"But you didn't."

"No. I . . . Well, another runner came along. He was young. Big. He saw me, and my light, and what was happening. He didn't even hesi-tate—he kept on running, grabbed the flashlight out of my hand, and beat the other man half to death."

"Then you did help her, in a way."

"That's what I've told myself a thousand times since then, that in the end it worked out the same for her as if I'd . . . acted. I've even convinced myself that if I hadn't been there with my light, the other runner never would have seen. But I've always lied to myself. I remember all this like it was yesterday. I've never been so horrified in my life, so outraged. Yet I didn't hit him with my light, or scream, or throw a rock, or run to a house and call the police. It must have been two minutes from the time I saw them until the other runner arrived. And all I did in that two minutes was . . ." Allison brushed back a tear. "I wet my pants, Ruth. I just stood there holding that light, and I peed all over myself. The only time in my life I'd been tested, and my courage failed me. I froze, Ruth. I found out I'm a coward."

Ruth started to say something, but Allison held her hand up, to finish. "And now there's Wen Li. There's no rapist after her—just life, just China, just the whole damned unfair world. I'm here, right now, when she needs help. I can't pretend I haven't seen, and right now it doesn't look like anyone's rushing to save her. I'm so scared that I'm shaking inside. I know I'm not going to be able to sleep. I want to be brave, to stand up to the Chinese government and dare it to try to take her back. I was just beginning to believe I could do that, when I talked to Marshall. Now all the wind has gone from my sails. I don't know if I can do this without him. I've always had him to lean on. He's always been so strong, so wise for me, for us both. What haunts me is that maybe I should listen to him. Maybe this wasn't meant to be. Maybe we should just turn ourselves in now and minimize the damage."

Ruth burned hot at that. "That's ridiculous. I've never been in this situation, either. I don't know exactly what to do, but I do know what *not* to do. I'm not giving her back, not until they rip her from my arms. I don't care what anyone says—I believe what we're doing is right. We'll find some way to do it. And I'm not afraid of the Chinese, either. You think they're going to burn some fat old lady like me with the world looking on?"

Allison laughed through her tears.

"Well, they won't. Like I said, I'm an old 'fraidy cat, too, Allison. If I thought this was physically dangerous, I wouldn't do it. Nash lost it with the driver, and I guess we'll be in trouble for that. But *we* didn't do anything. Besides, we can't take it back. What's done is done. We need to go on, now, to Guangzhou. If Yi Ling can get her uncle to help us, and if she'll be with us the whole way, I'm sure we'll be safe. And maybe while we're on our way to Guangzhou someone will sit up and take notice, and help us. Another runner, who sees what's in our light. But even if no one does, we have no choice. Right now we have only one chance for these babies, and we're taking it."

"I know. But there's Tyler, too. Marshall made me feel terrible about doing this with him. And he's right. I'm being selfish and inconsiderate."

"You're doing what you have to do under the circumstances. Don't worry about Tyler. For a nine-year-old, this is high adventure. And even if they arrest us, what will they do to him? Think about it. He's just a boy. They'll release him to your husband, or to the consulate. It isn't what you want, but is that really so bad? He'll be fine, Allison. We all will."

They hugged, and sat on the cool floor, and talked. As always, Allison felt better after talking to Ruth. But she knew Ruth was wrong about one thing. Even if she found the courage to run with Wen Li, she couldn't do it with Tyler.

CHAPTER 5

AT FIRST Colin Chandler couldn't tell whether he had a story or not.

He was sitting in the Suzhou hotel bar, between a majestic waterfall that was leaking all over the marble flooring, and a grand piano, where a singer in a red silk dress was trying to lift her reedy little voice above the roar of the water. The effect, Chandler thought, was typical of the Chinese government, which ran the hotel: an extravagant effort, producing entirely the wrong result.

Chandler had acquired Roger Lawton by accident, the way one does drunks at bars, unwelcome intrusions even when boredom is the only alternative. Lawton ranted for twenty minutes, driveling his hatred of all things Chinese. The drunk Texan wasn't simply obnoxious. He was barely coherent and racist to the core.

But then he mentioned the babies, and the reporter's interest shot up. His tale was intriguing, vastly more so than the Suzhou Trade Fair, which Chandler's editors at CNN had sent him to visit. He was doing background on a high-level bureaucrat in the Ministry of Commerce, a comer thought to be in line for premier. Definitely a pit assignment for a slow news day. Cameron hadn't even brought a cameraman.

"Here. Have another one." Roger Lawton accepted his fifth Scotch and soda. After the second drink he'd stopped grimacing at the taste, but not at the bartender, who didn't have real soda but instead used tapwater with some kind of pond scum floating on top. It didn't matter. The Scotch was real enough and killed the germs.

"Your wife up in your room?"

"Yeah, still blubbering. Upset, but I'm damned if I know why. Thinks she's getting another baby in the morning, but I've had it. We're out of here. First fucking plane I can find, even though I hate flying on Chinese planes. They're always late and they crash more than anywhere on earth. Did you know that? More even than Russia, and God knows the Russians can't fly. Commies and planes don't mix."

"The Russians aren't Communist anymore."

"That's what you think."

Chandler didn't have time to argue. "Tell me more about the others. They took the babies?"

"Yeah, looks like. The cops were here, asking questions."

"Which cops?"

"How should I know? Cops, that's all. Chink cops, wearing Chink uniforms. Asking Chink questions. Chink Chink Chink." He swirled the ice in his glass and took another swig. "That's all you get here. China Chink stuff."

"Where did they go?"

"How should I know? They sure didn't tell me. I don't care where they went. What's so fucking important? If they took the kids, they're stupid. If you ask me—"

"What was the name of the orphanage?" Chandler held his notepad ready, scribbling in it whenever something coherent happened to emerge from Roger's alcoholic haze.

"I don't remember. Shang-something. Or was it Dung-something? Dunno. Whatever. Stupid name. Stupid orphanage. I have the director's card somewhere, if I didn't throw it away." He rummaged through his wallet and pulled out a business card. "Here."

The reporter glanced at it. "This is for an insurance agent in Fort Worth."

"Really? Oh yeah. Sorry. Here's the right one." He fumbled with it and slid it over, and then he brightened. "Hey, am I gonna get on TV?"

"Maybe." The reporter copied the information from the card into his notebook. "What were their names?"

"Whose?"

"The Americans who left with the babies."

"I dunno. Branch something. No, Nash. Prime asshole. Pushy as hell. And Ruth. Bollard. Billiard. Something like that. Old broad, foul mouth. Too old for a baby, if you ask me. They'll let anyone do this shit. Too many babies, they've gotta give 'em to anybody with a heartbeat. And Allison Turk. From Denver." Roger remembered that name. He'd looked at her figure, at her light brown hair and green eyes, and wondered what it might be like to get into her pants. She was a looker. He noticed women like Allison.

Chandler mined the drunk for other details, then threw some bills on the bar and slid off his stool. "Thanks, Roger. Have a few on me. I'll be in touch."

Roger nodded into his drink. "Yup."

Colin Chandler rushed off to talk to the hotel's night manager. He'd get their names right and then call the orphanage. Then the American embassy. And the police, although the police never talked. They'd send him to the Foreign Affairs Ministry, which would try to drown him in its swamp of noninformation. But then there was Allison Turk, from Denver. Maybe he could get a line there.

His reporter's heart was pumping now. There were a hundred things to do. If the story checked out, he'd dump the trade fair. He looked at his watch and calculated the time difference. Plenty of time to get on the air while it was still Sunday in the States. Nothing much happened on Sundays. His story would get good play.

He was already thinking visuals. They were tough in China. He'd never get inside the orphanage, but he could do something in front of the fence. If they had a fence. If not, he could fake it. The hotel had a great garden for the lead-in. In the right light the greenery set off the color in his hair and made it look golden.

He pulled the cell phone from his pocket and dialed the bureau in Shanghai.

He needed a cameraman, in a hurry.

The Nanjing Public Security Bureau officer couldn't immediately locate the summary information card for Yang Boda because the card was misfiled under Tang. Finally he found it and copied the information. Yang Boda was a busy man. Most people had one index card only. For Yang Boda there were six, all well-worn and stapled together. There were multiple cross-references to other files, other names. The crimes of Yang Boda were not detailed, as this was not his *dàng àn,* his complete file, but smuggling and unspecified "antisocial acts" were noted. He'd spent seven years in the *laogai,* a reform-through-labor camp. Evidently, the officer noted, if Yang Boda was wanted again, he had labored, but not reformed.

According to the card his home was Wuhan, but it was known that he sometimes lived in his father's home in Nanjing. The officer copied the address, then refiled the card. He filed a request for the full *dàng àn,* which would be in Wuhan. The shift was just changing. He left the file room and went in search of the new shift supervisor.

It was late when Yang Boda arrived with Yi Ling and Nash. Yang Boda was a weathered man with stubble on his chin and grime on his clothes. He had long wiry hair stuffed beneath his cap. His face was deeply lined and his hands were thickly callused. He was a chain-smoker. Great clouds of smoke billowed endlessly through crooked yellow teeth. He had thick eyebrows and slits for eyes that missed nothing.

He regarded the waiting *lao wai* without expression, acknowledging them with a slight nod, and then greeted his father, Grandpa Yang. As they spoke, Allison listened in bewilderment. She couldn't tell whether they were angry at each other or just animated. The language and even its tones were impenetrable to her, just as their faces were. Only if they smiled could she sense any emotion at all between Chinese. They might be angry or sad or upset, and she wouldn't have any idea. Once again she felt helpless on her own, totally dependent on others she didn't understand. She wondered whether she'd have such trouble with Wen Li someday, whether such mysteries were etched in one's genes.

Yi Ling joined in the lively conversation between the men.

"He looks like a gangster," Ruth whispered to Allison.

"I hope he is," Allison whispered back. "We need one."

The discussion completed, Yi Ling introduced her uncle. "He understand some English but speak very little. He has agreed to help you. He say travel Guangzhou no trouble. We take boat to Wuhan. It is city on Chang Jiang—I am sorry, on Yangtze River. After that he have trucks to carry you." Yang Boda added something, and Yi Ling nodded. "Uncle's trucks owned by army. Special license. Never stop for roadblock. You will be safe in them. We ride in back. And now we must leave. Must wake babies."

"Tonight?"

"Yes. Police know Yang Boda my uncle. Know Grandpa Yang his father. They will come soon." Yi Ling was under great stress, though she did her best to hide it.

Her words chilled Allison as she suddenly realized what effect their situation was having on the Yang household. It hadn't really hit home yet, that each move they made added gravity to their situation, that others might now be endangered. She flushed. "We've put you in danger, I think," she said. "Will your uncle get in trouble for helping us?"

"I tell Grandpa Yang call police after we leave. Say we were here. Say he warn us to go to police station, that he make us leave. That way he not have so much trouble."

It was the only reasonable thing to do, yet Allison found the thought profoundly unsettling. Yi Ling was telling her own grandfather to betray her to the police. She wondered if the police would believe it.

"I am so sorry, but Uncle say first you pay. Trip very expensive. Very dangerous for him. Cost one thousand U.S. dollar."

"I thought it would be more," Ruth said, reaching for her bag.

"Each person," said Yang Boda, speaking for the first time in English. His voice was deep and thickly accented.

"Even babies?"

Yang Boda grinned. *"Ying er geng gui."*

Yi Ling translated. *"Especially* babies, he say."

Allison opened her money belt and counted out the cash. The bills were crisp, the new ones with an oversize Ben Franklin and an imbedded silver thread to combat counterfeiters. She'd seen few big bills in her life. Even so, these still looked funny somehow, as if they themselves were counterfeit.

She'd never carried so much cash and felt relieved to be parting with it. It was for the orphanage, when the adoption papers became final. Cash only, they'd said. In Denver she'd watched in awe as the bank teller counted out the money. *Thirty bills for a baby. Paper for a life.* A wonderful trade, in the circumstances.

But those papers weren't going to be final. Not yet, anyway. She handed the money to Yang Boda, who counted it with the practiced hand of a teller himself. Allison closed her money belt, much thinner now. She knew without counting that she had about $1,500 left, a reserve she'd brought for incidental expenses and to buy souvenirs. She had credit cards, but where she was going she doubted they'd be much help.

She hoped it would be enough.

She looked toward the bedroom where Tyler and the babies were sleeping, to be certain the door was still closed. There was one other item of business, over which she had agonized. "The money for Tyler," she said to Yi Ling. "It isn't to take him with us."

"*Allison!*" Ruth said.

Allison waved away Ruth's protest. "I've decided to send him to Shanghai, Yi Ling. To the American consulate. They can put him on a plane home. It should be very simple. Please ask your uncle to make the arrangements."

Director Lin stood in his darkened office, chain-smoking. The orphanage was quiet but for the occasional muted cry of one of the babies sleeping in a dormitory across the courtyard. The director couldn't sit because of his boils and had paced until his legs ached. It was nearly three in the morning. Nineteen hours since the *lao wai* had shattered his life. Nineteen hours the police had had to catch them, with no results. Impatiently he reached for the phone to call again, when it rang. He jumped at the sound, then snatched up the instrument. It had to be the police, with news.

"*Wei?*"

"You disappoint me, old Lin," said the familiar voice at the other end without preamble. Director Lin's heart skipped a beat. *Tong! How—*

"Perhaps you thought I wouldn't care about recent developments?" Tong Gangzi asked. "Or perhaps you thought I wouldn't find out?" The voice was quiet and muted, almost soothing. Director Lin felt the danger in the calm.

"I . . . I intended to call you, of course," he replied hastily. "I had hoped to be able to tell you the police had already made an arrest. That there was no longer any problem—"

"Ah, yes, the police. And why did you call them first, and not me?"

"I had no choice!" Director Lin said. "There were witnesses. The drivers, the nannies, the other families. And then one of the Americans assaulted a driver. After that the matter was out of my hands."

"None of which would have happened if you weren't such a fool in the first place, old Lin. You puzzle me. Once you knew they had the wrong babies, why didn't you simply let it pass? Why not let them go? Who cares about a few babies? You don't have enough?"

"They . . . they knew at the ministry," Lin said. His hand shook. He knew it was a stupid lie, an easy one to uncover, but it was the only one at hand, the only one that made sense. He could only hope it was unimportant, that Tong wouldn't check. "They brought it to my attention," he said. "I *had* to act."

"So you thought, apparently." Tong sighed. "A fly lands on the tiger's head, and you show the imprudence to swat the fly. It troubles me that I must remind you of the trouble we now face, if the tiger should notice."

Director Lin said nothing.

"I suppose now your best chance for a long life, old Lin, is that the Americans are caught quickly."

"*Hao*," Director Lin agreed with a nervous laugh. "That would be best."

"I will make a call, to be certain the matter is receiving the proper attention," Tong said. "Such calls are not inexpensive. You are deeply in my debt."

"I—" Director Lin started to say something, but the line was already dead.

He was sweating profusely now. He had to get his hands on the babies' files—before the police might think to look at them and, more important, before Tong did. He looked at his watch. Three o'clock Sunday morning. Without the help of his cousin Wu Hung, there was no way to get inside the ministry until Monday. *Monday!* More than twenty-four hours. He could only hope it would all be over before then. He raged inside at the black fortunes that had brought him to this precipice. If only Wu Hung hadn't gotten pneumonia. If only Wu Hung's substitute at the ministry hadn't been so efficient. If only Director Lin himself had not gone to visit Bangkok. If only he'd discovered the mix-up just a few days sooner. If only the cursed Americans had done as they were told. . . .

His boils flared and his stomach ached.

If, if, if. It did no good to wonder about anything now, except how long he had to live.

Inside the van, making its way toward the river through the dark back streets of Nanjing, Allison realized she still had the cellular phone in her pocket. She passed it to Yi Ling in the front seat. Yang Boda's eyes narrowed when he saw it.

"Where did you get that phone, *wài shéng nu?*" he asked.

"It belongs to the driver of the van, *Jiu Jiu.*"

"When was the last time you used it?"

Yi Ling thought back. "Mrs. Turk used it, to call the American consulate."

"Where were you?"

"I don't know."

"Think!" His voice was sharp. Yi Ling concentrated.

"This afternoon. Near Wuxi, I think."

The entrance to the Yangtze River bridge loomed before them. Yang Boda made his decision. "Turn around."

"Aren't the docks—"

"*Yòu zhuan!*"

Yi Ling turned sharply onto a side road, following his instructions through a series of side streets, then away from the river on the Jianning Lu. She pulled off next to a canal where small boats bobbed in the darkness, and parked the van. Yang Boda walked a block to the long-distance bus station, head down and cap low as he passed two guards. They paid no attention as he hurried inside the station. Night travel was considerably lighter than in the daytime, but the cavernous hall was still chaotic, with hundreds of travelers milling about. Bored gate attendants checked tickets, clearing passengers to pass through to the concourses outside.

He studied the schedule board that filled the wall above the gates, scanning the listings until he found departures for Tianjin and Beijing. Four buses were scheduled in the next two hours. He bought a newspaper and ambled slowly down to that end of the hall. He sat on one of the long wooden benches. As he pretended to read the newspaper, he slipped the cell phone from his pocket. After partially wrapping it in one section of the paper, he set it down on the bench, leaving the edge of the phone just visible. Then he got up and, without looking back, walked quickly away.

Ten minutes later, Wei Lin, a traveler on his way to Beijing, sat down near the abandoned paper. As he reached to pick it up, he saw the phone. He looked around to see whether the owner might still be nearby, ready to claim it.

No one showed any interest.

Wei Lin scooted down the bench to get nearer. He partially draped the phone with his jacket. He waited, looking thoroughly bored. A moment later the phone disappeared into his pocket. The announcement sounded for his bus. He made his way through the throng of travelers with his arm pressed against the phone, lest some unsavory pickpocket try to relieve him of it. He produced his ticket for the gate attendant and hurried up the steps onto the 884 express for Beijing. Five minutes later the bus departed the Nanjing station and roared to the northwest, up the Jianning Lu and over the Yangtze River bridge.

Grandpa Yang never had a chance to call the police. Fifteen minutes after the van had pulled away from his house, two police cars roared up, one blocking each end of the passageway closest to the house. Three uniformed officers jumped from each car, their boots clattering on the cobbled streets as they ran through the darkness to the target house. They pounded on the door until Grandpa Yang's frightened wife opened it a crack and peered out. They burst through, shoving her aside and racing into the courtyard, where they split up and quickly searched every room. They rousted the sleepy inhabitants, herding them into the courtyard. Outside in the street, a few remaining pedestrians heard the commotion and melted into the night. No one wanted to be noticed by the police on such a mission.

Ten minutes later, the police emerged with Grandpa Yang in tow. They hadn't given him time to put on a shirt. His hair was disheveled and his eyes were wide with fright. He was disoriented but knew that his opportunity to protect himself by calling the police as his son had instructed was lost. As always, he was stooped at the waist. His joints were stiff in the cool night air, and because he couldn't move fast enough, two of the officers half dragged him toward one of the cars, holding him beneath his armpits.

"I have not seen Yang Boda since yesterday," he protested weakly in his reedy voice. "Please, let me go. You are hurting me." They ignored him. He was shoved into the back of one of the cars. A door slammed and the car roared away.

The officers in the other car stayed behind, pounding on gates and doors in the neighborhood. In China a thousand eyes watched everything, saw everything. If foreigners had passed this way, the police would soon know. Such things were not long kept secret from the PSB.

Yang Boda left them huddled in an abandoned shed that stood below an elevated wooden boardwalk that ran from a fence near the frontage road down to the river's edge. At the water the boardwalk joined to a dock near a small inlet of the river where there was relatively little activity. Yang

Boda walked back to the van and drove it to a warehouse he often used. On his return to Nanjing he intended to grind the serial numbers, apply new paint, and sell the vehicle in Shanghai. If his niece complained, he'd tell her the van had been stolen. And that would be the truth.

His human cargo waited and whispered and listened to the sounds of a river that never slept. There was no ventilation in the shed. They were bathed in sweat, their nerves taut. Now and then they heard the footsteps of rivermen coming and going on the boardwalk, and occasional low voices or laughter. Each time, they held their breath and stood rock still.

Only Tyler was enjoying himself. In Denver they lived in Park Hill, a venerable neighborhood of brick homes, narrow alleys, and ancient elms. Tyler was Park Hill's master spy. He knew every inch of every block, and every block held a thousand secrets. He could travel long distances without being seen, skulking through backyards and slithering over fences. He knew all the hiding places, all the enemy attack dogs, all the trees where he could pick apples, all the secret forts hidden in abandoned alley incinerators. He wrote coded notes and left them behind loose bricks for his best friend, Will, who was Park Hill's second-best spy. And on summer nights Tyler peered in neighborhood windows to see what the enemy was doing. Sometimes he could tell no one except Will what he saw. Sometimes he didn't even tell Will.

Now he was doing the same thing, almost, and with a bunch of grown-ups at that. Even his stepmom was going along. At home she never sneaked around with him. She just worked. But now they were hiding above a mysterious black river in a gloomy shed where they could see out and no one could see in. It was grand. He felt the others tense when horns sounded or engines drew near, or when headlights illuminated a stretch of the wooden fence above their heads. He'd heard the strain in their voices all day. Even their whispers betrayed their fear. For some reason they weren't enjoying themselves. Adults could suck the fun out of anything.

He heard Wen Li stir in her sleep, crying just when footsteps sounded on the boardwalk. Tyler winced. The stupid child was going to give them away. He reached out to cover her mouth, but Allison caught his hand.

"She needs to be quiet," he hissed.

"*You* need to be quiet. Let me worry about her."

"Well, then, you'd better," Tyler grumped. "She's gonna get us caught."

"*Please, must be still,*" Yi Ling whispered.

In the darkness Tyler sensed rather than saw Allison glaring at him. He didn't care. She was too easy on Wen Li. He wished she'd ever be that easy on him. Through a crack in the shed, Tyler saw Yang Boda returning. At first the man was just a shadow, moving through an opening in the fence. Tyler instantly knew who it was. A cigarette glowed between clenched teeth. A cloud of smoke wafted upward, illuminated by the lights of the street behind him. The man slipped easily over the railing of the gangway, making no sound as he slid down the steep embankment near the fence. The man impressed Tyler, who thought he was about as close to a real spy as he'd ever seen.

Yang Boda opened the door. *"Kuài,"* he said, beckoning them outside. They followed him down the slope toward the water, keeping close to the wooden piers supporting the boardwalk. It was difficult going. The river had been running high and they were ankle-deep in muck, struggling with each step as they balanced babies and baggage. Yi Ling fell once, saving herself from a mud bath only by landing on her overnight bag. Tyler helped her to her feet. Near the water Yang Boda found a place where they could climb up onto the walk.

They scrambled up in silence, passing bags and babies, breathing hard from the exertion. Yang Boda hustled them onto the dock, where for the first time they felt the Yangtze, sensed its presence and immensity. The air near the river was heavy and humid and smelled of oil. Black water lapped against the dock.

On the opposite shore of the river, more than two kilometers away, lights blinked on the factory chimneys, construction cranes, and smokestacks of Puzhen. Upstream a ferry boat, its four decks brightly lit and smoke billowing from its stacks, was embarking passengers at the Number four dock. Downstream they saw the pride of Mao's China, Nanjing's massive bridge, as it soared over the river, the lights of a night train flickering as it traveled silently along the lower deck.

The river played tricks with noise. An eerie silence belied the city on the shore behind them. The lights of Nanjing glowed brightly against the sky, reminding them of its nearness, yet the sounds of the city were muffled by the night or by the water. By contrast the sounds coming from the river were sharp. A dozen different motors rumbled in the darkness—a launch, a tug, a freighter, the sounds distinct and crystal clear. A whistle blew and a tinny-sounding American song played on a radio. Despite the hour, the river was alive.

Yang Boda checked his watch and looked impatiently back up the shore toward the city. He was waiting for someone.

A battered dinghy with a small outboard motor was moored to a wooden bollard on the dock. It was there to carry them out to where Yang Boda's river boat was anchored. The dinghy was too small to carry them all, so he decided to take the first load immediately. He issued instructions to Yi Ling, then stepped nimbly into the dinghy. Tyler started to jump in, but Yang Boda waved him back, shaking his head. He reached to take Claire's hand, steadying her and the baby in her arms as the craft rocked precariously beneath her step. She sat heavily. Nash climbed in behind her.

"Ask your uncle if I can go now," Tyler asked Yi Ling eagerly. "There's room."

She avoided his eyes. "You must wait here," she said.

Yang Boda pulled the cord to start the engine. It coughed to life with a cloud of oily smoke. Crouching in the stern, he steered away from the dock and headed out into the river, toward the dark form of a ship a hundred meters offshore.

The others stood in the dark, feeling very exposed. Tyler knelt at the edge of the dock, watching the river. Yi Ling kept looking up the boardwalk and spoke quietly to Allison. "My uncle's friend An Rushan coming for Tyler. Uncle Yang trust this man with his own life. He will take very good care of Tyler. But he is very late."

Allison knew she could no longer postpone telling him. There might not be time later on. She handed Wen Li to the guide and walked over and crouched next to Tyler.

"Tyler, listen to me. I need to tell you something. It's important." He looked at her.

She was holding a nylon valuables pouch with a strap looped through one end. She hung it around his neck and tucked the pouch beneath his shirt. "You've got to keep this safe. Your passport is inside, and money, and a letter."

"What are you talking about?" he said. "What's going on?"

Allison steeled herself. "You need to be brave. A man is going to meet us here. He's a friend of Yi Ling's uncle. He's going to take you to Shanghai tonight. To the consulate. You need to give the letter to the consul there—he's the man in charge."

"What? What do you mean? Why? Where will you be?"

"They'll put you on a plane for home. Your father will pick you up." She felt awkward and knew she was handling it badly.

Tyler looked at her dumbly, slow to comprehend. "No!" Tears of disbelief welled in his eyes. He looked up at Yi Ling and then back at Allison. He looked to Ruth for support, but she'd walked with Tai to the other end of the dock. He knew it was no accident. They were ganging up on him, and he hadn't seen it coming. He shook his head. "You can't do this!"

"I can't take you with me," Allison said. "It might not be safe. Your father and I—"

"No!" Tyler said again, more loudly this time. The disbelief and fear on his face gave way to anger at his betrayal. "I'm not going with somebody else! I won't!"

"You have to, Tyler. It's the only sure way to keep you safe." Her voice wavered and she had to clear her throat.

"But I'll be safe with you!"

They looked up as the dinghy returned, bumping up against the old tires slung from the dock. Yang Boda let the motor fall to idle and stepped up onto the dock. He frowned when he realized An Rushan still hadn't arrived. He was anxious to be off.

"I don't know what's going to happen where we're going, Tyler," Allison said. "It's a long way."

"So what? We've already come a long way. I don't want to go to Shanghai. You can't give me up!"

"Don't be ridiculous. I'm not giving you up."

He snorted at that and pointed at Wen Li. "Then why are you keeping her and not me?"

"You know very well why! She has no papers! I can't send her! That's what this is all about." Allison brushed the hair out of her eyes. She took a deep breath and looked up into the night sky, trying to collect herself. "You're not being reasonable, Tyler."

"Well, neither are you. This is crap."

She wished An Rushan would arrive so that the argument could be cut off. She felt her resolve crumbling and tried to put a harsh finality into her voice, to stop the argument before she lost her will. "You watch your mouth, young man. You'll do as you're told."

"I'm sorry! Just take me with you!" he pleaded. "Please, don't leave me!"

Allison tried to give him a hug, but he pulled away. "Try to understand," she whispered. "I love you. I just want what's best—"

"No, you don't!" he cried. Tears began streaming down his face and he wiped his nose. "My mom would never leave me!" She flinched as if she'd been slapped. He buried his face in her chest then, sobbing. He clenched his fists and tried to hit her, but there was no violence in his blows, only frustration. He gave up and put his arms around her waist. She held him and stroked his hair. She started to say something but couldn't find words.

Yang Boda's gaze had been alternating between the river and the boardwalk. He knew something had gone wrong. An Rushan was long overdue. He couldn't afford to wait much longer. Suddenly his cell phone rang, the sound muffled by his jacket. He flipped it open quickly. "*Wei?*"

"Your father has been arrested," said the voice at the other end.

Yang Boda grunted. "Already," he said grimly. He asked a few questions of the caller, then hung up. There was no longer any question of waiting for Tyler's escort. Yang Boda hustled Ruth and Tai into the dinghy. As he did so, he saw the flashing lights of a police boat downstream, making its way upriver. "*Jǐng chá!*" he said curtly to Yi Ling. "*Kuài!*" He told her about Grandpa Yang.

Yi Ling put her hand on Allison's shoulder. "My uncle say we must go," she said. "Police on river. Maybe come this way. No time for more talk."

"What about An Rushan?" Allison asked, startled. "What about Tyler?"

"Cannot wait. Very sorry. Tyler must come with us now."

Tyler pulled away from Allison and wiped his eyes. He looked at her with a blend of anger and relief. He scrambled to his feet, anxious to be gone before An Rushan showed up and his fortunes changed. "Let's go," he said. He hurried to the dinghy and nearly leapt aboard, ignoring Yang Boda's outstretched hand. The motion of the boat threw him off balance and he nearly toppled into the water. Yang Boda caught him by the back of his T-shirt and set him down effortlessly. A moment later the others were seated, and Yang Boda set off once again.

As they pulled away from the dock, Allison held Wen Li and watched Tyler, who knelt in front of the boat. She was distressed, relieved, and fearful at the same time.

All that, and for nothing. He'll never trust me again.

From a distance it was just a dark ghostly mass looming on the water. Then, as they drew nearer, things began to take shape—first a wheelhouse, then a series of masts, then the low silhouette of the river freighter's hold. As they approached, Yang Boda cut the dinghy's engine and called out softly to unseen crew. Two figures materialized on the deck and lowered a wooden ladder over the side. Rough hands helped them on board. The men smelled of cigarettes and sweat.

The only heartening thing about the *432 Springtime Flower,* the flagship of Yang Boda's little fleet, was its name. The boat was of indeterminate age and uncertain origin, sixty meters of rotting wood, rusting iron, and broken glass. It looked as if it must sink the instant it began to move, or perhaps as if it had already been sunk and then salvaged. It was splintered and worn, its paint long since faded. Among the newcomers only Tyler smelled pirates and adventure; the others smelled the awful decay of a corrupt river.

Claire had been waiting on deck for them, afraid to venture away from the side rail for fear she'd put a foot through the decking. She held tightly to the rail with one hand and clutched Katie in the other. "Is this actually going to float?" she asked Yang Boda fearfully as he climbed aboard.

"Float good," he replied in one of his rare utterances.

"It's awful," she said. "How can we carry *babies* on this?"

"*Springtime Flower* make trip from Shanghai to Wuhan many times," Yi Ling said. "Not so pretty, but strong boat. Uncle very happy with it."

"I keep thinking Humphrey Bogart is going to show up from belowdecks," Ruth muttered.

The police boat had passed far to starboard, its business elsewhere. The first rays of dawn were streaking across the sky. Yang Boda said something to Yi Ling, then beckoned toward a companionway. "Getting light," she said. "Uncle take us to room. Say very small, so sorry. All share. Must hide during day. Not be seen." They ducked through a narrow wooden hatch and climbed down a steep ladder, into an overpowering stench of rot and salt air. Ruth straightened at the smell as if she'd hit a wall and tried not to breathe. On the wall belowdecks a kerosene lantern burned on its lowest setting. The glass was blackened with soot and provided little light for their passage, but the kerosene added plenty of acrid smoke to the air.

Yang Boda moved quickly and they had to hurry to keep up. The hatchways were low and treacherous. Allison banged her head twice, even though she ducked. She held Wen Li tightly to her chest, protecting her head with one hand. Once she reached out to brace herself and recoiled at the feel of the wood, which was clammy and cold. As she pulled away she gave a little cry as a splinter pierced the fleshy part of her palm.

They traversed a short passageway and climbed down a wooden ladder, getting deeper and deeper into the boat. Tyler, walking a few steps behind Allison, spotted two men watching them from a tiny room, their faces visible only when they puffed on cigarettes. He saw whiskers and narrow eyes. He shivered. He thought the boat was pretty wonderful but moved quickly to catch up with the others.

Their cabin was aft and low, near the engines. Yang Boda had banished some of the crew from the room to make way for his passengers. There was no door, simply a torn, grimy sheet that hung from the doorway. The cabin was hellish hot, the air stifling. Bunk beds lined the walls. Yang Boda flicked a switch and a dim, battery-powered light came on. Allison's heart sank. The place looked even worse than she'd imagined in the dark. The bunks were covered in filthy rags. The walls were black with age, the deck more than anyone could bear to look at.

To Yang Boda, all was in good order. He nodded happily, smiling and proud. "Okay?" he said. Without waiting for an answer, he turned and left.

Ruth surveyed their quarters, her fingers nervously working her bag. "Goodness," was all she could say. She was afraid to do anything, to let loose of her bag, to put Tai down.

"Very sorry," Yi Ling said, upset herself at the state of things, feeling personally responsible. "Uncle not prepared for passengers. Make better tomorrow. Try sleep now."

"What did you expect?" Nash shrugged. "This'll get us there." He tossed his bag onto an upper bunk and pulled out a couple of shirts. He stretched them over a lower bunk and beckoned to Claire to get in.

"Check it for bugs," she whispered. "I don't want to sleep with bugs." Her lip was quivering. "I don't want to sleep here at all."

Nash made a show of rustling the bedding. He shook out one of the sheets and felt everywhere with his hand. "It's all right." Claire approached but couldn't do it. She stepped back into the passageway. It seemed a little cooler. "I can't sleep in there," she said. She sat down on the floor, crossing her legs to make a bed for Katie. She pulled clothing from her bag for padding and busied herself changing the baby's diaper.

"Suit yourself." Nash climbed into the bunk. He was asleep in an instant.

Allison was too tired to worry about her surroundings. She helped Tyler rummage through his bags for enough clothing to make his bed. He chose an upper bunk above Yi Ling, Allison a lower. Yi Ling helped Ruth settle Tai.

Exhausted, Allison sank into her bunk, settling herself in with Wen Li, who was still oblivious to everything. Above they heard Yang Boda barking orders. The sun was just peeking over the horizon when they heard the sounds of the crew preparing to get under way. There was a ratcheting as the dinghy was lifted onto the boat deck, and then the whine of a winch and the clanking of the anchor chain as the links clattered through the hawseholes in the bow. Directly behind the bulkhead of the little cabin, the engines of the *432 Springtime Flower* rumbled to life. The bunks reverberated with the crankshafts. Nash's bag fell to the floor with a *whump* that woke Katie, who started to cry. As she lay there, Allison thought she heard Claire crying, too. She wondered if it could get any worse.

"I have to go to the bathroom," Tyler said from his bunk.

Allison groaned inwardly. "Go back up," she said. "You can probably go over the rail. But be careful and hold on, okay?"

Tyler squirmed but didn't move.

"What's the matter?"

"I have to go number two."

"Oh." Allison closed her eyes. She started to get up, but Yi Ling was already up. "Come," she said to the boy. "We find together."

"Thanks, Yi Ling." Allison relaxed gratefully, listening to the throbbing engines. The vibrations were strong but soothing. The little bunk was actually quite comfortable. Wen Li nestled in the crook of her arm next to the wall, where she couldn't fall out. Allison had never slept with a baby, and she worried about rolling over and crushing her. She sighed and started to shift.

"What's the matter?" Ruth asked quietly.

"I'm afraid I'm going to roll over on Wen Li."

"For God's sake, Allison," Ruth snorted, "she'll manage. She hasn't come all this way just to get squashed in her sleep."

Allison laughed. She looked at the ceiling, from which bits of wood were hanging loose, ready to fall. The boat was a horror. She thought of their earlier conversation. "I think this *proves* we're crazy, Ruth."

Ruth laughed. "Absolutely. Lunatic level, riding in the first-class cabin. But I still think we're right."

"I hope so."

"I know so."

A distant ship's horn sounded, the blast muffled and somehow comforting.

"Good night, Ruth."

"G'night."

The engines surged then and she felt a slow, steady roll as the boat gathered speed. Even in her fatigue, she found it hard to sleep. Her mind was still in turmoil. The day had been a disaster. Vaguely she heard Tyler and Yi Ling return, and then the beeping of Tyler's video game. Ruth started to snore. Allison thought of Claire, cowering in the passageway, hiding from the bugs. She knew it was none of her business, but it made her angry that Nash wasn't with her.

Allison realized she'd been awake for twenty-four hours. She hadn't done that since college. It had been the most remarkable twenty-four hours of her life—hours in which, for better or worse, a choice had been made, a line crossed. There was no going back. Each time she thought about it, she felt the same strange shock: she was a straitlaced civil engineer from Denver, huddled in the bowels of a broken-down cargo boat on the Wàn Li Chang Jiang, the ten-thousand-*li* Yangtze. Hunted by the police, with her stepson and a baby that wasn't legally hers.

With all that, she wasn't even heading toward Shanghai, toward home. Instead she was heading upriver, deeper into the heart of China.

CHAPTER 6

W ITH A ROAR two motorcycles and three cars arrived together at the PSB station in Hukou. The last car was a gleaming black Audi with official plates and flags waving from the front fenders. Before it stopped moving, a guard jumped out of the passenger side and opened the rear door. A man stepped out. His Western suit was striking because it was pressed and fit perfectly. His Italian leather shoes were highly polished and his fingernails were carefully manicured. His hair was slick and black and combed straight back. There was nothing casual in his air, nothing coarse, and somehow he showed no sign of the heat that made the men standing near him wilt. Amid the others he was a glittering island in a shabby sea.

Moments later Colonel Quan Yi stood in a corridor inside the police station, looking through the glass window at the prisoner slumped in the chair.

So this is the fearsome Ya Ming, he thought. The lettuce farmer who so distressed Beijing. Ya Ming had stood quietly in the road, leading other farmers in a protest against a waterworks. First one farmer, then ten, then a hundred. From such humble origins were revolutions born. Already an article had appeared in the *People's Daily.* The minister wanted it finished quickly. Colonel Quan had been flown in on a small government jet, to give the minister what he wanted.

They'd taken the prisoner's clothes and he sat naked in the chilly room, his body covered with cuts and bruises. His cheek was purple, the skin swollen and stretched like an overripe plum. One eye was puffed shut. The other stared without focus at the floor. There was spittle at the corner of his mouth. The fingers on one hand were broken. He'd soiled the chair and the room smelled of it.

The colonel wrinkled his nose and frowned. He generally found the methods of the provincial police brutal and primitive. Thugs without finesse. He turned scornful eyes upon the captain. "Is this the only way you know to handle such men?"

"He brought the injuries upon himself," the captain replied defensively, squirming inside at the awful loss of face. "In the street disturbance."

"Yes, of course. It is always so, *neh*? A pity he didn't die there, too. See that he's cleaned up, that he has something to eat and drink. And get him a doctor. Quickly. If he dies, you'll wish you had as well."

"But Comr—"

Quan Yi cut him off. "I understand his wife is here?"

"Yes, Colonel."

"Bring her to me."

Quan ignored her for a few moments. He lit a cigarette, carefully tapping his ashes into a precise little pile in a glass tray. He sipped delicately from a cup of tea as he studied a single sheet of paper.

Presently he looked up at her. "You are Su Xiao, wife of Ya Ming?"

She nodded, too terrified to speak.

"Su Xiao, I am Colonel Quan Yi. It is my wish that you be comfortable here. There is nothing to fear. You would like a cup of *cha*?"

"*Xièxie, bú yào*," she said, shaking her head. "I only want news of my husband."

"Please, I insist. It will soothe you." He took a glass from a tray on the desk and wiped it carefully with a handkerchief, then poured for her from a pot.

She was faint from hunger, and the tea was steaming and she couldn't resist. "*Xièxie*," she said, accepting it with two hands. With the first sip she knew she'd never had better. She drank only *hua cha*, a weak flower tea from Jiangsu.

"You approve, then," he said, noticing how she savored the hot drink. "It is Black Dragon, from Fujian. Wu Long. I carry a supply wherever I go. Here, Young Su, you may take some with my compliments." He withdrew a small paper packet from a wooden box in the drawer and handed it to her in a gesture of respect. Then he filled his own cup and sat down. He sipped his tea and smoked, and the neat pile of ashes in the glass ashtray grew, and he watched the farm woman in silence.

She kept her eyes down and sipped the tea. She felt his gaze, and it made her uncomfortable. She didn't know what to make of kindness from such an obviously powerful cadre and tried to retreat behind her little glass, hoping she might somehow keep her wits.

He turned his attention to the paper he'd been studying. He lifted it carefully and placed it in front of her. He produced an expensive fountain pen from his pocket and unscrewed the cap. He held it out for her.

"You may use my pen." His voice was velvet and his eyes were kind, almost sympathetic.

Su Xiao looked at the paper, then at him. "I beg your pardon, but I cannot read," she said. "What is it?"

"Your husband, Ya Ming, has acted to the detriment of the state. I have personally reviewed the case. It would be the easy thing for me to shelter and detain him without trial. Or to have him tried. He would be sent to the *laogai,* of course. But I believe Ya Ming is not a common criminal who needs reform *or* labor. I believe he is ill. As his wife, you must declare him so, for his own good."

"Ill!" Su Xiao let out a little gasp and her hand flew to her mouth. "But he is *not* ill! He is healthy as an ox. He works—"

"The doctors have already examined him. You are a peasant woman. Perhaps you have not understood the signs. While in custody he has already hurt himself. A sane man does not do this."

"He was hurt in the street! The police beat him! I saw! The others saw!"

"You are mistaken. I have the official report. There is no mention of this."

Her heart sank. These were arguments she could not hope to win. "My husband is only a farmer. If you'll just let him go, he will make no more trouble. You have my word."

"He has already made trouble. Written letters, stirring sentiments against the state." He opened a desk drawer and extracted a thin sheaf of papers that he tossed on the desk.

She had begged Ya Ming not to write them, but he'd insisted, emboldened by stories he'd heard of farmers in other provinces who'd written letters without reprisals. He'd sent them off to officials in the provincial capital. The only response he'd received had been the roar of the bulldozers' engines.

"He was only trying to protect our farm."

"You were offered a price for your land," he said. "The welfare of the county demanded that you accept, but you did not. Instead your husband sought to make trouble, to organize others. He is guilty of counterrevolutionary incitement."

"But our land is good and the price was not," Su Xiao protested. "We would lose everything, and have not enough to build another farm."

"The price was determined by the state. How could it be other than fair?"

She had no idea of Quan Yi's exact authority, but she knew him to be a man who could ruin her family or save it. She took a deep breath and plunged ahead. "The state does not farm our land. What they offered is no good. My husband went to see. Half the year it sits in water. It is almost all rock, honorable Quan, and nothing will grow. There's a battery factory nearby that poisons the soil."

He smoked in silence, blowing neat rings. "I am a reasonable man, Young Su. I am empowered to offer you more money," he said. "And I myself will see that you receive better land."

She brightened, hopeful for the first time. "What about the other farmers? Their land is no better."

"I cannot help the others. But I can help you."

She had tried. "That would be wonderful! My husband will be so grateful."

The colonel tapped the paper with the pen. The ruffian Ya Ming was not part of the bargain. "You must only sign this," he said, "and I will give the order myself."

"But I told you! He is not insane! His place is with his family. Please, Colonel Quan. *Qing.*"

"If you do not sign, your farm will be bulldozed and you will receive nothing in exchange. Do you understand me? *Wo bú zài hù!*" The colonel opened a file on the desk. It was Ya Ming's *dàng àn.* It was very thin, only a sheet and a half tracking an entire life. "You mentioned your son. Anlan, I believe," he said, reading from the file.

"*Shì.* He is very bright."

"The son of a felon will be denied permission to attend secondary school. And the family of a felon will be fined thirty thousand yuan, for antistate activity." He looked up from the papers. "Do you have thirty thousand yuan, Su Xiao?"

She gasped. "No, but without my husband—"

"This is all quite unnecessary," he said, his voice soothing. "You can do

Ya Ming a kindness with your signature. He will be well cared for. He will have the best doctors. When he recovers he will come home to a better farm, and he will have you to thank."

Su Xiao knew that if Ya Ming ever came home at all, it would be as a cripple, his mind or his body or both destroyed, the way they all were when the authorities finished with them. She knew it was not just a pen but the very future of her family that now trembled in her hand. If she signed, her husband would be destroyed. If she refused to sign, her entire family would be destroyed. Her eyes watered, and the words on the paper blurred.

There was a knock at the door. The captain of the PSB stepped in briefly. "I am sorry to disturb you, Colonel," he said. "There is a call—"

"*Xiàn zài bù xíng!*" The colonel snapped his impatience at the interruption.

The captain squirmed. "It is the deputy minister, Colonel."

Quan turned to Su Xiao and spoke softly. "If I leave this room without your signature, I will forget my inclinations of generosity." He rose from his chair.

Su Xiao closed her eyes. She leaned forward and signed the paper.

"*Wei,* Deputy Minister. I am Quan Yi."

There was an echo on the phone. The connection was bad, but Colonel Quan had no trouble recognizing the raspy voice at the other end.

"The disturbance is settled?"

"It was nothing, Deputy Minister. A minor matter."

"*Hao,*" came the reply. "Good. There is something else that presses me."

"Of course."

"I have received a call from Yu Zhiding," the minister said. Quan knew him to be the provincial head of the PSB in Nanjing. "He tells me that American visitors have kidnapped three children from an orphanage in Suzhou."

Colonel Quan raised his eyebrows. "*Dà bíng zi?* What were big noses doing with the children?"

"They were to have adopted them, but the bumpkins in the Civil Affairs and Justice Ministries have gotten into a power struggle. It seems to be a procedural matter. Apparently the Americans were given healthy babies, in violation of the rules that said they were to receive children with medical needs. The error was discovered and an exchange was ordered."

He sighed, the irritation in his voice clear. "As if there aren't enough babies to go around, and they have to choose. Something which should have been simple has become something difficult. But that is quite another matter, of no concern to me. What is of concern is that the Americans have taken the children and disappeared."

Quan grunted, surprised. "Disappeared! How is that possible?"

"You ask me? I wouldn't have known about it except that the governor received a call from a reporter with the American news agency CNN. The governor denied everything and then quietly made his own inquiries. He discovered the captain of the Suzhou gong an ju was trying to handle this himself. He didn't report to the PSB foreign affairs bureau. He will be dealt with later. In the interim the Americans have vanished."

"I see."

"You must act quickly, before the situation gets worse. The case has quite unpleasant potential. We must not be made to look like fools who cannot protect our own babies. When I brief the minister he will want to know it is you handling the matter. Quickly and quietly, as always. If you require more than the usual resources, you will have them. You are to drop all other assignments. I have already dispatched Major Ma with a file containing the relevant information. He will meet you in Nanjing."

Quan was surprised and troubled. He was working on several critical cases, including one involving state security at the very highest levels of the government, an investigation sanctioned by the premier himself. Now he was being ordered to drop everything to chase a few *lao wai* and some babies—the sort of thing junior officers handled routinely. It seemed an extraordinary use of his talents, but he said nothing.

"Of course, Deputy Minister. I'll leave at once."

"*Marshall?* It's Clarence. You'd better turn on CNN."

"What's up?"

"Just turn it on. A friend of mine from CNN called me a minute ago with a heads-up."

Marshall Turk was in his study, sitting in the gloom. Books and files littered his desk. A legal pad sat in the middle of the pile, filled with doodles he'd made while trying in vain to work on a client's case that was scheduled for trial in four days. He was behind with his preparations, but concentration had been impossible. The telephone startled him. Clarence Coulter was senior partner at Coulter Grogan, Marshall's law firm.

Marshall picked up a remote and flicked on the set in the bookcase, clicking through the channels until he had CNN.

" . . . others tentatively identified as Ruth Pollard of Los Angeles, and Allison Turk, of Denver."

Marshall's blood ran cold. He watched the set in shock. A bronzed reporter's face filled the screen. At the bottom it read, "Colin Chandler" and "Live, Suzhou, China."

"Chinese authorities have refused comment on the report, but CNN has confirmed through sources who requested anonymity that the American families, who had been given babies from this orphanage"—he indicated a three-story white tile building behind him—"were caught in a struggle between bureaucracies. They were ordered by authorities to return the babies, whose ages we understand to be under one year, to the orphanage. Instead the families have disappeared with the children and their present whereabouts are unknown. They are being sought by the police."

"Jesus Christ," Clarence breathed. "Are you still there, Marshall?"

"I'm here."

"What the hell is going on? Is it true? Is Allison all right? I had no idea—"

"Just a minute. Let me listen."

"Officials at the American consulate in Shanghai have confirmed they talked with the missing Americans but refused to provide details. From Suzhou, China, Colin Chandler reporting." The image switched to the Atlanta news desk, where the anchor introduced a story about teen violence. Marshall pressed the mute button on his remote control and sat watching the screen, trying to take it in. He coughed and felt needles of pain shooting through his inner ears. His head pounded.

"Marshall? Are you all right?"

"I don't know," Marshall said, his voice thick. "I'll call you back."

The first time they met, Marshall made Allison furious, and in turn she embarrassed him. Allison worked for a large civil engineering firm, Brady & Wesson, which had hired her straight out of college. The firm put dams and roads and bridges in impossible places. She loved her work, loved to shut herself in her office and do battle with the tough problems of her clients—spanning more space with less steel, supporting a building without destroying the beauty of the rocks on which it stood, sketching beauty and grace into the structures she designed. She was good at it—too good—and kept getting promoted. She had a staff of ten designers and was a project manager for some of the firm's biggest endeavors, when a bridge her team had designed collapsed on an interstate highway. Allison knew her staff had not been responsible, but the lawsuits filed threatened the survival of her firm.

Coulter Grogan was Denver's biggest and most political law firm. Its letterhead boasted two former governors and a senator. Upon an early foundation of legal work for large businesses, the firm added lobbying and international affairs to its résumé. It had offices in Washington, New York, London, and Hong Kong, representing governments from the Ivory Coast to Zaire to Singapore. Its partners organized fund-raisers for the political elite. When Air Force One came to town, it was Clarence Coulter who emerged from the jet one step behind the president, often even before the state's governor. When the president was just a governor himself, one of the first heavy hitters to believe was Clarence Coulter, who tirelessly raised funds for the obscure politician. Coulter opened doors and made introductions. After the governor won, there was no more influential law firm in the country.

Marshall Turk, the youngest partner at the firm, was a driven, apolitical attorney who specialized in trial work. He defended the white-collar problems of his firms' biggest clients: the indictments from the EPA, the interrogatories from the Department of Energy, the subpoenas from the Department of Justice. It was rare that he handled a matter like a collapsed bridge, but the owner of the engineering firm for which Allison worked was a fraternity brother of Clarence Coulter, who insisted that Marshall handle the case.

Marshall strode into the conference room where Allison and her team were assembled. As always, he entered the room with arrogance and flair, his suit impeccably tailored, three junior attorneys trailing behind, carrying his files and ready to take notes. Marshall immediately assessed Allison as a meek office engineer. He began questioning her staff methodically, rudely, almost adversarially. As he skimmed over technical details of the bridge design and its subsequent collapse, he saw her bristle, and then, to his astonishment, she called him on a technical point. He'd been bluffing about his knowledge of an obscure engineering matter—something he'd read during his preparation—and she tripped him up. He did his best to cloak his discomfiture, but it was clear she'd hit him.

In the hallway after their meeting, she drew him aside. "Excuse me, Mr. Turk, but I'm afraid I don't understand your methods. I thought you were on our side," she said.

"I am," he assured her, his eyes intense.

"Then I'd very much appreciate it if you'd stop being such an asshole. My staff isn't the enemy."

"In litigation assholes get the job done."

"Then I'm sure you've won a lot of cases," she said. "But I've got a good team in there and don't need you tearing it up."

"I do what I think is necessary to win."

"Then you'd better start by doing your homework. Your little bluff in there was transparent to the most junior engineer in the room. I hope you do better in court."

He looked at her more appreciatively after that, realizing that her unassuming manner masked a core of steel. Their relations did not warm during the trial. He was endlessly demanding and found her professional but cool. There were countless late night calls and summonses to hurried conferences and requests for an infinite stream of documents. She helped him develop charts and graphs and slides, so that by the time the trial started he was able to render a complex case comprehensible to the jury.

As always, his questioning of witnesses could be savage or funny or downright embarrassing for the person on the stand. What surprised him was that he cared whether she noticed. In court he found himself glancing discreetly in her direction. If she noticed, she gave no sign.

The night after they won, he called her at home. He was nervous. "I wondered if you might consider dinner with an asshole," he said.

"Absolutely not."

He persisted until she relented. "All right, just once," she agreed. "To say thanks." To their mutual surprise, they had a wonderful dinner, with no lingering animosity. They laughed easily and talked about everything, without arrogance or shyness or artifice. He was most surprised to discover he could relax with her. There was no need for him to perform, and she noticed.

"Now you've confused me," she said over wine. "I don't know which Marshall is real—the one I saw during the lawsuit or the one sitting with me now. I keep hoping you have an evil twin who plays the lawyer."

"I assure you, both of me are real," he replied, laughing. "But I leave the bad guy at work. Away from all that I'm just a cupcake."

As he looked into her twinkling eyes, he knew she believed him.

*   *   *

After Marshall's wife had died of cancer, he shunned the social circuit at the firm and buried himself in two tasks: raising his son, Tyler, and devoting himself to the needs of his clients. He loved his son deeply, spending every spare moment with the boy, while his intensity and skill at work won him a full partnership by the time he was thirty-five.

Allison was the first woman he had seen socially since his wife's death. For their second date they went to a movie with Tyler, who didn't warm to her at all. He was polite but distant, distrusting this woman in whom his father seemed so interested. He responded in monosyllables when she tried to make conversation.

"I'm sorry," Marshall said when he dropped her off that night. "He'll like you, I know it."

"You needn't apologize," she said. "This is difficult for him."

Over the next few weeks Marshall spent far less time than normal at work, and the three of them went rowing on the lake at City Park and bicycling in the mountains, but Tyler remained reserved. Then one weekend they went fishing on the Crystal River. Allison had never been fishing. Marshall got her started, then moved down the river with his own pole in hand, his motions beautiful and fluid. From the riverbank Tyler watched as Allison fumbled with her equipment, line tangled hopelessly around her reel, her hook caught in a bush.

"Jeez," he said at last, disgusted, "I thought you were a scientist."

"Engineer," she said lamely. Marshall pretended not to hear and kept casting.

Clearly unimpressed with her education, Tyler waded into the water. "You'll never get it that way." He got things straightened out, showed her how to tie a proper knot, and helped her cast a few times until she got the hang of it. Later that morning, when Allison caught the first fish of her life, she got so excited that she fell into the river. Without a shred of grace she disappeared beneath the frigid water and came up sputtering, and when she'd gotten her footing she realized she'd dropped her rod. Some of the fishing line was still tangled around her arm. Quickly she pulled it in, hand over hand, and at the end there was a sixteen-inch brown trout, flapping in the sun. Soaked to the bone, her teeth chattering, she whooped and Marshall cheered, and both of them saw Tyler smiling.

That night when Marshall was tucking Tyler into bed, they talked about her catch. "She's okay for a girl, I guess," Tyler said. "But I'd rather just have you."

"You'll always have me."

Soon after the marriage, Allison found herself pregnant. She and Marshall were delighted, and at thirty-five she knew she was ready to forgo her career for a while, if not forever, and become a full-time mother. As her stomach grew, she decorated the nursery, hand-painting mobiles that she hung above the crib, trying her hand at embroidering pillows, shopping for clothes. She let Tyler feel the baby kicking inside, and he was fascinated, if not too thrilled, to have a brother or sister around the house.

She was seven months pregnant when she went into labor while at work. Something had gone wrong, and the baby was stillborn. They named her Anna and buried her. The shock from that had barely subsided when the doctor told her she couldn't have any more children. Devastated, numb, Allison returned to work. Marshall was quite content with Tyler and didn't share Allison's level of desperation for another child, but he loved her, and he loved the idea of having a baby with her. They decided to adopt privately. They used a reputable agency that found a sixteen-year-old girl who was pregnant but not yet ready to be a mother. She didn't know where the father was. She thought he might be in jail in another state, but she hadn't seen him since the night the baby was conceived. He didn't even know she was pregnant. Marshall was uneasy about the father not being present, but under the circumstances it didn't seem there was an undue amount of risk. Marshall and Allison paid for doctors' appointments for the girl and took care of her other expenses.

The papers were signed while the mother was in her eighth month of pregnancy. A check for $15,000 changed hands, and on a bright summer morning a new Turk was born: eight pounds seven ounces and a world-class set of lungs. They named her Mary. Allison took indefinite leave from work to stay at home with her.

Then, with a knock at her door, her world collapsed. She opened it to find a pleasant-looking man standing on the porch. "Mrs. Turk?" he asked. "Mrs. Allison Turk?"

"Yes." The process server handed her the papers. She read them in horror and disbelief. She tried to reach Marshall, but he was in court. She called the lawyer who sent the papers, a rude Legal Aid attorney. The mother had found the father, he said. He wanted to keep the baby. The young couple was getting married.

"But they can't," Allison protested, fighting the sour bile rising in her throat. "We have papers. The adoption is final."

He sneered. "The papers don't mean anything."

She'd been in hysterics by the time Marshall got home. He held her and promised everything would be all right. She slept in Mary's room, her arm draped between the slats of the crib. She had to touch her.

Marshall had intended to prepare the case himself, but Clarence Coulter had prevailed on his better judgment, reminding him of the most basic lesson of law school, how the lawyer who represented himself had a fool for a client. Marshall relented only when Clarence assigned two of the firm's top attorneys and a paralegal to the case. Marshall let the others take the lead, but he was involved in every aspect of the depositions, the discovery, the pretrial motions. As was customary in its legal battles, Coulter Grogan swamped its poorly funded opposing counsel with a blizzard of paper. Marshall left no possible argument overlooked. He dissected each detail of the case with Allison, the coming trial dominating their lives.

A detective hired by the firm discovered that Mary's biological father had been arrested for the suspected abuse of the infant child of yet another girlfriend. The mother was uneducated, unemployed, and dirt poor. As the trial date approached, Marshall grew ever more confident, while Allison found it progressively harder to put Mary down at all. She clung to the baby all day, even while cleaning or cooking or running errands. At night they sat together in a rocker until Mary fell asleep in her arms.

The trial lasted two days. The judge ruled that the rights of the biological mother and father took precedence over those of the adoptive parents. The judge was still speaking when Allison became so upset that she had to be led from the courtroom. "You promised, damn you, you promised!" she screamed at Marshall. She knew it wasn't his fault, but the devastation was more than she could bear.

She didn't sleep for three days. Coulter Grogan filed an immediate appeal, but custody of the baby was granted to her biological parents pending the outcome. Nothing in Allison's life had been as difficult as handing Mary over to the court-appointed social worker. Marshall was still consumed with the legal battle and too busy to let himself fall into depression, but Allison had nothing but her grief to occupy her. For days she was heavily sedated. She wandered around the house, each reminder of Mary welling up inside her until she thought she would burst, but she refused Marshall's suggestion that they go away.

Marshall knew he had done everything possible, but the pain of failure, of losing to an opponent he thought he should easily have beaten, ate at his conscience. He tried to make Allison get angry at him, to accuse him of botching the case, but she wouldn't, yet she wouldn't talk about it, either. She retreated into her own private world of grief and wouldn't let him in. It had always remained an unspoken issue between them. For months they sought desperately to regain the closeness they'd shared before Mary, but they couldn't find it again, and for a time Marshall thought he was going to lose Allison, too. But Allison was not melancholy by nature, and as the months passed she shook the worst of her depression. They left Tyler with Marshall's sister and took a vacation together in Mexico, where through long days on the beach and long nights of making love they found themselves again. Afterward she went back to work, but it was a long time before she could laugh again, and she never got over the pain.

The appeal dragged on. After a year Allison told Marshall to drop it. "I couldn't take Mary from her new home now even if we won," she said. "It would just be selfish of me, and not fair to her. She's gone now. I need to let her go."

Now Marshall sat in his study, staring at the picture of Tyler in his Little League uniform, bat draped nonchalantly over his shoulder, cheek swollen with bubble gum, a seven-year-old's invincible grin on his face. He thought of his wife and son thousands of miles away, alone and running. No, they weren't alone, he had to remind himself. There was Wen Li now. There wasn't a picture of her in his study. It wasn't intentional, just an oversight, but that was indicative of his dilemma. He knew that what Allison said was true, that Wen Li didn't mean to him what she meant to Allison. He felt guilty, and he didn't like the fact that it was true. But it was.

Tyler was his son, but Wen Li was not yet his daughter. She was the cause of their trouble and not yet, in his mind, a partner in it.

It took all the discipline of his years as a lawyer to keep from going crazy. For the first time in his life, he wasn't sure what to do. He had never known Allison to act so out of character. He'd often ribbed her for being so predictably straight about everything. They'd never discussed it, but he knew she had never considered running away with Mary rather than turning her over as ordered. Other mothers had run. But not Allison. She had trusted Marshall, trusted the legal system to do the right thing. Even when the system failed her, as awful as it was, she obeyed, because she always obeyed. The judge's decision was the law. In Allison's life that was the order of things. The bizarre thing was that she'd had to travel all the way to China to go insane and test her new wings of defiance.

He picked up the phone and called Clarence back.

"What are you going to do?" Clarence asked.

"I don't know. I want to go find them."

"That's ridiculous. They could be anywhere. You'd never find them. The police will have them before you can even get to the airport."

"I know that. I'm just feeling helpless. Maybe I ought to get to our Hong Kong office. At least I'd be closer when something happens."

"Can you fly yet, with your ear problem?" Clarence asked.

"Doctor says no. He thinks I'm not recovering like I ought to be, and wants to do more tests."

"Then wait a day or two. There's not much you can do there now, anyway. She'll call again, and when she does you need to convince her to turn herself in."

Marshall closed his eyes. "I already tried that. She won't."

"I'll call Warren," Clarence said, referring to the secretary of state. "They sure as hell need to be doing something to help."

"They're going to be in an awkward position."

"Not awkward, impossible. But he owes me."

"We should get someone at the firm working on Chinese law. From what I know of it, their law is only as good as the man making it up."

"I'll get Eric Bader on it."

"He's pretty young."

"I used him on the Alter case. He's the best."

"Okay. Get him started on adoption law."

"Adoption law? Obviously your head *is* still stuffed. I'll start him on criminal law, Marshall. Kidnapping, for starters."

CHAPTER 7

WHERE THE *432 Springtime Flower* began its journey upriver, the Yangtze was more than a mile and a half wide. It ran fast and deep and created its own weather. On its currents flowed the history of a nation. It was one of the great highways of the earth, where for centuries the winds that blew from the east allowed the sailing junks of imperial China to trade silks and tea all the way upriver to Wuhan. Fed by hundreds of rivers and spanning ten provinces, the Yangtze was subject to moods as epic as the poems composed about it. The river brought life and death to a third of China's people and divided the country, north from south.

The river swarmed with107 traffic. Freighters of five thousand tons headed upriver, passing four-deck passenger ferries headed down. Neon signs and bright lights were strung along the sides of the ferries, illuminating passengers who could be seen peeing over the side, or taking pictures, or smoking and chatting at the rails. Some of the tiniest craft carried ricks of wheat so large that the boats beneath were all but lost to view. Rusty barges rode low in the water, bearing lumber or coal or dredged-up river soil that was dumped on the banks, from which it was hauled away by coolies, two buckets at a time.

The bulk of the Yangtze fleet was composed of small cargo boats, most no more than six meters in length and quite shallow in draft, looking like floating Confederate hats with long bills. Most had shanty cabins jutting from the rear from which laundry fluttered, while cookfires and old engines trailed plumes of smoke. Whole families lived on board year-round. The little boats swarmed in packs, and the deep thrumming of their engines could be heard long before the boats could be seen.

There was nothing picturesque about the lower Yangtze. It was a utility, a foul pipeline through which flowed an endless grimy commerce. There were dreary towns and power plants and docks where modern rigs that resembled giant praying mantises plucked cargo from boats to railcars and back again. Farmers toiled in fields sandwiched between factories. Water buffalo wallowed in the deep mud near the shore and grazed on lush grasses, beneath smokestacks that belched noxious fumes. Goats and pigs foraged in groves of mulberry trees where silkworms were bred and raw sewage from Shanghai was dumped. At water's edge a woman balanced on a bamboo raft, doing her laundry. Her young son squatted nearby, shitting into the water.

Yang Boda stood at the helm of the *432*. His wheelhouse was more shack than bridge, standing above and behind the hold. Inside there was a bunk for the first mate, Shidao, who took turns at the wheel. A book of well-worn river charts hung from the wall. The wheel was teak, worn smooth and black from years of use. Next to the wheel stood a compass mounted in an old brass binnacle. Above it, hanging from a crossbeam, was an ornate wooden bird cage. Inside, a canary hopped through a field of sunflower seeds, chirruping gaily. Yang Boda whistled back through yellow teeth. His father had run junks, and his father before him, in an uninterrupted line stretching back hundreds of years. While Yang Boda's boat had modern engines and navigation aids, it also bore the traces of generations of superstition. Strips of colored cloth hung from the canary cage, fending off evil spirits. The strips were as old and tattered as the boat, their colors long faded but their effectiveness never in doubt. Beneath their shield, the *Springtime Flower* had survived floods and fire and the endless imprecations of a hostile river. On the port side, the side of honor, there was a niche in the wall, inside which stood a statue of Chen Jiang Wang Yeh. The potbellied Chen was the river guardian king, a twelfth-century pirate whose spirit served to protect crew and cargo. By captain's orders, a joss stick burned at Chen's feet whenever the boat was under way.

Every so often, when some mishap befell the *432 Springtime Flower*—when a generator failed or a bearing seized—Yang Boda would attempt to shake the water ghosts responsible for the bad luck. He would seek out a bigger ship on the river. Then, pushing his engines until they screamed, he would steer the *432* perilously close to the bow of the other boat, often avoiding a collision by less than a meter as he crossed in front, leaving the captain of the other vessel apoplectic with rage. By so doing, Yang Boda would cut the string that tethered the spirits to the *432*, freeing them to infest the other boat. Cackling, Yang Boda would leave the other ship in his wake and speed upriver, free of trouble. That some of his beliefs sprang from superstitions long dead among other rivermen only proved to Yang Boda that they were worthy of retaining.

Having taken every celestial precaution, Yang Boda used all his earthly skill to navigate the cruel river passages that changed with the seasons, sometimes almost daily. He peered through the grimy windows of the wheelhouse, seeking to avoid the sandbars that could form overnight, and the treacherous chop-chop that sometimes gave the only hint of the swirling currents that could take the unwary boatman to the bottom. No matter how many times he made the trip, he never let his guard down— not for the dangers of the river or for the authorities who patrolled it, both of which threatened him this day.

Soon after embarking at Nanjing, he had heard an alert on the police maritime frequency. Already they were searching for him on the river. He had known they eventually would be, but their speed surprised him. It did not bode well for his father's well-being. The PSB would care nothing for his father's age or infirmities, and Yang Boda feared for him. It would be expensive to free him, and he hoped the PSB wouldn't be too hard on him before he could make the arrangements.

On the river he had the advantage of traveling under assumed identities, both for himself and for his vessel. He carried three separate identity cards, all in different names. They were quite genuine, issued by the police themselves. He had taken similar precautions with the papers for the *Springtime Flower,* the pride of his little fleet. When he heard the alert he dispatched one of his crew to retrieve the three battered wooden placards that he used on such occasions. While it was still nearly dark they were quickly screwed into place over the others—one port, one starboard, the other aft. With the last turn of the screwdriver, the *432 Springtime Flower* became the *Fragrant Moon* of Shanghai, whose papers were issued by the maritime authority and quite as legitimate as his own. The police might accuse Yang Boda of many things, but they could never say that his various sets of documents were not in order.

Now, as he navigated the buoys that marked the channels, he mulled over his strategy for passing the next inspection station at Xingang. His sources had told him surprise inspections were scheduled there for the next forty-eight hours. Already he had made it past Wuhu station without incident. There were certain customs stations where he was required to stop, but Wuhu was not among them. The real danger lay in being hailed by a bored shore officer marking his passage, or in a surprise inspection by one of the *kuài ting,* the "fast crab" police boats that patrolled the Yangtze, looking for unpaid duty and smuggled cargo. He had taken great pains not to attract attention: his vessel looked as seedy and innocuous as any on the river. But just to be sure, before reaching Wuhu he had laid up behind an island just below the city, waiting until the precise moment the shift would be changing and his passage might attract less attention. He knew all the shifts at all the stations along the river, and most of the officers within them. He knew which could be bought and which could not. As he reviewed his precautions, he was confident he'd done everything possible.

His passengers had arisen in the early afternoon when the sun was hot and the air lay on the river like a wet, fetid blanket. He'd ordered them to stay belowdecks, but his niece had grown stubborn after the difficult night. She insisted that a proper place be made for them in the stern behind the wheelhouse, so they could sit outside. A tarp was stretched over the stay cables that ran aft from the wheelhouse to the boat deck, providing a canopy that was low enough to protect them from prying eyes on the river but high enough to permit a breeze of Yangtze air, which, although gray and tasting of minerals, was fresher than the air below. Next Yi Ling stripped the grimy bedding from the bunks and washed it herself, hanging it over the starboard rails, where it flapped noisily in the breeze. She badgered one of the crew into hosing down the cabin. Finally, over the protests of the cook, she confiscated the only electric fan from the galley and placed it inside the cabin.

Yang Boda glared good-naturedly at his niece. "You would make a good first mate," he said. "But you should never anger the cook like that. He'll put something unsavory in your soup. Or worse, in mine. Besides, cargo does not merit such special attention."

"These are my honored guests, Uncle," Yi Ling reminded him.

"As you wish," he said, patting the thick wad of currency in his pocket. "Your guests. My cargo." He peered out at the river and made a slight adjustment in their course to avoid a coal barge. "You have risked much for these *lao wai,*" he said. "Your mother would thrash me for letting you place yourself in such danger."

"It is for the children."

"Orphans!" He snorted. "For orphans you give up everything? Your job, your apartment, your future? Your freedom? If they catch you—"

"I know, Uncle," Yi Ling said. "But I cannot explain what I do not fully understand myself. They needed my help. I was able to give it. I could not turn my back on them."

"I hope that is enough, when you are working in the *laogai*," he snapped, referring to the labor camps in which he had spent so many years. "You are just a foolish child. This cause is not worthy of your life."

"Then I do not know of one that is," she retorted.

Yang Boda started to disagree, then thought better of it. He neither understood nor approved of his niece's actions. He had helped her because she had asked, because she was family, because he could. But for him that was as far as it went. He did not understand extending help outside one's family except for money, and she wasn't doing it for money. He sighed. One fugitive in the family was enough, but as he studied the face of his sister's daughter, he realized she was a woman now instead of the mere girl he always thought of. Her determined expression told him further argument was futile. Whether she knew her way in this matter or not, for Yi Ling there could be no turning back.

"When this is finished and you have delivered the *lao wai* to their destiny, then you must come to work for me. I can hide you. Protect you. You have many skills I can use."

Yi Ling had given little thought to her predicament, but she heard the concern in his voice. She took his rough hand into her own and pressed it to her cheek. "You are wonderful to me, Uncle. Thank you for your kindness."

Yang Boda grunted. "Kindness is for fools. I am a businessman looking for a good employee, that's all." He pulled a small well-worn notebook from his pocket. He flipped through the pages until he found what he was looking for. "These are friends of mine," he said, copying addresses and telephone numbers onto a piece of paper. "Guard them carefully. Should you ever need help, call them. One lives in Jiujiang, one in Guangzhou, the other in Xiamen. They are well connected and owe me many favors. They will climb the mountain of knives and swim the sea of fire for the niece of Yang Boda." A smile flickered briefly. "More than that, if she brings money."

Yi Ling took the paper. "*Xièxie* I will keep it. But we are safe with you now. What could happen?"

"Something always happens," he replied.

*   *   *

Nash felt the old surge of adrenaline that always accompanied danger. He was exhilarated by their flight, by the idea of being a fugitive in China, testing his skill and luck against that of the authorities. He believed that if they were caught, the worst that would happen would be expulsion from the country, without the babies. He was certain the Chinese had no stomach for imprisoning a group of parents trying to protect children. The world press would never let them get away with anything other than a symbolic detention and a quick release.

But Nash didn't expect to get caught. As always, he expected success. He studied the maps he'd brought, intending to sit down with Yi Ling and her uncle and talk about their route. He needed to be involved, to understand Yang Boda's plans, to help improve on them if he could. He had no intention of being passive cargo. He'd never been passive in his life.

His estimation of Yang Boda was rising, beginning with the man's boat, which had looked so defective in the darkness. While the women tended the babies beneath the tarp, he had done his best to explore and had soon realized that the outside of the boat was a masterpiece of deception. The *432 Springtime Flower* looked like any of a thousand other broken-down boats that plied the Yangtze, except that this one boasted powerful engines and modern electronics. He had seen Yang Boda in the wheelhouse, sliding back a panel behind which was hidden an array of modern electronic equipment. Radar, he thought, and probably sonar, too. He scanned the boat, and his eyes stopped at a compartment above and behind the wheelhouse. As he looked more closely, he saw the panels were plastic or fiberglass and not deteriorated wood as they appeared. He guessed the antennas would be hidden there. The crew—he counted eight—were veteran sailors, tough and weather-beaten, moving about their duties with a skillful air. But they looked rougher somehow, as if their true skills went well beyond simple seamanship.

Nash wondered what Yang Boda carried beneath the canvas tarps in the hold. Drugs? Arms? A cargo within a cargo, he guessed. He started down a ladder to investigate but found his way blocked by a surly sailor whose expression left no doubt that further explorations were unwelcome. Nash turned and climbed back up.

Tyler had no such difficulty. He made friends easily with the crew, communicating with smiles and gestures. They liked the young blue-eyed boy and let him have the run of the boat. In the engine room he winced at the noise of the big diesels as he held a pot of grease for the oilman, who slopped it on a bearing. Later, he helped feed the ducks tethered to a beam on the forecastle, and he watered the chickens confined in a wooden coop that hung from the bowsprit.

Twice he'd been herded belowdecks with the others, when small motorboats hailed the *432* and pulled alongside, selling fish, vegetables, and melons. Tyler watched through a porthole as the farmers in the boats haggled with Yang Boda, their banter friendly as they passed baskets up and down on ropes.

"Can I fish?" Tyler asked Yi Ling hopefully when he saw the fish.

"Not many good fish in Yangtze," she replied. "Most grown by farmers in ponds. They bring to river and sell to boats."

In the galley he watched as the cook worked over an open fire in a stone hearth, tending steaming iron cookpots. Every so often the cook stopped to suck at the long tube of a hookah that sat on a ledge above the fire. The cook grinned at him and beckoned at the pipe and the sweet-smelling smoke that rose lazily in the galley. *"Sài guò huó shén xian."*

"I . . . I don't smoke," Tyler said, shaking his head. The cook laughed through a mouthful of crooked yellow teeth. He handed Tyler a knife, and together they scaled and gutted the fish. Knives flashed as they lopped off heads and chunked flesh, then plopped everything, heads and all, into a sizzling wok.

Toward evening the first cool breeze of the day fanned the deck. Allison watched Wen Li sucking hungrily at her bottle and felt an overpowering tenderness. She stroked the child's dark hair and found herself wishing that she could breast-feed her. It was silly, she knew, but it was an almost sensuous need that brought a flush to her face.

Ruth watched her. "She has your eyes, you know," she joked.

Allison smiled. "Yes. But Marshall's ears, I think."

The cook and a helper appeared, bearing trays of food and tea. There were vegetables and rice and a rich fish stew, the cook's specialty.

Claire poked at her stew. "Isn't that an eye?" she asked in horror. "Oh God, and look!—that's an *antenna* or something." She pushed it away in disgust. The cook looked puzzled. He picked up the bowl, offering it to her once again. She shook her head and winced. The cook gave her a withering look and chucked the uneaten meal over the side, where a pair of gulls instantly appeared, diving for the scraps before they disappeared beneath the surface.

Tyler took his bowl and sat on the deck near the railing, staring into river water that looked as thick and strong as the stew. He saw trash and bits of wood, all the flotsam of the river on its journey to the sea. There were plastic bottles and clumps of vegetation and a cardboard box with Chinese characters and a picture of a television on the side. A pair of old trousers was caught up in the branches of a floating tree limb. A gull perched expectantly, waiting for dinner.

He started to toss it a piece of his stew when he stopped cold, the spoon frozen in his hand. He looked carefully, to be sure. It was hard to make out, because it was tangled up with some fishing net and what looked like an oil filter. He gave a little cry and scooted backward, his bowl clattering to the deck. Startled, the gull flew off.

"Tyler, what is it?" Allison called out.

He shook his head, his face white. Allison hurried to the rail. "Tyler? What—" And then she saw. She gasped and fought back the bile rising in her throat.

The legs and arms were puffed up, stretched shiny almost beyond recognition. The little torso was bloated and covered with a cotton shirt that had been partially torn away. Something—a fish or a bird or a crab—had taken the eyes and most of the face. But there was no mistaking what remained. It was the body of a child.

Claire's hand flew to her mouth, and she leaned over the rail and vomited.

"Dear Lord," Ruth whispered, turning away, shielding Tai's eyes as if the baby might see. Yi Ling arrived and saw what was in the water. She took Katie from Claire and helped her to sit down. Allison put her arm around Tyler, who was still staring at the river.

"Sometimes they bury that way," Yi Ling said.

She knew that when they were girls, sometimes the babies weren't dead when they entered the water.

The technician from China Telecom waited patiently in the darkened room in Shanghai, wishing he could smoke. The room, filled with Motorola TACS switching gear and IBM computers, was one of the few places in China where one could not light up. He stifled a yawn and watched his video screen, which, upon the order of the Ministry of Public Security, was now monitoring all mobile telephone traffic in the more than two hundred cells that covered the rough triangle that bound Nanjing, Shanghai, and Beijing. Hundreds of thousands of phones were active in that area, but his computers would quickly find the one he wanted. When turned on, even while no conversation was taking place, a cell phone made a perfect homing device, periodically sending a weak radio signal to the nearest cellular station. A chip in the set identified the telephone to the network, so that calls made to the number could be routed to the correct cell. Assuming the person holding such a phone was moving, such a signal could be tracked.

Suddenly the computer emitted a long, insistent beep. He tapped in a few commands and waited. There it was! The screen flashed a series of numbers. He scribbled furiously on a notepad. He moved to a second monitor and punched in a command. An instant later he had what he wanted. He turned to a large wall map and checked reference grids. The phone was moving in a northeasterly direction, approximately three-hundred kilometers outside Beijing. It passed the number thirty-one station in Tai'an, and then the forty-seven Linyi tower. He timed the intervals between stations and calculated the caller was moving at ninety-two kilometers an hour. As soon as the signal hit Linyi station he knew the caller was on the freeway and not the train, since a phone on the train would have picked up the Gao station.

He keyed in a final request and copied the number the cellular phone was calling. It belonged to an import-export firm in Beijing. In a moment the police would be listening to the conversation.

Chewing furiously on an unlit cigarette, he dialed the PSB.

"I only want something to drink." The old man whispered the words.

"Yes, of course, *lao ren jia*. All you need do is tell us of your son's activities and you shall have anything you wish to drink. As much as you want. Anything at all."

"I only want water."

"Yes, *lao ren jia*. I know, water. Now just help me. I will write what you say."

Major Ma Lin, Colonel Quan's deputy, did not enjoy what he was doing to the old man but knew it was much better than what he would have been forced to do to him as recently as five years earlier. Then, there would have been no gentle persuasion—not even with an old man. Instead he would have used all his gruesome tools of persuasion: tubes and probes and sharp instruments. But Colonel Quan was firm: this was the new China. There was to be no violence, nothing overt. Organizations in Hong

Kong and throughout the world scrutinized such things carefully, creating trouble that was, the colonel insisted, almost always unnecessary. By nature Ma Lin was a gentle man, and that suited him just fine.

Anyway, there was no need for violence with Yang Boda's father, Grandpa Yang. He was eighty-four, frail and failing quickly. He had been detained for nearly eighteen hours. In that time he hadn't slept or eaten or relieved himself. The room in the PSB headquarters was sweltering. There were no windows or fan. Sweat streamed from the old man's brow.

"I cannot help you," Grandpa Yang replied in his reedy voice. "My son tells me nothing. He is away. He is always away."

"Your neighbors say he was home last night."

"No! They are mistaken."

"Four of them have said it." Major Ma tapped the file on the wooden table. "They all say the same thing. Yang Boda was there, and there were *lao wai* with him."

"I only want water."

"You can lose your house for helping a fugitive to escape. You can go to prison. Do you want that?"

"Just water. . . ."

"You must tell me."

"Please, I am tired." Old Yang trembled. The veins stood out on his skinny arms. He was close to tears, weak and near collapse. "I must pee, and then I want to lie down."

Major Ma considered what to do next. He stood and rapped sharply on the door, which was opened instantly by a guard. The major whispered something and the guard hurried down the hall.

"Come now," Major Ma said. "You can relieve yourself." Old Yang rose unsteadily and stumbled, and the major caught him by the arm. The old man nodded thanks and mumbled something.

They entered a long corridor lit by a row of bare fluorescent tubes, more than half of which had burned out. Major Ma directed him toward the far end. Along the way they passed other rooms, all identical to the one they had just left. In each cubicle others were being interviewed, anonymous troubled souls coping with the PSB. They walked past one, then another, and Old Yang paid no attention. But at the third room Major Ma hesitated.

"You must look, *lao ren jia,*" he said, nodding toward the glass. Old Yang blinked as he looked through the one-way mirror. It took a moment for things to register. It was his wife inside the room. He didn't know they'd brought her, too. She was eighty-seven, three years his senior. They had been married for sixty-eight years. She had borne him eight children, and together they had survived famines and floods, revolutions and the rape of Nanking by the Japanese. He knew every nuance of that beautiful face, every expression. What he saw there now made him burst into tears.

Twenty minutes later, after Old Yang had finished talking, Major Ma gave him water and let him pee, and then the old man sank onto a cot for a nap.

Ten minutes after that, two carloads of *bian yi,* the plainclothes police, roared out of the PSB compound.

Colonel Quan Yi was quite good at what he did. His work made China strong, allowing her to move forward in the world in her own way, untroubled by excesses of Western justice. His superiors feared him and needed him. He knew their secrets and kept them; he knew their enemies and destroyed them. His power was nearly unchecked, and despite a modest salary as a colonel in the Ministry of Public Security, he had the trappings of a wealthy man. Helicopters and small jets stood at his disposal, along with uncounted funds to use at his sole discretion. He moved about China at will, wielding the iron hand of her authority.

He was neither old guard nor new guard, but a bridge between Chinas, a pragmatist, skillfully navigating the winds of reform blowing slowly across his nation. His loyalty was to order, his goal the efficient destruction of China's internal enemies. He had survived because he had no politics and because he was incorruptible.

He had studied in the West, receiving degrees in psychology and criminology at the University of Chicago. He left the United States with an enduring preference for finesse over brutality, persuasion over force, subtlety over the garish excesses of the old guard. But in the end, if laws needed to be broken to serve the interests of the state, he himself would break them.

Now the colonel from Beijing sat one floor above the interrogation rooms, personally supervising the hunt for the *lao wai.* He was methodically casting his net for the quarry, using a makeshift if naive staff from the Nanjing PSB. At his orders they had sent faxes, alerted bureaus, and sifted through reports as the state security apparatus shifted into gear.

Between Nanjing and the city of Jiangyin, two hundred kilometers downriver, boat traffic on the Yangtze was disrupted as double the usual number of ships were hailed for surprise inspection. Ferries were boarded, cabins searched, and passenger manifests scrutinized. The pilots, pursers, and crews of each of the ferries that had sailed downstream from Nanjing in the past eighteen hours were questioned aboard their ships. All were shown pictures of the fugitives. They had not been seen. Police launches drew alongside other ships and barges, chosen at random, the unlucky vessels standing to while grim-faced police boarded to make their hasty searches. Holds were opened and tarps thrown back. A score of arrests were made and more than eight tons of contraband seized, but there was no sign of the Americans.

Armed now with visa photographs of the fugitives, police revisited train and bus stations, interviewing crews, drivers, guards, and ticket agents. At the Nanjing airport gate crews and security personnel were interviewed. The pictures proved to be of little use. Most big noses looked identical to each other, although most people said they would have remembered the babies, especially babies traveling with *lao wai*. But no one remembered a thing.

In Shanghai, on the busy Huaihai Zhonglu, a dozen plainclothes police were on the alert, poised to make quick arrests. With no attempt at subtlety they peered over the tops of newspapers and listened to police reports over the miniature receivers they wore in their ears. Officers with binoculars perched inside office windows overlooking the area, scrutinizing vans, buses, and taxis. In Beijing, outside the American embassy, such surveillance was routine. There was always a heavy presence of plainclothes and uniformed police near the embassy compound. All nonsecure telephones inside the embassy were tapped, including all landlines with which the embassy communicated with anyone inside China.

As Quan was reviewing these measures, a junior officer knocked. "Excuse me, Colonel. There is a report from China Telecom. The cell phone stolen from the chauffeur has been located."

"How long ago?"

"Less than ten minutes." The officer pointed to a section of road on the wall map. "They must be heading for the American embassy," he said.

"Did they get the number the phone was connected to?"

"Yes, sir. It's an import-export firm, in Beijing."

"I want to know everything about the company—its owners, its employees, its customers. And I want to know if Yang Boda has an interest in the firm."

"*Shì.*" The officer scribbled notes.

"Prepare the authorities in Dezhou. As China Telecom verifies the position of the device, wait until it has passed from one highway toll station to the next. Then block all traffic front and rear, and search every vehicle."

"Every vehicle? The *lao wai* are fleeing in a van, are they not, Colonel? Shouldn't we simply stop all vans?"

Colonel Quan forced himself to patience. Officers such as this were the future of China; part of his duty was to help them, to teach. He smiled thinly at the young man. "There is an old saying," Quan told him. "Perhaps you know it: 'A peasant must wait a long time with his mouth open before a roast duck flies in.'"

The officer stared at him eagerly, expectantly, but blankly. "Yes, sir?"

"You think they would not steal a vehicle? Borrow one? Or perhaps in Nanjing City fugitives wear a sign, to make your job easier?"

"Of course not, honorable Quan," the officer replied, embarrassed. "It's only that—to stop every vehicle on that highway—there could be more than five or six thousand . . ." His objections shriveled in the harsh glare of the colonel's gaze. "I will transmit your order at once. Is there anything else?"

Quan shook his head dismissively, and the officer hurried from the room. Quan lit a cigarette and poured himself a fresh cup of Black Dragon tea and turned his attention to a file on his desk. It was already late Sunday afternoon. More than thirty hours had elapsed since the Americans had disappeared with the babies and more than twelve hours since they had been seen at the house of Yang Boda's father. Locating the telephone was the first positive development they'd had. But as he read the *dàng àn* of Yang Boda, he was certain his quarry would not be caught so easily as that. *Known contacts with Sun Yee On triad in Shanghai, Xiamen, Canton,* the dossier read, referring to the organized crime societies. There were addresses and dates and suspicions, all outlined in minute detail across two full pages. *Arrested 1986 for smuggling, bribery, and environmental crimes . . . animal skins . . . currency violations . . . sentenced to seven years in the* lao-gai. There were names of associates, suspected accomplices, and family members—all of whom, at Colonel Quan's order, were now being picked up and interviewed by their local PSBs. Within a few hours, Quan would most certainly know what they knew.

*   *   *

"My interview with the father of Yang Boda was productive," Major Ma Lin reported. His manner with the colonel was informal. The two men had worked together for years.

"Ah?"

"We have detained an associate of his son's," the major said. "The man keeps some of his records. He has not talked, but there were files and papers in his house, records of business transactions. We're going through them now."

"Do you have the names of the boats?"

"Only three, those the associate knew. We believe there are at least three others we don't know. We do have the names of the companies he owns. We're searching the registry in Shanghai to see if we can find any vessels in their names."

"What do we know about the three boats?"

Ma Lin consulted his papers. "All river vessels, nothing oceangoing. Small freighters ranging from one to five thousand tons, all purchased after 1994. Light enough to trade between Wuhan and Shanghai. Their manifests usually show light manufactured goods going upriver, agricultural products downriver. We're checking registrations, but most of the records in Shanghai are not computerized. I have seven men working on it, but it will take them hours. Perhaps a day or more."

"Very well. Notify me when you have it. Alert all police and customs on the river. I'd be surprised if most of them don't know of Yang Boda anyway. Certainly they know his money."

"I have already given the order. And there is more."

"Oh?"

"The father told me they're not going to Shanghai or Beijing. Yang Boda is taking the Americans upriver. They're going to Guangzhou."

"Canton! A long way, *neh?* Do you believe him?"

"Few men journey ten *li* when one will do as well, Quan Yi. It seems unlikely, although I believe *he* thinks it is the truth."

"Certainly he knows we would be concentrating on the east." Quan Yi lit a cigarette and paced the room. He stopped before the large wall map. With his finger he traced the Yangtze to its junction with Poyang Hu, the great freshwater lake almost five hundred kilometers upstream. It would be a bold move, however unlikely it seemed. "Jiujiang," he mused aloud, thinking of the port city near the mouth of the lake. "From there to Nanchang. After that, anything is possible—Xiamen, Canton. Waterways, rail, highways. The whole of the southeast would be open to them."

"I thought it wise not to ignore the possibility, Colonel. I have already passed the alert to the upriver stations all the way to Jiujiang."

"All right, although I must confess to skepticism. I believe the father is toying with us. Yet we have found nothing in the other direction. There is only one positive report, involving the telephone stolen from the orphanage driver." He quickly related what he knew.

"Yang Boda doesn't strike me as the sort of man who would make such a mistake with a telephone," Major Ma said. "He would know we could trace it."

"Of course he should. But fortunately for us, such mistakes are made all the time, Ma Lin. We must not ignore the possibility, anyway. Meanwhile, you must keep working on the father."

"*Hao.*" Ma Lin turned to leave, then hesitated. "By the way, I called Civil Affairs, to see what they could tell me about the regulations involved in this matter. I don't know the law in such things."

"And?"

"I tried to reach the director, but as it's Sunday I was only able to reach a clerk. He's bringing me a summary of the adoption code when he gets off duty. I'll have it copied for you as soon as it arrives."

Quan nodded. Ma Lin was as thorough as he himself.

"Apparently there is some error. As I say, it was only a clerk on duty, but when I gave him the names of the kidnapped children, he checked them against his log. He said it was impossible, that I couldn't have the right names."

"And why not?" Quan didn't look up.

"He said those children had already been adopted. Two weeks ago, by Canadian families."

Quan grunted. "Incompetence is a long-standing virtue at Civil Affairs. Only indifference is more highly prized. They've probably gotten the lists mixed up."

"I suppose so. There's certainly no question the Americans have kidnapped the babies. All the man had was the file log, not the files themselves. He said he'll pass it on to the duty clerk Monday morning. It's probably nothing. Anyway, I'll have someone follow up at Civil Affairs, and cross-check with the orphanage."

"Very well."

CHAPTER 8

BEIJING, MAY 26—(REUTERS WORLD SERVICE): The Foreign Ministry has confirmed that five Americans are being sought for questioning in the abduction of three infants from an orphanage in Jiangsu province. The fugitives have been identified as Nash and Claire Cameron, from Colorado Springs, Colorado; Ruth Pollard, of Los Angeles; and Allison and Tyler Turk of Denver, Colorado.

Local police in Suzhou refused comment and would neither confirm nor deny that the Americans are being sought. Orphanage officials could not be reached for comment. Sources say that the fugitives will seek asylum for the children in Beijing. A spokesman at the U.S. embassy stated that no contact had been made by the Americans with embassy officials there and refused to speculate on what would happen if they did. "American citizens traveling in China must obey Chinese laws," the spokesman insisted.

BY SUNDAY MORNING in Denver, Marshall Turk had taken eleven phone calls from reporters seeking information about Allison. Each time the phone rang he snatched it up, hoping it might be Allison or news of her, but each time it was another reporter. They seemed to know or care nothing of the local time. The calls came in all night, the last one at four in the morning. He was used to dealing with reporters in the course of his work, providing background and analysis on various cases. Generally he liked them and had no hesitation about using them for his ends, but now he found their questions blunt, impertinent, or stupid, and all of them quite unsettling.

"Is it true your wife kidnapped a baby? . . . Why a baby from China? . . . Does this have anything to do with the case you lost? . . . Had your wife been under medical care? . . . Did you know she was going to do this? . . . Why didn't you go with her?"

He put them all off with curt no-comments. He got out of bed at seven and took a shower. He still hadn't shaken his ear infection. His head ached and his ears were beginning to ring. He took the antibiotics and drops the doctor had prescribed, along with the handful of vitamins he swallowed every day.

He hated to be alone in the house on Sunday morning. Since he and Allison had been married, their sacred routine had never varied. With Tyler they stretched out on the thick carpet in the den. Marshall and Allison traded sections from the newspapers, while Tyler worked on the comics or one of his video game books. In the winter they'd make a fire; in summer they sat on the sun porch. They listened to music and ate fruit and cereal for breakfast. Tyler would inevitably complain about their music, which ran to classical or jazz. Then he would get to choose, and it would be the adults' turn to complain. After breakfast they'd all climb on their bicycles or load the car for a day trip to the mountains.

Marshall picked up the newspapers from the front porch and flipped through them for stories about Allison. Both carried the same brief Reuters wire service story that had no new information. In the breakfast room he turned on the television, clicking through the talk shows until he found the news. As he listened he rummaged through the cupboards, not hungry but knowing he ought to eat. He found some of Tyler's cereal and was reaching for a bowl when he stopped. He heard the words *fugitives in China* and turned to the television.

The reporters had succeeded in reaching the brother of Claire Cameron at his home in Oxnard, California. A veterinarian, Ralph Whittaker was heavyset and blunt spoken, his jaw set like a bulldog's as he confronted the camera on his front porch and lectured the reporter who had caught him on his way out. His wife stood at his side, their small daughter peering out from behind her skirts. No, he said in response to a question, he hadn't heard from his sister since she'd left for China. He had learned of the situation only from other reporters. He had already called the U.S. State Department, which had assured him only that it was aware of the situation and investigating.

"But let me tell you this. Claire is no criminal," Whittaker said, shaking his finger at the camera. "Whatever she has done, it's for the baby. She's dreamed about this adoption for months. She and Nash have prayed for it. It's outrageous what the Chinese have done. To give her a child, and then take it back—my God, I can't imagine what she must be going through. As if they don't have enough kids to go around. What kind of monsters are they, anyway? Now if you'll get off my steps, we're on our way to church, to pray for her."

The report shifted to Washington, and Marshall perked up. Even without the subtitle he recognized the face on the screen. It was Congressman Fred Pollard, a ranking Democrat on the House Committee on International Relations. *Pollard!* He hadn't made the connection. The congressman was livid, his features sharp as he wagged his finger at the camera. "I've seen the Chinese government pull some dumb-ass stunts before," he said, "but this—this is beyond dumb. It's incomprehensible. I am shocked and outraged at their actions. I can assure you, they will be brought to account in the court of world opinion, just as they will pay in the Congress of the United States. I will get to the bottom of this. I just pray my sister is all right. But I'll tell you, they're picking on one tough woman. She'll give them more than they bargained for, that's for sure."

Marshall listened to the rest of the report. He kept the sound up and wandered aimlessly through the house in his slippers and robe, carrying the bowl of cereal with him. Finally, restless and impatient to be doing something, he got dressed, forwarded his phone, and drove downtown to his office.

Even so early on a Sunday morning there were half a dozen lawyers working. Coulter Grogan never rested. Marshall went directly to Eric Bader's office, on the hunch Clarence would already have him at work. Sure enough, the young associate sat at his desk, dressed in running clothes. Evidently Clarence had found him at his athletic club and ruined yet another Sunday for an associate, something Clarence felt a need to do on a regular basis.

Bader sat behind a pile of books from the firm's law library, peering intently at his computer screen, which could tap into law databases all over the world. He looked up when Marshall came in.

"Hi, Mr. Turk," he said. "I'm sorry to hear about . . . things."

"Thanks," Marshall said. "And thanks for working Sunday. What do you have?"

Bader grimaced, waving at the pile of notes on his desk. "Nothing good, I'm afraid. The Chinese have made a few reforms over the last few years, but for the most part it's still a nightmare for defendants. I'm sorry to be so blunt, Mr. Turk, but your wife picked one hell of a place to fuck with the law."

A dozen police swarmed onto the 884 express from Nanjing when it was still 250 kilometers outside Beijing, expecting to find the fugitives and their cell phone.

Half an hour later Colonel Quan received their report.

"It was a businessman, Colonel," Major Ma told him. "He swears he got the phone on a bench in the bus station. He says someone left it there in some newspapers. He didn't see who it was."

"What time?"

"Last night, just before the bus departed. Around three forty-five."

Quan nodded. The time was right; Yang Boda would have been fleeing Nanjing at three forty-five.

"It is as we thought, Colonel," the major said. "Yang Boda has kept his wits."

Quan's attention was focused on the huge wall map. He smoked his cigarette and sipped his tea. It was Vivid Green Spring, from Fujian. Late day tea, soothing and mild. "Indeed he has," he said. "And now he tests us, to see if we can keep ours."

The engines of Inspection Cruiser Six surged as the boat pulled away from the quay at Jiujiang, a busy tea and rice port on the Yangtze. The ship's master, Captain Li Tang, stood outside the small bridge on the upper deck, leaning on the railing. Below him, the crew scurried to rig the boat for patrol, making fast the lines that had been cast off the quay's bollards, tending the engines, checking pumps, and, of course, brewing tea. It was just after four in the morning. They were setting out hours earlier than usual, in response to an alert from the Nanjing PSB. The fax machine in the Jiujiang Supervision Station had churned out a short list of ships, which, if located, were to be stopped and searched.

The *432 Springtime Flower* headed the list. The *Fragrant Moon,* registered in Shanghai, was not mentioned. But it didn't matter. Captain Li knew the vessel in question, whatever its name of the day, just as he knew the others on the list, just as he knew Yang Boda. He had done business with them all. In fact, he had been expecting Yang Boda, but not until later in the morning. They had made their customary arrangements by telephone the previous day.

For the name of Yang Boda's ship to appear now, in an official alert, was indeed a pity; it meant the captain's hands were tied. Arrests would have to be made, ships impounded. This time, the bribes would go to those much higher up the food chain than Captain Li Tang. But the captain knew his misfortune would be short-lived. The alert would soon pass, and the life and business of the river would return to normal.

They had been under way only a few moments when the watch officer summoned him to the bridge. He pointed to a blip on the radar. "Captain, I have a freighter ahead, midchannel. It is the *Yonglin,* bound for Shanghai. She's identified herself properly. The captain has complained about a smaller vessel on his port side. I've picked her up, when she's strayed from the *Yonglin*'s radar shadow. Very faint, but I've seen it twice."

The captain stepped outside to the bridge deck. The air was fresh, the moon full. He peered out over the water through high-powered binoculars, scanning the river. He quickly made out the starboard lights of the *Yonglin,* but nothing behind her. "Course and speed?"

"Oh-one-oh, sixteen knots."

The captain smiled. A thousand times he had seen this trick; the smugglers thought themselves so clever. To avoid detection they would hide their vessel behind a larger ship and run without lights. It was extremely risky. Lacking proper navigation equipment for night travel, the smugglers relied on the mother ship for steerage, in effect borrowing its ability to see at night. Mistakes or a fickle river often sent one or both boats to the bottom, but the smugglers never stopped trying.

Captain Li considered his orders. The *Yonglin* and its shadow were moving downstream, the direction from which Yang Boda would be approaching as he made his way upstream. The hours before dawn were always the quietest time on the river. With so little traffic, there was certainly time to troll for commerce. He glanced at his watch. It was 4:24 A.M.

"Very well. Set a course to intercept. Let us see what leech sucks at the belly of the *Yonglin.*"

*   *   *

Five minutes later Li Tang had the boat in sight. He ordered the powerful searchlights trained on the stern. The boat was the *River Swan,* registered in Wuhang. He saw the dim form of the pilot in his cabin, hunched over the wheel. When the pilot saw the lights come on, he turned and looked, then turned back again. His stern dipped into the water as his powerful engines surged, churning a great frothy wake as he rammed the throttle home. His boat leapt forward, cutting across the freighter's prow. By the time the freighter's horn blared, the *River Swan* was already well past.

"Ahead full!" Li Tang shouted. He felt his ship respond as he heard the radio operator ordering the *River Swan* to heave to. The police boat had to make a wide turn to avoid the freighter. By the time they were clear, the smuggling boat was far ahead, racing across the moonlit water. Li Tang knew they couldn't call for help. At this hour, theirs was the only cruiser on the river.

The captain soon realized where the smuggler was leading him. There was a cluster of small islands at the confluence of the Yangtze and the mouth of the big lake, Poyang Hu. Shallow channels ran between the islands. Some, including one at Hsin Chou, were not dredged and were never used by river traffic. Either the *River Swan* would try to elude him there or she would make her way into the mouth of Poyang Hu itself, where hundreds of inlets and coves might protect her forever.

A moment later he saw the *River Swan* veer toward the lights of a temple that stood on Yang-chia-chou island. So it was to be the channels, then. The smuggler wanted to test Li Tang's stomach for adventure at high speed. The captain's pulse quickened. It was a deadly dangerous chase. He knew the channels and was certain his craft could make the passage without running aground. He swallowed and felt the old adrenaline surge. His boat was fast, he knew the river, and his searchlights were bright. Yes, he had the stomach.

Gauging distances and depths, he raced on, calling out orders to the crew behind and below him. The other boat was several hundred meters ahead, but he was closing the gap.

Engine roaring, the *River Swan* flew into the first short channel, its desperate pilot running without lights. An instant later, Inspection Cruiser Six followed him in.

At that moment, the moon disappeared behind a bank of clouds, cloaking the river in darkness.

*   *   *

Nash awakened just after three in the morning, too hot and restless to sleep. He got up, taking care not to step on any of the sleeping forms on the boat deck. Even though Yi Ling had washed the crew's cabin and installed a fan, it was still dank, foul smelling, and hot. After some scouting they'd settled on the boat deck for the night. Ruth and her Wee Duck and Claire and Katie slept inside the dinghy, which hung at the stern from thick ropes attached to a winch from which the little boat could be lowered into the water. They raised it a little so it hung free. It swayed easily with the boat on the river's gentle swells, like a cradle. Allison, Tyler, and Wen Li were nestled together on the deck just forward of the dinghy, surrounded by a low wall of wooden crates Nash and Tyler had stacked behind the wheelhouse.

Nash walked forward along the port rail to the bow. On the forecastle deck he tripped over a cord and heard the angry hiss of a duck he'd disturbed. "Sorry," he whispered. He made the full circuit of the boat, stopping every so often to savor the cool breeze and listen to the rush of water against the hull. When he reached the wheelhouse, he stopped.

"Ni hao." Happy for company, First Mate Shidao beckoned Nash to sit.

"Ni hao," Nash replied. They watched the river and drank bitter tea from a battered steel thermos. A thousand meters to port, a big ferry passed them on its way downstream, its sides lit by bright strings of lights.

Nash pointed. "Big ship," he said.

"Beeg sheep?" the first mate repeated.

"It's a ferry."

"Derry?"

"Yes. Ferry."

"Hao." Shidao flashed a wide grin of rotting teeth, happy to be learning English. "Beeg sheep derry."

The mate worked the wheel tirelessly, making adjustments constantly to avoid hazards that Nash could only guess at. Near four o'clock he motioned to Nash, questioning whether he wanted to take the wheel. They were in a broad stretch of river, the view clear in the moonlight. The mate pointed at a light on a distant shore and indicated that Nash should aim for it. Nash nodded. "Okay." Shidao watched long enough to satisfy himself that the big nose wasn't going to steer in circles. Then he stepped out of the wheelhouse and went to the rail, where he peed into the river.

"*Yi jí duò shou*," the first mate said with a nod of approval when he returned. His apprentice had done well. He let Nash keep the wheel, and with one eye always on the river, he slid back a panel behind the capstan. As Nash had suspected, a small array of instruments was exposed. Nash recognized the radar screen but had never seen sonar. "Deep?" he said, indicating the screen, then pointing, first out at the river and then down, toward the bottom.

"Ah hah." The mate nodded. "*Sheng nà*. Deep." He pulled some charts from a hook and checked them quickly with a penlight. Nash tried to make out where they might be. Shidao pointed. "Poyang Hu," he said.

Again the mate checked the sonar. The channel was deep, the river quiet. It wouldn't be for long. He slid the electronics panel shut, then pointed outside. "Poyang Hu," he repeated. The chart showed they were at a junction where the great river met a great lake. Nash looked outside again, and now he saw it. The hills on the south shore dropped down to water level, where the moonlight danced off a large body of water stretching away to the south. As big as the Yangtze was, Nash thought that what he could see of Poyang Hu might simply have been more river, but the chart said otherwise.

The first mate tensed as they reached the confluence of the river and the lake. If the levels and temperature of the water were perfect, the junction could be glassy and calm. If not, they could merge in a turbulent deathtrap, a cauldron where the river boiled and whirlpools could slam a boat to shore or suck it to the bottom. He coaxed the engines carefully, feeling his way through light chop. Nash could feel the mate's tension, as he could feel the shifting currents through his feet on the deck. They passed the junction without incident, and Shidao breathed easier.

He checked his watch. Four-thirty. It would soon be dawn. He made a slight course correction and a moment later trimmed the boat to lay in behind the island of Hsin Chou, just downstream of the city of Jiujiang. Yang Boda had ordered him to stop there, to await the morning's shift change in the Jiujiang Supervision Station, when Captain Li Tang would come on duty. Once on patrol, the captain would order Yang Boda's boat to stand for inspection. The police would board the *432*, where the two crews would share tea and exchange gifts—money for signatures on manifests—and then part until the next time.

A shallow channel cut behind Hsin Chou, one never used by river traffic. Sheltered by high levees that protected the island from the periodic floods that ravaged the Yangtze, the island created an ideal shelter behind which they could wait, concealed from the view of passing ships. The mate slowed the engines to near idle, giving the lee shore of the island a wide berth, cautiously avoiding the sandbars that built up there. Once again he checked his watch. Four thirty-five. At any moment, Yang Boda would appear to relieve him.

First Mate Shidao noticed something terribly wrong. The joss stick had burned out, the one that sat at the base of the statue of old Chen Jiang Wang Yeh, the river guardian king. The mate wasn't worried about the joss stick itself—he believed in nothing of the sort. What worried him was the reaction of Yang Boda, who believed in it deeply. Yang Boda's opinions ran hard where such matters were concerned. While he was on board, that joss stick never went out.

Shidao felt for matches on the ledge above Chen. He found a pack, but it was empty. He felt again, farther back. He cursed. He looked over at Nash quizzically, making the motions of striking a match. Nash shook his head. "I don't smoke."

Shidao decided to get some from the cook, who was already stirring, preparing breakfast. They'd seen him a few moments earlier, pitching something over the rail into the river. Shidao beckoned to Nash, indicating that he should take the wheel once more. Nash took his seat, and the mate pointed at a shore light: *Steer there.* They were well past the danger from the lake currents, and in a few moments the mate would drop anchor. They were barely moving at all; the *lao wai* was a good hand and would be just fine.

As Shidao stepped out of the wheelhouse, the moon slipped behind the clouds, and it was as if a heavy drape had dropped over the river. He looked at the sky, hesitating, and then climbed down a short ladder. He leaned out over the starboard rail just above and behind the hold. From there he could make out the rim of the galley porthole. He heard the clatter of pots and pans.

"Gei wo dian huo chai!" he called.

There was no response. He was about to shout again when he heard the onrushing roar of an engine. The *Springtime Flower* was just clearing the levee of Hsin Chou, puttering into the channel. The first mate looked over his shoulder, over the port rail in the direction of the noise. In the darkness he didn't understand what he was seeing: it looked like the silhouette of a boat, illuminated by the searchlights of another boat just behind.

Both were on a collision course with the *Springtime Flower.*
He screamed and started to run.

Allison stirred from her sleep, which had been light and unsettled. Something had changed. She raised herself on one elbow to listen. It took a moment before she realized it was the sound of the boat's engines. They'd been running steady all night, throbbing so that she could feel them through the deck, and now suddenly they'd gone nearly quiet. She looked at her watch, pressing the button to illuminate the dial. Four thirty-five. She looked at Wen Li, snuggled on the bamboo mat between pillows made of clothing. Pooh reclined at her side, choked as usual in the crook of her little arm. Tyler was on the far side of the baby, curled up into a tight ball.

She closed her eyes, letting herself drift with the low rumble of the engines, trying to get back to sleep. She heard someone calling out in Chinese. One of the crew, she thought. Then, vaguely, she heard the sound of a motor, the motor of another boat. At first it was faint, lost in her subconscious, but gradually she realized it was growing louder, and very quickly at that. Then there was another sound, a different engine, and she could tell they were racing, and straining, and coming closer.

When she opened her eyes, she realized the moon had gone behind some clouds. She lifted herself up on one elbow, but it was dark and she could see very little through the crates. The engines sounded as if they were nearly upon them. She wondered if she ought to get up and look.

Then she heard a scream. An instant later, the entire world seemed to explode.

CHAPTER 9

NASH SAW THE oncoming danger at the same instant as the first mate. Although blinded momentarily by the searchlights of the other vessel, he reacted instantaneously and would have made the first mate proud. He gunned the engines and spun the wheel hard starboard, but it was too late.

The *River Swan* was making nearly thirty knots, its prow leaping up and down on the waves as it sought to elude the police boat, which had now nearly pulled abreast of its port side.

The *River Swan* struck the *432 Springtime Flower* broadside, just behind the hold near the wheelhouse. The impact punched a gaping hole in the hull of Yang Boda's boat. The rear of the *River Swan* lifted almost completely out of the water as it slammed into the bigger object. With an awful tearing of metal and splintering of wood, the side of the *432* was opened to the river, the hole extending three feet above the waterline and six feet below.

The force of the collision telescoped the smuggler's boat, the cabin of which was sheared off by the *Springtime Flower*'s hull. The pilot's body was ripped in two, his head and torso caught in the cabin while the rest of him stayed with the hull, which was swallowed inside the bigger vessel. His precious cargo, swords and pots and armor, ancient relics from the Tang dynasty on their way to Hong Kong, were ejected into the dark water of the river, drifting downward into the murk to bury themselves for the next millennium in a thick bed of silt.

The *Springtime Flower* began sinking immediately. Water poured into the massive wound in her side and quickly overwhelmed the bilges.

The impact threw Nash against the port window above the statue of the river god. The glass shattered, tearing a great gash all the way through his cheek. He felt the wound with his tongue; he thought half his face must have been ripped away. There was no pain, yet, but he felt fire in his shoulder—his collarbone, he thought, where it had slammed against the window frame.

Then there was a second collision, not nearly as powerful as the first, but he was exposed, helpless, dangling in the opening, and this time it was his ribs that took the brunt of the impact. He tried to free himself, gasping in pain, but without luck. He realized the force of his body had ripped loose some of the wall boards and now his shirt was caught in the planking. The harder he tried to free himself, the more firmly the planking clamped down.

He rested a moment, gathering his strength. He turned his head. The moon darted in and out of the clouds, illuminating the scene briefly. Ahead he could just see the outline of the other boat. From the search and emergency lights he'd seen just prior to the impact, he had guessed, correctly, that it was the police. Having not seen the smaller smuggling boat, he mistakenly thought it was the police boat with which they had collided. As for the second impact, he could only surmise they'd run aground. It didn't matter, not really. Now the lights of the other boat were out, and he could see tongues of flame licking at its side. Acrid smoke filled the air.

He heard someone crying hysterically. It sounded like Claire. The sound galvanized him into action. Once again he gave a mighty pull, and his shirt tore free. He tumbled back into the wheelhouse, landing on his back on the binnacle and falling to the floor. Gasping, he freed himself and crawled outside. Holding on to the rail, he pulled himself up. He worked his shoulder. He could still move it. *Not broken after all,* he thought. *Just bruised.* He put a finger to his cheek. The gash had seemed gruesome because he could feel it with his tongue, from the inside, but his finger told him it wasn't very long. For a man with his history of injuries, he'd come through it all nearly unscathed.

He wasn't frightened, not at all. His senses were alert, and despite his injuries he knew he was all right. He saw the flames and smelled the smoke and knew the danger, and it exhilarated him. He felt the boat already listing. The engines had died. He had to get the others to the lifeboat. They had to get away.

He heard a scream. This time he knew it was Claire.

*   *   *

The galley was directly behind the hull where the *River Swan* had struck. The cook was killed instantly as he prepared the morning tea, his galley sheared in two by the impact. The cold black water of the Yangtze swept him away as it poured into the ship. Within seconds the roaring water found its way into nearly every compartment of the ship, filling the crew quarters, the storerooms, and the companionways. The sides of the hold were breached, and nothing stood between it and the water. Three of the crew were swamped. Unable to swim, to find an escape, to grab hold of anything that would float, they drowned instantly. In the engine room, the oilman reacted quickly after the first collision, slamming shut the watertight door. But then the second impact ripped a spare engine block from its anchor. It landed on him, pinning his legs to the deck. He drowned there, in diesel fuel pouring from ruptured tanks.

The mechanic, still able to walk, managed to escape the hell below. Once on the main deck, panicked out of his mind, he ran for the side and jumped into the river. He couldn't swim.

The police cruiser's radar had not detected the *432 Springtime Flower*. It had been hidden behind the island's levee and had emerged without warning into the channel. The cruiser had been in the deepest water, its searchlights trained on the boat it was chasing. The crew was scrambling for ropes and weapons. The first collision caught them completely by surprise, virtually destroying their quarry before they had a chance to absorb what had happened. Only the lightning reflexes of the captain, Li Tang, who had seen the dark hull of the *432* with not five seconds to spare, kept them all from certain death; but as quickly as he reacted, it wasn't quickly enough. "Hard to port!" he screamed to the watch officer. They swerved sharply, nearly foundering as the wake overtook their craft. One of the crew, unprepared for the maneuver, toppled overboard. No one noticed.

Despite the captain's evasive action, the *Springtime Flower* struck the cruiser a fierce blow amidships. The impact crushed the outer railing, collapsing it into the superstructure, severing the conduits carrying the main electrical cables. The ship lost all electrical power, disabling the radio and the radar and plunging the searchlights into blackness. A fuel line ruptured and flames shot skyward. The engines died abruptly.

The cruiser had sustained heavy damage, but all of it above the water-line. While the boat was not sinking, fire threatened to do what the collision had not. Two of the crew closest to the flames sprang into action, desperate to extinguish the deadly blaze. One ran below to close the valves that fed the fuel, but he had no flashlight. Without power, he had to feel his way. Thick smoke billowed up from below, forcing him to retreat. Above him, the other crewman ripped a fire extinguisher from its wall anchor and turned its chemicals on the fire. It wasn't nearly enough. He threw it aside and tried to engage the boat's river hoses. He tried desperately to start the auxiliary motor that ran the pump. Cursing, working furiously, he pulled again and again on the cord. The motor only sputtered. Behind him, the flames worked their way up the side of the boat toward the bridge, where the captain slumped unconscious over the rail. Inside the bridge, the dazed watch officer was trying to pick himself up off the deck, mumbling orders that no one was there to hear.

The other officer aboard the cruiser had struck his head on a stanchion. His scalp was bleeding profusely. Holding his forearm to the wound, he had leaped onto the deck of the *432 Springtime Flower*, where he staggered as he tried to get his bearings. He heard voices rising out of the confusion—men shouting, women screaming, babies crying. He could hear the fire behind him growing as the flames joined with the moon to dimly illuminate the features of the *432*. He knew she was sinking quickly. As he moved forward, he tried to understand what had happened. Had there been two boats or three? Was this the smuggling boat or a different one? It didn't matter. Now there was only smoke and noise and shouts of fear. Someone ran past him. He patted for his flashlight, but it was gone, lost somewhere in the collision.

Then he came across a woman holding a baby. Instinctively he grabbed her by the arm, to propel her in the direction of the police launch, toward the safety of its two lifeboats. He brought his face close to hers and was astonished to realize it was a *lao wai* woman. Overcoming his shock, he barked at her. "*Chū qù! Kuài diǎn, nèi biān!*" He pointed at the cruiser, ordering her once again to abandon ship. Out of her mind with panic, understanding nothing, Claire screamed and shrank away from him, her back against the wheelhouse wall. Clutching Katie tightly, sobbing with fear, she slipped to a sitting position. Still shouting, the officer grabbed her by the arm, trying to lift her up.

At that moment Nash appeared. He saw the uniform, saw the man wrenching at Claire's arms, saw Claire holding Katie. Misunderstanding the officer's intentions, his own mind fixed on escape, Nash slammed into him, knocking him to the deck. The two men struggled, the officer overwhelmed by Nash's greater size and strength and by the complete surprise of his attack. Nash hit him in the face and then again in the stomach. The officer managed to get his hand on his club. He wrenched it free and started flailing at his attacker, all the while bellowing for help.

In the pitch darkness of his cabin, Yang Boda sought to establish the extent of damage to his leg. He had been knocked from his bunk, and his leg had got caught in the steel frame. He heard the bone snap, not like a twig but like a great bough, up high, and then as he fell to the floor he'd heard the sound of his own flesh ripping. He tried to pick himself up, but the pain was too great and he collapsed. He groaned. The pain was soaring. He put his hand and felt the sharp edge of bone. His hand came away warm with blood.

Too much blood, he knew. The fracture had severed an artery.

"Yi Ling!" he called. He realized how weak his voice was. He took a deep breath and called again, this time more loudly. "Yi Ling! Are you all right?" She couldn't hear him; he knew she had been sleeping in the crew quarters. He pulled off his shirt and tied it around his leg, high up the thigh near his crotch, and tightened it with all his strength. He felt the area around the wound. There was still the hot rhythmic pulse of blood—less now, but still something. He tightened again, groaning in pain from the exertion as the bone ripped at his skin. He felt the strong impulse to rest, to sleep, but struggled against what he knew was the pull of death.

He hauled himself across the floor toward the cabin door. Sweat poured from his brow, though he felt cold. Through his pain he tried to understand what was happening. Already he could feel his boat listing, but beyond that he felt a faint vibration through the floor, a vibration that resonated inside his soul. He knew his ship well. He knew she was dying.

And then he understood: It was water, rushing belowdecks, water engulfing his ship, water pounding against steel and wood. There were muffled shouts and cries. Had there been an explosion? A collision? He hoisted himself up using the latch on the door and pulled. It didn't budge. He pulled again, so hard that he screamed out in pain. His leg, dangling midthigh at an impossible angle, tormented him with each movement. Again he yanked, but the door wouldn't give.

Whatever had happened to his ship had cocked the structure and jammed his door.

He was trapped.

Water started pushing its way into his cabin, first through the gap between the door and the floor and then quickly, very quickly, higher up the door frame as well.

As the water swirled around his broken leg, Yang Boda pounded on his door.

Yi Ling had been in the crew cabin, and her night, like that of so many others aboard the ship, had been restless. She slept, then awoke, then slept again, the sleep punctuated with unsettling dreams and half-conscious thoughts. She was plagued with worry about their flight, about whether she and her uncle—no, her uncle alone, really—could succeed in getting the Americans to safety. She closed her eyes and saw checkpoints, road-blocks, spies, obstacles—a thousand hurdles to clear. She knew very well there was nothing to be gained from worry. Such problems weren't solved with night terrors in ships' cabins, but she couldn't clear her mind.

She got up and had stepped into the passageway when she heard a scream. She didn't hear the engines approaching. The impact flung her backward onto the companionway deck. She hit flat on her back, banging her head. The breath was knocked out of her. She tried to draw a breath, but her lungs wouldn't work. She sat up quickly, clutching her chest, cer-tain she was going to suffocate. Then came a second jolt, less powerful than the first. She slid along the deck and hit the wall. At last she began gasping and choking. She braced herself, fearing another shock.

What she heard then frightened her more than anything in her life.

She heard water roaring into the ship. She was terrified of water. She couldn't swim.

She struggled to her feet and started back up the stairs, holding tight to the rail with both hands. At the top she hesitated, her mind racing as she debated what to do first. She knew nothing about boats but knew the ship was in terrible trouble. She thought first she ought to find her uncle, who would know exactly what to do.

But then her decision was made for her, as she saw what she had only heard before—the black water of the river was already rushing up from below, bursting through doors and swirling through the companionway. It was too late. Her uncle could take care of himself better than the *lao wai*. She had to help them. She had to help the babies.

She emerged to the sight of flames. She didn't know they came from another boat; she still hadn't grasped what had happened. Plumes of thick smoke wafted through the darkness. She caught a lungful and began to cough and gag. She heard yelling nearby, someone hollering for help in Chinese. She bent over and raced aft, toward the deck and the dinghy where the *lao wai* had bedded down for the night.

She tripped over something and fell headlong to the deck.

"*Shén me!*" she cried out. She sat up and saw two men battling, gasping and grunting as they fought for advantage. She had no idea who they were. Then they got up, and for the first time she began to make out what was happening. The first thing she saw clearly was that one of them wore the uniform of the police. She looked past him, toward the blaze, and realized there was another boat, its superstructure now engulfed in flames.

The policeman broke away from the other man, and she saw it was Nash. The officer ran toward the fire, screaming for help. Yi Ling watched in horror as Nash tackled him next to the railing, just as the officer was ready to leap. The force of Nash's blow sent both men over the rail. Together they toppled into the water. A moment later the two boats, drifting without power and subject to the whim of the river's currents, came together with a gentle thump, closing the gap where the two men had disappeared. The boats separated once again and moved apart.

Yi Ling shook her head in disbelief, as if that might clear the nightmare unfolding in front of her, but nothing changed. She ran to the rail. There was no sign of the men, only the black water, its roily surface reflecting the light of the fire. She realized that the water was much closer than it ought to be. They were sinking faster than she'd thought.

"*Jiu Jiu!*" she cried. "Uncle!"

There was no answer. Yi Ling turned and ran aft.

The collision jolted Ruth and Claire awake. In the dinghy, lined with blankets and hanging from its ropes, they barely felt the impact.

Even before Ruth was fully awake, she instinctively sheltered Tai, tucking her into the crook of her arm. Startled, Tai began to cry. Ruth couldn't see any of what had happened. She was too stunned to move, and from the screams and other awful sounds that filled the darkness, she wasn't sure she wanted to. She could see the top of the wheelhouse, and in one of its windows she saw the reflection of flames. That was enough to propel her into action as her instincts for survival kicked in. She wriggled out from beneath the wooden seat, just as she saw Claire trying to do.

Claire's eyes were wild with fear. "Nash?" she said. "Where's Nash? Oh God, Nash, are you okay?" Clutching Katie, Claire stood up, lost her balance, and sat down heavily. "Nash!" she cried again, ignoring Ruth's hand on her shoulder. She half crawled and half fell out of the boat, clutching the gunwale with one arm and Katie with the other. Once on the deck, she didn't turn to help Ruth get out.

"Wait," Ruth said. "I'll come with you!" But Claire rushed forward into the chaos and darkness.

Over Tai's cries Ruth heard a baby in hysterics. It had to be Wen Li. Ruth yelled, "Allison? Tyler?" Then she heard Tyler crying.

Ruth struggled awkwardly out of the dinghy onto the deck, holding Tai. On unsteady legs she made her way port, following the sound of the boy's cries. She waded into the rubble of crates that had been stacked neatly on the deck the previous evening.

Allison had been sleeping on the left, the port side, the children beside her. Their mattress was a bamboo mat, which in the collision had whipped across the deck like a puck on ice, pushing some of the crates before them. The impact slammed them into the deck rail, the blow cushioned somewhat by the crates, which exploded in a shower of splinters. The children were lucky. Allison's back struck the steel rail posts where they met the deck, and the children slid into her. Wen Li hit the softest place possible, Allison's stomach. Tyler was less fortunate, striking his head against Allison's. Both were now seeing bright flashes of light. Tyler was the first to sit up. He pushed away the boxes, rubbing his head and crying. "Why did you do that?" he demanded angrily, unreasonably, having no idea what had happened. As Ruth arrived Allison was just sitting up, dazed.

"Tyler, I'm sorry—God, are you all right?"

"Yes! No! I hit my head!" He sobbed, rubbing the big lump he could feel rising at his hairline. He seemed more frightened than hurt. Wen Li was screaming. Allison held her up and brushed her face. "Her eyes!" she cried. "There are splinters everywhere! Is there a light somewhere? Ruth, can you see? Is she okay?"

Ruth shoved aside some of the wood planks. "Give her to me," she said. Allison handed up the baby, and Ruth, now with a baby in each arm, stepped carefully back a little and found an undamaged crate to sit on.

Allison tried to stand but couldn't. Dizzy, she sank to a sitting position, trying to collect her wits. Her neck and legs felt as if they'd been whacked with a baseball bat, and her head was pounding. She felt hysteria welling up inside. She could see the light of flames, and they could all feel the boat listing.

"Is she all right?" she asked again.

"I think so," Ruth said. "I've got a penlight, if I can find it." Balancing the babies on her lap, she fished in her pants pocket. "Got it!" She flipped it on and directed the beam onto Wen Li's face. The baby had a little scratch on her nose and wriggled madly when Ruth shined the light into her eyes. Her cheeks were red and streaked with tears. "She's okay," Ruth said. "Her eyes are fine. She's just pissed off."

Allison finally made it to her feet. She steadied herself against the rail and rubbed her neck. "What happened?" she asked Ruth.

"Damned if I know. I was asleep. The whole goddamn world blew up. There's a fire over there. All I know is we'd better get in the dinghy. This ship is sinking."

A wave of nausea overcame Allison. She closed her eyes and breathed deeply and touched her head where it felt on fire. Ruth's words registered then. *Fire. Sinking.* "Where's Claire? Wasn't she with you? And Yi Ling? Where is everybody?"

"I don't know." Ruth got to her feet, and Allison, a little more recovered now, took Wen Li and tried to comfort her, to stop her crying. She put a hand on Tyler's shoulder, expecting him to push it away, but he surprised her and put his arms around her waist, letting her comfort him.

At that moment Yi Ling appeared, her arm around Claire, who was holding Katie. A look of relief passed Yi Ling's face when she saw they were all right. "Quick!" she said. "Take little boat! Quick now!"

Claire shook her head. "Not yet!" she cried. "Where's Nash?" She was confused and in shock. "There was a man," she said. "Nash hit him. I fell. I couldn't see. The smoke . . ." She appealed to Yi Ling. "Do you know where he is? Did you see him? I can't find him anywhere."

Yi Ling propelled her toward the dinghy. "Take little boat," she said again, not ready to answer her question. She didn't *know* the answer, she realized. Not about Nash, not about Yang Boda. She couldn't allow herself to think about it—she needed to get the others to safety.

At the dinghy Claire wouldn't climb in. She turned and stood with her back to the little boat, still looking, her eyes lit by the flames. Claire pointed to the burning boat. "Could he be over there?" No one answered.

Allison looked at Yi Ling. "Where's your uncle? And the rest of the crew?"

"Don't know. Not matter—we cannot all fit anyway. I will come back to look. Now must please get in!" she commanded.

"She's right," Ruth said. "We've got to get away, or we're all going down and there won't be any chance for the others."

Allison and Tyler climbed in first. Then, sobbing, Claire allowed herself to be helped in behind them.

"Here, Allison, take Tai," Ruth said, passing the baby over. "I'll help Yi Ling get the dinghy away."

"Our bags!" Allison cried. Ruth ran over and found two bags in the rubble of crates and tossed them into the dinghy.

"There should be two more," Allison said. "Your big one isn't here."

Ruth nodded, out of breath. "They must have gone in the river." Then she and Yi Ling started pulling on the levers that held the ropes. Yi Ling's side released easily, but a gear on Ruth's side jammed and the ropes wouldn't budge. The bow stayed tight while the aft end of the dinghy swung free, nearly pitching everyone inside into the water.

"I can't get it!" Ruth panted, straining on the lever. "It won't move!"

Yi Ling ran to help her. "Try again with me—now!" Together they shoved. The rope stayed fast.

They were running out of time. The boat deck of the *432 Springtime Flower* was now only a little more than a foot above the water. They would be under in another minute or so. As the ship sank it would take the dinghy with her to the bottom if they couldn't get it free. Ruth groaned. "It won't give! Does anyone have a knife? We can cut the ropes!"

"I do!" Tyler knelt up in the dinghy, bracing himself to keep from tumbling overboard as it swung once again over the water. He found his pocket knife, got it open, and scurried forward. Ruth took it and began hacking at the rope. The blade was sharp and the fibers started to part at once, but the rope was thick. "Hold on to the back!" she called to Yi Ling. "If this goes, the dinghy will shoot away!" Now on her knees, Yi Ling used one hand to hold on to the boat while she held on to a stern chock on the deck with the other. Twice the dinghy slipped from her grasp, swinging out over the water, then returning again, where she grabbed it.

Ruth sawed madly as she felt the Yangtze swirling at her feet.

"Hurry!" Yi Ling gasped. "Cannot hold!"

"Okay, get ready! It's com—"

At that moment First Mate Shidao appeared at a dead run, his feet splashing in the water covering the deck. The collision had knocked him into the hold, where he'd been pinned briefly by the cargo. He had managed to free himself and climb to safety. In vain he had tried to help another crew member, who had been swept from his grasp and lost in the blackness. After that he'd managed to get up the ladder and onto the main deck, where he'd assessed the situation quickly. There was nothing to be done for the ship. He couldn't get below to help any of the crew who might be trapped there. He sprinted straight for the lifeboat.

"Jìn lái!" he barked as he saw what Ruth and Yi Ling were trying to do. He pushed Ruth aside and yanked at the lever holding the rope. Under his strength it parted abruptly, dropping the front of the dinghy, which slapped on the water. Pitching forward with the motion, Allison yelped but managed to hold on to Tai and Wen Li, while Tyler clung to the gunwale. Ruth tumbled in clumsily, banging her knees and falling flat on her face as she fought for balance in the violently rocking craft.

Shidao had caught hold of the bow of the dinghy. Now floating free in the water, pulled away stern first. He leaned out, trying to hold it and reverse its course, but he lost his footing on the watery deck of the *432* and fell face first into the river. He went under for an instant and then came up again, flailing and splashing.

"Help him!" Ruth shouted. "He'll drown!"

Yi Ling reached out to catch his hand. "Aghhh!" he sputtered, taking a mouth full of water. His arms thrashed ineffectively. Like so many sailors, he couldn't swim; like so many drowning people, he did all the wrong things.

Without its engine running, the dinghy couldn't be maneuvered toward him. Allison yelled at Claire, who was sitting nearest the outboard. "Claire! Start the motor!" But Claire was paralyzed, transfixed by the ship sinking behind the drowning man. She clutched Katie to her breast and looked for some sign of her husband.

Allison felt the cushion of blankets still piled in the bottom of the boat. She picked one up and held one end while flinging the other toward the first mate. He almost had it, then lost it. Now drenched, the blanket was heavy and difficult to maneuver. Grunting, she heaved again, and the end slapped the water near the mate. This time the first mate caught hold.

Yi Ling and Allison reeled him in. Shidao got his arms up over the edge. With another heave that nearly capsized them all, the two women got him on board. He landed in the bottom, sputtering and coughing. He was slimy with diesel fuel that had leaked from the ruptured tanks of the *432* and covered the surface of the river. Noxious fumes filled the air and invaded their throats and mouths, and Allison and Yi Ling were now covered with it as well.

Shidao hawked and spat into the river. He blinked, trying to clear his stinging eyes. He scrambled to the back. After two pulls the outboard engine popped into life, smoking heavily. He turned the throttle and spun them around, intending to have another look to see whether anyone remained in the water or was trapped on the ship.

The dinghy rode dangerously low in the water. As it made its little circle, those on board turned to stare. The clouds had thinned and the moon was back out. By its light they could see what was left of the *432 Springtime Flower.* The ship was nearly submerged, tilting to port. The main deck level had already been swallowed by the river, with only the upper deck and the wheelhouse, rising above that, still visible. From a pole among the masts atop the wheelhouse, a Chinese flag fluttered softly in the light breeze.

They saw no one, and there weren't many places left where survivors could be. On the far side of the ship, they saw the police boat, its wooden superstructure engulfed in flames. Fire rose eerily from the water, fed by the fuel of ruptured tanks. Debris floated everywhere. A bamboo deck chair bobbed past, a canvas shoe caught in its slats. There was a life preserver, probably from the police boat, as the *432* had carried none; and cardboard boxes, and clothing, and bits of plastic and wood. They putted quietly through the flotsam, looking for a head, an arm. For anything.

There were still two men on the police boat. They were quite distant now, the cruiser having floated more quickly with the current than the *432.* They were abandoning ship, yelling back and forth as they maneuvered their starboard lifeboat into the water. Over the noise of their voices the survivors in the dinghy heard other sounds, awful sounds: creaking and sighing and popping, and breaking glass, and the muffled noise of massive streams of bubbles coming from compartments and holds beneath the water. And, above that, something else, from near where the forecastle was now slipping beneath the water. They heard the chickens and the ducks making a terrible racket, as, caged and tethered near the bowsprit, they were going down with the ship. Amid all the death and destruction, it was, somehow, a particularly wrenching sound. And then it stopped.

A moment later the *432* stopped as well, coming to rest on rocks or a sandbar in the shallow channel. Only a portion of the wheelhouse now remained above the water. They could see its broken windows, jagged and desolate and final in the moonlight.

A silence descended on the river, and for long moments no one said anything. They listened for a shout, for a cry for help. There was nothing but the *put-put* of the dinghy's motor.

From the moment of impact until the *432 Springtime Flower* came to rest on the river bottom, less than fifteen minutes had elapsed.

Yi Ling kept looking. She had not lost hope. There was much they could still not see: debris floating in the water to which survivors might cling, and the shore of the island of Hsin Chou not far distant. Yang Boda was tough and resourceful. Possibly he had gotten out of his cabin all right but had not had time to make it to the dinghy. Perhaps he had gone into the water near the forecastle, where she couldn't have seen him. Anything could have happened. She wouldn't permit herself to despair. It would be light soon, and then they would know more.

Her attention shifted to the distant police boat, where she could see the two officers had made it into their lifeboat. "We need to get to shore, quickly," she said to Shidao. "This boat is full now, and we couldn't get anyone else in even if we found them. Maybe we can come back and look for the others."

"*Hao ba.*" The first mate nodded. It wouldn't be long before other boats passing by in the main channel of the river saw the flames. Most would stay out of the channels by the islands, fearful of running aground, but their radios would be crackling with news of the fire. Whatever could be done would have to be done quickly. He gunned the throttle and made for the south shore of the river, preparing himself once again for their passage through the treacherous currents.

Behind him, the wreck of the *432 Springtime Flower* grew smaller. Yi Ling moved next to Claire, and together they watched until it was gone.

The dinghy ran with the heavy current, bucking through rough water as it passed the mouth of Poyang Hu, the freshwater lake. Shidao crossed the passage at an oblique angle, trying to guess where the best landfall might be. He could see the great Stone Bell Tower, a famous landmark that rose from the bank. The sun rose behind it, silhouetting the hill like a beacon for him to follow. That would put them on the east side of the lake, away downstream from Jiujiang, which on the south side of the river could be reached only by ferry. His passengers held on tightly and huddled low in the boat. Claire was sobbing.

"First mate go back to look," Yi Ling said softly, trying to comfort her.

"He's dead, isn't he?"

"Could be in water, holding on. Many things floating. Could swim to Hsin Chou island. In daylight we see." Yi Ling knew that in the daylight the scene would surely be crawling with authorities. At least, she thought, if Yang Boda and Nash and any of the crew had survived, they would be rescued quickly.

"He would have come if he was all right," Claire sobbed. "I know he would. He wouldn't leave me. He wouldn't. . . ."

Tai was wailing like a banshee. Ruth felt around the bottom of the dinghy for the bottle of formula she'd had when they'd gone to sleep the night before. She found it beneath one of the soaking blankets. The nipple had gotten encrusted with grunge. There was nothing to be done about it. She wiped it with her fingers and rubbed it on her sleeve. "Let's hope this dirt has some iron in it," she cooed softly. "Iron's good for a Wee Duck. . . . Don't tell social services on me now, promise? They'd have my butt for this. Shhhh. . . ." Tai sucked at the bottle, content at last.

Shidao got the boat safely through the chop and turned sharply to shore. He saw a deserted gravel beach and ran the boat aground, scraping the bow until it found purchase in the soft rocky earth. Yi Ling hopped out into the knee-deep water. She helped the others, passing bags and babies in the growing light of dawn. On the beach they sank immediately up to their ankles in mud. It sucked at their feet as they struggled up the beach to solid ground. Behind them the first mate pulled the dinghy farther up the shore, and then he joined Yi Ling.

They turned to look back across the river, hoping to make out the *Springtime Flower*. They saw no trace of it, but there was a boat, a kilometer or more away, headed downstream. They saw its flashing blue lights, and a strong spotlight trained from its bridge toward Hsin Chou. A shrill blast of a horn shattered the dawn, and then two more, in quick succession.

There was to be no rest. Yi Ling looked hopefully at the first mate. "We must get the *lao wai* to safety. Do you know where we are?"

"*Zhì dào.*" He nodded. "Poyang Hu." He beckoned to the southeast, and she could see the lake. A ferry was making the first journey of the day across the mouth of the lake, carrying cars and people and livestock from the town of Hukou toward the Jiujiang shore. Yi Ling knew the area vaguely. She had taken tour groups to Lushan, the breathtaking garden in the clouds that nestled in the mountains on the east shore of the lake.

The first mate considered their options. He didn't know the lake the way he knew the river. "There are many fishing boats, just past Hukou," he said, pointing straight south. "If you can get the *lao wai* there, you can wait. It isn't far. No one will see you. I'll take the boat back and try to find Yang Boda." Yi Ling nodded gratefully. It was their only chance.

She turned and explained to the others, who had seen the police boat. Everyone agreed except Claire.

"I'm not leaving," she said.

"Just to wait, near Hukou," Yi Ling told her. "First mate take little boat, find Nash. Bring there."

"I'm not leaving," Claire repeated firmly. "I'm going to wait here for Nash."

Yi Ling was growing desperate. It would be only a short time before the survivors from the police boat alerted the others as to where the little dinghy had gone. They might have only twenty or thirty minutes before the second police boat radioed shore authorities near Hukou, who would soon be everywhere.

Yi Ling decided. "I think Nash dead, Claire," she said, her voice wavering. "Saw him fall in fight, fall into river. I not say before, because of hope. But now we cannot wait. Police come."

"Did you see his body?"

"Too dark. Water took away."

"You're lying," Claire said, her anger flaring. "God*damn* you! How dare you destroy my hope?"

Yi Ling held Claire's gaze and shook her head. "Not lying. I am sorry."

Claire blinked back tears. She set herself firmly, her voice breaking. "I don't care what you say or what you saw. He might still be out there. What if he's hurt? What if he's swimming? What if he's holding on to some piece of wood, and no one's there to see him? He wouldn't leave *me*, and I'm not leaving him."

"Even if you see him, nothing you can do. Police will get him."

"How do you know that? Anyway, I don't care. I'm not going."

Allison and Ruth tried to reason with her, but it soon became obvious that the only way they would get her to move would be to carry her, along with Katie. It was out of the question.

"What is it?" Shidao asked, sensing the disagreement. Yi Ling explained. "You go now with the other *lao wai*," he said. "No one will be about at this hour to see them except fishermen. Find a fishing boat and hire it. Get them on board, and then come back. Until then I'll watch this one"—he indicated Claire—"up there, where we can see the river." At the top of the slope leading up from the Yangtze was the northern base of Stone Bell Hill. Steep cliffs descended from the temple on top to the water's edge. There were caves there, many places to hide and watch the river, out of sight. "When you come back, you hide with this one and I'll see what I can do with the boat." The first mate didn't say that if he saw the police approaching, he intended to abandon the *lao wai* woman to her fate and disappear into the streets of Hukou. While he cared nothing for the *lao wai,* he was willing to help the niece of Yang Boda—a man he revered, a man who was most certainly dead by now—but not at the price of his own freedom. And there was more than freedom at stake. He knew the true cargo in the hold of the *432.* If the arms were discovered and he was caught, it would earn him a quick bullet to the brain.

Short of giving up, it was the only option they had.

Once again, Yi Ling offered a hurried explanation to the *lao wai.* This time, Claire agreed.

CHAPTER 10

REN KAI tinkered with the old engine. Its belts were brittle and cracked, its gaskets leaking, its piston rings as loose as his grandmother's teeth. Most of the time—also like his grandmother, he thought—it worked without protest. But this morning it would not start. He pulled the end of the gas line off the fuel pump and turned the key to crank the engine. A strong stream of gas spurted from the line. Next he checked the spark plugs. They were ancient, relics from some forgotten dynasty, their porcelain shields cracked, their tungsten tips marred and worn by countless adjustments and cleanings—but for all that, they still sparked bright blue fire when he held them to the engine block and cranked the motor.

"*Tā mā de!*" He cursed at the engine and shook his head in puzzlement and frustration. He'd been at it over an hour. "Fuel! Fire! Fuck!" He slammed the hull with his fist and cursed again. He looked out to the lake, where he could see the other boats, already departing. They would soon settle in all the best places, and his catch would suffer. He banged on the carburetor with his mallet. Something inside gave way or freed itself, and in the inscrutable manner of his engine, whether by some miracle of mallet technology or the simple workings of spirits, it sprang to life at last. He laughed to himself, vowing to buy the parts the carburetor wanted, and closed the engine compartment cover. He wiped his forehead on his sleeve and his greasy hands on a rag.

"Child's mom!" he shouted over the engine to his wife. "Child's mom, pick up the nets! Let's go!"

"You'd better come up!" his wife yelled back. "Turn off the motor! We have company! Big noses!"

"Turn it off? I just got it going!" Ren Kai climbed up the three-step ladder and poked his head through the deck platform. His wife, Mei Ling, was standing by the wheel. They were moored with their stern to the shore. Mei Ling pointed. Ren Kai squinted into the rising sun. The glare was blinding, but there was no mistaking: there, running across the beach between piles of green nets awaiting repair, were a Chinese woman, two big nose women, and a big nose boy, their Western features prominent even from a distance. They carried bundles that looked like babies and bags that looked heavy. Ren had never seen a Westerner in person, only in the movies. He leaned back down and killed the engine. He wiped his hands and went topside to meet them.

Allison and Ruth stood by as Yi Ling engaged in an animated conversation with the fisherman, whose wife stared with unabashed curiosity at Tyler. The grin on her face was immense. Tyler shyly lowered his gaze. Mei Ling laughed. Her teeth, like those of her husband, were bright white and perfect. Ren was a slight man in his mid-forties, his face and arms darkened by a life spent in the sun. His hair was thinning, curled slightly from the humidity. He had cultivated a mustache since his youth, but it remained tentative, wispy, and thin, as if it were still trying to find a foothold on the lip of an adolescent. His eyes were wide and brown and, except for when he was working on his engine, showed kindness and warmth and humor.

Yi Ling did not understand Ren Kai's dialect, so they tried to communicate in Mandarin, the official language of China. Neither Allison nor Ruth could even tell there was difficulty; it was all strange to their ears. Yi Ling had started by showing him her official identification as a guide for the CITS, the government travel service. He looked at it and nodded. He knew of the CITS. He rarely saw anyone from the government except in his village, where he paid taxes.

"I would like you to take the *lao wai* out onto the lake," she began.

"What?" He didn't understand her. Clearly she was a bumpkin from one of the wretched northern provinces. Her Chinese was horrid.

Yi Ling tried to simplify her speech, to talk more slowly and clearly to the simpleton from the south. She used little words and short sentences and sounded to herself like a fool. "The lake, Poyang Hu. Take the *lao wai* onto the lake."

"Fish?"

"No. Maybe. They just want to see," she said.

"See what? Just Poyang Hu here. Water, no more."

"Lake pretty. They tourists. See everything."

"No fish?" he asked again.

"No. Yes. Very well. Take them fishing. Bring back four o'clock afternoon."

"Big noses not catch fish."

"Try."

"They fish I cannot fish. Cost fish. Cost money."

"We pay."

"How much?"

"Fifty U.S." Ren's expression barely flickered, but Yi Ling knew he was hooked.

He thought it over. Fifty U.S. was a stupendous sum. He had heard of the insane wealth of the West and now had proof of it. "Hundred," he said.

"Seventy-five."

"Hundred fifty."

"You said *hundred* before."

He grinned. "This bargain take too long. We talk, I not fish."

"Okay, hundred twenty-five."

"*Hao.*"

Yi Ling reported the deal to Allison and Ruth, who quickly produced it from their money belts. Ren beamed as he saw the cash materialize. He wouldn't need to fish for a month, and he could even fix his carburetor.

Yi Ling realized she was making arrangements without a plan. If the fisherman brought them back at four, and she wasn't there to meet them, what then? What if the police were there, combing the beaches for them? She felt knots inside as she tried to work it out. "Where is your village?" she asked him.

"South lake. Youlan county." He said it proudly. It was the center of the world; all fishermen of Poyang Hu knew Youlan. But Yi Ling gave him a blank look. "Near Nanchang City," he said.

"Do you have a map?" she asked.

"Map? What for map? I know the way," he said.

Yi Ling turned to the Americans. "Do you have China map?" Ruth nodded and fished her Nelles map from her bag. Its scale was large, so Poyang Hu was tiny, but Yi Ling took it and pointed to the lake. "Where?"

Ren studied the paper carefully, trying to understand what he was seeing. There were no Chinese characters; all place names were Pinyin and meant nothing to him. The coastline of Poyang Hu changed with the seasons, as floods took it from big to huge and back to just big again, all the while altering its shorelines. On this map it was a clean, sharp form, and he might as well have been looking at a map of Venus. He shook his head. "Where Nanchang City?"

Yi Ling found it at the southwest corner of the lake. She pointed.

"And Gan River?"

She found that as well, a tiny blue line flowing into Poyang Hu.

"Hah!" he said triumphantly. "Then my village Youlan is here."

He put the tip of his finger on a spot that covered a hundred kilometers, but it was just to the east of Nanchang. Yi Ling knew she could find it. She produced paper and pencil from her bag and asked him to write his family name and house number.

"At four o'clock you come back here," she said. "If I not right here"— she pointed to the beach—"you not wait. Understand? Not come to shore. Take *lao wai* to Youlan. Meet me there."

"*Youlan?*" Ren was puzzled. "Youlan far. Two, three days. More when I fish." Normally he returned to his village only every six months or so, depending upon the fishing; just now the best money was to be made where they were, near the great river Yangtze.

"Yes. Youlan."

"This boat not good for honored foreigners. Too small. Dirty. No place to sleep."

"Good enough. These *lao wai* not choosy."

Ren wouldn't know; he'd never been so close to a foreigner. But his eyes narrowed just the same. "Cost more money. Trip there, trip back, Ren Kai not fish whole way. Hundred fifty not good. Must feed guests. Must see babies not fall into Poyang Hu. Plenty trouble for Ren."

Yi Ling closed her eyes, hoping for guidance from—she didn't know—wherever it was her inspiration came from when she was making impromptu arrangements. Only the stakes had never been so high. She regretted leaving Claire behind; now her own duty was split, and she couldn't see to them all. There hadn't been much choice, but that fact didn't make things easier. She hoped that Claire would return with her when she realized her husband was gone. Yi Ling was certain he had died and hoped for Claire's sake—for the sake of them all—that the first mate would see something to verify it. The longer they all remained in the area, the more dangerous it became.

Four o'clock ought to give her enough time. If not, it would mean that she would have to get Claire to Jiujiang or one of the towns to the south. From there they could make their way overland to Nanchang. She knew the way, past Lushan. She had been there before. It should be easy. They could even take the train. No, not the train, that was too risky. They would hire a private taxi, keeping to country roads, where the risk of being stopped would be small. She didn't know exactly how, but she knew she could get to Nanchang and from there to Youlan, where she could meet the boat.

She had to trust this simple fisherman, to leave the welfare of the Americans and their babies to a man about whom she knew nothing. She believed she had failed in her duty, and the thought tormented her almost as much as the disaster on the river itself had. But she didn't know what else to do. At least it was a plan, and behind the plan was a backup.

Once again she turned to Allison and Ruth. "I am sorry, but must pay more," she said. They had ready the bills she'd already requested.

"How much?" Allison asked, not inclined to argue.

"Maybe five hundred. Maybe more. He take you near Nanchang. Very far. I try to make the best bargain. Okay?"

Ruth looked at Allison; there was no decision to be made. "Of course. Whatever you think."

Yi Ling looked at Ren Kai and plunged ahead. "Before finish money talk—important see no police."

"Unh?" Once again, Ren was completely puzzled by this tour woman from the CITS.

"Police. Must see no police. Must stay away."

"Why?"

"Just important. *Lao wai* visas not good."

"Visas?" He didn't know the word.

"Travel papers. Big fine. I meet you village, take to Nanchang. Fix there. Before that, no police."

Ren thought it over. It was easy enough to avoid the police, who were rarely seen on the lake. No Chinese he knew needed to be persuaded to avoid the police anyway. But if there was trouble for the *lao wai*, that meant there could be trouble for him. For Ren Kai trouble, of course, meant money. He considered what the present trouble might fetch. He studied the American women and their babies—a part of the bargain he couldn't begin to understand—and the boy, the beautiful boy, sitting so quietly beside them. He considered their Chinese guide, Yi Ling, who wasn't coming along. He considered what portion of the truth she might be telling him and concluded it must be very little. None of it added up to a sum he could understand, so he decided to ask for a great deal, to cover his ignorance.

"Two thousand U.S.," he said.

Yi Ling gasped inwardly but showed no sign of it. She began to bargain and failed quickly, caving in when it appeared for a second time that the fisherman had decided the price ought to go up rather than down. She did gain one concession. "One thousand now, one thousand when *lao wai* safe in Youlan."

He nodded his acceptance, and again she turned to the women and told them. Each of them produced five one-hundred-dollar bills. Yi Ling counted it carefully in front of him. Once he shook his head, rejecting a bill with a creased corner. Afterward he carefully wrapped the money in newsprint stained with fish oil and handed it to his wife.

Yi Ling took another moment with her pen and paper. Using the paper her uncle had given her on the *432 Springtime Flower*—it seemed a year ago now—she copied names and addresses. She wrote them first in Pinyin, the anglicized version of Chinese, and then wrote the Chinese characters as well. She was reluctant to do it, because of what had happened to her uncle after he had made a similar paper for her. It seemed final, somehow. An omen. She dismissed the foolish feeling; she had to give the Americans every advantage.

She handed it to Allison. "Keep paper," she said. "Uncle's friends. Good help. Help you, if ever you need." She explained each name and what she'd written on the paper. She added a contact of her own in Nanchang, for whom she had only a telephone number.

"You're not coming with us?" Ruth asked her uncertainly.

"Must wait for Claire," Yi Ling said. "Good fisherman," she said, indicating Ren. "I come back later today. We meet. Any trouble, fisherman take you to village, where I meet you. See—I have written name here of village Youlan, and of Nanchang City. I have family name of fisherman. You wait with him. He take care of you. I find you."

Allison's heart pounded at that. She hadn't expected they might part from Yi Ling, not even for an instant. She had been everything, done everything, arranged everything. She was their only security, their lifeline. The thought of even one afternoon without her was terrifying.

Yi Ling stood, refusing the fisherman's offer of tea. "You must hurry, I must hurry. Four o'clock, yes?"

He nodded, and then Yi Ling noticed he wore no watch. "You have no clock?"

Ren snorted at the question. Northerners were as wasteful as they were ignorant. "Have sun. Why clock, too?"

In the Chinese way, Yi Ling did not stop to say good-bye. Instead she gave a brave smile. She kissed Tai and Wen Li, lingering as long as she dared, and her eyes misted a little. Then she turned and climbed down from the boat to the beach.

Below, Ren made his preparations with his old engine, which started immediately but with a clatter of sloppy parts. "Sounds like the motor has tuberculosis," Ruth joked, trying to ease her own nervousness. She and Allison sat in the cabin and clutched their babies. They watched the preparations, lost in thought. Mei Ling threw the nets that had been drying on the beach onto the prow and unwound a rope from one of the tree stumps that served as bollards. Wading through the water, she climbed up to the deck on a ladder made of wood and rope. She grinned at Tyler as she hauled up the ladder. He was watching her intently. This time, shyly, he grinned back.

The little boat pulled away from the beach near Hukou. Allison and Ruth watched as Yi Ling hurried up the slope, until she disappeared.

The captain of Cruiser Two radioed a request for the immediate assistance of small, fast search vessels and rescue boats with divers, in the event that someone on the freighter might still be alive and trapped below. All hands stood at the rails, looking for survivors. Their sister ship was still aflame. They had picked up her two crewmen. One was badly burned and in shock. The other had described the chase and the ensuing collision and reported he thought a lifeboat had managed to escape the sinking ship.

"Body in the water! Ten meters off the starboard beam!" The cry came from the bridge.

A dark mass drifted in the river, from a distance all but indistinguishable from the other debris. As they drew near, it appeared to be a man floating facedown, arms and legs outstretched. The cruiser slowed and the crew stood mute. They could all see the uniform of the police.

A gaff with a barbed hook was extended over the rail. The man holding it slapped the water twice before he caught hold of the uniform's collar. With strong arms he pulled the body toward the ship. Two men were lowered over the side. They slung ropes around the shoulders and arms of the corpse. As the crew above hoisted it from the water, another body surfaced, one of its hands caught on the first man's belt. The second corpse was faceup.

They all stared in amazement.

The second body belonged to a *lao wai*. His eyes were wide open, his face contorted in agony. The flesh of his cheek was ripped open, one finger of the dead officer still inside the gaping wound. The two bodies were quickly lifted to the deck and laid out, side by side, faceup. They all knew the policeman, Chen. There was a red European-made pocket knife sticking in his belly. His features, too, were twisted in death. Both men had died hard.

The captain had seen a shipping alert issued earlier by the PSB regarding the fugitive *lao wai* and instantly made the connection. "Find his papers," he ordered. They searched the dead man and found a thick wad of yuan in his pockets and a nylon pouch hung round his neck. The captain unzipped the pouch. Ignoring the wallet, he carefully opened the water-logged blue passport with the gold eagle embossed on the front. Inside the cover he found the photo page, still flat and perfect beneath its plastic laminate, the personal information still clear: *Cameron, Nash. Passport No. 07411983, Colorado, U.S.A.* He separated the warped and swollen pages behind the photo page one at a time. Near the rear he found the stamped Chinese visa, its numbers still legible. He hurried to the bridge, where he checked the name on the passport against those on the alert. He had to compare the unfamiliar characters slowly. The fourth name on the list matched: *Cameron, Nash, Colorado, USA, Passport 07411983, Visa 030182 . . .*

He picked up the radio microphone and made his report. From Jiujiang Control the report was transferred to Jiujiang PSB, which immediately flashed it to Nanjing. The junior officer sent to summon Colonel Quan in his quarters in the Jinling Hotel found him already awake in the lobby, working through the finishing motions of tai chi.

Quan read the report and was pleased. At last the net was tightening. He awakened Major Ma with a flurry of instructions. "You must visit once again with the father of Yang Boda," he said. "He was telling the truth after all. Find out what truth he has yet to tell us."

"Unfortunately that is impossible," Major Ma said.

"Oh?"

"He died last night."

"His wife is still with us, *neh?*"

"Of course. I'll see her at once."

"Make certain she knows nothing of his death. I have no wish to cloud her memory with sorrow until her memory has served us first."

Thirty minutes later Quan was airborne. The small jet that had brought him to Nanjing was out of commission for maintenance, so he requisitioned a fast French-built Aerospatiale helicopter from an army training base. It would take him just over an hour and a half to make the 360-kilometer flight. Before the pilot had even lifted off, Quan had donned earphones and was monopolizing the aircraft's radio, issuing a stream of instructions to the Jiujiang PSB. The helicopter swung out across the great river, over the bridge and then south, its nose low. The sun was up only a few degrees above the horizon, and already it promised to be a sweltering day. The shadow of the helicopter flitted through rice paddies and over smokestacks and down the long, high-voltage transmission lines that ran along the river.

Quan called Beijing to report.

"You say the American stabbed the officer?" The deputy minister was sour, gruff, and impatient.

"Yes, Deputy Minister, although I have not yet seen the bodies. I am told there was apparently a struggle. The American's knife was found in the officer's body."

The deputy minister sighed. "Your situation is getting worse, not better," he said. "First kidnapping, now river disaster. People dead." He coughed, trying to dislodge the phlegm in his throat. Even over the radio Quan could hear the click of his platinum lighter as he lit another cigarette. "The American embassy has contacted the Foreign Ministry, which is now bothering me," he said irritably. "Reporters are making a nuisance of themselves. One even called *me*. At my *home*."

"I regret the inconvenience," Quan said. "I expect to have the matter resolved shortly."

"I expect so as well," the deputy minister replied coldly, and he hung up.

Your situation, the deputy minister had called it. Quan didn't like that, not at all.

CHAPTER 11

"I WANT THESE FILES."

Director Lin stood in the busy ministry office, having entered the moment the doors opened. A counter separated him from a large room in which a dozen workers were just settling themselves into the day's routine, pouring tea from battered thermoses, discussing the weekend's soccer matches, and contemplating the huge stacks of paperwork that awaited their attention.

Director Lin pushed a list across the counter, toward the cold-eyed bureaucrat. It was this man, Director Lin knew, whose unwitting efficiency had brought him so near disaster. It was this man who had substituted for Lin's cousin Wu Hung, who had worked at Civil Affairs for seventeen years, the last six in the adoption bureau, where he'd handled the files of thousands of babies who'd been abandoned and orphaned. During those six years they'd worked together smoothly, without a hint of trouble. Then, two months earlier, while Lin was in Thailand, Wu Hung had developed pneumonia and died, leaving critical things undone and bringing Director Lin's world perilously close to crashing down around him.

The bureaucrat studied the names. His eyes showed recognition. "Those files are not available," he said.

"And why not?"

"It is a police matter. We have been notified. They require the files."

"Of course they do," Lin said imperiously. "You know very well it is my orphanage from which the children were kidnapped. The police are coming to interview me later this morning. I agreed to pick the files up first."

"Sorry. This is not what I was told." He turned to go.

"Wait, please." Director Lin smiled thinly. Prepared for this eventuality, he drew an envelope from his jacket pocket. He pushed it across the counter, the bills just visible beneath the flap. "You were told wrong," he said. "Your instructions are detailed more clearly inside. Please check again."

The man opened the envelope. He looked at the thick pile of yuan and made his decision instantaneously. "Just a moment," he said, deftly pocketing the envelope. "I'll get the files." Director Lin nodded. Things never changed at the ministry. The man disappeared into the file room.

He was gone longer than Lin expected, and then he reappeared with a puzzled look on his face. He checked a file drawer in the common area, then two large stacks of files sitting on a table, flipping through them quickly. He stopped at the desks of two co-workers, asking questions.

At last, empty-handed, he returned. "I don't understand," he said.

"What is it?" Director Lin tried to keep his voice calm.

"The files are gone."

"*Gone?* How could they be gone?"

"I don't know. *I* didn't give them to anyone."

"Have the police already been here?"

"No. We've just opened, and I would know, anyway. They were not to pick them up until later, and they would have asked for me."

"Then look again, you fool," Lin snapped. "You've misplaced them."

"I'm telling you, the files aren't there!" the man hissed. "I've looked everywhere! No one has seen them!"

Director Lin felt his head spinning. He leaned on the counter to keep his balance. The files could be missing for only one reason. Forgetting his money, he turned and half ran, half staggered from the ministry.

Yi Ling sat with Claire on the rock ledge at the base of Stone Bell Hill, waiting for the first mate to return. It was a good vantage point, offering a sweeping view of the lake and the river with its islands. The limestone hill was pitted with underground fissures and caves. Trees and bushes sprouted from crevices in the rock, providing excellent shelter where they could see without being seen. Had Yi Ling not known where to look, she never would have found Claire. Atop the cliffs above them, they could just make out the golden tip of the seven-story River Subduing Pagoda.

Because of seasonal flooding, there were no roads nearby; the only traffic was on the water.

Claire was near collapse. Yi Ling offered to take Katie, but Claire declined, holding the baby close. She stared at the water, which looked gray and depressing. Ships and boats plied the channel well past Hsin Chou and the much larger island beyond. They could just make out the vague form of the top of the *Springtime Flower*. In the river near her uncle's boat, Yi Ling could see four police boats—two small ones, which were patrolling the shorelines of the islands, and two bigger ones, anchored near the *432*. She couldn't tell what they were doing.

Neither woman lost hope. Yi Ling believed that her wily uncle would certainly have outwitted the river and found a way to survive. Even now he would be eluding the police, lying in a clump of bushes somewhere or dug in behind a log. He had survived worse disasters in his life, including starvation and torture in the *laogai*. He would find a way to join them. She knew he would.

Claire didn't allow herself the thought that if Nash had survived and caught hold of something, he would already be well downstream. "Do you think we'll see him, if he's there?" she asked Yi Ling in a tortured whisper. "I'm afraid I won't be able to see."

"My eyes very good," Yi Ling told her. "I will see." Keeping one eye on the river, she busied herself making formula for Katie. She used the last of the bottled water from Claire's bag. She doubted Allison and Ruth had very much with them, either, and knew she would have to slip into Hukou to get more.

They heard the helicopter long before they could see it, its blades whipping at the heavy air of the river valley with a steady *whump-whump*. They couldn't tell where it was coming from, and then it appeared from directly behind and above them, thundering out past the top of Stone Bell Hill. Even though they were both expecting it, it still made them jump. They felt the air pressure of the blades, the noise direct and deafening. It flashed by, the sun reflecting off the blades, and swooped quickly across the river toward the wreckage. The craft circled the islands several times as its inhabitants surveyed the scene below, then set down gently on Hsin Chou. One of the doors opened. A man climbed out and walked to the water's edge. One of the smaller patrol boats raced toward the shore nearest the helicopter. The man got into the boat, which sped back to one of the rescue vessels.

Instinctively, Yi Ling thought the helicopter a bad omen. Its arrival told her that the authorities knew this was no longer a simple case of a river collision. Watching its spinning blades, and the police boats swarming around the scene, she began to feel for the first time the power of what they were up against and the unlimited forces that would be arrayed against them. It was not cold, but Yi Ling shivered.

In the hours that followed, as they awaited Shidao's return, police activity in the area increased dramatically. More boats arrived and patrolled the shorelines downstream. Every so often Yi Ling could see one of the boats' occupants climbing out, wading in the shallow water near the shore, exploring the sorts of vegetation and obstructions behind which she imagined her uncle hiding. One of the boats beached exactly where the first mate had landed a few hours earlier. Two men got out and explored the area near the water. They stared up at the cliffs, then got back in their boat and left.

Yi Ling was growing concerned about the first mate. She didn't see how he could possibly find out anything near the wreck with all the police there. She checked her watch. It was already almost noon. She left Claire there and hiked around the hill to the village of Hukou, where the ferryboats landed from the Jiujiang side of the river. In the village she saw three policemen, but they weren't looking for a single woman. No one stopped her or even looked her way.

In a small shop she purchased bottled water, a few tins of sardines, and half a dozen Styrofoam cups of dried noodles. In another store she found a cheap shawl and a straw peasant's hat for Claire. It wasn't much of a disguise, but they were going to have to walk in the open soon. That morning just after dawn, when Yi Ling had accompanied Ruth and Allison, it had been so early that no one but the fisherman Ren Kai and his wife had seen the two women up close. Now there would be more people, some of them looking for *lao wai,* and any disguise was better than nothing. She thought if Claire kept her head down and they kept to the beach and away from the village, no one would think anything of it.

She walked out of the village and made her way back to their hiding place in the rocks. To her relief, she found the first mate had returned. His expression told her his news was not good.

"I wasted hours trying to learn something by going around the island and trying to see from the top of one of the levees on the big island," Shidao said. "But I could see little and hear less. So I got back in the dinghy and went directly up to their boat. I told them I had seen the fire from Hukou. I asked if I could help. They laughed at me and sent me away, but not before I could ask some questions. The American man is dead. They found his body with another—a *gong an*. They took them to Jiujiang. The small boat that sank the *Springtime Flower* was a smuggling boat, being chased by the police cruiser."

Yi Ling was almost afraid to ask. "What of my uncle?"

Shidao shook his head. "They have found no survivors on shore or down stream. They found some bodies under the water in the wreckage but haven't recovered them yet. They are sending more divers and equipment so they can cut into the compartments." He looked at his employer's niece, and his voice grew soft. "No one could have survived," he said.

"What's he saying?" Claire asked.

It was a moment before Yi Ling could even look at Claire. Yi Ling struggled to maintain her composure. She still thought there was a chance for Yang Boda, but there was nothing to be done waiting here. Even if he were alive, she couldn't help him now. She debated lying but saw no use in it. If Claire didn't know the truth, she would want to remain where they were, and that was the one thing they could not do.

"I am sorry," Yi Ling said at last. "Your husband was killed. First mate say they found his body. They have taken him to Jiujiang."

Claire jerked a little at the news, and then her gaze clouded. She seemed to hug Katie even more tightly. She started to rock back and forth with the child, lost in some distant place.

Yi Ling sat beside her and touched her shoulder. "We must go soon," she said. "Nothing left for us here."

Claire shook her head. She wiped her cheek with the back of her hand. "There's nowhere to go," she said. "Not without Nash."

"He died to bring Katie home," Yi Ling said. "You must finish."

Claire broke down then and dissolved into her grief.

Colonel Quan stood on the deck of the salvage boat. Below him, divers explored the wreckage of the *Springtime Flower*. Farther out on the river, two men on a small boat were tossing a grappling hook into the water. For an hour they had trolled in an ever widening arc. Mostly they had found thick clumps of vegetation. But then, floating alone, they found an arm. They would be days at the grisly chore.

One of the deck hands behind Quan shouted, and another man picked his way across coiled ropes and equipment stacked on the deck to join him. Together they pulled on a rope, lifting a crate the divers had found in the hold of the wrecked freighter. As it came out of the river, its sides gushed water. They set it on the deck and untied the rope, then removed the top.

One of the officers removed an assault rifle. Quan immediately recognized the gas return tube above the barrel, the box magazine, the folding metal stock. It was a Kalashnikov AK-47, an old design but highly effective nevertheless, capable of firing six hundred rounds a minute. He might have guessed. Yang Boda had been carrying more than a few *lao wai* up the river. From what the divers said about the quantity of arms they'd found in the hold, it appeared the rebels in the troubled Muslim province of Xinjiang had just been deprived of a great many weapons.

Quan was soon joined by a captain from the Jiujiang PSB, who arrived on a launch to make his report to the colonel in person. He gaped open-mouthed at the weapons. He knew that Quan's very presence signified that something unusual was afoot, but the sight of the arms, and of the Aerospatiale helicopter on Hsin Chou, had rammed it home. He walked with Quan to the bridge, where he unfolded a map and laid it out on a table.

"We have searched this entire area," the captain said, running his finger from the mouth of the Poyang Hu downstream nearly ten kilometers. "If someone had been holding on to floating debris, we would have seen them by now. At the hour when the accident occurred, it is likely the passengers were sleeping. Some of the cabin doors jammed. This ship sank very quickly, Colonel. I think we will find the *lao wai* trapped inside, drowned before they could escape."

"How long before the divers can cut into the compartments?"

The captain looked at his watch. "Another hour at least before their equipment arrives, Colonel. After that, another hour. Maybe two."

"We don't know who was on the boat that was seen leaving."

"No."

"How big was it?"

"The men didn't see it clearly. It was still very dark. But most of these freighters carry just a small dinghy, if they carry anything at all."

"Assume it carried Yang Boda, his niece, and the *lao wai*. That would make one man, four women, a boy, and three babies. Could they all fit?"

"Yes, but not easily. With such a load the boat would be in danger of capsizing. To cross the lake to Jiujiang, they would need something bigger."

"Or they might just make two trips." Quan studied the map, absorbing the magnitude of the difficulties that faced him. He was certain Yang Boda had escaped, that even now he was making his way with the *lao wai* toward Jiujiang, or to Nanchang farther south. Nearly four hours had passed since the collision—plenty of time for his quarry to have made two trips across the mouth of the lake or to have hired a larger boat, or to have disappeared into one of the myriad streams, inlets, or marshes in the area surrounding the lake. For that matter, there was no reason to suppose they were staying on the water. There were roads everywhere, on both sides of the lake: primary routes, like the major highway connecting Jiujiang and Nanchang; and hundreds of secondary roads, meandering through the province connecting small villages. In addition, there were countless dirt roads, roads that during flood season were underwater and not even shown on his map. On any of those roads, one might board buses or hire taxis or even a private car. Infinite cracks and holes through which his quarry might slip. For the moment he could not worry that they had eluded him. He decided to sweep the immediate area and then to concentrate on the Jiujiang-Nanchang corridor, where he was certain Yang Boda's network of accomplices and contacts would be the greatest.

His finger swept an area of river on the map. "Search every vessel, from here to here. *Every* vessel. And all fishing and cargo boats on the lake within"—he looked at his watch and made some quick mental calculations—"a thirty-kilometer radius."

"We don't have enough boats to do that."

"Do not tell me what you cannot do!" Quan snapped. "Get more from Wuxue!"

"Even if they will give them, they will never arrive on time, Colonel. Wuxue is two hours upstream."

Quan knew it was true. The farther one traveled from Beijing or Shanghai, the more impoverished were the local governments' resources. This was particularly true in a poor province like Jiangxi, where the police had an excess of manpower but precious little equipment. "I will contact them myself to see they give you what they do have. Until they arrive, use the boats you have to patrol the eastern shore, here. Unless I am mistaken, they will make for one of these inlets and try to find land transport to the

Nanchang highway. Set blockades on the roads—here, and here. All vehicles are to be searched."

"Of course." The captain nodded. A land search was much easier than water.

"Your men are covering all the ferries?"

"*Shì,* as you instructed when we spoke by radio earlier, Colonel. We have men on the Jiujiang side, and on the north side of the Yangtze, in case they are trying to confuse us. Our men got there quite quickly. We've checked every passenger. They couldn't have gotten through that way."

"Unless they had already passed."

"Traffic has been light this morning. We have talked to the ferry crews. They saw no *lao wai.* No babies."

Quan nodded, unconvinced. "Be certain that all offices of the PSB in every county on both sides of the lake have been alerted. Bus and truck drivers are to be interviewed. Neighborhood captains are to be notified." It was a colossal task. Quan knew that his best chance for success lay not in the direct efforts of the police, but in reports that would inevitably filter in from rural communities, where big noses would be highly conspicuous. The mere sight of them would cause instant comment, comment that would soon be overheard by the local PSB. No foreigner could hide for long in a nation of curious informers; of that he was certain.

He lit a cigarette and poured himself a cup of tea from the stainless-steel thermos he carried. He preferred his tea freshly brewed, but here there was no alternative. He stood at the rail of the boat and watched the two men tossing the grappling hook into the gray water. Twice it came up empty. The third time a blanket dangled from one of the hooks. It was bright pink, decorated with blue flowers. A baby's blanket. One of the men pulled it free and tossed it into the bottom of the boat.

Quan stared out across the river toward the south shore. The day was hazy, but already hot and humid. A pair of white tick birds raced up the river, their wingtips almost touching the water. Quan admired the precision in their flight, the grace and skill with which they echoed each other's movements, no matter how slight, as some sixth sense guided them along the same invisible meandering path. As one they turned suddenly toward the south, where they disappeared behind an imposing rock outcropping that stood sentry at the mouth of Poyang Hu. "What is that?" he asked the captain.

"Stone Bell, Colonel."

"So. The famous hill." He had never visited the site but knew the story, of the hill where waves broke against the rock, causing an eerie bell-like sound. From Stone Bell the Taiping rebel Shi Dakai had routed a dynasty's finest navy, 150 years ago, during the bloodiest of China's bloody rebellions.

"What's there now?" Quan asked.

"Along the base, caves, and rocks. Nothing. Above it, as you can see, a pagoda, and a shrine. There is a path to the top from Hukou, on the back side."

"Your men have searched the caves?"

"Only a cursory search, Colonel, along the area you can see, and ten kilometers each way up and down the shore. Our men are still out there."

Quan took the captain's binoculars and scanned the rocks. Perhaps he was overestimating his quarry. Such rocks were a good place to hide, to plan, to recover. A perfect place to rout the dynasty's forces. "Call the Hukou PSB. Tell them to search there again. Every cave. Every rock."

"At once, Colonel."

Ren Kai spent the day puttering in circles with his cargo. He was trying to do as the CITS guide had asked, but his passengers were making it difficult. Only the boy showed an interest in fishing, and although Ren had moved the boat three times, stopping where he knew the fish would almost jump into the boat uninvited, the boy had caught nothing. The two women had sat talking to each other in soft voices, holding their babies, barely responding as his wife, Mei Ling, had tried to make them more comfortable. He knew nothing of *lao wai,* and couldn't begin to read their expressions, but they seemed subdued, sad somehow, and paid little attention to their surroundings. There was a complete language barrier, of course, but that wasn't the trouble. They were polite enough, but he could sense they carried some great burden. Mei Ling cooked a hearty lunch, but only the boy showed an appetite. The women fed their babies but barely picked at the food themselves. If he ended up carrying them all the way to his village and their moods didn't improve, it was going to be a long, awkward voyage. He should have charged more money.

He squinted at the sun. It was just after two o'clock, time to head for the rendezvous with the CITS guide. He pulled in the fishing line for the boy, who removed the bait from the hook and tossed it back in the water.

Ren went below and pushed the starter. The engine cranked but didn't fire. He tried again. The battery was strong and the engine turned over quickly, but still nothing.

He cursed. It was getting old, this mechanical trouble. He opened the engine compartment and leaned over the recalcitrant motor, fiddling with wires and hoses. Everything looked good. He decided to try his mallet. He gave the carburetor a hearty whack, then another for good measure. He tried the starter once again. The motor turned obediently but did not start.

He sighed and found new curses and pulled down his tools, which were wrapped in burlap. He put them on the deck, removed his shirt, and set to work.

The officer of the *gong an ju* got close enough that Yi Ling could see his eyes, and the mole on his cheek, and the tiny beads of sweat on his brow. He picked his way gingerly across the rocks, stopping every few paces to catch his breath and look around. Once he looked directly at where she stood, but with the vines and heavy vegetation that covered the hollow in the rocks where they stood, he didn't see her. She stopped breathing when he looked, touching Claire's arm, hoping her fingertips would communicate the need for absolute silence. Katie had fallen asleep only fifteen minutes earlier, after spending the long hours of the morning and early afternoon fussing and restless. Now she was quiet, bundled in the crook of Claire's right arm, dead to the world.

The officer was nearly upon them by the time Shidao spotted him. The officer had approached from the south, the lake side, while their attention had been on the river. With an urgent whisper the first mate alerted the women, and they scooted back up the slope into the shelter, where they'd spent most of the day.

The officer stared down the hill at the water. He drew a pack of cigarettes from his pocket and lit one. When he had smoked half of it he stood and stretched, the cigarette dangling from his mouth. He turned directly toward them and unzipped his fly. He took a long piss into the vegetation at their feet. The first mate's face was impassive; he was as silent and still as the rocks in which he stood, ready to leap if necessary. Claire was certain the officer could hear the blood pounding in her head. Yi Ling closed her eyes, willing the man away.

With a sigh the officer shook himself and zipped up. He blinked as the smoke from his cigarette irritated his eyes. He took it from his mouth and then, thoughtfully, deliberately, picked his nose. He leaned down and wiped his hand on a bush. Then he turned back to the river and saw one of his colleagues coming from the other direction, down the hill near the beach. "Hah!" he called, waving. He started down to meet him.

Claire was trembling and weak and began to sob again. Yi Ling took Katie and helped Claire sit down. The policemen poked around the terrain below them for nearly thirty more minutes, before disappearing behind the rocks to the east. Yi Ling looked at her watch. It was almost three-thirty. They needed to hurry. She had intended to lead them back around the hill and through Hukou, but with all the police she decided they would have to cross the base of the hill the hard way, to avoid people.

With Shidao on one side of Claire and Yi Ling on the other, they made their way through the rocky slopes and vegetation. By the time they cleared the base of the hill, their faces were scratched and their clothing ripped by thorns. Twice more they saw the police, searching on foot on the shore below them. They crouched in the brush, waiting for the danger to pass, then moved as quickly as the difficult terrain allowed. They walked almost two kilometers to the south, until they could no longer see the Hukou dock.

At four o'clock exactly they arrived in a stand of mulberry trees at the top of the slope above the spot where she had agreed to meet the fisherman. The shore in each direction was mostly deserted. Some of the fishing boats that Yi Ling had seen earlier had returned, their owners tending their nets. There was no sign of Ren's boat. Once, Yi Ling saw a police boat hailing a small fishing vessel. Her heart sank. If they were inspecting every boat, Ren would either be caught or avoid the area. At four-thirty she convinced herself that without a watch, the fisherman was simply late, even though she knew better. She squinted as she scanned the water, upon which the sun's rays sparkled painfully. They watched and waited.

Yi Ling was famished. Without hot water she couldn't eat the dried noodles, so she opened a tin of sardines. She offered some to Claire, who wrinkled her nose at the oily fish and wouldn't eat. The first mate dug in hungrily. Together they finished off three tins.

No matter what spirits Ren Kai cursed, no matter the gods he invoked, no matter the epithets he remembered, no matter the promises he made or the penalties he swore, his engine would not start. Three o'clock came and went; his wrenches clattered and sweat poured from his brow. He started pulling hoses, to rinse them and clear any obstructions. At three-thirty his carburetor lay in pieces on the deck. Venturi jets, screen filters, adjusting screws, floats: he checked each piece, and blew through every orifice, and carefully wiped everything clean with his shirt-tail.

One of the *lao wai* women stuck her head in the cabin. She pointed at her watch and said something. With an apologetic look and a sweep of his hand, he indicated his dilemma. *"Ma shàng hao,"* he said, his smile full of promise. "It will run soon. There is still time." Patiently he reassembled everything, then carefully cut a new gasket from a sheet of cork.

"We have finished our inspection of the wreckage, Colonel," the PSB officer reported. "All compartments have been cut open and searched by our divers. We found thirty-eight cases of weapons. More than six hundred guns in all."

Quan didn't care about weapons. "What of the bodies?" he snapped.

"We think we recovered six."

"Think?"

"There were . . . pieces, sir. Until the doctors can tell us for certain, we can only guess. But one of them—one of the whole bodies, that is—matches the description of Yang Boda."

"And the *lao wai?*"

"There was no sign of them, or the babies."

"Any Chinese women?"

"No. They were all seamen, judging from their clothing."

"You say one looks like Yang Boda. Did he carry identification?"

"Yes, Colonel, but the name did not match." The officer read a name off the card; it meant nothing to Quan. "We will make inquiries, of course," the officer said. "His fingerprints have already been taken."

"Bring him to Jiujiang," Quan ordered. He wanted to see the body for himself. He had seen the photographs in Yang Boda's *dàng àn*. He had studied his face. Identification or not, he would know the man when he saw him.

Quan considered the developments. So it was the *lao wai* and the guide Yi Ling who had escaped in the dinghy. Their bodies were not going to wash up downriver. But if the body the divers had recovered was indeed Yang Boda, then the man's resources, his network of criminal friends, would be lost to the others. While Quan did not underestimate the CITS guide, every instinct told him the fugitives were still nearby.

He picked up the phone and called the Hukou PSB.

At five o'clock Yi Ling allowed herself to think Ren wasn't coming at all. Boat traffic on the lake had thinned considerably. The fishermen had all returned to their night berths. Only an occasional small boat passed through the channel at the neck of the lake. Every half hour she saw the ferry that linked Hukou with the road to Jiujiang. By five-thirty she knew that she must do something else. She considered hiring another fishing boat to take them to Youlan but thought she could do more if she could get to Jiujiang. She remembered that one of the names her uncle had given her had been of a friend who lived there. She thought that Yang Boda, having been separated from them, might make his way there. And she herself had friends in the city, friends who might give them shelter.

She wished she'd made different arrangements with the fisherman that morning. Now she saw great holes in what had seemed a reasonable plan. She had no idea what might have become of the two American women, and she imagined they must be terrified. She wasn't good at this, she realized.

Shidao checked his watch. "Your fisherman is not coming," he said impatiently. "We should not wait any longer."

She nodded reluctantly. The first mate agreed it was best to go to Jiujiang. There was anonymity in a big city, safety in crowds where even *lao wai* didn't stand out as much. They decided it would be safest to cross the lake in the dinghy. By now every fisherman in the area would have been alerted to their presence, making it risky to approach one of them for passage, and the ferry was very likely being watched. So Shidao left alone to get the little boat, which he had left moored in the midst of twenty other small boats tethered at the Hukou dock. The dinghy had no markings from the *Springtime Flower.* If the police were searching for it—as he was certain they would be—they likely wouldn't have noticed it among so many others just like it.

In that estimation the first mate was correct. The police hadn't known that particular dinghy didn't belong there. But the dock attendant, a garrulous, white-haired old man who walked with a stoop and sold gasoline and diesel to small watercraft, and who knew every boat and fisherman who ever stopped at Hukou, had. Only the locals kept their boats where Shidao had left the dinghy. Passing vessels that bothered to visit Hukou at all used a different dock, one that faced the river. The attendant had mentioned the dinghy to four other people by the time the PSB heard of it. They had sent a plainclothes officer to talk with the old man, who obligingly pointed out the foreign craft and then rambled on about the unseasonably heavy rains in the south that were already beginning to make the lake rise. The officer examined the boat. He thought the little craft insignificant but dutifully called in his report. He was ordered to wait and watch. He borrowed a pole and line from the attendant, who showed him where he might fish. During the late afternoon various boat owners came and went. The fisherman watched them carefully, but none approached the dinghy. The officer wasn't perturbed, however. While he was waiting he caught three fish.

It was nearly six when he saw yet another man approaching. The man seemed quite nonchalant as he strolled down the dock. Upon seeing the fisherman, he inquired politely about the catch. The officer smiled and nodded and pointed to a line in the water on which dangled his three fish. Shidao laughed and waved. He stepped into the dinghy, cast off the line, started the engine, and set out onto the lake. He had not gone ten meters before the officer, his catch forgotten, was speaking urgently into his radio.

At dusk Yi Ling set the straw hat on Claire's head and wrapped the shawl around her shoulders. They had to make their way across the open slope, to where the first mate had just beached the dinghy. They moved as one, Claire right on Yi Ling's heels as they hurried toward the water, feeling naked and vulnerable without the shelter of the trees. Yi Ling watched the lake. There were only a few boats in sight. Fishermen, she thought, wondering absently if they worked after dark, too. On the opposite shore, the lights of a small village began to flicker on. She strained to make out detail in the gathering darkness. Everywhere she looked she thought she saw something moving, someone threatening. She knew it was her nerves, but the knowledge didn't help.

After what seemed an eternity, they reached the dinghy. Shidao quickly got the boat turned around and out into the lake again. Once under way they all felt better, as if some shadow of danger had passed. The lake, while quite as open as the shore, seemed safer somehow; a boat attracted little attention.

The first mate steered a course well to the south of the ferry landing, intending to ditch the boat in one of the coves on the western shore. He planned to find a place there for the women to hide and then proceed alone by taxi or bus into Jiujiang. He knew several of Yang Boda's contacts there, one of whom owned a fleet of six taxis. He would return to the lake in one of them, pick up the women and the baby, and then hide overnight in Jiujiang. Meanwhile he would try to reach Yang Boda's partner in Wuhan, the man who was going to provide the army truck in which Yang Boda had intended to conceal the *lao wai* on their overland journey to the south. If he could reach the man and make arrangements, he would see Yi Ling safely onto the truck. If not, he intended to part company with her after making the attempt. Even Yang Boda would not ask more of him, and Shidao knew it was madness to compound the danger he already faced by traveling with such a conspicuous figure as Claire.

Shidao steered the dinghy on a straight line, watching the distant lights of the ferry as it departed the west shore, swinging around on its hundredth passage of the day across the lake. He hunched over, nervous and intent. Just another ten minutes and the darkness would swallow them completely. Ten minutes after that, they would be safe on the western shore.

They all heard the speedboat at the same instant, its powerful twin engines drowning out that of their little outboard, even from the distance. The boat, its prow lighter than the surrounding darkness, was approaching fast from the northeast. Shidao couldn't see any markings or make out the type, but the speed of its approach fed his worst fears. He twisted the knob further, trying to coax more speed from half a horsepower, but the little outboard was already going flat out.

The speedboat bore directly down upon them. The first mate changed course, swinging to the west, in case the other boat simply hadn't seen him, but as he did the bigger boat changed course as well, to compensate. It seemed as if it were going to run them over. They were still more than half a kilometer from the shore. He couldn't outrun the other boat.

Yi Ling looked at him inquisitively. "Maybe it's a pleasure boat," he said, without conviction. A moment later they were blinded as an intense searchlight blazed on. The light was trained directly upon them. The other boat slowed. A tinny voice came over a loud hailer. *"Ting xià!* Stop your boat at once! Identify yourselves!"

Shidao had no weapons, nowhere to run, and he would not soon forget what it had been like to be in the water just that morning, when he had nearly drowned. Even if he could swim, there was no escaping, nowhere to hide. They were in the open, caught like a hare in the headlights of a car. He shut down the power. He would wait until the other boat came along- side, and then, with luck, a moment would come when he could attack the men in the other boat. He had nothing to lose.

The speedboat swung around in front of their prow and then circled back, its searchlight blinding as it bathed their little boat in light. The powerboat made one complete circle and then its engine dropped to idle. Claire hunched over, her face hidden beneath her straw hat, Katie invisible beneath her shawl.

Fear tightened Yi Ling's throat. She knew their luck had run out.

CHAPTER TWELVE

THE MOMENTS TICKED RELENTLESSLY BY. Every so often the motor would crank again, each time to no avail. Allison looked in on the fisherman's efforts. What she saw left her almost in tears. "He's got the engine in pieces," she reported back to Ruth, who, uncharacteristically, was too shaken by the thought to make her usual light comments. They sat and waited and listened, helpless.

It was nearly five when a cloud of black smoke preceded what sounded like the death rattle of a sick machine. But after rumbling and cranking and clanking, the engine began to churn. It belched clouds of noxious smoke, then started to run more smoothly, and at last sounded as if it might actually power the boat. Allison's and Ruth's stomachs were in knots; they found themselves saying silent prayers as they chugged northeast across the lake. They'd missed their appointed time with Yi Ling and Claire but hoped that somehow they would still be waiting. They simply *had* to be. The alternative was unthinkable.

Once, Ren spotted a police cruiser, moored next to some other boats. He waved the women inside the cabin and kept his course. They never got close enough to see whether there was even anyone on board.

They neared the beach outside Hukou. He kept his distance at first, navigating a large arc in the water. All eyes scanned the terrain for any sign of Yi Ling.

Ruth squinted through weak eyes. "Do you see them?" she asked Allison.

"No." Allison's voice was soft, concealing the terror she felt. "Tyler? Do you?"

"Huh-uh," he said, unconcerned. "Can I fish some more while we wait?"

But Ren was cautious, and there was no waiting. He headed off to the west, then cut south until he knew his craft would be lost to the view of anyone watching from the shore, then turned northeast and approached the spot once more. He saw the other fishing boats, belonging to his friends with whom he berthed at night.

Again Allison's answer to Ruth was the same. "No," she said, heartsick. "There's nobody there."

Ren steered away once more, only this time he didn't double back. His boat chugged straight south.

"Go back, please," Allison pleaded, beckoning toward Hukou. "Just wait a little longer. Try once more."

Ren shook his head. Their engine trouble was most regrettable, but his instructions from the CITS guide were clear. "Youlan," he replied, pointing, nodding. He flashed his brightest smile, trying to coax a happier look from his unhappy passenger. Then Ruth joined in, and the two women gestured and pleaded and chattered their foreign babble. Ren heard the urgency in their voices, but his wheel never wavered. The sun was setting, the huge globe burning golden through the haze as it brushed the hills that rose from the lake. He saw how beautiful it was and pointed, trying to put their minds at ease. They barely looked.

Mei Ling gave them a sympathetic smile. *"Cha?"* she said. Tea?

Allison took a deep breath and gave up. She hugged Ruth and brushed back a tear.

Again Ren Kai wondered what troubled the *lao wai* so. He didn't have any reason to think the CITS guide a liar, but he didn't think the trouble was for something as simple as bad papers, as she had explained. People he knew didn't act this way about their papers.

He intended to go just another few moments and then stop for the night. He wanted to drop anchor near some crab nets on the eastern shore, where the water was shallow and usually calm. A good friend of his owned the nets but never stayed there at night. Ren knew they would be undisturbed there.

Years on the lake had made him quite farsighted, so that he had to hold a newspaper at arm's length just to read the boldest type, but across the water his eyes were as sharp as a hawk's. With those keen eyes Ren saw the boat approaching long before another man might have noticed anything at all, and he knew instantly from its shape what it was.

Police. The boat was coming from the western shore, from his starboard side. It wasn't moving at top speed. But it was moving quite purposefully on a course that would directly intercept his own. Ren felt his knees go weak. Only rarely in his years of fishing had he ever even seen the police, much less been stopped. But now, today, he knew what was going to happen.

They *were* going to stop him. And, he knew with equal certainty, it had everything to do with the *lao wai.* He thought quickly. There was a choice to be made. He could try to hide them or he could just turn them in.

Ren Kai was not a criminal. He had never been in trouble for anything, not since his fourth year in primary school when he'd broken a window. But he had no love for the authorities, either. And the guide had paid him well. He had the briefest thought that he should have refused her request, that he never should have placed himself or his wife at risk. But such thoughts were too late. He had done what he had done, and everything he knew of the police told him that no matter what the truth of it, his fate would be sealed by the mood of the officer in charge and that nothing Ren might offer in his own defense would make any difference.

Which left him with only one choice.

"Mei Ling!" he shouted. "The *ji̇̌ng chá!*"

Quan Yi finished a peaceful meal of curried squid at the hotel in Jiujiang. He had spent the last part of the afternoon straightening out an ugly incident at the train station. Three Dutch couples with children they were adopting tried to board the express to Nanchang. An overzealous young officer, seeing the unmistakable foreign faces and the Chinese babies they carried, had produced his automatic weapon, which he'd leveled menacingly at the shocked travelers. At gunpoint, shouting and near panic, he'd ordered them down onto the floor of the station. One of the women had fainted and hit her head against a bench.

It had been almost an hour before medical attention arrived, and nearly half an hour after that before the terrified Dutch had been allowed to leave. Already Quan could imagine the call of outrage he was going to receive, after the Dutch government finished venting its anger. Quan knew it would take great luck to prevent a hundred similar cases of mistaken identity all over eastern China. The last thing he needed was to create a tourist scare out of his hunt.

Quan personally apologized to the offended tourists and saw to it that their hotel rooms in Nanchang were provided compliments of the Chinese government, the full cost of which he ordered taken from the officer's salary. The young man would be eight months paying for his mistake but would, the next time he was confronted with a simple suspect description, remember to consider such trifles as sex and age before he started fingering the trigger.

Quan had just ordered tea when his cellular phone rang. He withdrew the instrument from its leather carrying case and flipped it open, extending the antenna. *"Wei?"*

It was Major Ma, calling from Nanjing. "I sent an officer to pick up the babies' files at the ministry late this morning," he said. "The files were missing."

"Oh?"

"Our officer was told by the bureau director that the files must have been sent back to the Justice Ministry by mistake. Justice used to handle some of the adoptions, so I had him check. They weren't there, either. It took most of the day, but he found the bicycle courier. The man had delivered some documents between the two ministries this morning, but not these. He had his delivery log to prove it. Either they were lost at Civil Affairs or someone took them."

Quan pondered that. "Why would anyone care about such files? And I don't know what this might have to do with our Americans," he said. "This seems a matter involving the ministries, not the fugitives."

"I agree, Quan Yi, but first a clerk at Civil Affairs tells us these are the wrong babies, and now their files are missing. It appears more than incompetence now, or coincidence."

"So it might seem, although the files may still be sitting on some desk, buried beneath the soccer scores."

"Civil Affairs went through every file in the bureau twice, with our man watching. The files aren't there."

Quan thought for a moment. "All the babies came through the same orphanage?"

"Yes. The Number Three Children's Welfare Institute, just outside Suzhou."

"Certainly the director keeps copies of the files, *neh?* He should be able to clear this up."

"Apparently he was here in Nanjing for the day, visiting the ministry. I've already asked the Suzhou police there to question him when he returns."

"Hao." Quan hung up. The waiter arrived with his tea and was pouring for him when the phone rang again.

"Colonel Quan, I am Captain Liu Hui." It was the head of the Hukou PSB, his voice pitched high with excitement. "We've caught them!"

Quan immediately feared another grotesque error, like that with the Dutch. "And exactly whom did you catch, Captain?"

"I have their papers here, Colonel." There was a pause as the captain sorted through the documents arrayed on the desk in front of him. "Sorry, sir . . . ah, here it is. Yi Ling," he said, "of Jiangsu province." Quan leaned forward in his chair. "And there is a Shidao Ying, of Hubei." Quan didn't know the name. It could be a crew member, he supposed.

"Anyone else?"

"Yes, sir," the captain said, keeping the best for last. He had personally verified the name against the alert before he called. "Cameron Claire," he said. "From Colorado. The United States of America. U.S.A."

"You *have* them, you say? You have seen them yourself? Where?"

"They were apprehended in a boat on Poyang Hu, half an hour ago. They were crossing from the east shore to the west. The man Shidao resisted arrest. He has sustained serious injuries and is being treated at the hospital. The women are being detained here, at Hukou PSB. I have just left them. Oh yes, there was a baby with the American. She has been taken to the Hukou Social Welfare Institute."

"And the other Americans?"

"Not yet, sir. We are still looking. I have thirty men out now, searching the marshes and coves on both sides of the lake. Obviously the fugitives were waiting until it was nearly dark, and trying to get across the water in two groups."

"I'll be there at once." Quan stood and threw a wad of yuan on the table, his tea forgotten. As he strode for the door, he permitted himself the briefest moment of satisfaction. Despite the deputy minister's impatience, Quan had been fishing for less than two days and already his net was filling. But he had to give the *lao wai* credit. He had fully expected to apprehend them within hours of beginning the search. That they had eluded capture for so long was a remarkable achievement.

"Heh, fisherman!" The small two-man police launch slowed, its helmsman nursing it along until it nudged against the old battered tires hanging from the side of Ren Kai's boat. The engine stopped, and the officer in front tossed a rope to Ren, who looped it around a wooden bitt on the foredeck, lashing the two boats together. "How is the catch?" the officer inquired. He wore khaki pants and a short-sleeved shirt bearing the emblem of the Jiangxi provincial police.

"Not for shit," Ren replied, smiling broadly. "Too many fishermen, not enough fish." Mei Ling stood at the door of the cabin and waved. The officer nodded and waved back. He stepped across the gap between the boats. His helmsman remained seated in the launch.

"You are checking for electric nets?" Ren asked. Such nets were the primary reason for most surprise inspections on the lake. They were legal on the rivers, but never on Poyang Hu. "With electric nets my catch would be sufficient that I could offer you dinner. But as you can see, I have none."

The officer shook his head. "No. I am looking for *lao wai.*"

Ren gave an involuntary nervous laugh. "*Lao wai?* The government thinks we are catching *lao wai* now in Poyang Hu? It is hard enough to catch crabs."

The officer chuckled. "Just orders. I must inspect all boats." But he made no move toward the cabin, to look around. Instead he sat on the gunwale. He removed his cap and wiped his brow.

Mei Ling appeared through the cabin door carrying a thermos and four porcelain cups. "You must take tea with us," she said politely.

The officer grunted his thanks. He called to his companion. "*Cha?*" The other man shook his head. He had leaned back in his seat, arms behind his head, feet propped up on the instrument panel. He closed his eyes for a quick nap.

They drank tea and chatted about the weather as dusk settled on the lake. The officer said there were heavy storms reported in the south of the lake, near Nanchang. It was the time of year when storms moved quickly, raising the level of Poyang Hu and inundating the adjacent croplands. To Ren the biggest danger of such storms was the winds they brought. On the shallow waters of the lake, such winds could whip up waves that might easily overturn a fishing boat. "With luck they won't make it this far north," Ren said. "Not until next month, anyway."

The officer was in no hurry. He finished his first cup and extended it toward Mei Ling for a second. As Mei Ling poured she glanced at her husband, her eyes imploring him to find a way to send the unwelcome visitors packing. But Ren Kai could do nothing without raising suspicion. The officer slurped noisily at his tea and chatted about everything and nothing.

Presently he stood, and they assumed he was going to go. Ren stood with him. "You are welcome on our boat any time," the fisherman said politely.

"You are very kind. And now I must see your registration papers and fishing permit."

"I'll get them," Mei Ling volunteered, turning to go inside.

"I'll come along," the officer said. He followed her through the sliding door into the cabin.

The boat was made of wood. Its hull consisted of long pine logs. In the middle of the deck stood the sole structure, a shedlike cabin that provided shelter for Ren and Mei Ling, who lived on board ten months of the year. Nets in need of mending and drying laundry hung from bamboo rails.

The cabin was barely tall enough to stand up in. The roof was arched, made of bamboo woven into eight watertight sheets, each of which spanned the cabin from port to starboard. The sheets telescoped across each other, sliding in grooves that ran the length of the walls. It was an ingenious design, permitting the roof to be opened to the sky and stars or closed off during the rains. On the forward bulkhead was the stool where Ren perched while steering the boat. Just below the wheel was an access panel for the engine compartment. Tyler was hiding inside.

Wall shelves held cooking utensils, candles, and books. Below the shelves, built-in wooden benches lined the perimeter of the cabin, concealing the boat's storage compartments. Normally the benches contained food; freshwater fish and turtle tanks; clothing and bedding; and nets, tarps, and fishing tackle. Now the port side contained Allison and Wen Li, while the starboard held Ruth and Tai. Brightly colored pillows and thick quilts were piled on the benches. At night they were stretched out on the highly varnished floors to make a comfortable bed. For that reason, shoes were never worn inside the cabin.

"Very nice," the officer said as he stepped inside. He noticed that Mei Ling had removed her slippers. He bent down and started unlacing his shoes. "Oh, don't worry," Mei Ling said quickly. "I'll have the papers in a moment."

"No bother," he said, setting his shoes to one side of the doorway.

Mei Ling took the boat's papers and registration placard from a drawer. Her hands trembled as she handed the documents to the officer.

He didn't seem to notice. He took a pen and notebook from his pocket and looked for a place to write. Mei Ling beckoned toward the little ledge above the wheel, but he ignored her. He sat on the bench over Allison's head. He spread out the papers and began copying the information into his book.

Allison heard him sit and held her breath. Wen Li was sucking on her two middle fingers, quite comfortable in the darkness. Allison closed her eyes and forced herself to calm.

Tyler was on his hands and knees, his face pressed up to the louvered panel that covered the access hole. Through one of the slits he could see the man's feet. He moved his head around, trying to see more. He was having a great time. He had sensed Allison's tension when she'd told him they had to hide, but he hadn't been afraid, not at all. He could hide from cops and spies all day long.

Claustrophobic and streaming sweat, Ruth was going mad. It was stifling in the pitch-blackness, and something was pressing painfully against her back. Her legs, drawn up toward her chest, were cramping. But much worse than her own discomfort was that Tai was congested, her nose stuffed up. She'd sneezed half a dozen times during the afternoon. She couldn't keep a bottle in her mouth for very long because she couldn't breathe through her nose, and she generally wasn't feeling well anyway. Now, in coffinlike confinement, she was squirming, miserable and hot. Ruth could tell from her whimpering that she was about to cry. Ruth patted her and held her close and with her fingers guided the nipple of the bottle to Tai's mouth. Tai wanted nothing to do with a bottle. She wanted up. She wanted out. She wanted to cry.

Mei Ling, afraid some sound might come from the hiding places, had been chattering nonstop about inane, disjointed subjects—birds and porcelain and straw bedding. Anxious to be done with her, the officer finished his notes and stood up. He handed her the papers and started for the door. He stopped suddenly. Mei Ling, just behind him, stiffened. He patted his pocket, realizing he'd forgotten his pen. He turned to retrieve it from the bench. A soft swell on the lake made the pen roll off and onto the floor. Mei Ling quickly bent to get it, but he was there first, his head not six inches from Ruth's. Then he had it. Mei Ling smiled and indicated his shoes. He stepped into them and knelt to tie them, his fingers seeming to take forever as he worked one knot and then the other, while Mei Ling rattled on about fish soup.

At that moment Tai let out a little cry. To Ruth it sounded like a roar; she couldn't imagine they hadn't heard outside. She pulled Tai closer, putting her hand over her mouth, trying to find a way to let her breathe without letting her cry. It was impossible. As Ruth clamped her hand tighter, Tai resisted more vigorously. Ruth withdrew her hand for an instant, trying to let Tai catch a breath. But by now the baby was so angry that she'd expelled all her breath and couldn't get a new one. Ruth knew if she did, Tai would scream so loudly this time that they'd hear her in Jiujiang. Desperate, Ruth clamped down and began to sob herself, a muffled cry of panic and horror as she debated what to do. How could she subject the baby to this? There was nothing more important to Ruth than Tai's welfare, and here she was choking the child in an attempt to protect her. She felt Tai's hot mouth on her hand, felt the little body struggling beneath her arms, and now the tears streamed down Ruth's cheeks. She *had* to sit up, even if it meant getting caught. But what of Allison? What of Tyler and Wen Li? She prayed and sobbed, and Tai squirmed beneath her grip.

The officer finished his laces, straightened up, and stepped outside, Mei Ling right behind him, still jabbering. Near the bow he stopped and turned to Ren Kai. "If you hear of *lao wai* with babies, anywhere near the lake—"

"I will report it, of course," the fisherman replied dutifully. "But it is more likely I'll see a dragon out here than a foreign devil." The officer laughed and stepped off the boat into his own. Ren quickly unwrapped the line from around the bitt and tossed it over. The helmsman, stirring himself from his repose, started the engine, which smoked instantly to life. Then, with a wave, they were gone.

Mei Ling darted back into the cabin. She slid the door shut and crossed to the compartment in which Ruth was hiding. Before she could get there the lid burst open, and Ruth shot up with a cry of anguish. Frantic, sobbing uncontrollably, she lifted Tai from the compartment. The child was limp. At the noise, Allison and Tyler opened their own compartments.

Tai's eyes were closed and her skin had a bluish pallor. "Oh dear God, I've killed her!" Ruth shrieked. Disabled by panic, she made no move to help. Allison handed Wen Li to Mei Ling and took Tai from Ruth's arms. "We've got to help her breathe!" She set Tai on the deck and leaned over her. Just then Tai coughed, choked in a breath, and then coughed again. Her face surged with color as she screwed up her mouth and let forth with a piercing yell. Allison picked Tai up and held her, patting her on the back. Ruth was so hysterical by then that she didn't seem to notice.

"She's all right!" Allison said sharply. Ruth kept blubbering and Allison shook her hard on the shoulder. "Get hold of yourself! She's all right! Stop it! Stop it! Here, take her!"

The presence of the baby reduced Ruth's shrieks to low sobs as she tried to collect herself. She slumped to the deck and touched Tai's cheeks and stroked her hair and looked into her eyes. "Forgive me, forgive me, forgive me," she whispered, rocking back and forth, clutching Tai to her breast. "Oh, Wee Duck, please forgive me."

Allison took Wen Li back from Mei Ling. She sat next to Ruth on the deck and put an arm around her friend's shoulder.

Tyler couldn't stand all the crying and carrying on. He went outside, to watch Ren set the nets.

At long last peace descended on the little fishing boat on Poyang Hu. And then it was swallowed by the darkness.

CHAPTER 13

THE AMERICAN NETWORKS were full of the story, which had touched a raw national nerve. Marshall flipped through the channels as he packed, catching bits and pieces. Using equal parts hysteria, hyperbole, and rumor, politicians and pundits were arguing about human rights and most favored nation status for China, as pictures of the fugitives flashed on the screen.

Marshall stopped when he saw Congressman Fred Pollard on the CBS Evening News. "The one-child policy is just another capricious violation of human rights, and has led to the most horrible consequences: babies abandoned, families ripped apart, women forced into clinics for involuntary abortions, women sterilized," Pollard said gravely. "The Chinese government's disregard for the sanctity of human life is long-standing. And now my sister and two other women have simply tried to rescue infants from the Chinese torture chambers, and the government has made them criminals." Pollard looked at the camera. "When the Congress votes on MFN next month, I don't think the issues could be clearer. What is most important to our nation? Do we vote for morality, or money? God, or godlessness? Babies, or the butchers of Beijing?"

There were clips of demonstrations outside the Chinese embassy in Washington, while inside, a spokesman read a statement. "The Chinese government, with an earnest and responsible attitude, has always shown great concern for children's rights and interests. The intrusion of other countries into the internal police matters of the People's Republic is unwelcome, unwarranted, and unwise. The fugitives are wanted for violation of the laws of China, nothing more. To suggest they are victims of Chinese repression is inflammatory, ignorant, and misleading, and insults the Chinese people and legal system."

Every time Allison's and Tyler's names were mentioned, Marshall felt the same sense of unreality he'd felt all day, yet it was all too real. The eleven calls he'd taken the previous night from reporters had been the trickle before the flood. The calls had continued nonstop, until he'd taken his listed phone off the hook. Allison used their private line, of course, so he didn't have to worry about missing a call, but then the calls started coming in on that line, too, as frustrated reporters scrapped for an interview. Now there were television cameras on his front lawn and reporters peeking in the windows. Eric Bader called to say there were even cameras in front of the Coulter Grogan offices. So far, he hadn't talked to any of the reporters. He didn't intend to until he knew whether doing so might somehow help Allison and Tyler and not hurt them.

Marshall glanced at his watch. Another two hours before his flight. He called Clarence Coulter to tell him what he was doing.

"You should wait until you're feeling better," Clarence said.

"I can't wait. I can't stand just sitting here, doing nothing. I'm going to Hong Kong."

Clarence sighed. "Of course. I understand. When does your flight leave?"

"There's a Cathay Pacific red-eye out of San Francisco that leaves at ten tonight. I'm confirmed on it, but most of the Denver–San Francisco flights are booked solid until eight. It's going to be tight, but with luck I'll make the connection in time."

"Nonsense. If you insist on going, you can use the jet, of course," Clarence said, volunteering the firm's six-seater. It was a gesture he rarely made: the jet was for him and him alone. "It'll get you there in plenty of time. It'll be waiting at DIA by the time you can get there."

"Thanks, Clarence. And I need you to get somebody to cover a couple of cases for me—Abbott and Strongfield. I've got the briefs here at the house. I'll leave them in the milk box so somebody can pick them up. I think we can get a continuance on Abbott, but Judge Wakefield is not going to tolerate—"

"I'll take care of everything. Don't worry about it. I'll call Victor Li and tell him you're coming." Victor Li was the managing director of Coulter Grogan's Hong Kong office.

"Thanks. I've never met him, but I worked the Lambert case with his son, Li Kan." The complex case had brought Marshall and Li Kan close together for nearly six months as the litigation had wended its way through both U.S. and Her Majesty's courts. In the process they had become good friends. The first time they had met, Marshall had asked him whether to pronounce his name "Can" or "Con." Li Kan had laughed and suggested he decide for himself after the case was finished. Marshall had concluded that while both pronunciations were correct, "Con" was most accurate.

"He'd have been all right except that he's Harvard. Drove his old man nuts."

"They occasionally get a good one out the door." Marshall grinned. Clarence was New Haven to his toes. "But I guess Li Kan isn't practicing anymore anyway. He sent me an e-mail a few months ago saying he was leaving the firm. I haven't heard from him since."

"I know. He likes playing the ponies better. Victor has threatened to disown him. He tells me Li Kan is involved in a lot more than horses."

"Well, I'd better get going, Clarence. I'll stay in touch."

"Do you want my mobile phone? It works everywhere. I can meet you at the airport with it." Clarence knew Marshall refused to carry a cell phone.

"I already stole it," Marshall admitted. "You left it in your office. I've got our private line forwarded so that if Allison calls, I'll get it. I've got my pager. Let me know if anything develops."

"I will. Godspeed, Marshall. And keep some cotton in your ears."

"Of course, Colonel. I will be there at once."

Major Ma closed his cellular phone and placed it back into his jacket pocket. He sat on the bench in the tiny holding cell of the Nanjing PSB. He looked down at the floor, where the old woman, Yang Boda's mother, lay curled beneath the blanket he had brought for her. He watched to see if she was still breathing. He thought he saw the blanket rise, then fall again. The movement was little more than a flutter. The doctor had been in once, angry at having been called at such a late hour. Summonses to that particular warren of holding cells usually came well after he could do anything to help. He checked her pulse, then examined her tongue and skin. "She's hypoxic," he said. "Her heart is weak. If you don't get her to a hospital quickly, she'll die." The doctor left without doing anything more. Major Ma summoned an ambulance and waited now for the attendants to appear.

He had spent hours with her, trying to determine what she knew of her son's whereabouts. From the beginning of the interview, it was as if she had known that her husband was dead, even without being told. Major Ma knew she couldn't have known, because he alone had spoken with her. Yet since her detention the previous evening, her eyes had dimmed, and she had wept, and for the first time since being arrested she had stopped asking for her husband. When she looked at him, he saw it in her eyes. She knew. She did not protest, or plead, or display the sullen anger that even elderly prisoners so often showed. Instead her mind seemed to wander, and over a very short period of time she deteriorated before his eyes. She mentioned Yang Boda once, and Major Ma listened intently, but then she carried on about a duck, and the major realized she was remembering something about Yang Boda the boy, forty years or more ago. She made little sense, her sentences clipped and disjointed. Patiently he tried to coax her back to the present, but she lingered wherever it was her mind had drifted.

Then she very politely announced she was too tired to talk anymore. She rose from her wooden chair and lay down in the corner of the room, curling up on the cold concrete floor. She closed her eyes and stopped responding. He shook her gently by the shoulder. She wasn't asleep, and she wasn't dead, but somewhere in between. After that he summoned the doctor.

Ma Lin was neither a cruel man nor a compassionate one. Instead he had been numb for thirty years. His life had begun to unravel when he was twenty, at the very instant the world seemed so full of promise. At that time, he lived in a comfortable neighborhood of Beijing with his father, a widower who was a renowned cellist and composer who had studied music in London before the liberation. Their house was small, lined with scores and books and LP recordings. On the walls hung musical instruments from around the world. Ma's father had collected some himself during his overseas concert tours; others had been sent by admirers from Cape Town to Moscow. Ma could remember his father carefully taking the instruments from a shelf or the wall or a glass case. He would dust them lovingly and then play them, exhibiting extraordinary facility with instruments of all kinds, from the *yueqin,* or moon lute; to the *sheng,* a mouth organ; to the *zummara,* an Indonesian double clarinet. But it was his gift with the cello that brought people from all over China to hear him play.

Ma Lin had never cared for music in his early youth, but at the age of sixteen he fell in love with the piano when he heard one of his father's colleagues play Rachmaninoff's Second Piano Concerto. After that his father had gladly made room in their small house for a piano. Lin studied earnestly and was a solid player, showing promise, if not the sheer brilliance of his father.

In 1966 his idyllic life ended when he made the discovery during the Cultural Revolution that he was not a musician, but a coward. Angry crowds of young revolutionaries had begun to turn the country upside down. There were denunciations and book burnings, suicides and executions. Month after month it grew worse as neighbor turned against neighbor, student against teacher. One evening, two days after Ma Lin had seen a university professor hanged by a crowd drunk with revolution, a friend had come to warn him. The Red Guards were coming: Ma Lin and his father were to be next.

Ma Lin had felt the terror running through his veins. His father was not at home. Desperate to keep from being branded a criminal for his music, he started carrying instruments from inside the house out to the street—a mandolin, a violin, a flute, a trombone. He dumped them in a pile, adding books from the shelves and scores from their drawers, running inside and out again as fast as he could. He heard the crowd and then saw it coming in the dusk. He lost himself in the madness and began chanting their slogans. He found kerosene and then a match.

His father had come home to the incredible scene of his own son torching the precious relics of his life, and even as he cried out, Ma Lin threw his beloved cello on the pile. The strings snapped in the fire. Ma Lin's eyes had gone hard, and his denunciations burned his father worse than the fire. "My father has tried to ruin me!" Ma Lin cried, whipping up the crowd. Some of the students helped him break the piano into pieces, and soon it crowned the bonfire. His father had sunk to his knees, the tears streaming down his face turning to steam in the heat of the fire. A fire brigade formed, a river of insanity down which flowed every stick of furniture, every book, every remaining instrument on its way to the inferno.

Ma Lin himself shaved his father's head, which was fitted with a dunce cap. The old man was paraded down the street with a sign hanging from his neck. At the square he was made to kneel and confess his crimes. The foreign books and music recordings in his home were proof of his counter-revolutionary loyalties. His instruments confirmed his desire for self-aggrandizement. He was a vain and vile man.

The venom of Ma Lin's accusations against his own father demonstrated the strength of his sentiments, and Ma Lin himself escaped condemnation. He watched his father's disgrace with a curious detachment, coupled with a definite sense of relief for himself. Before long he convinced himself that his father's crimes were real. And then he forced himself to stop thinking about it altogether.

He never saw his father again and heard later that he had died in prison.

He never touched another piano. The only song he sang was "Raise the Iron Broom of the Revolution," of which he believed not a word. He sang it for his life.

Afterward he was sent with a trainload of students to the countryside, to work alongside the peasants. He spent four years in the northeast province of Heilongjiang, trying to grow onions on a farm where, despite the orders of the Party, onions wouldn't grow. No one had enough to eat, and each winter there were some who froze to death. Ma Lin discovered that by informing on others caught hoarding food or expressing sentiments that fell short of revolutionary, he could supplement his diet and wear warmer clothes.

He had sacrificed family, friends, and truth. But he learned to survive.

Upon his return to Beijing, he joined the *gong an ju*, the Public Security Bureau, which was the only job he could find. There he had been a solid performer, and it was also there that he had been noticed by Quan Yi, a rising star of the state security apparatus. His early assignments ranged from undercover work as an informer to the detection and apprehension of subversives and smugglers. Ma Lin's outwardly gentle demeanor was belied by the fact that, as time progressed, Quan used him more and more often for interrogations. Although Ma Lin didn't relish the duty, he was good at it, using whatever tools his subject and the times required: gentle persuasion, dire threats, drugs, scalpels, drills, rubber truncheons, or electric prods. More often than not, persuasion or threats were sufficient. People looked at his face and trusted him instinctively. His smile was kind, and he was easy to talk to. He tried, when he could, to keep the promises he made to suspects in exchange for their cooperation. He tried, when he could, to deliver on the threats that he made as well. Through it all he was careful never to care about the people he interrogated, careful to remain numb. It was a job.

He had married in his early thirties. Those years had been good to Ma

Lin and his wife, as the country passed from beneath Mao's shadow of madness. He was able to move into a two-room apartment and was among the first in his building to acquire a television set. He and his wife had had one child, a cheerful girl whose intellect had shone brightly from the moment of her birth. As Quan Yi and Ma Lin had moved together up the ranks of the PSB, Ma Lin's daughter moved up in school, passing the difficult entrance exams for the University of Beijing, where she studied architecture.

Then had begun the second crisis of Ma Lin's life. His daughter began to come home with ideas critical of the government. Ma ordered her to forget politics and tend to her studies. He didn't care about the criticisms themselves; he had no politics. But he knew all too well what such ideas could cost. His daughter ignored him. All her life he had praised her beautiful, thick black hair. To spite him she cut it short and ragged. She left pamphlets in the house where he would find them. Ma Lin felt stirrings of the same terror that he had kept buried for twenty years. One night he slapped his daughter so hard that she fell down. After that she stopped coming home. He scanned all the classified intelligence reports of the Beijing PSB, dreading the day her name would appear.

And then had come the nightmare of Tiananmen. Ma Lin was spending endless days and nights at Quan's side, analyzing photographs, orchestrating arrests, conducting interrogations. The state security services sought desperately to keep tabs on what was happening in the great square, alert for signs that the unrest might be spreading beyond the students to the workers. The Soviet leader, Gorbachev, was coming for a summit, and the officers of the PSB were overwhelmed with work.

One day he picked up a photograph from a pile taken in the square by intelligence agents. The image was blurry, snapped through a telephoto lens, but there was no mistake, and his blood ran cold. She was leaning against a replica of the American statue of liberty, her face set in proud rebellion. Wearing plain clothes, Ma Lin had tried to enter the square, to approach his daughter and reason with her, intending to remove her by force if necessary. He was turned away by student guards before he could even get near.

One night the tanks rolled in. Gunshots echoed through the streets of the capital; students fled into the night or stood fast, their fists raised in impotent defiance. The guns had hardly fallen silent when Ma Lin received an urgent summons to the hospital. Barely daring to breathe, he walked down the long corridor, its concrete floors and tile walls stained with blood. He stepped around the injured and over the dead; there were too many for the gurneys. It was the longest walk of his life. He kept his eyes forward and his mind blank. He did not find his daughter in the postoperative recovery room, as he had been directed. She had already been moved downstairs, to the morgue.

Ma Lin was shamed by his daughter's behavior, at the same time not understanding it. The child felt passions that had never burned at the father. Even so, it was the second time in Ma's life that he had to struggle at all to bury an emotion. For his father, Ma Lin had never cried. For his daughter, his tears were hidden at night.

At the very least, his own job should have been forfeit then. The families of other dissidents had lost their homes, some their jobs, others even their freedom. But Colonel Quan had known his daughter well. He had bounced her on his knee when she was a small girl. He had taken her to the cinema. Upon her matriculation at the university, he had presented her with an expensive Japanese engineering calculator that had cost him half a month's salary. Quan was genuinely saddened at her death and intervened quietly, saving Ma's job. Ma's already intense loyalty to the colonel increased after that kindness.

His wife was shattered. She stopped speaking to him, blaming him personally for the tanks and guns. She lost weight and aged ten years in two, then died bitter, sick, and alone. Without a family, Ma Lin devoted himself to his work. He continued to shun ideology but occasionally caught himself wondering about the *why* of things he did in his work. Often he felt, and justifiably so, that something he had done had benefited the state or preserved someone's life or safety. Other times, like now, in this room with an old woman who knew nothing important and had curled up to die, he felt old and tired and worn out.

The attendants arrived at last. They were joking with each other and at first handled the old woman somewhat roughly. Their banter died when the PSB major snapped at them. They immediately turned to business. One produced an oxygen mask, the other a blanket to cover her, and then they were gone.

Major Ma Lin closed the door to the little room and hurried down the corridor. It had been Colonel Quan on the telephone earlier, summoning him to Jiujiang. Yi Ling and one of the American women had been captured. Quan, because he spoke English, was going to handle the American, but for Yi Ling he preferred the subtle talents of Major Ma. "You are to use whatever means necessary to induce her cooperation," Quan had told him. "There is little time."

Working beneath the bright lights of the fire truck, the police and fire inspectors stepped carefully through the still-smoking rubble. The apartment building was in one of the wealthier neighborhoods of Suzhou but was poorly constructed, allowing the blaze to spread swiftly. The fire had raced unchecked through floor joists that had no fire blocking, then up walls filled with cheap paper insulation. The roof collapsed onto the second floor, which then crashed onto the first, so that the authorities were now picking through what used to be upstairs bedrooms. The blaze was already out of control by the time flames were spotted. Two apartments had burned to the ground before the first fire truck arrived; two more before the blaze was controlled. Large sections of exterior brick walls had partially given way as well.

The investigators stepped on roof tiles and over smoking rafters as they searched for victims. One of the firemen found the first body. It was a smoldering husk of ash and bone, laying over the springs of a steel bed frame. The teeth were bared and charred black, the remains scarcely recognizable as human. By the time dawn lit the eastern sky, nine more bodies had been recovered from the four houses. They were quickly wrapped in sheets and carried away.

The police interviewed neighbors from adjacent apartments as they stood, packed and chattering, in the narrow street in front of the building, aware how lucky they were the fire had been controlled so rapidly. The man who called in the first report told police he heard screams even before he saw smoke or flames. He couldn't say from which apartment the screams had originated.

The neighborhood watch officer provided information about the residents of the apartments to one of the police. By midmorning a preliminary report was on the desk of the Suzhou PSB section chief. He reviewed the names, stopping at one he instantly recognized. Twenty minutes later he reached Major Ma Lin, in Jiujiang.

"Are there signs of arson?" the major asked.

"Arson, sir?" the chief said. Arson was an extremely rare crime in China. "None in the report. Someone smoking in bed, most likely. There were screams, but that could have been someone trapped by the flames."

"Have it investigated," Major Ma said.

"I'll have to bring in someone from Shanghai," the chief said. "No one here—"

"Yes," Ma Lin said. "And cordon off the area. I want it thoroughly searched for evidence. And autopsy the bodies. I'll need positive identification."

"There isn't much to work with," the chief said. "The fire was hot and the structures were totally destroyed. There's very little left to autopsy."

"Just see it's done quickly."

Ma Lin called Colonel Quan with the news.

"I think we've found the orphanage director," he said.

BEIJING, MAY 30—(REUTERS WORLD SERVICE): The Chinese Foreign Ministry has announced that one of the American fugitives being sought for kidnapping three infants has been killed in a violent collision at the confluence of the Yangtze River and Poyang Hu lake. In addition to the dead American, more than six Chinese citizens are said to have perished in the collision, including officers of the local public security bureau.

In a startling development, officials said the remaining American fugitives may now face additional charges of accessory murder, because the officers' deaths occurred during the commission of the crime of kidnapping. Charges of complicity in the smuggling of arms may also be filed, officials said. Both are capital offenses in China and potentially carry the death penalty. Details were not immediately available regarding the nature or cause of the collision. Foreign reporters have been refused permission to visit the scene but have received unconfirmed reports that salvage operations are proceeding around the clock at the site.

Authorities have not released the name of the dead American. Officials at the U.S. embassy in Beijing have demanded that the Chinese government disclose information they may have concerning the whereabouts or fate of the remaining fugitives. "This is an internal Chinese police matter," said the spokesman at the Foreign Ministry. "No information will be forthcoming until arrests have been made."

Marshall had great difficulty hearing Clarence as he read the wire service story. The plane was two hours out of San Francisco, over the Pacific.

Clarence's voice faded in and out over the air phone's satellite link. Static roared in waves. Marshall could barely hear anyway; his ears were pounding with infection. He could hear nothing at all out of his left ear and held the instrument to his right, feeling pain from even that gentle pressure on his outer ear.

"I'm sorry," Clarence said, "but I knew you'd want to know. A friend of mine at the *Denver Post* woke me up with it. He faxed it to me at home. I paged you the instant I read it."

"You did the right thing. Thanks."

"I know Allison and Tyler are all right, Marshall. I don't know why, but I'm sure of it."

Marshall closed his eyes. "Yeah."

"The story seems to have struck a popular chord here. The Chinese have kicked a hornet's nest. It's all over the television. My guy at the *Post* told me the *New York Times* is running a picture of the three babies above the fold on the front page. And I hear from our London office it's even getting coverage in Europe."

"I assume that's good."

"Maybe, maybe not. It could just make the Chinese dig in their heels. They get their asses out of joint when they catch outside flak. They always play hardball, and there's the fear they'll decide to make an example. At the moment, we're certainly not having much luck through official channels. But the secretary promised me he'd—" The line crackled and went dead. Marshall tried to make another connection, but this time he got only static.

Grimacing, he hunched over his tray table, rubbing his temples and trying to ease the excruciating pain in his ears. The medicine hadn't helped. The flight on the firm's jet from Denver to San Francisco hadn't bothered him at all, and he thought everything was all right. But from the moment the 747 lifted off the runway at San Francisco, he'd been in sheer agony. Now he felt tightness in his chest as well as he wondered about the fate of his wife and son. Incredible words clanged in his head. "One American fugitive killed . . . Murder . . . arms smuggling . . . death penalty."

They'd have said if it was a boy, wouldn't they? Or a woman? Surely they'd have said.

He damned himself for getting on the plane. He should have listened to Clarence. His head was bursting, his lungs were in pain, and he was helpless anyway. He worried that Allison would try to reach him just then, while he was in the air. He wouldn't be there to help her. *Goddamn you, Allison, for doing this, for jeopardizing so much.* His fingers worked his wedding ring. They had matching bands of white gold and gold, fashioned by a Navajo craftsman. Allison had chosen them in Santa Fe. He remembered the delight in her eyes when she'd slipped it on his finger. Absently he rubbed at the rough images engraved in the band. *God, help her, please, God help my son. I love them so much.* . . . He had never felt so vulnerable or known such consuming fear. He had always been in complete control of his life. But not now, and the feeling of impotence gnawed at him. He fought it back, trying to channel his thoughts productively, just as he would for a client. But this was Allison, his love. And Tyler, his flesh. "Capital offenses . . . salvage operations around the clock . . ."

The pain in his ears grew worse. He ordered a double Scotch from the attendant and downed it quickly. Another followed.

This can't be happening.

Over the Aleutians he finally nodded off. Over Japan, his left eardrum ruptured.

CHAPTER 14

"**M**AKE A FIST FOR ME," the kindly voice said.

Yi Ling felt the cold swab of alcohol on her arm. *Another shot? Oh yes, please. Another.* She flexed her muscle, but she didn't know whether she'd made a fist or not. Then she felt the sting again, followed by a hot rush that overtook her in waves. It was a wonderful feeling. She closed her eyes and let her mind go with it. She was flying, but there was no plane, nothing to hold her up but her own arms, outstretched, and she felt the breeze on her face, the air rippling through her hair. Somehow she had gotten out of the cold damp room with its dreary tiles and stained floor. Now she could see water below, the small waves sparkling in the sun, and it was beautiful beyond imagination.

"Yi Ling, do you know who I am?"

Yes, I know. Was that her voice? She didn't know. It was silky, with a pleasant tone. If it was her voice, she liked listening to it.

"Who am I?"

You are Ma Lin. My father.

"Yes, Yi Ling. And you remember what I want, don't you?"

To make me feel good, Father. You are very kind to want to do that.

"Yes, I want that, Yi Ling. I want nothing more."

May I have more, Father?

"Not yet, my child. You have just enough for now. Later, if you are good, if you help me, there will be more. I promise."

She felt something touch her chest, above her heart. They were listening to her heart. She could listen, too, but from inside. She could hear her own heart beat; she could hear the blood rush in her veins. She could even hear the air touching her skin. She had never known such a thing made a sound. It was hushed. One had to listen with care, but it was there.

"You must tell me, now, about the babies."

The babies?

"Yes. I want to help them. They are lost. Alone. I want to bring them home."

I wanted to help them, too.

"Of course. It was the right thing to do. But now they do not have you to help them anymore. They have me. I will help them."

Yes, Father. You are good.

"Where did you leave them? Where were you to meet?"

In a safe place.

"Which safe place? I have looked for them. I fear they are in danger."

A tear welled in the corner of her eye. She felt it growing until it quivered, and then it ran down her temple and into her hair. She felt it touch one hair, and then another, until it stopped. *I tried to help them. I couldn't help my own baby. They took her, Father. They took her from me, before she was even whole. I remember. The table was cold, and they took her from me and put her in a jar.* There were more tears then, a river of tears, and she heard someone crying. Were those her cries? The cries of her baby? It was hard to tell. Her chest heaved a little, and she sobbed. She wanted to wipe the tears, but her arms wouldn't move. She opened her eyes and blinked, and her vision wavered too much to see. There was light. She could see it through the clouds. Or was it water? Her eyes burned then and she closed them again, and she felt a soft hand on her forehead. It calmed her.

"You must not think of that, my child. You must think of those who have lived, not those who have died. You can only help the living."

Yes, I must try. I will try.

"You were on a boat. Where had you been?"

Hukou, Father. We were hiding.

"Who was hiding?"

We were.

"All right. Where were you going?"

To Jiujiang. They stopped the boat. The memories came in a rush. She could feel the waves lapping at the side; feel the light blinding her; hear the harsh voices of command from the other boat. She heard her heart pounding, as it had then.

I dropped my bag into the water, Father.

"And why did you do that?"

She stirred, straining against the pressure on her wrists, the memory

assaulting her, overwhelming her. First Mate Shidao lashing out at someone on the other boat. The sound of wood against bone. *Because there was
blood, Father. I got it on my face. It was more than blood. There were lumps of
something. It was sticky.* There were names on the paper in her bag. Her
uncle's friends. She wiped the mess from her face and let the bag disappear, swallowed by the black water. She wanted to tell her father about the
names, she truly did, if it would help the babies, but the images of the
first mate were stronger and made her forget. *They hurt him.*

He saw she was gasping then, laboring to breathe as she began to
panic. He was losing her. Such a delicate balance, the drugs. He would
have preferred an IV drip, so much easier to regulate than the short bursts
of a syringe, but one had not been available. He knew how to make do; his
touch was as practiced as a physician's. Always careful to prevent infection, he quickly swabbed her skin again with alcohol. There was no time
for a tourniquet, but her veins were good and he smoothly administered
the contents of a different syringe. Then he leaned over her and talked
softly, soothingly. "Don't think of the blood, my child. Think of the
babies. See their faces. Hear their cries. Help them, Yi Ling. Help the
babies." He covered her hand with his own and felt her fingers intertwine
with his. She squeezed his hand. It was a good sign.

Yi Ling's moment of fear passed. She calmed, floating again at a different level. It was quite pleasant, and then suddenly she felt emotional. It
wasn't sadness or fear or anger. It was a fullness in her heart. She saw Tai's
face. She started to cry, but she didn't know why. Just tears, and they
poured out.

He let the tears come and didn't intrude.

I'm sorry, I don't mean to be weak. I will help, Father. I will.

"Of course you will."

Through a hole in the door, Quan watched Major Ma practice his craft.
Quan hoped the major was correct in selecting drugs over more forceful
means with this woman. If the drugs didn't work, hours would pass before
they could question her with more traditional methods. The crewman
Shidao was beyond questioning; he had died of the injuries he had sustained during his arrest.

Meanwhile, two hundred police were combing every centimeter of the
lake's shore within twenty kilometers. They were slogging through

swamps and marshes, exploring caves, checking the empty seasonal straw huts that had not yet been inundated by the rising waters of summertime, and every boathouse and paddy.

With Yi Ling in custody and her uncle and most of his crew dead, Quan knew he was, in all probability, chasing two American women, a young boy, and two babies, who were as alone, helpless, and out of place in south China as they would be on the face of Mars. By themselves they would probably not last another hour on the run. Even if another of the *Springtime Flower*'s crew had survived and were helping them, it would be a low-level crewman, lacking Yang Boda's contacts and resources. They could not last long. It was possible that they had all perished in the collision. He doubted it, although a dozen boats and crews were trolling the river bottom with grappling hooks.

The captured American woman was in a room down the hall from Yi Ling. The guards had reported that since her arrest she had alternated between hysteria and quiet sobbing. As Quan had ordered, her cell was one of the worst in the Hukou PSB. There were no windows except for a small opening in the door to the hall. The walls were caked with years of grime, the floor rough concrete. A fluorescent light fixture, its ballast failing, flickered and buzzed on the ceiling. There was a hole in one corner of the floor for the latrine, and a water faucet next to it with a broken handle. In the sweltering heat and without ventilation, the stench in the room was overpowering.

When Quan entered he saw that her face was drawn and pale, her eyes dull with grief. Yet she sat erect, with dignity, and seemed not to be cowed by her confinement. He admired her courage and set about the task of shaking it.

She had been visibly relieved to hear his excellent English. He had been courteous and correct.

"I trust you have been treated well?" he asked.

"No one has hurt me."

"Have you been fed? Are you hungry?"

"I want to see my husband's body."

"That is not possible, Mrs. Cameron."

"They took Katie from me."

"The child Xiao Bo is safe," he said, using the baby's orphanage name.

"Her name is Katie and she was already safe. I want to see her."

"First I need to know where you were going. What your plan was. Where are the others?"

"I don't know."

"Where were you going to meet?"

"I don't know. Yi Ling made those arrangements."

"With whom?"

"I didn't see."

"Where did she go to make these arrangements?"

"I want a lawyer."

"I am afraid this is not Colorado Springs, Mrs. Cameron."

"You can say that again. I want to see my embassy, then."

"Let me explain something to you, Mrs. Cameron. You are in serious trouble. I assure you your American citizenship will have no bearing on the matter. Your sense of your legal rights are quite misplaced in China. You are fully subject to our laws, whether you wish to be or not. In this country we deal with kidnappers with a bullet to the back of the head. There are no appeals. Sentences are carried out instantly. And I can assure you—it will not help that you are a woman."

Her eyes glistened. He could see her struggling to maintain her composure.

"You must be thirsty," he said gently. She nodded. Quan beckoned to the guard standing outside the door, and he passed in a plastic bottle of water and a tin cup. Quan broke the seal and poured for her.

"It would be best if you cooperate with me. It will go easier on you. You will be moved to more suitable quarters. Your best hope for earning the court's mercy is that we catch the others quickly. You can help us do that, before someone else gets hurt. Do you understand?"

She sipped at her water, and then she nodded. "Yes."

"That is very wise. You have my word I will do everything I can to help you. And now I must know about your plan. Every detail, everything you can remember. Where were you going? What was your route? Your destination? Were you going to Guangzhou—to Canton?"

Claire was as afraid as she'd ever been in her life. There was a catch in her voice, and she had to clear it before speaking. "Please, can I ask your name?"

"Of course. I am sorry to be impolite, Mrs. Cameron. I am Quan Yi."

"Well, Mr. Quan Yi, you need to understand something, too. My husband is dead and my baby is gone. I know I'll never get her back, no matter what you say. So I really don't care what you do to me. I hate your country and I'm not going to help you find the others. So go fuck yourself, Mr. Quan Yi."

*　　*　　*

"CNN has learned that one of the five Americans being sought by Chinese authorities after disappearing with three babies from a Suzhou hotel has been killed and another captured by police in Jiujiang, a one-time tea port on the Yangtze River. Sources have identified the dead American as Doctor Nash Cameron, a surgeon from Colorado. Cameron was reportedly killed in a confrontation with police. His wife, Claire, has been arrested. Her present whereabouts are unknown. The events occurred on this spot in the river, where authorities are now salvaging the boat on which the Americans were said to be passengers." The camera shot zoomed past Colin Chandler's shoulder to an extreme telephoto shot of the distant river, in which the wavering image of the salvage boat could be seen next to the partially submerged hull of the *432 Springtime Flower.* "The boat in the photo reportedly collided with a police launch that was pursuing it in the darkness. There were several other fatalities in what has been described as a dramatic nighttime chase and fiery collision on the river. Chinese authorities have refused comment on the story, and have denied permission to reporters to visit the scene."

Chandler's face once again filled the screen. "This means that two women—Ruth Pollard, sister of Congressman Fred Pollard, and Allison Turk, wife of a partner in the prominent Denver law firm of Coulter Grogan—are still on the run, traveling with their two infants and Turk's son, Tyler." Chandler paused, relishing the drama of the moment. He had paid nearly $500 for his information. Chandler's hair blew in the wind. The camera panned from its vantage point over the river, taking in a partial view of Poyang Hu and the hazy hills beyond.

"Two women, a boy, and two babies. Desperate fugitives in south China, the subject at this hour of a massive manhunt.

"Reporting from Jiujiang, China, this is Colin Chandler, CNN."

The police entered Colin Chandler's room at the Nanhu Guesthouse with a key produced by the manager, who cowered in the hallway behind them. Chandler, sound asleep, was awakened rudely.

"What the hell—" Chandler said. "What is this? Who are you?" No one replied. One of the men started opening drawers, pulling out his clothes, and dumping them on the floor. Another stood at the bureau, flipping through Chandler's notebook and papers. "Get away from those!"

Chandler said, getting to his feet and struggling into his pants. The man ignored him. With his pants up but not zipped, Chandler started across the room, but another officer blocked his way. Chandler stopped, glaring. Soon every drawer in the room was opened. The contents of his shaving kit were strewn on the bathroom floor. His tape recorder was opened, the cartridge inside removed.

"Who are you?" he asked again, knowing quite well what the answer was. "How dare you come into my room like this!" Down the hall, he heard the outraged voice of his cameraman as he, too, was roused and ejected from his room. With considerable commotion the cameraman appeared in the doorway of Chandler's room at the head of a group of three police, one of whom carried his camera bags and equipment. "Be careful! You'll damage that! You'll have to pay, by God!"

"I'm a reporter!" Chandler said. "You can't—"

"I know very well who you are," said the officer in charge. "I have received notification that your Foreign Ministry accreditation is out of order. You are here illegally."

"The hell you say!" Chandler pulled his papers from the belt pouch and thrust them at the officer. "There—accreditation, passport, everything. All current!"

The officer studied the papers indifferently. "These appear to be forged," he said. "Where is your permission to work outside Shanghai?"

"That's ridiculous! You know very well reporters work all the time outside their home cities without permission! This is arbitrary and outrageous! You can't do this!"

"Your presence in Jiujiang is a contravention of Chinese law. You and your cameraman will be returned to Shanghai under escort. Your case will be reviewed there by the appropriate authorities."

Protesting loudly, Chandler and his cameraman were hustled down the hall.

It was the middle of the night in Suzhou when the medical examiner finished the last of the autopsies. As instructed, he called his report directly to Quan Yi. "Three of the bodies in Director Lin's house were too damaged for a specific cause of death to be established, Colonel. The fourth was probably that of an adult male. I found a lesion on the anterior portion of the second cervical vertebra."

"Meaning?"

"The fire didn't kill him, Colonel. His throat was cut, his head nearly severed. He was dead before the fire started."

"Do you have a positive identification on the other bodies?"

"Not yet. We're seeking dental records, but it may be days before we have them, if at all. I can only tell you that one was an adult female, and two were children."

Quan hung up, puzzled. The man was certainly Director Lin, the woman his wife. No doubt her throat had been cut as well. Burglary was unlikely. He wondered if the murders had anything to do with his case, with the baby files missing from the ministry. He saw no connection, yet he was not a man who believed in coincidence. There were too many unusual things associated with the case to think that, and now they were multiplying. He did not yet have the report of the arson investigators, but he had no doubt what he'd hear when he did—they would find evidence the fire had been deliberately set, to cover the murders.

Whatever was going on with the orphanage, Quan regarded the matter as a secondary issue, not directly related to his pursuit of the *lao wai*. Nevertheless, he called Major Ma and sent him to Suzhou.

CHAPTER 15

"XĬNG XING, lao wai! Zǎo fàn!"

Allison opened her eyes to Mei Ling's smiling face, inches above her own. Sunlight streamed through the window of the cabin. Even first thing in the morning, Mei Ling's grin was infectious. Allison smiled back. She was startled to see Wen Li in Mei Ling's arms. Wen Li was sucking on her knuckles, drooling heavily and obviously quite pleased with the world.

"What?" Allison said. "I don't understand."

"Zǎo fàn! Mei Ling made a motion with her free hand, bringing it to her mouth, and then rubbed her stomach. "Chī ba!"

"Oh. Breakfast." Allison sat up in the thick pile of quilts. "Where's Tyler? And Ruth?"

Mei Ling pointed aft. "Wài miàn." She laughed and pointed at Allison. "Nǐ qǐ wǎn le!" She tilted her head sideways, resting it on her free hand and closing her eyes, mimicking Allison asleep. She pointed at the sun, indicating how late it was. Allison checked her watch. It was only just after six. She thought of Marshall and smiled: fishermen rose early.

Allison stood and straightened her clothes. She took Wen Li from Mei Ling, who started making breakfast, and made her way aft. She found Ruth sitting on an upturned bucket with Tai, watching Ren and Tyler fishing.

It was a beautiful morning. There was a slight chill in the air. Low hills hugged both shores, which were heavily wooded and seemingly primitive but for massive power lines suspended between steel towers. The boat was still anchored near the oyster traps where they had stopped the previous evening. The surface support lines for the traps stretched out over vast distances on the lake, pulled into long graceful arcs by light winds that rippled the shimmering water.

Tyler and Ren were hauling in a net. The fisherman was stripped bare to his waist, and his pants were rolled up. He'd already been in the water, freeing the net where it had snagged on one of the traps. He watched Tyler struggling and called out to the boy. *"Shǒu yá shǒu, xiàng zhè yàng!"* he said, showing him how it was done. Tyler changed his grip, and the net came more easily then. Soon most of it lay in a pile on the deck, dripping with water and wriggling with fish. Ren quickly freed each one from the mesh, tossing some back into the lake, pitching others into a bucket of water on the deck. Two crabs scurried across the net and plopped back into the water. Tyler saw something in the webbing and whooped in excitement. He wrapped his end of the net around a post and scampered to catch it. As he lifted it triumphantly, he saw Allison. "Lookit!" he called. "A turtle!"

It had a mottled brown shell and a colorful underbelly. Ren smiled approvingly as he hefted it. It weighed nearly two kilos. *"Zhèi gè hǎo,"* he said. He patted his stomach and called over his shoulder. "Mei Ling!" She emerged from the cabin, and he handed her the reptile. *"Gěi kè rén da yá jì!"*

"Uh-oh," Allison said. "I think he might be inviting it to breakfast."

An uneasy expression grew on Tyler's face. "You're not going to cook it, are you?" he asked Ren, making a motion of eating. "No! Please!"

Ren looked uncertainly at the boy. He said something to Mei Ling, who held it out with a questioning look. *This?* "Yeah." Tyler nodded, smiling. He took the turtle and set it on the deck. He nudged it, trying to get it to walk. The turtle was in no mood to oblige him and kept its head and feet tightly withdrawn. Tyler stroked its shell and talked softly.

Ren laughed. "A curious breed, these *lao wai*," he said to Mei Ling. "They'd rather entertain food than eat it!"

Ren stowed the nets and turned to Tyler, his new apprentice. *"Youlan,"* he said, pointing south. *"Wǒ mén xiàn zài yào zǒu la."* He gestured at the line that disappeared over the side of the boat and pretended to haul it in. *"Qǐ máo!"*

"Oh, the anchor," Tyler said. He hauled in the line as Ren disappeared into the cabin. This time the engine started right up.

As they got under way, something on the lake caught Allison's eye. "Look!" There was a rare classic junk, the first they had seen, its three white sails spread wide against the perfect blue sky. It was majestic on the sparkling water, ancient and well traveled, looking as if its teak decks might once have borne an emperor. Its pilot sat aft on the high poop deck, guiding the large rudder. The sails were made of well-worn linen panels, held flat with bamboo battens. A wood railing ran around the open deck. A few men sat along the rail, legs dangling over the sides. The bow jutted out and upward, ending in a carved dragon's head. Beneath the head, water curled from the prow as the junk sailed north.

Mei Ling saw the ship and hurried from the cabin, carrying a rattan hat for Allison and a scarf for Ruth. She pointed at the junk and then at her eyes. Then she wagged her finger: *No.* They understood at once. Although they were some distance from the junk, in China a *lao wai* stood out like a beacon. From a distance the headgear would help, at least a little. Allison gestured at Tyler, "What about him?" she asked. Mei Ling thought for a moment. She disappeared into the cabin once more, returning with a Mao cap that had belonged to Ren's grandfather. It was old, ugly, and mildewed.

Tyler regarded it with undisguised contempt. "You want me to *wear* this? It's stupid looking, and it stinks. Can't you see if he's got a baseball cap?"

"Put it on," Allison ordered.

Tyler sighed. The hat was so big, it slipped down around his head, settling on his ears and all but blinding him. "You can't even see me now!"

"That's called being inscrutable," Allison said. "It's very Chinese."

"You'll grow into it," Ruth added.

They *putt-putted* south, their engine always tentative. Ren kept to the east shore of the lake, avoiding both the more heavily used channels in the middle and the fishing grounds where his acquaintances worked. In the early afternoon he saw another police boat. The launch passed three hundred meters off the port side and never slowed. Neither Allison nor Ruth saw it.

The lake widened until they could no longer see the western shore. On the eastern shore there were cotton fields and rice paddies nestled in the low hills and mile after mile of swamps and grasslands. They saw an island on which stood a lone pagoda. Ren launched into an animated series of hand signals, gesturing at the sky, indicating a falling star that landed in the lake, and then pointing at the pagoda and signing that it would bring good luck. At least that's what Allison and Ruth thought he was trying to say.

Both Ren and Mei Ling were unfailingly cheerful and quick to laugh. After the tensions and strain of the first day, everyone got along beautifully. Ruth got out her English-Chinese dictionary and tried out some words. She pointed at the lake and said, *"Chéng chuán,"* and he shook his head and chuckled and said something entirely different, so quickly that she couldn't tell whether the word was the same or not. "I think my pronunciation sucks," she said, handling Allison the little book. "Here. You try it."

Allison found the word for boat. *"Xiǎo chuán,"* she said, choking out the words, and Ren laughed as if she'd told the funniest joke he'd ever heard, but he gave no sign he thought the joke might be about the boat.

"Obviously he didn't understand," Allison said, flipping through the pages as she looked for another word to try.

"You probably said something about his underwear," Ruth said.

"Or my own."

They did manage to learn each other's names, and when one of them would look quizzically at a bird or a place or a mountain, Ren would nod and say something unintelligible, which they would repeat in execrable Chinese, which would send him into fits of laughter, and which word they promptly forgot anyway. Only Tyler showed any aptitude for the language. He was shy about repeating the words, but at Ren's prompting he tried anyway. Tyler adored the fisherman and followed him around like a puppy dog, watching, copying, and helping when he could. Ren taught him a new knot that awed the boy. He could tie a rope around a post, cinch it tight, and then release it with just a flick of a finger. Tyler tried it four times before he got it and was delighted—it was as much a magic trick as a knot. Until Allison objected, he practiced by loosely tying Wen Li's legs together and then releasing them when she wiggled too much.

The lake was serene, and that afternoon no one intruded on their little world. Poyang Hu was the largest freshwater lake in China, with plenty of shoreline to hug. Most years there were massive floods in the summer that swelled the lake to twenty times its winter size. There were countless coves and innumerable streams that emptied into the lake. They saw a swan, and two egrets, and other birds they couldn't begin to identify. The water was quite clear, and they could see turtles and fish swimming beneath the surface. They saw a lone water buffalo standing in the tall grasses, watching them as they passed. Fishing boats glided one way or another in the distance, some propelled in the shallow water by poles, others by small outboard motors, their arched bamboo roofs providing their occupants shelter from the hot sun. Thickly forested hills could be seen on both shores of the lake, an occasional village visible on their slopes. There was no sign of the congestion or pollution that so dominated the lower

Yangtze; this was a pristine place without smokestacks or factories or crowds. Allison and Ruth reveled in the healing tranquillity of the lake.

Allison and Wen Li spent the afternoon continuing their discovery of each other and the world around them. They counted clouds and made silly rhymes. A flock of geese swept into view from the west, passing just beyond the bow, their wings *whooshing* on the wind. Allison couldn't tell whether Wen Li saw them or not. Sometimes her eyes seemed to wander aimlessly, but occasionally she'd focus intently on Allison's eyes, looking as if suddenly she could see inside Allison's head and was quickly picking it clean. Or she'd get a very wise look on her face—her Confucius look, Allison called it, quite profound, quite Chinese—and nod at Allison's lessons, as if she knew the answers all along and was just tolerating Allison's primitive tutorials. They counted fingers and touched noses and named eyes and ears. They had a little plastic toy Allison had brought from Denver. It had a windmill and little figures of ducks and a smiling woman, figures that spun round and changed colors, bright yellows and greens and reds, and beads inside that rattled and shook. Wen Li watched it for hours, fascinated, almost expectantly, as if waiting for it to catch fire or something.

Allison put Wen Li down on the quilts in the cabin and let her move around. She'd been holding her almost nonstop since—since when? She had to think. Suzhou. It seemed a year ago. Allison guessed Wen Li's legs must have been tightly bound in the orphanage, because they were just starting to come to life. They'd jerk and wander and be completely spastic. Then she'd bring them both up at an impossible angle, holding on to her feet with both hands, and start sucking on her toes, which she'd just discovered. Then she'd scoot across the floor like a worm. She'd look immensely pleased with herself, then pass some gas. Tyler loved it when she did that, thinking that if that's all a little girl could do in the world, it was enough, and all right with him.

In the late afternoon Ren Kai stopped in a little cove surrounded on three sides by gentle hills and hidden from the view of boats on the lake. He and Tyler dropped the anchor and set out the nets for the night. As the sun dipped low it seemed to grow in the haze, turning bright orange. The wind had died and the water became a great sheet of dark glass, without so much as a ripple. A lone stork stood on one leg in the shallows, lost in the shadows that were beginning to envelop the water. It stood so still, they almost didn't see it.

Despite the hour, the heat remained oppressive. Tai was suffering from a heat rash, which gave Ruth an idea. "It's time for the evening bawth," she announced formally. "Let's clean up these little buggers!"

With a little sign language Mei Ling understood. She produced an iron wok and an aluminum pot, which she filled with warm water from the stove. They stripped the babies and plopped them into the water, Wen Li in the pot and Tai in the wok. Wen Li's shoulders and head stuck up just above the edge of the pot, while Tai lounged in the wok, her neck just supported on the rim. She stared up at the sky, trying to make sense of the clouds. "She looks like a country club matron," Ruth observed. "Positively born to leisure. After the manicurist gets done I'm going to take her out to play nine holes."

The mothers shampooed and scrubbed the babies. Wen Li splashed and shrieked and threw toys away just as fast as Tyler could fetch them and bring them back. Allison watched them together, amazed at how Tyler could change so totally. Sometimes he seemed genuinely delighted by her, playing and teasing, while the next moment he could be bitter or hateful and plain mean. "He's fine," Ruth said when Allison mentioned it. "Just like a real big brother. When I wasn't much bigger than Wen Li, I remember my own brother used to shoot me with a BB gun. He'd tell me to run, that I had until he counted to ten. He always cheated and shot at five. Later he told me he was just teaching me how to run fast." Tai giggled as if she'd understood. The bathwater was soothing her rash. Ruth surveyed the cookery. "This looks like dinner for cannibals," she said. "Just throw in some carrots and onions and light a fire underneath, and we've got baby stew."

Tyler brightened. "Want me to get some matches?"

"Yeah, but then you have to hop in, too," Ruth said, giving him a gentle pat on the rear end.

"How is it you came to adopt Tai?" Allison asked.

"I'd always wanted a child, but it just never happened. I got married, twice, but it never worked out. My first husband decided he liked Jim Beam better than me, and of course he'd have made a shitty father. The next one was the most wonderful man I'd ever met. I never understood what he saw in me, or why he asked me to marry him, or why he stayed, but when we were together it was heaven. I was madly in love with him. I would have died for him. And then, four years to the day after we got married, he ran off with another woman. He took everything we had. Cleaned out the savings accounts. Kept the car, which was in his name anyway. I even had to move out of the house. He'd borrowed against it, borrowed more than it was worth, and hadn't kept up the payments. It was just as well. The rooms there had too many memories. Every time I turned around I'd start bawling.

"I guess I was lucky we didn't have kids. When he left I wouldn't have been able to take care of them and my own blubbering self as well. I got very depressed for a long time. I ate like a pig until I weighed two hundred pounds. I was about ready for the asylum when I finally got disgusted and shook it. I opened my antique store and got back on my feet. After that the years just passed. And then I decided I wanted a child. I looked for a man, but the harder I looked, the worse they seemed. I went out with a few, but either I didn't like them or they didn't like me. I knew my ovaries were getting as tired as I was, and that I was running out of time.

"Then one day I decided I was approaching motherhood all wrong, thinking for some crazy reason that I needed a man first. I read that China would let people like me adopt. Nobody else in the world was doing that. It sounded perfect. So I did the paperwork and jumped through all the hoops, but then I had to get past the next problem—I didn't have enough money. That's when I made the mistake of asking my brother for a loan."

"The congressman? The one who used to shoot you with his BB gun?"

"The very same asshole. He told me I was crazy. He said these kids were all retarded or crippled or had reactive attachment disorder. I think he was just worried about Commie genes, that the Chinese were planting little Mao clones in America who were going to grow up and throw people like him out of power. When Tai sleeps I'm already telling her subliminally to do just that, by the way. Anyway, he went out of his way to make me feel like I was making a horrible mistake. He was so passionate about it that he almost shook my own faith that what I was doing was right. He said the biggest kindness he could do for me was to give me no help. That's when I *knew* I was right. I haven't talked to him since.

"I went to a bank, but they wouldn't give me anything, either. I almost gave up. But then my aunt Sally's jewelry saved the day. I never knew Sally. She died when I was a girl—slipped on some stairs and broke her neck. I have pictures of her in big fur coats and flamboyant hats. She wore tons of rouge and smoked cigarettes in silver holders. When you look at the pictures, you can see the strong family genes—I'm almost as glamorous as she was," Ruth joked, patting her own coarse hair pretentiously. "When she died my father gave me her jewelry. It was the ugliest stuff I'd ever seen—everything from diamonds to rhinestones all of it in gaudy settings. I wouldn't have worn that crap on Halloween. I put it away and forgot about it. And then, just when my finances seemed worst—I'd just finished lying about my assets on the adoption application—I came across the key to the safety deposit box and remembered the jewelry. I got it out and took it downtown to one of the big stores. I thought the jeweler would probably call the cops on me for trying to pass glass, but he gave me almost fifteen thousand bucks for it. I definitely underestimated Aunt Sally's taste in jewels. It was a miracle. Suddenly I had enough.

"And that was that. I'd conceived a child with paperwork instead of intercourse. I suppose screwing would have been a lot more fun, but then I'd have been stuck with the man afterward."

Allison laughed. "And at least the paperwork doesn't lie about how it'll feel about you in the morning."

"Tai and I have had long talks about it," Ruth said. "After we get home and get settled, we might look for a man, or we might not. If we find one who doesn't drink or gamble or run around or smell too bad, the Wee Duck and I can raise him together." She held Tai up high overhead and clucked her tongue. The Wee Duck grinned and gurgled, then had a coughing spasm. Ruth wiped her mouth.

"It'll be a lucky man who gets the two of you," Allison said.

Ruth snorted. "Some jewel thief down on his luck, more likely."

After dinner Tai sounded congested and miserable. "Is she okay?" Allison asked.

"Her fever's gotten worse," Ruth said.

"Do you want some drops?"

"I gave her some already. They don't seem to have done much. I wish I had a thermometer. I lost mine in the collision."

"Mine got smashed," Allison said. She felt Tai's forehead. She was hot to the touch and her skin was red. Mei Ling also felt the baby and cooed sympathetically. In the cabin she found something that looked like tea leaves. She boiled them, stirred in some white powder, and mixed it in a bottle with formula. Tai took one drink and pushed it away. When she cried her nose bubbled up and she coughed. Ruth cooled her forehead with a wet cloth.

Allison saw the concern in Ruth's eyes. "She'll be fine," she said.

"A woman stopped me in the market—my God, it was only four days ago," Ruth said. "She looked at Tai like market meat. Poked at her and looked in her eyes. She said she didn't think Tai was warm enough."

Allison smiled. "I know. A hundred degrees and they want to see the babies bundled up anyway. They've done the same thing to Wen Li and me."

"But then she told me she didn't think Tai was healthy. That she looked sick to her. That I should have gotten a better baby." She looked up then, and Allison could see her eyes brimming.

"Forget it. People say stupid things."

Ruth wiped at the corner of her eye and forced a smile. "I know. Tai's going to live to be a tough old broad like me. I just want to get her home."

They watched the moon rise over a glassine lake. "I wish we could stay here forever," Ruth said, speaking softly so as not to disturb the spell. Tai was asleep on Ruth's lap. She had finally accepted some of Mei Ling's concoction. It seemed to have helped, but they could still hear her ragged breath in her congested air passages.

Allison was bouncing Wen Li lightly on one knee. Wen Li was trying to eat Allison's wedding ring right off her finger. The shiny metal fascinated her. Allison watched her and thought wistfully about Marshall. She knew how worried he must be. She wondered where he was, and what he was doing, and whether he was thinking about her too. Of course he was. She imagined him in their living room, in a scene she could call up at will. In her vision it was cold and wintry, a blessed relief from the oppressive heat and humidity of China. The snow was falling softly outside the French doors that led to the garden. They were sitting before the crackling fire, talking and drinking coffee and laughing together, about the news, or their work, or nothing at all. It seemed so distant, now, a different time in a simpler world. She wondered if things would ever again seem normal.

"What a mess we've made," Allison said absently. "How complicated this has all become." They worried for the hundredth time about Claire and speculated about Nash. Of all the things that might have happened to him, they could think of none that were good.

"What are we going to do if Yi Ling isn't in Youlan to meet us?" Allison wondered aloud.

"I've been trying not to think about that."

"How much money do you have left?"

"I don't know, after we pay Ren the rest of what we owe him. A few hundred in cash, I think. A few more in traveler's checks."

"I've got about the same. It won't be nearly enough if we have to pay anyone else to help us."

"I don't know how we'll *find* anyone else to help us."

An exhausted Major Ma Lin rubbed his eyes. It was just after dawn on Tuesday morning. He hadn't slept in thirty hours. At Colonel Quan's order he had flown from Jiujiang to Suzhou, to examine the files of the Number Three Children's Welfare Institute, the orphanage run by Director Lin until his death. "I would have the Suzhou PSB do it," Quan said, "but I don't know what we're looking for, if anything. They'll never see beyond the obvious."

Ma had arrived to find the task more difficult than he'd imagined. Files and papers were scattered through boxes, cabinets, and drawers. There were thousands of them, spanning years of operation. He'd had no idea there would be so many. Some dealt with current residents of the orphanage, while others, filed just next to them, were for children who were long gone. There were gaps in the drawers, as if certain files had been taken, but there was no way to know whether the gaps represented missing files or were simply indicative of the general anarchy of paper. No one in the orphanage had been able to shed much light on the situation. If there were rosters or master lists, they couldn't be found. Director Lin, he learned, had always run the administrative affairs of the orphanage without help from his staff. Either he had intentionally sown disorder or else he had desperately needed assistance.

The major immediately summoned four officers of the Suzhou PSB to help him gather and organize the files. While waiting for them, he took a quick tour of the orphanage, which was spartan but seemed well run. The floors were concrete but clean. There were toys and a few books, all worn from heavy use. Clothing and bedding were clean but threadbare. Fresh laundry hung outdoors from balcony rails. Windows were set high in the walls and provided little light. Incandescent bulbs hung on cords suspended from the ceiling.

Ma Lin was guided by one of the senior aunties, a woman in her sixties who'd said she'd worked there twelve years. She was in charge of the infant ward and led him through their dormitory. He walked between rows of cribs. The babies lay two or three to a crib, the cribs packed three deep along each side of the room. Despite the daytime heat, the children were tightly bound in blankets to keep them warm at night. They lay on their backs like scores of cocoons, waiting their turn for a moment's attention. A few were beginning to raise morning cain as hunger overtook sleep. Most were quiet. A few smiled up at him. Others were bored or listless, indifferent to his passage. Some played with rattles or stuffed animals. Others held their hands out in front of their faces, turning their palms back and forth, staring at their fingers, playing some quiet game only they understood. There were coughs and cries and baby noises.

Two aunties worked the room like an assembly line. They moved steadily down the rows of children, changing diapers and wiping noses and cooing and feeding and burping, two babies to a shoulder. To some of the children they administered eyedrops as they worked; to others they added medicines to bottles from cluttered steel trays. The aunties were a blur of motion, well organized but overburdened. They showed great compassion in caring for their charges, whose sheer numbers simply overwhelmed their ability to keep up.

Ma Lin counted sixty cribs. "Today we have one hundred and fifty-five in this ward," the auntie said. "One hundred and forty-eight girls. All less than a year old. Sometimes we have more." There were different wards for toddlers, she explained, and wards for children up to the age of six, and others for children between ages seven and sixteen.

"There's no one older than sixteen?" he asked.

"Not at this orphanage," the auntie said. "If they haven't been adopted by then, they're sent away."

"Where?"

"To the streets."

"How many get adopted?"

"Never enough. Maybe a tenth overall. Almost none older than four."

He spoke with the aunties in the different wards, asking questions and taking notes. He saw stuffed animals piled in corners, and a broken bicycle, and a single brightly colored mobile hanging from the ceiling of one room without furnishings, where young girls played together. They all stared at him as he passed, some with hopeful looks, others haunted, others without expression at all. The older they were, the quieter and more subdued they seemed. There was something not at all childlike about them. He had trouble bringing himself to meet their gazes. The babies had made him want to smile. The older children just made him want to hurry, especially the ones kept off in a room by themselves, with cleft palates or misshapen limbs or the vacant stare of profound retardation. He looked through the doorway at them but couldn't bring himself to go inside. He picked up the pace as he completed his tour, growing more uncomfortable with each room.

Finally, the four officers he'd summoned arrived in the courtyard. He quickly put them to work organizing the mountains of paper. They hauled files from cabinets and piled them on long worktables. Each file contained all the paperwork tracking the life of a displaced child—a child orphaned, abandoned, or lost and subsequently placed in the care of the orphanage. Ma Lin flipped through the files, which, depending on the circumstances of a child's case, might contain three items or a hundred. Most were painfully brief: *Parents: unknown. Hometown: unknown. Age: approximately 7–8 months. Medical history: unknown. Distinguishing marks: none.* A few had photographs; most had none.

Some files contained police reports, detailing authorities' efforts to find birth parents. Some held medical statements, prescriptions, and doctor's notes. Many contained the original anonymous notes that had been pinned to the babies' clothing by the birth parents who abandoned them, telling the hour and date of birth, so that their futures could be seen by whoever might someday want them.

Birth certificates were usually those created by the province, using guesswork when necessary as to a baby's age. Other papers officially designated the children as abandoned, so that they might qualify for adoption. A tiny fraction of the files had copies of adoption papers and were stamped "Adopted," with a date, and contained details and pictures of the adoptive families. Ma copied some of their names into his notebook.

There were drawers of files in Director Lin's office, and more drawers full in the adjoining room, and more still downstairs: unknown, unresolved, uncertain, unwanted, and mostly female. Endless files, nearly all the same:

Subject found on steps of Xinhua People's Hospital, 3 May, 5:10 a.m. . . .

Subject approximately 2 1/2 yrs. of age, discovered wandering in Jiaxing market . . .

Subject diagnosed with spina bifida . . . cerebral palsy . . . congenital maldevelopment of the brain . . .

He looked at the blanks stamped on the inside cover, marked "Disposition."

Subject transferred, Shanghai Children's Welfare Institute . . .

Subject transferred, Xiaoshan . . .

Subject transferred, LD . . .

Subject released, age 14 . . .

Subject adopted . . .

Subject transferred, LD . . .

The senior auntie came in, bringing a thermos of fresh tea. He thanked her and pointed to an entry. "What is LD?"

"I don't know," she said. "Maybe another orphanage."

"And there are no deaths reported in these files," he said. "Surely—"

"Those are downstairs." She led him down one flight and pointed to yet another row of cabinets. "In there."

There were more files, many more, cabinet after cabinet of them. "How many?" he asked.

"I don't know," she replied. "Perhaps the director kept figures."

"What happens when a child dies?"

"Sometimes the doctor comes, sometimes not. A truck comes, from Civil Affairs. It takes them away. Sometimes to the hospital, but usually to the crematorium, I think."

"Always the same doctor?"

"Sometimes. Not always." She looked uncomfortable with the discussion and excused herself to go feed babies.

Ma Lin began going through the death files and found them as inconsistently documented as those of the living, upstairs. Some contained causes of death, while others did not. *Pneumonia . . . meningitis . . . malnutrition . . . dehydration . . . cause of death not established . . . leukemia . . . cerebral palsy . . . hypothermia.*

The files were arranged chronologically, by date of the child's death. He moved down the row to the most current drawers. He flipped through them, wondering what he should be looking for. The deaths seemed spread evenly among age groups. He thought that a little odd; he would have expected most to be for the very young, as they were presumably the most vulnerable. He counted the files in the most current drawer. Seventy-eight. He thumbed backward through adjoining drawers until he found a file six months old, then counted forward. Two hundred and thirty seven files in half a year. He wrote the number down. He wondered if all the files were there. Without master logs he had no way to know, and there had been no such logs among Director Lin's papers. The clerks at Civil Affairs should know, he thought. Civil Affairs brought most of the live babies to the orphanage, and Civil Affairs took them away when they died.

After half an hour of it, Ma Lin sighed. As depressing as he found the files, what did it matter to his investigation anyway, how many babies had died or how?

"Those are the wrong babies," the clerk at Civil Affairs had said.

How could they be wrong? Why would anyone switch their identities, and how would anyone know? There were often identical names assigned by the orphanage; upstairs he had seen seven named Jiang Yu: "Pretty Jiangsu." Jiangsu was the name of the province. Fifteen were called Mei Ming: "No Name." Only dates set the children apart from each other— assumed birthdays, and dates of admission, and dates of death, dates buried in an avalanche of detail.

And what did any of it have to do with the American fugitives?

None of it made sense. He had begun his search thinking Director Lin might have sold babies to couples desperate to adopt, couples who couldn't qualify legally. But why would anyone kill him for doing that? If it weren't for the death of the director under suspicious circumstances, he would have concluded that the clerk was mistaken and that the files had simply been lost.

He scanned endless reports of death, chronicled on pink crematoria slips and white doctor's notes. *Malnutrition . . . encephalitis . . . malnutrition . . . congenital maldevelopment of the brain . . . cancer . . . respiratory failure . . . severe malnutrition.* He wondered about the high incidence of malnutrition. He'd seen no sign of it among the living children upstairs. He copied down the names of two of the doctors whose signatures appeared in the most recent files, intending to ask them about it.

He spent a few more hours in the orphanage, taking notes and asking more questions. For a second time he went through every paper in Director Lin's office. He reopened a ledger he'd examined earlier in the day. The book detailed routine payments made by the government to assist in the care of the orphanage's children and payments to vendors and suppliers of food, medicine, and clothing. There were notations for toys, others for coloring books—scores of transactions for minor amounts. There seemed to be nothing out of the ordinary. He had one of his officers make a copy of the ledger. He ordered a copy of the orphanage's bank records, as well as those of the director, and a copy of the director's international travel authorizations from Beijing.

He left his men to the massive task of cataloging the files, listing disposition and dates of entry and departure from the orphanage. He assigned one of the men to visit the Ministry of Civil Affairs and local police stations, to compile similar lists from their records so that they could be cross-checked. It was probably a futile exercise, he knew, as babies occasionally came from other sources and would not always be listed in standard agency files.

Too many children.

Ma Lin drove across Suzhou to the ruins of the director's house. Uniformed police stood by to keep curiosity seekers away. The site reminded Ma Lin of photographs he'd seen of Nanjing after the war. A score of men worked amid smoke plumes that still rose lazily from the rubble, sifting for evidence and carting off debris. Even with such a large workforce, it would be several days before they'd gone through it all.

The lead fire investigator sought him out and briefed him. His findings weren't surprising. "Definitely arson," he said, "and very professional." He indicated a vague trail of accelerant behind the remains of the kitchen and a neatly clipped, blackened cable end. The apartment's electrical power had been cut prior to the blaze.

Ma Lin called Colonel Quan in Jiujiang to report on his activities. "Nothing about this feels quite right, Quan Yi," he said. "Obviously the director was killed by professionals, but if it was for something to do with the affairs of the orphanage, I haven't found it yet. Possibly there's something else about his life that led to his death. Gambling, perhaps. I'll stay longer, if you wish."

"No," the colonel said. "Without something more solid, the orphanage must remain a secondary concern. The deputy minister is pressing for progress on the *lao wai*. Keep your men working the files, but you have unfinished business with the guide Yi Ling."

Half an hour later, Ma Lin sank wearily into the comfortable seat of the small jet carrying him back to Jiujiang, but the sleep he so desperately sought would not come. His eyes closed to visions of babies in their cribs—row upon row of them, room after room, all but swallowed in the shadow of a sad infinite mountain of files.

CHAPTER 16

ROPER GROGAN and Clarence Coulter had always made a perfect team. Where Clarence was the glad-hander, the fund-raiser, the genial front man who stood at the side of presidents, Roper was the hard-driving, ruthless, nuts-and-bolts brains behind the scenes at the firm. Neither partner practiced much law. Clarence did the PR, which kept the firm connected. Roper did the throat cutting, which kept the firm profitable.

Now Roper Grogan sat in his thirty-eighth-floor office, staring out at the snowcaps of the Continental Divide. On a clear day he could see from Pike's Peak to Long's Peak and beyond; it was the most spectacular view in Denver. As he talked—listened—on the telephone, he watched angry clouds beginning to billow over the Indian Peaks. A storm was moving in over the Rockies, a storm that seemed weak next to the one on the phone.

Ethan Mallory, chairman of the Terabyte Corporation, a Fortune 100 firm, had been blistering his ears in a tirade that had lasted for twenty minutes. Mallory was neither soft-spoken nor subtle. He was always volatile, and now he was angry as well.

"Do you know how many drives I sold last year in China?" Mallory asked him.

"No, Ethan. How many?"

"Three hundred thirty thousand. Do you know how many I can sell next year, if I can get the Shanghai factory going? I'll tell you," he said without waiting for a response. "Just over eleven million. That's better than a thirty-two hundred percent increase, at two hundred and thirty bucks a pop. I've got a hundred and sixteen million invested in that factory right now. Do you know how many drives that factory is going to produce next year, if most favored nation status does not go through for the Chinese?"

"I'd—" Roper started to say.

"Mother-fucking none, that's how many. A big fat bullshit zip." Mallory was just getting heated up. Roper had never heard him so exercised about anything, and certainly not about his own law firm.

"And that isn't all. Did you watch those syrupy shows over the weekend about this baby business? Did you hear MFN withering in the storm? Well, I did. Christ almighty, there was no end to it! CNN, NBC, CBS, God knows where all else. I wasn't the only one watching. So were my investors. Do you know how much damage that storm caused this morning on the Street? We opened at ninety-nine and five-eighths, Roper. *Ninety-nine and five-eighths!* We closed Friday at a hundred and eight and a half. Do you know what eight and seven-eighths points means to me? A little over three hundred million dollars, all over some baby bullshit."

"Calm down, Ethan. MFN is taking hits all across the spectrum. The baby story has only—"

"What did you bill me last year, Roper?"

Grogan closed his eyes. He hated it when his clients did this. "I don't know, exactly. About twelve million, I think." Of course he knew the exact answer, but that was close enough.

"More like fourteen two, if you're only counting Terabyte," Mallory said. "But I mean *all* of it—the subsidiaries, the joint ventures, the foreign stuff. Everything. What was the total?"

"About thirty."

"Thirty-one four and change," Mallory said. "I don't pay you that money to make problems. I pay you that money to solve problems. And this morning's news flash is that my own goddamned law firm is part of the problem."

"Come on, Ethan, the firm—"

"You need to rein him in, Roper. Pronto."

"Marshall Turk didn't even make the trip," Grogan said. "It's his wife. We aren't even certain what's happened."

"Honest to Christ, do you need *me* to tell *you?* It's in all the reports. I don't give a furry rat's ass if he's there or not. Turk, Turk's wife—it's all Coulter Grogan to me. Your own goddamned lobbyist called me from the Hill this morning to say that Jenkins and Baker are both wavering on the bill over this business. And Ballard was for us, but now he's had to go ballistic about China to appease the pro-lifers in his district. I chewed your lobbyist's ass, and then realized the sonofabitch didn't even know it was his own firm fucking things up! You need to get this over with. Not tomorrow, not next week. Now! I don't care what you have to do. Do something. Make my pain stop, Roper. Make the story go away."

Roper Grogan listened to another five minutes of thunder, trying to tame his client's furies without success. The worst of it was that this was the third call he'd taken already that morning, all over the same thing. Make my pain stop, they all said, and they weren't even as civil about it as Mallory. Roper Grogan knew, as they all knew, that it was quite unfair to blame the firm. Completely unreasonable. But that didn't matter. It was his name on the shingle. They paid him to take care of business, and this was business.

After Mallory finally dismissed him curtly and hung up, Roper Grogan punched the button on his intercom. "Get me Congressman Pollard. And then Victor Li, in Hong Kong," he said.

The Cathay Pacific 747-400 pulled up to the jetway. A cluster of officials stood inside, waiting for the doors to open. The flight's crew had called ahead, requesting medical assistance for one of the passengers. Customs officials were standing by to expedite debarkation. A private ambulance waited on the tarmac outside the concourse to take the patient to the best private hospital in the colony.

After his eardrum ruptured, Marshall's fever climbed steadily. The cabin lights had been dimmed as most passengers slept on the long flight, so it had not been until the aircraft was over the Sea of Japan that the flight attendant noticed how ill the passenger in first class was. There was a nurse on board who briefly examined him and took his temperature. It was high enough that the attendant summoned the pilot. After a discussion with the nurse, the pilot decided not to divert the flight to an alternate airport; they were best to head straight for Hong Kong. Marshall heard none of the discussion. He was stone deaf in his left ear, could hear little more than the shriek of tinnitus out of the other. He was shivering violently, uncontrollably. Sweat poured from his brow and he had begun to cough, a great hacking cough that sent needles through his lungs. They wrapped him in blankets and gave him aspirin for the fever. The nurse gave him a hot-water bottle and told him to keep it next to the ear, but the pain was too great and he let it slide. The aspirin did not reduce the fever over the next few hours, but the fever didn't rise, either.

Marshall went through the blur of arrival only half-aware. He sensed rather than saw what was going on around him. A wheelchair. The chatter of Cantonese, the whine of an aircraft engine, louder even than the ringing in his ear. Fluorescent light panels. Officials in police uniforms, Chinese faces. *Chinese. Allison. Tyler.* The terrible vision came again, the night, the boat. A corpse, floating down the river, turned on its stomach so he couldn't see who it was. Too dark to tell whether it was male or female, big or small. Just a body. He leaned over, trying to reach down, to turn it over, to see who it was . . . then felt strong hands beneath his armpits, lifting him back into his wheelchair. A lump grew on his forehead. Someone produced a strap, to keep him from falling again. There was an ambulance. White doors and the smell of astringent. A siren, shrill and odd sounding, nothing like the sirens in the States. Dry mouth, pounding headache. Spots of light, flashes of color. A tile building, a canopy overhead. A hallway, more voices, a needle in his arm. Something cool, blessedly cool.

And then darkness and sleep.

He awoke sometime later, to a Chinese doctor with a bow tie and white frock who was listening to his heart. "Ah, Mr. Turk," the doctor said, smiling. "You are among us once again." The voice was not distinct, as voices usually were, but Marshall could tell the doctor's English was better than his own. British English. Clipped, precise. Marshall blinked and tried to sit up. He felt horrible. Everything ached. "What happened?" he said.

"A bacterial infection, Mr. Turk. Acute otitis media. Your eardrum ruptured on the flight. By itself that is not normally serious. But evidently the medication you were taking was not effective against this particular strain. Either that or you weren't taking your dose regularly. In any event, there is some involvement with your mastoid process."

Marshall looked at him blankly. "What?"

"Just here, behind your ear." The doctor tapped a finger to his head, to show the place. "A small bone. The infection has involved it. Between that and your upper respiratory infection, you managed to become quite ill. I've given you IV Mefoxin for the infection, and something for your fever, which had climbed to thirty-nine five Celsius. Nearly a hundred and three Fahrenheit, I believe. You were quite dehydrated, so we're running a saline drip. Oh yes, and I've given you a decongestant to help unblock your eustachian tubes. Quite the pharmacist's dream, you are. And you've responded quite nicely, Mr. Turk. There shouldn't be any permanent hearing loss in your left ear, but we won't know for certain for a few days."

"I can't hear very well out of my right ear, either. Your lips are moving, but you might as well be underwater."

"That ear was becoming involved as well," the doctor said. "But it should respond quickly. I've also given you some Demerol. You were thrashing about a bit from the pain. Made quite a scene for a bit. You'll be groggy for a while, but you're well out of danger. In fact, your recovery should be quite rapid. Unless you sprout some ghastly new symptom—which I doubt—you'll be out of here tomorrow. Day after, latest."

Marshall closed his eyes. Demerol. That explained why his head seemed stuffed with sand. He struggled to think. "What day is it?"

"Tuesday."

Marshall felt a twinge of alarm. "My wife . . . did she call? Have I had any calls?"

"I'm afraid I don't know. And now if you'll excuse me, I have other patients to attend who are *truly* ill. I'll look in on you later. Good day, Mr. Turk." The doctor adjusted one of the drips, hastily scribbled a note on Marshall's chart, and left the room.

A few moments later Li Kan, Victor Li's son, breezed in. Kan was nattily dressed, as always, and still as round as Marshall remembered—round face, round eyes, round glasses. Now even his stomach was getting round. He was always outrageous and outgoing, and now he was getting fat, too. He lived high.

"Hiya, Turk," he said. "Don't get up on my account."

Marshall opened his eyes. "Okay."

"I heard about your trouble. I just wanted you to know I'm here if you need me. I won't stay. Doc says you need sleep. I wondered if you need anything else besides that."

"Don't know. Probably, but my brain doesn't seem to work right now."

"It never did, as I recall," Li Kan said. "Anyway, I was on my way to Sha Tin. Just stopped in to see if they've poked you with enough needles and medicated you with enough powdered yak penis that I can go bet on the ponies without feeling guilty." He chattered on for a few moments, but Marshall barely responded, his head floating. He smiled a few times at things Li Kan said, but he wasn't sure at what.

"I've left you my pager number, and my mobile. Call me when you're not so stoned. Or when you at least want to share your drugs with an old friend." Li Kan squeezed Marshall's shoulder, and then he was gone.

After that Marshall floated in and out for hours, half aware of a hazy succession of nurses and orderlies and shots. The only thing that brought him near the surface was the phone, but it was not the call he'd hoped for.

"Marshall? It's Roper Grogan."

"Hello, Roper. Speak up, will you? I can barely hear. My ears—"

"I know. They told me. I won't keep you. I wanted you to know that even though you had a bad flight, I'm glad you're in Hong Kong. I think it's the right thing."

"Clarence thought I was crazy."

"He doesn't have your perspective. You must be sick with worry. But I called because I've got some good news for you."

"I could use some just now."

"They announced it was a man named Cameron who died on the river. That means your wife and son are safe . . . or at least, I mean, that it wasn't them."

Marshall couldn't say anything at first. The fever or the drugs were making him emotional, and now it all flooded over him in great waves. He had never expected to feel relief over another man's death, but he didn't care. He couldn't help it. He tried to blink back the tears but found himself weeping.

"Are you there?"

Marshall fought for control. His voice cracked. "Yes, yes, I'm here. I'm just . . ."

"I know. Have you heard from Allison yet?"

"No. I've got the phone forwarded from the house. I hope the signal will follow me here."

"It should. I've made the trip with mine, and it worked fine. Do you have the phone with you?"

Marshall looked around his room. He saw Clarence's cellular phone in a plastic bag with some of his other belongings, on the window ledge near the bed. "Yes, it's here."

"Hold on, then. I'll try to call you right back on it." The bedside phone went dead. With an effort Marshall dropped it in its cradle. He sank back into his pillow, giddy with relief and Demerol. A moment later the cellular phone rang.

"Roper?"

"You sound like you're just across town. Amazing, isn't it? Anyway, I won't keep you long, because I know you're not feeling well and I'm sure she'll call. When she does, what are you going to tell her?"

"To turn herself in, of course. But I've already done that and she refused. Maybe after what happened on the river it will make more sense to her."

"I think you need to do more than that."

"What do you mean?"

"I'll be blunt. Look, I admire Allison and her courage in doing this. I can only imagine how difficult it must be for her, running and hiding. But Tyler is there with her, Marshall. The best thing you can do for him—for both of them—is to see that they're caught without further incident. We've already had one fatality. God knows we don't want more. If the authorities know where she is and who she's with, they can plan properly. They can apprehend her safely. But if she persists in running, God knows what might happen. More accidents. More happenstance."

"Christ, Roper. You're suggesting that I turn her in?"

"I'm suggesting that you act in her best interest. She's not thinking clearly, Marshall. She's on the run. You need to think for her now. It's the best thing. It's the only thing."

Marshall rubbed his eyes, still so relieved at the news that he couldn't think of anything else. It was hard to think, anyway. Roper's arguments were sailing around in his head on currents of drugs. "I don't know if I can do that."

"I understand how difficult this is for you. But you must realize that nothing good can come of her continued flight. It only increases the chance something will go wrong. There's no possibility she'll escape. None whatever. It's inevitable they'll catch her. They can either do that sooner, on favorable terms, or later, on terms over which you have no control. You know, of course, which of those is best."

"Can we get her a deal?"

"I don't know," Roper lied. "If you're okay with it, I'll have Victor Li look into it."

"I have to think about it."

"Do that, but you may not have much time. Get some rest now. I'll call you later. Victor assures me you're in the best medical hands in Asia. If you need anything at all, he's there to help you. We all are. Good luck, Marshall."

*   *   *

What Roper Grogan hadn't told Marshall was that his conversation with Victor Li had had only one purpose, that together they had settled on a course of action that would seal the fate of the fugitives—with or without Marshall's cooperation.

Victor Li, born in the city of Canton, now known as Guangzhou, had lived in Hong Kong since the 1950s, when his family had fled Mao's mainland. Victor had been Roper Grogan's roommate at Yale. He understood, as no Westerner ever could, the workings of the Chinese mind, and now he ran the Coulter Grogan office in Hong Kong.

"There are three possible outcomes as I see it, my friend," Victor had told Grogan. "The first and best—and altogether most unlikely, in my opinion—is if Marshall's wife and her friends manage somehow to arrive in Canton. To do so they will have had to elude what is an intensive manhunt in a country where they cannot hope to blend in or escape notice. I know of the man who is hunting them. Quan Yi, from Beijing. I know him by reputation only. He is quite capable and totally ruthless. He will catch them before they get to the city, if he hasn't caught them already."

"Surely we'd have heard."

"Not necessarily, my friend. But assume he does not catch them outside Canton. Once in the city they still have to get into the consulate, which is located on a narrow peninsula that is easily monitored. By now every visitor to the building will be watched, photographed, and studied. A reasonable man might conclude it is simply not possible."

"They've already been on the run longer than anyone thought possible."

"True enough," Victor said, "and let us hope they succeed. But even if they do, they're not home free, of course. The American consulate said they'll follow Chinese law. Technically that means they should hand the women over to the police. Of course, that's only their public position. The U.S. State Department and the Chinese Foreign Ministry would try to work something out. Their problem would be a thorny one, but at that point the matter would be in the hands of diplomats rather than police. Bargains could be struck that were not possible while they were still fugitives. In the end, I think Beijing would let them go. Whether or not they were permitted to leave with the babies, the women would seem heroic. The whole thing would be quickly forgotten, and the world would soon return to business. But it isn't going to happen. That leaves us with two alternatives, barring an accident.

"The first is if the women decide to give up, to turn themselves in. World sympathy would swell for them and the babies, as it already has. Having chased the women and then having failed to catch them, the Chinese would look both heartless and incompetent. Worst of all, they would lose face in the eyes of world opinion. I must emphasize, Roper, that there is nothing so dangerous to the outcome as such a loss of face. It would, inevitably, leave the Chinese no maneuvering room, and make them intractable. They would have little choice but to bring the full force of law against the fugitives. I think there is a very real possibility the women would spend time in jail, while the boy would be deported. Even if the government relented in the end and made some sort of humanitarian gesture, there would first be the necessity of a trial, of a public affirmation of China's absolute mastery of her own affairs. While Chinese trials can move at lightning speed, any delay at all could be potentially fatal for the MFN vote coming up in Congress—and we would not have served our clients.

"That leaves a final possibility. If the authorities catch the women on their own, they would save face, and—with a suitable blend of indignation and mercy—be able to bring about an honorable end to an ugly affair by making a magnanimous gesture. I don't think anyone in Beijing wants to see this drawn out. It's a public relations disaster for them, coming at the worst possible time. I certainly wouldn't want to be in the place of the official who made the decision to exchange the babies in the first place. He's probably already in a labor camp. But as much as everyone might like, what he did cannot be undone. Therefore the whole affair must be concluded gracefully by the Chinese, with honor. Capture would permit that. They could free the women and the boy, with or without the babies. Face would be preserved, laws upheld, order restored, everyone freed. The world community could not object to such an outcome. Best of all, it would be over with quickly. The threat to MFN would diminish."

Victor Li paused for a moment. "So my advice to you, my friend, is that for the good of our clients, for the good of the women themselves, we need to help the Chinese catch them." In this statement, Victor Li was being disingenuous with his old roommate. One of his most valued clients, a man of great power and influence in Beijing, a man whose illegal activities Victor suspected but never questioned, and whose legitimate concerns earned the firm substantial fees, had, only that morning, given Victor Li a speech much like the one Roper Grogan had received from Ethan Mallory. The difference was that Mallory just wanted the whole affair concluded quickly, while Victor's client had been specific about how.

"I want them caught," the client said. "The babies must never leave the mainland." As Victor Li listened, he could picture the man speaking, could see the one eye boring into him with such intensity. The man had lost the other eye in some sort of accident or fight; Victor never inquired. He never covered the missing eye socket, never had the horrible scars surgically repaired. The effect served to unnerve his audience, which was, Victor knew, the very effect it had on him and was precisely the way his client wanted it.

Victor Li saw no reason to share this information with his partner, for it didn't change what he already saw as the best solution to everyone's problem.

"I see your point," Roper told him. "And I quite agree. But how can we help?"

"I assume one of the women will call relatives for help, if they can. What about Congressman Pollard?"

"I talked to him before I called you. He won't be of any use. He says his sister's a lunatic. He doesn't say that in public, of course. But he told me she's there against his advice and better judgment. He says she'll never call him for help, and if she does, he's not inclined to give it. Whatever happens, he says it's just tough shit for her, that she'll have to pay the price of ignoring his advice. Meanwhile he's going to do all he can to torpedo MFN, which he'd be doing in any event. His sister's situation just adds fuel to his fire. I think he loves it."

"Nice guy."

"Quite. So anything we can get the women to do will have to come through Allison Turk. She's already called Marshall once. I think she will again."

"Then I will arrange things." Victor Li explained what he had in mind.

"All right. By the way—any possibility we could cut a deal up front?"

"Not a prayer. The Chinese would never buy it. It would make them seem weak in their own house."

Roper had thought as much and knew immediately he wouldn't tell Marshall that.

Within half an hour after the two partners hung up, as Roper Grogan was talking on the phone to Marshall, a private detective working for Coulter Grogan crouched in a van outside the hospital, recording all telephone calls coming to or from Marshall's room.

Roper Grogan was not particularly fond of the need for subterfuge with his own partner. He genuinely hoped Marshall would voluntarily turn his wife in. But if not, Roper was prepared to act on his own. It was business.

If Allison Turk called her husband and revealed anything of her whereabouts or her plans, the police in China would know almost as soon as her husband did and plan a reception for her.

Either way, Marshall would never know.

They drew near the fishing village of Youlan at dusk. Ren piloted them through a seemingly endless labyrinth of interconnecting coves, a waterway that crisscrossed the marshes to the east of the city of Nanchang. The maze had no signposts, no markers of any kind. The boat passed through channels that only a longtime resident would even suspect existed. As they sailed, they watched a pageant of peasant life in the Chinese countryside. The landscape was dotted with lakes and fishing ponds and rice paddies carpeted in flowers and separated by dikes, along the tops of which ran rough roads too narrow for motor vehicles. Peasants rode bicycles or pushed handcarts loaded with mountains of straw, or slung farming implements from their shoulders as they made their way home from the fields before dark. Their houses were made of red brick with maroon roof tiles. Plumes of smoke rose lazily from the cookfires inside. Most houses had pigsties and brick shanties for their water buffalo. Children too young to work played in the mud. Chickens ran through the yards, chased occasionally by dogs.

Some fishermen were beginning their night work, poling their canoes into position, their lanterns flickering above the water. Their silhouettes were just visible against the darkening background as they cast their nets, which floated to the water and splashed down gently, making barely a ripple.

As the waterways narrowed and the shore pressed in on their boat from both sides, Ren Kai motioned the *lao wai* to stay inside the cabin, lest they be spotted. Mao cap pulled low over his brow, Tyler stood next to the fisherman at the wheel and peered out the window.

Allison and Ruth rode in silence as they neared the village, their tension mounting. They feared losing the safety and comfort of the boat and the idyllic lake, which had for a brief time sheltered them from a hostile world. Now both worried about Tai. Her cough, always persistent, had grown ragged and rough. Her cheeks were flushed scarlet, and her cry was miserable and heartbreaking. Ruth fretted and fussed but could do little to help. She had faithfully given Tai the antibiotics prescribed by the orphanage doctors in Suzhou, carefully mixing the drops into Tai's formula. But it was becoming clear that Tai's problems ran deeper than just a cold. In the rare moments when she felt good, Tai was spirited, quick to play and respond to Ruth. But for the first time, her eyes had lost their luster and there were moments when she was listless, and that worried Ruth most of all.

At length Ren slowed the engine and carefully guided the boat to its berth alongside a rickety wooden jetty that projected out from the shore. Mei Ling jumped out and secured the line to a wooden bollard.

"Youlan," the fisherman said, pointing. The village proper lay beyond the cove; near it, half a dozen fishing boats were berthed together. A narrow peninsula led out to where Ren Kai had tied up. At its tip there were two houses, isolated from the village by a narrow strip of rice paddies. He pointed at one of the houses and then at himself. *Home.*

Ren motioned to Allison and Ruth to remain inside the cabin. It was beginning to rain lightly, and the only people they could see were walking along the paths near the village. Because of the rain and the isolation of Ren's house at the end of the peninsula, it was unlikely that anyone would be coming that way, but he didn't want to take any chances. He and his wife hurried along the path to their house. A light appeared in a window and then went out again. They crossed to the next house, and again a light went on and then off. Evidently no one was in either house. Ren Kai then hurried down the narrow path toward the village, while Mei Ling returned to the boat.

Later, having shared gossip and tea with his village neighbors, Ren Kai returned. His news was not good. *"Yi Ling bú zài zhè,"* he said, shaking his head. The guide Yi Ling had not been there asking about him.

Allison and Ruth exchanged a forlorn glance. They had both feared as much, but the reality was worse than the fear and it settled over them like an icy blanket. Even with Yi Ling's help they didn't have much hope. Without her, it was hard not to lose faith entirely.

"Well . . ." Ruth sighed, trying to seem cheerful. "Now what?"

Allison wanted to curl up in a blanket and hide. She forced herself to suggest something she didn't really want to do at all. "Yi Ling gave me the phone number of someone in Nanchang," she said. "I could go into the city and call them. Maybe they'd let me come see them. I could try to get their help."

"Couldn't Ren do that alone?"

"Sure, but I need to see if I can get us some more money, too. Maybe there's a hotel where I could use my credit card. And I need to call Marshall. I think I have to go."

Ruth thought it over. "I suppose you're right. You'd better leave Tyler and Wen Li here." The thought was paralyzing, but Allison had to agree. The children would only slow her down and increase her visibility.

They found a hotel in Ruth's guidebook, and Allison communicated to Ren what she wanted. He saw the hotel name in Chinese characters and nodded. He knew the place.

There was another order of business. "I need five hundred," Allison said. "We still need to pay Ren what Yi Ling promised him for getting us here."

Mei Ling and Ren talked as Allison counted out the money. "I don't know if you should do what she wants," Mei Ling said quietly. "We know they're in trouble. We could be arrested for helping them. The police could take our boat. Arrest our son. You know how they are. We have brought the *lao wai* here, as we agreed. Maybe we should ask them to go."

"And just where would they go?" Ren asked gently. "They have nowhere to turn. We have come this far with them; surely a bit farther can do no harm. Their trouble cannot be so great that we should turn our backs on them. I can take this one to Nanchang easily enough, and maybe then we will be done with them. And besides, there is little Tai. Who would help her?" They looked at the baby in Ruth's lap. "If she gets any sicker tonight, you should take her to Jin Shan." Jin Shan was a doctor who lived up a hill on the other side of the cove.

Ren knew that no matter what his wife might say about turning them out, she agreed with him. She liked the odd foreigners as much as he did. She adored the boy and doted on the babies. Despite the danger, she nodded. "All right," she said. "But I'm afraid."

As Allison counted out the money Ren saw how little she had left. He took the bundle of bills she offered. He knew he had charged a thousand times the value of the journey. He looked at his wife with a question, and she answered with her eyes. He counted out half the bills and gave them back to Allison. Confused, she stared at him. He spread his hands in satisfaction. "*Gòu le,*" he said.

Ren went into the village once again to borrow a vehicle. Then he led Allison out into the light night rain beneath the shelter of a bright pink umbrella that Mei Ling produced from the house. Allison wore her rattan hat and a cotton jacket of Mei Ling's that was too small but had floral prints that looked more Chinese than the one she was wearing. Self-conscious about her height, Allison hunched over as she walked, as if somehow she might seem smaller. She struggled to keep close to the fisherman, who moved quickly despite the darkness. He led her on a roundabout route in order to avoid the village, trudging between rice paddies on an uneven path that was wide enough to walk only in single file, and hardly wide enough for that. She wondered how he could see well enough to know where to go. The surface of the path was soft and slippery, and she soon lost her footing, ending up with her backside in the mud and her shoes in the water. He took her by the arm as she stepped over a channel in which she could hear running water. From the village she heard faint flute music, and laughter, and she noticed different smells, from raw sewage to woodsmoke and what she thought was boiling cabbage. Finally they clambered up an embankment and found themselves on a dirt road. A farmer hurried by, his head sheltered by a newspaper. Allison bowed her head deeply, hiding her face with the rim of her hat, but the man never looked anyway. He kept his head down and mumbled a response to Ren's greeting.

They walked in the direction of the village and came to a widening in the road where a few vehicles were parked. He led her to a motorized cart. The front was a motorcycle, the rear a wagon covered by an arched frame over which a tarp had been stretched. Ren helped her into the rear. The tarp was tattered and provided little protection from the elements, but it did help shelter her from view. Ren fired the engine and set off. She instantly discovered what an unpleasant journey it was going to be. The engine's muffler was missing or defective, and the racket was deafening. The road was awful, and there were no shock absorbers under the cart. She bounced around until her buttocks ached. She tried to get into a crouching position on her hands and knees, but the little cart bucked and jerked and jolted her around like a ball. She had to sit again and tried to suspend herself from the frame using her arm strength, which gave out quickly. Worst of all were the exhaust fumes, which seemed to be aimed directly inside the cart. She put her mouth to a rip in the canvas, trying to get what clear air she could.

Ren rode unprotected in the drizzle. His clothes and face were soaked. Every so often he called to her from the front, with one of the English words he'd learned on the lake. "Okay?" He sounded almost joyous.

"Okay!" she shouted back.

Eventually they arrived at an asphalt road. The ride got smoother and the fumes less noxious. There was a great deal more traffic—other carts, like theirs, and trucks that came barreling down upon them with frightening speed yet somehow missed them at the last instant. As they drew nearer to the city, the rain stopped. Pedestrians appeared as if by hidden command, walking in the dark, unafraid of traffic that missed them by inches. Some pushed carts and others led sheep.

They passed long rows of shops, the interiors of which were open to the street and flashed by like frames of a movie—a welder's shop, a seamstress hunched over her pedal-driven sewing machine, a brochette vendor, a carpenter, a canned goods merchant. They came to an elevated roadway, and she began to see neon lights, Kodak and Ford and Sony. Televisions flickered in streetside rooms as the kinescope continued its display of brief vignettes of urban Chinese life. Students hunched intently over textbooks, studying beneath bare light bulbs. The streets swarmed with pedicabs and handcarts loaded to near collapse with piles of merchandise. Barbers worked on sidewalks, their customers' chins tilted to the sky as straight razors flashed in the night lights. Mechanics banged on stubborn motors, and it seemed everyone had a horn. Men hawked and spat and played cards or billiards. Others smoked and drank tea, or read newspapers and gossiped. After the peace of Poyang Hu, it was a cacophony of sound and sight, everything busy and alive. The air was electric with urgency, with a sense of purpose and progress.

On one particularly busy street Ren found a hole in the traffic, pulled over to the curb, and stopped. He gestured down the street and said something. Allison looked and saw a sign in English: Jiangxi Hotel. It was the one she'd showed him in the guidebook. He helped her out of the cart. She stretched her cramped legs, thankful to be standing at last. At first she was fearful, thinking surely the police must be everywhere, all looking for her. But across the street she saw two different groups of foreigners. There were singles, couples, and even a few children, all clearly Western, gawking in shop windows and consulting guidebooks. The busy city would give her anonymity that was not possible in the country.

Ren leaned back against the frame of the cart and motioned her on. *I'll wait,* his posture said. Allison smiled gratefully and started across the street. Almost immediately a horn blared at her and she jumped back. A taxi fairly flew by, its driver honking and glaring at the stupid *lao wai* trying to get herself killed.

Much more carefully now, she crossed the street and entered the river of pedestrians. She had expected to blend in but noticed that everyone seemed to stare at her. Then she caught her reflection in the window of a shop and with a flush she realized why. She was a mess. She hadn't bathed in days. Most of her clothes had gone to the bottom of the Yangtze. She had only those clothes she wore, and they were filthy. Earlier that evening she'd fallen in the mud, which was now caked on her jeans. She brushed at the mud with little effect and did the best she could with a comb. She held the rattan hat self-consciously and decided not to put it back on. In the country it had provided a semblance of security. In the city it made her look even more awkward than she felt. She summoned her courage and walked up the steps to the hotel.

The Jiangxi was a modern hotel that catered to foreigners and rich Chinese tourists. The lobby was round in shape, made almost entirely of marble—the walls, the floors, even the elevator doors, all highly polished, reflecting the light of small chandeliers that hung from the ceiling. The signs were all in English as well as Chinese, and she read them with relief: there were half a dozen restaurants and bars, a bowling alley, a gymnasium, beauty salon, business center, swimming pool, shopping arcade complete with clothing store, food and sundries, and gifts. She felt rather than saw the concierge staring at her as she stood gawking at it all. She straightened her shoulders and walked ahead through the lobby, trying to appear as if she belonged. There were fountains by the rear entry and pay telephones. She hurried toward them, only to find signs that said the phones took only IC cards. She had no idea what such cards were. Certain the concierge was still staring at her, she walked nonchalantly toward the arcade. She found a sign for the bathrooms. Inside there were marble sinks and gleaming toilets. She washed her face and arms and took paper towels to the mud on her clothes. With a real mirror she made progress on her hair. Despite the grunge that remained, she felt much better.

She wanted to rent a room, to use its shower and phone, but she was afraid to use her credit card like that, fearing that somehow she might be hunted that way. She wondered whether changing money presented the same risk. She had to try. In the lobby she drew a deep breath for courage and approached the desk, where she was greeted brightly by a young clerk.

"Hello, may I help you?" the girl asked.

"Yes, please. I wondered if I might use my credit card to obtain money," Allison said.

"Change money? Yes, of course. What is your room number, please?" She turned to the computer terminal, ready to type. Next to her computer terminal, hidden from Allison's view by the counter, was a piece of paper from the *gong an ju*, the Public Security Bureau. The same list hung at every reception desk at every hotel in south China, from Jiangxi to Hunan, from Fujian to Guangdong. There were five names on the list. The name Allison Turk was among them.

"No, not change money," Allison explained, smiling. "I need to get new money. I mean, I want to use my credit card to get cash. You know, *charge* money." She tapped her credit card on the counter.

The girl took the card and studied it. "Oh, I see. Charge money." She looked crestfallen. She didn't see at all. She didn't know how to deal with Allison's problem and felt most impolite. Then she brightened. "I will ask the night manager." Still holding the card, she moved off before Allison could stop her. Allison felt a surge of panic—she didn't know whether she wanted to speak to a night manager at all. She didn't want attention, didn't want to stand out. She felt like a neon criminal, flashing her guilt for all the world to see—even though, in this hotel, at least, she had done nothing wrong. Even so, her palms were clammy with fear. *Don't be paranoid,* she told herself. *For God's sake, you're just trying to get some money.*

The night manager appeared then, a mousy little man with thick glasses and an ill-fitting suit but a ready smile. Everyone at the Jiangxi smiled. "I am pleased to assist you, madam," he said, looking at her credit card. "You wish money?" Allison explained again, and the night manager shook his head. "Perhaps that may be done at a bank, tomorrow. What is your room number, please? I will make inquiries on your behalf, and call you."

"Well, no, no thank you, that won't be necessary. What about a check? Might I cash a check?"

"A traveler's check? Of course." He nodded as the clerk reached for the change pad.

"No, I mean a personal check."

The night manager gave an embarrassed laugh at that. "No, I'm afraid that won't be possible. Again, I will be most pleased to make inquiries." His pen was poised. "Your room number, please?" he asked once more. He looked at her credit card and started to copy her name from it.

Allison reached out and plucked the card from his fingers. "Thank you, don't bother. Really. Maybe my husband has already gotten money.

I'm pretty sure he has." Face flushing, she backed away from the counter, nodding her thanks. She turned and despite weak knees walked as confidently as she could across the lobby, until she found herself stepping onto the elevator, whose doors had opened just in time. *This is crazy,* she thought as the doors slid shut. *What am I doing?* She got off at the first stop and found herself in another lobby. She was immediately enticed by the smell. A sign announced a buffet and she realized she was famished. She walked through the doors into the restaurant. A table in the center of the room was heaped high with meats and vegetables, fruits and salads, and steaming cauldrons of soup. There were only a few diners scattered around the room, all Chinese, and enough food to feed a hundred times as many. A hostess greeted her and showed her to a table. Allison immediately visited the buffet for fruit, salad, and soup and poured herself two glasses of orange juice from the carafe marked "Orunj." As she ate, a couple entered and took the table immediately next to hers. The man was big, barrel-chested, and bald, and his laugh shook the room. The woman was as slight and shy as her husband was massive and gregarious. From their conversation, Allison gathered the man sold machine tools and was in Nanchang making a sales pitch to one of the aircraft manufacturing plants. Allison tried to discern his home from his accent and settled on Texas. He talked nonstop, and his wife ignored him. He kept glancing over at Allison, and when he caught her eye gave a little wave.

"Howdy, ma'am," he said. "I hope you don't mind a little company."

Allison didn't want company at all. "Not at all," she said.

"Name's Purvis," he said. "Orville Purvis. This here's my wife, Gladys. We're from N'ohleans."

"I'm sorry?"

"Loozianna. Y'know, Bayou country. Cajun cousins."

"Oh, of course."

"I thought you were American. You got that look. California?"

"Colorado."

"I skied there once. Vail. Snapped my leg clean in two. Come to think of it, that was on the China Bowl. How 'bout that for a co-insy-dense? *China* Bowl!" His laugh boomed through the restaurant; the Chinese diners were too polite to stare. "Now I just ride the snow cat up to the restaurant on top. Only thing big enough and safe enough for this fat ass." Purvis reached for an egg roll, dipped it deep into a bowl of fiery mustard sauce, and got the whole thing into his mouth in one bite.

He chatted for a few moments, managing a one-sided conversation even while wolfing down huge portions of food. "You here on one of them tours?" he asked between bites. "Not much to see in Nanchang, unless you build airplanes or like seein' monuments to the revolution. Or maybe you here gettin' a baby? Lots of couples here in this hotel gettin' babies."

Allison put down her fork. She felt an unwanted tear welling in her eye and wiped at it. She stared at her salad and didn't know what to say. She envied the Purvises their freedom, their normalcy, the fact that they were worried only about weather and egg rolls and machine tools. Normal people, with a normal life.

"Orville, that ain't none of our affair," Gladys said with a pained expression.

"Jus' tryin' to be polite, hon," Orville said, wounded. "Makin' talk, that's all. Didn't mean nothin' by it."

"Well, I'm sure Allison don't need you prying into her life that way. Now we'd better get going, Orville," she said. She rummaged through her purse. "Oh dear, I've forgotten my phrase book," she said.

"Better go get it. You can't do much shoppin' without it."

"What room we in again? They ought to put room numbers on these cards."

"Seven eleven, hon. Like the store, remember?"

"I'll be back in a minute."

"We're going shopping," Orville explained after she left. "Trinkets for the relatives. Real-live 'Made in China' stuff. Hell, you can get more of that in N'ohleans than you can here, I think. But it seems to count more when it travels all that way in my luggage. Anyway, Gladys is trying to learn a bit of the language. She's one helluva bargainer—"

Allison summoned her courage. "Mr. Purvis . . ."

"Orville."

"Okay, Orville. I wonder if I might ask you a favor."

"Oh?" His fork stopped midair.

"I . . . I need money, Mr.—Orville. Cash. I was wondering if—if you had any cash you could spare, that is—if I could write you a check." She did it awkwardly and felt stupid.

"Hell, you can do that downstairs, honey," he said, waving his fork dismissively. "I do it all the time."

"They only take traveler's checks."

"You mean you tryin' to write a *personal* check?" Orville Purvis tried to digest that with the rest of his meal. "I expect they don't do much of that 'round here."

"It's all I have."

Orville nodded but said nothing.

"It's good, Orville. You have my word."

He smiled at that. "You don't look like the sort to come all the way to China to pass bad paper, little lady." He studied her face. "You . . . uh . . . in some kinda trouble or somethin'?"

"No. Well, yes, a little. It's a long story. I just need some cash."

"How much you talkin'?"

"As much as you can. Five hundred, a thousand—anything."

Orville laughed. "Hell, I ain't got but fifty bucks cash money, hundred tops. U.S., anyway. But you're welcome to it, if it'll help." He reached for his wallet and produced a wad of bills. "Sorry," he apologized, counting it out. "It's mostly ones and fives, for tips. There. Ninety-eight. Sorry it ain't more. You want some China money, too? I can get more of that easy enough."

"You're wonderful."

He counted out a pile of hundred-yuan bills. "Thirty-two. That's about four hundred, give or take."

Allison wrote him a check for five hundred dollars. "I can't tell you how grateful I am," she said.

He waved her off, folding the check and putting it in his wallet without looking at it. "Here's my card," he said. "You ever get to N'ohleans you look us up, heah?"

"I'll do that. I promise." Allison wondered whether to share more with him. She wanted desperately to do so, to ask for help, to at least have someone know what was happening. His would be a shoulder to cry on, if nothing else. But that was foolish. What could she possibly ask him—to hide her and the children in his baggage? He had already done her a great kindness, giving money to a stranger. Not many people would do that.

Gladys returned with her guidebook, settling the issue with her presence. Orville threw a wad of his remaining yuan on the table for the bill. "Nice meetin' ya, Allison. Gotta git before the shops close."

"And you. Thank you again."

"Don't menshunit," he said, and they were gone.

Allison considered what to do next. With cash she could buy a phone card—she'd decided IC must mean international call—and call Marshall from the lobby. She started to rise and then had a thought. At the buffet table she piled a plate high with cake, muffins, and apples. She saw the hostess watching and felt her face flush again. It always did that, a dead giveaway; it was one reason she was always so honest—she couldn't get away with anything. But she smiled and walked back to her table, where she casually sipped tea, stuffing the food into the bag at her feet whenever the hostess looked away. Each time she reached down to make another deposit, her stomach churned. *Now I'm a food thief, too.*

She stood to leave when something on the Purvises' table caught her eye. Gladys had left her hotel passport behind. It was a purple pocket-size folder with the hotel's name written on the front in English and Chinese. Allison had had one like it in Suzhou. She picked it up and glanced inside. There was a plastic room key.

At that moment the hostess approached her table with the bill. "Your room number, please?" Allison started to reach into her pocket, but then a shocking idea took root. She had to preserve her cash.

Like the store, Orville had said.

"Seven eleven." The hostess wrote it down. Allison signed the ticket in a scrawl.

Not allowing herself to think about what she was doing, she went downstairs to one of the shops. She bought diapers, formula, and a variety of medicines—aspirin, bandages, antibiotic ointment, and other supplies. At another store she bought a fresh set of clothes for herself and Ruth, clothes like she'd seen Chinese wearing. She found a new T-shirt for Tyler and batteries for his video game.

The purchases mounted up and the charges were always the same. "Seven eleven," she said.

A short while later, the elevator door slid open and she emerged onto the seventh floor. Using the placard for a guide, she walked past the floor attendant's desk, which was deserted, and found room 711. She knocked lightly, her heart beating wildly. Silence. She swiped the card through the lock. The little door light flashed red. She tried again. Red again. Flustered, she hesitated, afraid a third failure might make some alarm sound or switch the lock off. She glanced up and down the hall, to see if anyone was watching. She checked the room number again, to be sure she had the right one. She stepped back and examined the back of the key card by the dim light coming from the hallway ceiling. There was a little diagram, with arrows. She realized she was putting the card through backward. *Some engineer,* she thought as she swiped it again. The light flashed green and the door clicked open. She slipped into the room and closed the door behind her. She saw luggage and clothing and packages, and her guilt soared. Orville had trusted her, and now she was violating his privacy, his life.

She sat on one of the double beds and looked at the phone. To her relief there was a card on top that explained how to place both local and international calls. She wouldn't have to use the front desk. She started with the international call first. She was shaking and had to start over twice because of mistakes. A noise in the hall brought her heart to her throat. She hung up and stood, ready to bolt if the room door opened. She heard the click of a door closing down the hall and then silence. She closed her eyes and took a deep breath. She dialed again. As she heard the phone ringing, she realized she hadn't planned what she would say when—if— Marshall answered.

The telephone rang first at her house in Colorado. Through a miracle of communications technology the call was routed via microwave, satellite, and landline back through space and halfway around the world, where it rang in a hospital room less than five hundred miles from where she stood. In the parking lot outside the hospital, a tape recorder switched on.

Marshall's voice flooded her with relief. "God, I'm so happy to hear from you. Are you okay? How's Tyler?"

"He's fine. We all are. I left him with Wen Li and Ruth."

"Left him? Where are you?"

"A hotel room."

"Where?"

"Nanchang. It's near—"

"I can't hear you. My ears—"

"Nanchang," she said, louder. "Are *you* okay? You sound sick. Groggy."

"Yeah, I'm fine. Just glad to hear from you. The boat—it's been all over the news."

"We got off okay."

"They said Nash Cameron didn't. They said he's dead."

Allison gripped the phone. "We didn't know. We got separated. It was dark. We couldn't see what happened."

"People *died,* that's what happened. You've had me worried sick."

She heard the anger in his voice. "I'm know. I'm sorry. I called as quickly as I could."

"They say you were smuggling arms."

"That's ridiculous."

"I know that. But they don't, or at least they're not admitting it. They've got a massive hunt going on for you—kidnapping, murder—"

"Murder?"

"Accessory murder. Some police died in the collision. You were being sought for kidnapping when the crash occurred. That makes you legally responsible, too. This hole you're digging is getting deeper every minute."

"Oh God . . ." She sighed. "Marshall, we didn't have anything to do with that." She closed her eyes. "I know this is a mess. I'd give anything not to be in it. But I can't change what's already happened."

"Where are you going?"

"To Guangzhou, I guess."

"How?"

"I don't know, exactly. People have been helping us. A fisherman who lives near here, and I have a name here in Nanchang, that our guide gave us. I'm trying everything. If I can get to Guangzhou, I'm going to need help from the consulate there. Can you do anything? Can Clarence?"

"Allison, goddammit, you need to stop this. You need to turn yourself in, before you get hurt. You have no *right* to put Tyler through this—"

"I tried to get him to Shanghai," Allison started to explain, "but—"

"It doesn't matter! Jesus, you have no right to put *yourself* through this, or me! I'd die if anything happened to you. And the embassy has already said it's going to follow the law—the Chinese law. That means even if you do make it, they'll just turn you in. You're risking lives for nothing—you haven't any hope."

Allison was near tears now, her voice breaking. "I was hoping you'd say *we,* Marshall. Something about *our* hope."

Marshall was bitter. "I wish I had been there. I wish you'd asked me. I wish you'd thought about all this before you ran. But I wasn't, and you didn't, and now we're *not* in it together, Allison. You're making the decisions without me, and I think you're making bad ones. I think what you're doing is both dangerous and wrong, and I love you, but I'm so angry at you I just—"

"Can't you understand? I don't have a choice!" she nearly yelled in despair.

"Do you think this is easy for me? I don't want to be doing this. I certainly don't want to be doing it alone. But I've made up my mind. I'm not giving up Wen Li without a fight. I'm going to make it to Guangzhou, Marshall. I don't know how, but I'm going to do it. If it ends there, if they want to turn me in after that, they're going to have to look me in the eye first. At least I'll have that much before I give up." She was shaking again. "Look, I don't need you to tell me how screwed up this all is. I just need to know if you're going to help."

There was a long silence on the line. "Of course I am," he said at last. "I love you, Allison."

Allison pressed the phone to her cheek, to be closer to him. "I know you're angry with me," she said softly. "I wish I could make you understand."

"What? I can't hear."

"I love you, too," Allison said, more loudly. She bit her lip. "I have to go now. I'll call you again."

CHAPTER 17

"**S**HE'S BEING HELPED by a fisherman," Marshall said. "He lives near Nanchang. She's in a hotel there right now. She's going to Guangzhou. That's all I could find out."

"I know how difficult this is for you, Marshall," Victor said. "But you're doing the right thing. I'll call you later." With that he hung up.

Marshall felt his head swimming. *No, Victor,* he thought. *You don't have any idea how difficult it is.*

Victor Li called his private investigator and had him play back the recording of Marshall's conversation with Allison, to cross-check what Marshall had told him. Then he called his client on the mainland. More calls followed, and within moments Colonel Quan had the information.

Quan called the Nanchang PSB, dispatching officers to every hotel in the city. They were to begin with the half dozen that catered to foreigners and then sweep the rest as necessary. Every lobby was to be watched, every clerk and hotel shopkeeper shown the woman's photograph. As Quan issued his orders, scores of sheets bearing Allison's visa photo churned from a copy machine in the central police station. Officers grabbed copies and fanned out to Nanchang's hotels.

Quan hung up and sat thinking. An infinite hunt had become a finite hunt, a manageable hunt. *A fisherman who lives near here,* the Turk woman had said. *And a name that our guide gave us.* It wasn't much, but it was something. Yi Ling might have put the Americans on a fishing boat near Hukou; she most certainly had given them a name.

Yi Ling was the key.

He called Major Ma and gave him the news. "There is no time for finesse in your methods. Use whatever means are necessary. I need the information *now*, old friend. Do not disappoint me."

Quan hung up and turned to a map of Poyang. Without a name to go on, searching for a fisherman was next to impossible. Near Nanchang there were literally hundreds of villages scattered over a vast area lined with canals, rivers, inlets, and bays. Because the water rose sharply during this time of year, not all the villages were even accessible by road. If one included the Gan and Fu Rivers in the search—both navigable waterways that supported fleets of small fishing boats—the number increased dramatically. Despite the odds, Quan was undeterred. If nothing else, he had manpower.

As the search narrowed to one corner of the province, police were awakened and called to duty. He called the Hukou PSB at the northern end of the lake, where the Americans had disappeared. He ordered the dock master rousted from his bed and taken to his bureau. The man was to search records of boat registrations, for fishermen who used his docks in the summer but lived somewhere in the south of the lake in winter.

Officers were sent to board every fishing vessel docked for the night within ten kilometers of Hukou. Occupants were to be questioned about fishermen they knew who lived in the south—fishermen who had not returned to their normal berths in the past two days. PSB county offices along the southern reaches of Poyang Hu were dispatched to visit local docks, looking for signs of the *lao wai*. Somewhere, Quan knew, someone had seen them.

Twenty-six minutes after Marshall and Allison hung up, Quan was airborne once more, closing in for the kill.

At eleven o'clock Ruth knew it was time to do something. She didn't know what, only that she must do *something*. Tai was on fire, every part of her body burning up—her ears, her toes, her fingers. The infant fever drops weren't helping any more than the cool washcloths with which Ruth had been lightly rubbing her body. The child wouldn't take water. She was crying hoarsely and her cough was gathering strength. She was past any help Ruth knew how to give her. Ruth gently brushed back wet wispy strands of Tai's hair. The Wee Duck was *sick*.

Ruth crawled over to Mei Ling and shook her gently on the shoulder. Mei Ling awoke with a start. "Please," Ruth said. "It's Tai."

Instantly Mei Ling was alert. She looked at the baby and decided at once. *"Jin Shan dài fu,"* she said, pointing outside the boat somewhere. *"Wǒ mén zǒu."*

Ruth covered Tai in a light summer blanket. "We'll have to take the children," she said, nodding toward Tyler and Wen Li.

Mei Ling shook her head. She led Ruth to the cabin window. The neck of the cove was quite narrow. She pointed to a house on other side, just up a short hill. *"Jin Shan,"* she said, indicating Tai and then the house, making the connection. There was help at that house. Then she slid open the cabin door and showed her their transport to get across the neck of the cove. It was a tiny boat, more plank than canoe, too small for them all. With more gestures Mei Ling made it clear—she would take Ruth and Tai to Jin Shan, then return to stay with the children. *"Hai zi mèn zài zèr hen an quán. Wǒ mén cóng nàr néng kàn jiàn ta mén."*

Ruth's nerves were too shot for her to argue. She knew Allison and Ren ought to be returning soon anyway. She knelt by Tyler. "Tyler! Tyler! Wake up!"

She shook him and he sat up, rubbing his eyes. "Hunh?"

"Tai is sick, Tyler. I'm taking her to get help. We'll be just over there." She showed him the house. "Your mom isn't back yet, but she should be here soon. Tell her where we are. You need to stay here, with Wen Li. She'll sleep through the night, but you've got to look out for her, Tyler. Can you do that?"

Tyler was still half-asleep himself. "Yeah. I guess."

Mei Ling brought the little boat around and helped Ruth climb in. Mei Ling paddled across the narrow passage and then stood thigh-deep in the water while Ruth stepped onto the shore. They hurried up the hill.

The house of Jin Shan was in a compound with three others, surrounded by a low brick wall. They stepped over the broken wooden gate and into a courtyard muddy from the rain. Ruth could hear vague animal noises from inside a low shed with a thatched roof where the small animals found shelter. By the light of Mei Ling's flashlight, she saw the fluffy white forms of chickens asleep just inside the doorway.

Mei Ling knocked and called out quietly. She repeated her call several times until an old man answered. He peered out into the darkness without opening the door all the way.

"Old Jin, it is Mei Ling. Get your wife, please. There is a sick baby." When the old man saw who it was, and saw the baby in Ruth's arms, he bade them come in immediately. They stood in a cramped entry. He showed them into a small room where he wanted them to wait, then disappeared. The room was a tiny office, crammed to overflowing. The walls were lined with wooden shelves. Files and journals and thick books with curled pages were stacked on a table. Papers were stuffed in every opening, the overflow set in piles on the floor. On the desk stood a small mannequin, illustrating hundreds of acupuncture points. Charts above the desk depicted different views of the human ear, on which more hundreds of points were detailed, the significance of each explained on tiny marginal notes.

The room was partitioned by curtains that hid two tiny examination rooms, each of which held a cot. Steel shelves lined the walls, filled with plastic boxes. Lettering on the front identified the flowers, herbs, or insects inside. Other shelves held bottles and boxes of medicines. There were potted plants and flowers and bulbs. Drying leaves hung from ceiling hooks, stems tied together with string. A score of smells blended to give the room an indefinable yet pleasant fragrance.

They heard voices in the back, and soon a woman appeared, chattering rapidly. She was tiny, her hair snow white and drawn back underneath a scarf. She was ancient but full of energy and greeted Mei Ling with a broad smile. Ruth saw warmth and humor and intelligence all etched deeply into her wrinkled face. Her eyes melted in compassion when she saw Tai. She regarded Ruth curiously. "English?"

Startled to hear the word, Ruth nodded. "Yes . . . I mean, American."

"Sit there," Jin Shan said, indicating one of the cots. She turned on a light and drew a chair up beside the cot. Gently she began her examination of Tai, peering at the child through glasses whose lenses were cracked. She took her temperature and listened to her heart and lungs with a stethoscope, all the while peppering Ruth with questions in halting but clear English about the progression of the fever. She looked at the pills Ruth had been giving the child. Tai struggled angrily as Jin Shan prodded her tongue and peered into her throat. Ruth tried to quiet the child and felt immense relief to be so near a woman so radiant with confidence and whose touch seemed so sure. Instinctively she knew Tai was in good hands.

"The child is not strong," Jin Shan said. She touched the soft spot on the baby's head and noted it was somewhat recessed. "Very . . . I don't know the word . . . waterless inside. If we cannot get her to drink, we must give her drink through needle in veins." She turned to a small propane stove and started heating water, then busied herself making an herbal mixture. While that was cooking, she poked through some boxes in her pharmacy and soon found what she wanted. She crushed some pills with a mortar and pestle and poured the powder into a small cup of water, to which she added some honey. "*Yin qiao,*" she said. "Medicine very bitter." Even with the honey Tai wanted nothing to do with the concoction and batted angrily at the cup. "Ah!" Jin Shan chuckled and cooed. "Maybe not strong, but very filled of fire! Good sign." Deftly she held Tai's nose, forcing her to open her mouth. Timing her movements with the baby's cries, Jin Shan got the mixture down her throat. Tai sputtered and choked and her eyes watered.

Jin Shan then prepared a syringe, drawing a milky liquid from a vial she took from a small refrigerator. She turned Tai over and gave her the shot in her bright pink buttocks. At that Tai howled like a banshee, and Ruth cried with her, her tears falling onto Tai's hot skin. Finally Jin Shan filled a plastic bag with ice cubes. She showed Ruth where to rub, to help reduce her temperature. As Ruth began the rub, Jin Shan sat once again and took Tai's little hand in her own. She examined it closely, turning it over, and then repeated the process with the other hand.

"What are you looking for?" Ruth asked.

Jin Shan pointed to a barely discernible line on Tai's index finger. Ruth had to put on her reading glasses to see, and even then she wasn't certain she was looking at the right place. "Finger line of baby," the doctor said. "Very important. We watch tonight. Now it is light red, but short. It stops between first and second finger joint—there, you see?" Ruth didn't. "We must watch carefully," Jin Shan said. "Already bad enough. But if it darkens or grows longer, that mean trouble."

"I don't think I see what you mean," Ruth said, worried she might miss something.

"Not worry—it is for me to watch," Jin Shan said. She stood. "Enough medicine for Tai. Now some for you—you will have some tea?"

"I've already put you to too much trouble," Ruth said, but Jin Shan waved her off and soon the three women were drinking tea and talking quietly in a mixture of English and Chinese while Tai slept fitfully.

Jin Shan was full of questions. She asked about Ruth, about her home and family, about how she came to her front door in the middle of the night with a sick baby. Ruth had debated only briefly with herself about whether or not to tell the truth, since she realized that not even Mei Ling or her husband, Ren Kai, knew the true circumstances of their situation. But there was no real debate. Ruth told her everything. Jin Shan listened wide-eyed to the story, stopping periodically to translate for Mei Ling, whose own eyes grew at the tale. They sat together and talked late into the night. Several times Mei Ling left to check on the children asleep on the boat. They hadn't stirred.

Ruth learned that Jin Shan cared for nearly four hundred families near the village, using a blend of Western and Chinese traditional medicine. She had been to medical school in Taiwan and practiced acupuncture, massage, and herbal medicine. She stitched farmers' cuts and delivered babies. She said that seven years earlier, on her seventieth birthday, her husband had wanted her to slow down. But there had been no one else to do the work for the village, whose inhabitants would otherwise have to travel all the way to Nanchang to find another doctor. The work kept her young, she said, adding that her work probably did her more good than she did for the villagers. "Soon must quit, though. Eyes bad now. Hands not so steady. Sometime needles poke wrong spot." Her eyes twinkled, and Ruth laughed. She had watched every move of Jin Shan's, and there was no sign of tremor.

It was very late when Jin Shan finally dozed off. Ruth had seen her eyes growing heavy-lidded, but Jin Shan had waved off her suggestions that she go to bed, insisting on staying awake to check on the child. But then she fell asleep in her chair, literally in midsentence. Ruth and Mei Ling did what they could to make her comfortable, slipping a pillow between her neck and the chair.

A while later Mei Ling rose to check once again on the boat. Ruth smiled up at her, grateful beyond words for her help and sorry beyond words for the danger she faced as a result. Ruth said all that with her eyes and with her grasp as she took the younger woman's hand in her own. Mei Ling understood perfectly. She squeezed and smiled back.

Ruth checked Tai's finger, looking for the line. The light was not good and she didn't know anyway what she was trying to spot. She did see a line but didn't know if it was the right one. There seemed to be more than one. She thought it looked purplish, and the thought constricted her chest with fear. But Tai seemed to be sleeping all right, and she didn't want to wake Jin Shan. Ruth envied the woman her stamina and wished she had half as much. She turned off the light and sat in the darkness, listening to the light snores of Jin Shan and the sickness rattling in Tai's chest. She brushed the hair from Tai's forehead, a bit less fevered but still flushed. Ruth needed sleep but dared not let it come.

* * *

Allison hung up the phone in Orville's room. There was still no answer at the number Yi Ling had given her to call in Nanchang. She looked at her watch. She'd been too long already and ought to leave. She paced the room, waiting to call again, and saw her reflection in the mirror. She was still a mess; she wanted a shower desperately. She decided to wait five more minutes and try one last time to call. And in five minutes, she knew, she could take a shower.

She started the water running and stripped quickly, laying her clothes on the vanity. She stepped into the tiled enclosure, letting the water run over her, washing away days of accumulated grime. She shampooed twice and scrubbed her skin with a washcloth. The steam was relaxing, the water glorious. She lost herself in its soothing flow.

Downstairs in the lobby, the doorman pulled open the heavy glass entrance door. Huffing from his walk, Orville Purvis nodded at the man and stepped aside to let his wife in. Gladys started for the elevators. "Jus' a minute, hon," Orville said. "I got to change some money."

"My feet hurt," Gladys said. "Can't you do it in the morning?"

"Got an early appointment and I don't have any cash. I can't even buy a newspaper."

"You can't read the newspapers here anyway," Gladys whined. But she followed him to the counter and set her bags on the floor.

Orville told the clerk what he wanted and extracted six traveler's checks from his wallet. He began countersigning the checks as the clerk figured the exchange. She was counting out Orville's money when the front door opened again and three uniformed police entered. Orville paid little attention as they approached the desk. One of them rudely interrupted the clerk. The officer extracted a paper from a manila file and slipped it across the marble counter. Orville was turning away, bending to pick up his wife's packages, when he got a good look at the black-and-white photograph. It was grainy, but that didn't matter. The face startled him. "Lookee there," he said quietly to Gladys. "It's that woman from dinner." Gladys's eyes widened, but she said nothing.

As the clerk studied the photo, one of the officers studied the couple. Even if Western faces looked similar to him, it was clear the woman standing next to him in the lobby wasn't the one in the picture. He turned back to the clerk. She slapped her hand on the counter, indicating she didn't know. *"Duì bù qǐ,"* she said. "I just came on duty. I have not seen this woman."

"Where is the manager?"

"Upstairs in the buffet, I think I will get him."

"Be quick about it."

Dear Mr. and Mrs. Purvis:

I must ask your forgiveness. I have abused your kindness. You left your room card on the table at dinner and I borrowed it. I charged some things with it, in some of the shops downstairs. I also made some phone calls. I am leaving another check that will cover everything, along with something extra for your trouble.

Please believe I would never have done this if I didn't have to. I wish I could explain. Perhaps someday I'll have a chance.

Allison Turk

P.S. I also used your shower.

She wrote the note with the telephone cradled on her shoulder, waiting for an answer at the other end. She scribbled out a check, estimating the total and adding a hundred dollars. She set the check on top of the note and reluctantly hung up the phone. Maybe Yi Ling had written the number wrong. Without an address there was nothing more to be done. She rose and gathered her bags. She looked around one last time to be certain she hadn't forgotten anything.

She flicked off the lights and opened the door, and found herself staring into the startled, angry eyes of Orville Purvis.

"What the hell you doing in my room?" Orville thundered.

Allison stammered and stuttered and blushed. "I . . . I . . . left a note," she said, as if that explained something.

"Oh, good, a thief who leaves *notes*," Gladys said. "I think we should call security, Orville. She's been inside our room!"

"I can see that, hon," Orville said.

"I didn't take anything."

"Then what were you doing?"

"Please . . . I have to go." Allison started backing down the hall, ready to run. "Please don't call anyone. Read the note. I'll call you when I get back to the States. I promise."

"She's been *inside*, Orville!" Gladys said it again, looking fearfully down the entry hall into their room, half expecting Allison's accomplices to pop out of a closet with guns blazing and knives flashing. "Well, are you just going to *stand* there?"

Orville stared at Allison. He considered himself a good judge of character. At dinner he had liked her instinctively, but he was not a man to suffer abuse gladly—and this woman was beginning to smell powerfully of abuse. "Did you take anything?" he asked sternly.

"Who *cares* if she took anything?" Gladys snapped. "She was in our *room!* No wonder they're looking for her! I'm going to call the manager myself!"

"What?" Allison looked over her shoulder, toward the elevators. "Who's looking for me?"

Orville stood fast, uncertain what to do. From inside the room they heard Gladys on the phone, getting hysterical. "I want to speak with the manager!" she demanded loudly. "There's a burglar up here! No, dammit, I said burglar! T-h-i-e-f! Don't you understand plain English?"

Allison looked beseechingly at the big man. "You've got to believe me. I didn't—"

Orville made his decision. "You'd better git," he said. "But don't take the elevator. There's some cops in the lobby. They got your picture."

"God bless you, Orville," Allison said. She turned and raced for the stairwell. She flew down the seven flights of stairs as if on wings. At the first floor there was a steel door with a glass window that overlooked the lobby. Through it she glimpsed the police near the front desk. The night manager stood in their midst, talking animatedly.

Allison ran back up the stairs to the second level. She banged through a door and fled down a hall that led past a kitchen. More stairs descended to the hotel's rear courtyard. As she took them two at a time, she blew by a cook. Startled to see a hotel guest there, he stood aside to let her pass. At the bottom of the stairs a sign promised in bright red Chinese and English letters that an alarm would sound if she opened the steel door. She never hesitated. She shoved the brass handle and stepped outside. A bell rang shrilly as the door swung shut behind her.

In the lobby, one of the officers looked up at the sound. He looked quizzically at the night manager. "A rear door alarm," the manager said. "It is not uncommon to hear—"

"Quickly!" the officer snapped, dispatching one of his men in the direction of the bell. Before the door closed behind the man, the first officer was already phoning in his report. "The night manager has identified her," he said excitedly. "She was here, trying to change money. I need more men!"

At the sound of the alarm Allison broke into a run, keeping to the shadows. She rounded a corner and found herself back on the busy, well-lit street. She slowed to a fast walk, looking over her shoulder. Crowds of pedestrians bustled along the streets. No one emerged from the hotel driveway behind her. She walked the opposite direction from the front door of the hotel. She went the long way around the block, making her way back to where she'd left Ren Kai. To her relief she found him sound asleep in the back of the cart. She jumped in and shook him awake.

As he started the engine and pulled away from the curb, a police car rocketed past, siren blaring, lights flashing. It screeched to a halt in front of the hotel.

Ma Lin had misjudged her.

First, the drugs failed. The guide Yi Ling floated on them for hours, coming very close to where he wanted to take her. But she never arrived. When Major Ma had taken her as near to the edge as he dared, he switched methods, fearful that more chemicals would either kill her or send her into irreversible psychosis.

So late the night of her capture, as he was leaving for Suzhou to review orphanage files, Major Ma ordered a noise generator installed outside her cell. When used in conjunction with sleep deprivation, the device showed extreme promise. By itself, sleep deprivation caused temporary hallucinations, releasing stress chemicals in the LSD family into the brain. Subjects became paranoid, imagining that they were being devoured by rats or that their clothes were on fire. At the same time their powers of reason began to fail, making them more susceptible to manipulation, but sometimes it also had the counterproductive effect of disrupting the very memories that were being sought.

But the generator, developed by the Israelis for dealing with their Palestinian problem and further refined at the Ministry of State Security, added a promising dimension. It operated at the very fringes of the ranges that could be detected by the human ear, producing sound that was profoundly disturbing, sound that scarred nothing but the psyche.

Yi Ling was kept awake in a standing position, until her eyelids drooped and her muscles quivered uncontrollably. Her heart and respiration rates soared with her blood pressure. Her mind and body were near collapse. Now, after forty-eight hours of it, when Ma Lin applied different frequencies to the generator, the effect on her could be seen: she would stiffen, or begin to cry, or shake uncontrollably, or wet herself. Through it all he was there with her, soothing, prompting, promising her relief if only she would do as he asked. He was genuinely upset when she became incontinent. He gave her a towel to wipe herself, but she couldn't hold it. Her fingers wouldn't close over it, and it fell to the ground in the puddle. She bit her lip deeply, and he wiped the blood clean himself.

He skillfully wove threats through promises that were wrapped in rewards. He assured her that he alone could prevent harm to her grandfather Yang and his wife. He told her she could visit Yang Boda, who was recovering in a hospital. "He's been calling for you," Ma Lin told her. "He needs you. Tell me what I want, and then you can call him. And after that, my child, you can sleep."

But through it all he learned only two things from her.

He had misjudged her, and he feared her.

She was extraordinarily strong. Sometimes she was unresponsive; at others she babbled nonsense, or, briefly, she became lucid. And at those moments she haunted him with similarities to his dead daughter. There was a slight physical resemblance between them, certainly, and their ages were very nearly the same, and he felt an overpowering tenderness toward her.

But it wasn't that. It was their shared trait of defiance in the face of overwhelming odds. While Yi Ling was not in mortal peril, at least not from him, she certainly felt the agony of his ministrations. Yet she found the strength inside to resist. In her lucid moments her first question was always about her family or about the babies from the orphanage.

She doesn't even know those babies.

Her courage made him uncomfortable. Like his own daughter, she was driven by some invisible force he had never felt and would never understand. He rubbed his eyes, wondering if he hadn't been working too hard. He noticed his own hands were shaking and his stomach churned with acid. He was ready to give up.

But then Quan called, his voice brusque. His tone made it clear that

Ma Lin had let him down. Quan needed names: a fisherman; a contact in Nanchang. He needed it no matter the cost to Yi Ling.

Ma Lin understood his orders but could not bring himself to do it. He was a technician, not some bloodthirsty inquisitor. There was, of course, an easy solution, a lieutenant in the Jiujiang bureau who was not queasy about more vigorous measures. Such men were always readily available. Reluctantly Ma Lin summoned him. They passed each other in the hallway. The lieutenant pushed a cart that carried probes and heavy batteries. Wires dangled from the cart and trailed on the floor behind. Major Ma averted his eyes as he stepped aside to let him pass.

He waited down the hall, where he sat in a chair and studied the veined cracks in the stucco wall and lost himself in other places. Her shrieks brought him back from his reverie and he found himself running. He burst into the room as the lieutenant stood aside, a smug look on his proud young face.

"I am here now, my child," Ma Lin cooed as he removed the electrical leads and covered her naked lower body with a sheet. He loosened the straps that bound her ankles and wrists and helped her to a sitting position. She was sobbing uncontrollably. She bent over, cramping. There was a spot of blood. He gave her water and tried to quiet her. "There, there," he said. "It will be all right now."

"I want . . . tell you, Father," she said, crying and coughing. "I want to help you. Please don't let him hurt me anymore."

"He won't harm you while I am here." He waved the other man from the room. "There, you see? He's gone now."

She coughed again until she nearly choked. "I want to help, but I don't . . . I can't remember now what it was you wanted." She sobbed. He soothed her, whispering and stroking her hair. She told him everything she could remember then, names and places and details. She even remembered names from her childhood and started telling him those.

Ma Lin's tears were real as he held her close. He hated himself for this wretched work.

They aren't even her own babies.

Within seconds of receiving the report from the hotel where Allison was sighted, Quan further tightened the net of security around the city, ordering even secondary roads blocked and all vehicles checked. A cook reported seeing the woman fleeing the hotel. An army of police scoured the neighborhood, while more officers inside searched every room, corridor, and closet. Quan himself questioned the staff, many of whom were being summoned from home.

Quan was about to go upstairs to talk with some Americans named Purvis. The man's wife had reported a burglar at the same time Mrs. Turk had been in the hotel. Quan was just stepping into the elevator when his cell phone rang.

It was Ma Lin, calling from Jiujiang. Quan heard the weariness in the major's voice.

"The fisherman's name is Ren Kai," Ma said. "He lives in Youlan."

Mei Ling stood outside the house of Jin Shan, keeping watch over her boat. She was restless and knew there would be no sleep this night. After Jin Shan had explained things about the *lao wai* and their flight from the police, Mei Ling had understood at last the full extent of the danger they all faced. There had been a moment when she had been genuinely angry at the *lao wai,* but that passed when she asked herself what she would have done for her only child, a son who was now safely grown and working in a factory in Changsha because there weren't enough fish in Poyang Hu for him to follow in the footsteps of his father. Their lives had been simple and anonymous. They fished and paid taxes and once a year, at the New Year, visited relatives and shot off a hundred yuan's worth of fireworks. She had never done anything even remotely contrary to the law. Her life had been spent without risk. She had never thought about it before; it was simply the way of things. And then, two nights earlier, for the first time in her life and for reasons she didn't even understand at the time, she had lied to the police about strangers she was hiding. She wondered if she would do it again, and she knew the answer was yes.

Now that she understood their trouble, she felt a more immediate fear, that something had gone terribly wrong. It would soon be morning. Her husband should have returned by now with Allison. She watched the road beyond the village, expecting each moment to see or hear the motorized cart he'd borrowed from a village friend, but the night was quiet. There was nothing she could do inside the house. She watched the boat and waited.

She heard the noise before she saw what made it, and she knew it wasn't the cart. There were two distinct motors, a car and a motorcycle.

She peered in the direction from which they were coming and saw the flashing lights before she could make out the vehicles. The sight shot terror to the quick of her soul.

Police.

She hoped they would go past the village but knew instinctively why they had come and what they would do next. She was right. The lights stopped just past the turnout, the only place with enough room to park without blocking the narrow road. There was the sound of doors closing and distant muffled voices.

"Jin Shan!" she called inside. "The *gong an ju* have come! I am going for the children!" Without waiting for a response and without a plan, Mei Ling broke into a dead run, leaping over the broken gate, running headlong down the slope to the water. She saw flashlights on the other side of village, reflected off the walls of the narrow walkways between houses. She knew they would be a few moments coming; they would have to roust the village headman first, to ask directions. She leapt into the canoe and paddled madly, propelling the little boat across the neck of the cove. The paddle slipped in her wet palms, and her heart pounded. She was out of the boat even before it was all the way to the pier, grasping for a hold on the wooden supports. She nearly lost her grip but just managed to pull herself up. She scampered across the wooden pier and onto her boat. "Tyler!" she hissed, jabbing him more sharply than she had intended with her shoe. She flipped open a compartment and picked out a few things, throwing them into one of the babies' bags. She scooped up Wen Li and the blankets. "Tyler!"

He sat up, confused and cranky. "What? I'm tired. Lemme . . ." He started to lie back down again.

Mei Ling shook him, almost violently now, her voice an urgent whisper. *"Jǐng chá! Wo mén bì xu ma shàng zou!"*

Tyler heard the urgency in her voice and sat up. "Huh?"

"Jǐng chá!" Mei Ling hissed again.

Tyler didn't know what she was saying, but he could tell that she wasn't horsing around. He stood and looked out the window. Near the village he saw some moving flashlights. "What is it?"

Mei Ling didn't answer. With her free hand she thrust one bag and then another at him. He was awakening quickly as he realized they were about to go somewhere. Wen Li whimpered a little but didn't awaken.

"Where is everybody?" he asked. He didn't remember Ruth leaving.

"*Lái!*" Mei Ling pulled him out of the cabin and onto the pier.

She looked at the lights, desperately considering what to do. The finger of land on which their house was built was effectively a dead end. There was nowhere to run, except into the arms of the approaching police. There were two houses on the spit, hers and that of her sister and her family, who, she had learned the previous evening, had gone to see her husband's ill father in Jingdezhen. Mei Ling knew she couldn't hide the children there or in her own house, and she couldn't leave them in the boat. The police would search all of those places. Nor could she try to flee in the boat. By the time she got its cranky old engine started, they'd be all over her. There wasn't even time to take the canoe back toward Jin Shan's house. It was too late now, and surely they would be seen.

They were trapped.

The voices grew louder, and she felt the hot rush of fear. She started down the pier with Wen Li. Tyler hurried along behind, lugging the bags. Without a plan, she moved away from the police, across one of the low dikes that surrounded the rice paddy closest to the water. They made their way along the top, moving toward the dead end of the spit, and then circled back around behind the two houses. From there she could see back up the strip of land to the village. It was all open to view.

There was no way out, and they couldn't swim. She turned around and looked back in the direction from which they'd come.

She had an idea.

"*Lái lái! Kuài diǎn,*" she hissed at Tyler, and propelled him toward her sister's house. There was a separate enclosure behind the structure, between the dwelling and the water. It was surrounded by a wooden fence. Inside was a low mud-brick hut with a thatched roof and a couple of pens. As they raced for it, Tyler tripped and went down, yelping in pain.

"Dang it!" he called softly.

Mei Ling backtracked on the slippery dike, stooping to help him up and clucking her tongue. "*Xiao xin, bié shuāi dao.*" He got up and retrieved one of the bags that had fallen into the paddy water. It was sopping.

They crossed the last few meters to the enclosure. Mei Ling fumbled with the rope catch on the gate and led them inside. Tyler heard animal noises. He followed her cautiously, trying to figure out where he was. The stench was overpowering. Mei Ling bent down and disappeared beneath a low roof.

Tyler nearly bumped into one of the enclosure's residents and gave a little squeak of fright. They were in the pigpen. Tyler had never touched a pig.

Mind racing, Mei Ling knew she had only seconds to act. If Ren had already been caught, there was nothing she could do. But if not, she had to get back onto the road somehow, to warm him before he drove into a trap. If he was still free, she would divert him and Allison to Jin Shan's house.

That meant she had to leave the children, at least for a while. There was nothing else to be done.

She spread the quilt she'd taken from the boat near the back of the pen, shooing one of the grunting, sleeping occupants into the other side of the pen. She took the bags from Tyler and set them down, then caught the boy by the shoulder and hurried him to a sitting position. She handed him Wen Li. It was just beginning to get light. Tyler could read the fear on her face and feel it in her every move.

"*Nǐ bì xū dāi zài zhèr.*" With urgent gestures she made it plain—he was not to move, not to go anywhere. She showed him the three plastic bottles of water in one of the bags, and the formula for Wen Li, and the other supplies. Still somewhat dumbfounded by the night's events and thoroughly frightened himself, Tyler paid close attention. She signaled that she was going to leave and come back later. And she pointed to where they could now see the police, just getting to the boat. She held her hand to her mouth, and crouched even lower, sheltering her head. *Be still,* she told him with her gestures. *You must hide.*

Tyler understood. "*Shì,*" he said.

Mei Ling wanted to stay a little longer, but she'd already taken too much time. She squeezed the boy on the shoulder. "*Yī huìr jiàn,*" she whispered, and backed out of the shelter. She slipped out of the gate and replaced its catch. Half crawling, half crouching, she made her way to the water's edge. A moment later she was swimming quietly. Her head barely visible on the water, she moved away from shore, then turned and swam past the entrance to the cove. She heard voices on her boat, but no one shouted. No one saw her. She was a strong swimmer and made half a kilometer before she dared come back ashore at the edge of a field on the far side of Youlan. Already breathing hard and sopping wet, but with no time to rest, Mei Ling started to run. She flew over the dikes and along the bicycle paths, her feet falling softly on the muddy earth. Just as the sun was rising, she arrived at the road that led back to the village. A few farmers were already on their way to the fields. She hid in a culvert, to await her husband.

CHAPTER 18

KEEPING OFF THE MAIN ROADS, Ren Kai sped through Nanchang, making his way to the east along side streets. Allison barely noticed the jolting ride. Her eyes were closed in exhaustion, her body and spirit drained from the night's events. Suddenly Ren Kai lurched to a stop. Allison pitched forward in the cab. She heard his urgent whisper and looked outside.

They were on a narrow street that fed into a busy intersection. Police cars stood in the middle of the intersection, blocking the way. Traffic was snarled as far as she could see in the direction of Nanchang. She almost didn't believe her own first thought, that they were there for her. But she knew they were.

Ren Kai quickly turned the cart around and jounced back down the street, looking for a way around the roadblock. He got lost twice, asking directions from half a dozen different people as he made his way through a dizzying maze of alleys and back streets. It was almost an hour before they arrived back at the main road. There were no police in sight.

It was very late by the time they neared his village of Youlan. Numb with fatigue, Allison saw the sun peeking up over the horizon. She longed for a soft bed but reflected happily that she would settle for the children instead.

At that instant Ren Kai gasped and stopped the cart. Mei Ling, her wet clothes clinging to her body, climbed in beside him. She talked excitedly, gesticulating and pointing toward the village.

"Jǐng chá lái le! Tā mén zài chuán shàng! Zài wǒ mén jiā!"

"Zěn me huì zhèi yàng?"

Allison panicked, not understanding it all, but she thought she recognized *jǐng chá. Police.* "What is it?" she asked, leaning forward to touch Mei Ling on the shoulder. "Are the children okay? Tyler? Wen Li?"

"Okay," Mei Ling said, but then she launched into more unintelligible chatter.

Ren Kai quickly turned the cart around and drove a short distance to a junction with a road that was even narrower than the one to the village. It was more path than road and led through a patchwork of rice paddies toward the lake. They bounced and slid along it until they came to a ram-shackle brick storage building that farmers shared for tools and carts. The tin roof was shot through with rust. A lone water buffalo stood nearby, chewing something and quite indifferent to their passage. Ren parked the cart between a high mound of hay and the building, where it couldn't be seen from the road. The three of them hurried along the dikes to the lake shore, then along that to Jin Shan's house.

Allison was frantic by the time she got inside. She was relieved to see Ruth but shocked by her drawn appearance. Allison started to ask about Tyler and Wen Li, but then she saw Tai on the table, Jin Shan tending to her, and her hand flew to her mouth. "What—"

"She's close to pneumonia," Ruth said. "She's in bad shape, but she's in good hands." She told Allison about the doctor, who had administered both herbal treatments and antibiotics.

"I'm so sorry," Allison whispered, hugging her.

Mei Ling told Jin Shan what she'd done with the children. Mindful of Allison's desperation, Jin Shan led her to the window. She pointed out the pens and explained what had happened.

"Just the *two* of them? Alone?" Allison felt her terror welling out of control. She could see three police near the boat, one with a radio. Another officer had just emerged from the front door of Mei Ling's sister's house. He said something to the one with the radio and then hurried along the path to the village. Behind him, past the house, she could see the edge of the pigpens. The children were so close, yet she couldn't reach them, couldn't help them at all. They might as well be on the moon. She couldn't imagine what they must be going through, how terrified Tyler must be. She worried about the pigs, about the wet, about whether they had enough food and water. She came very close at that moment to giving up, to running down the slope to the water and swimming across to them, to surrendering and bringing an end to their awful ordeal.

She leaned her forehead on the glass. "It was so stupid of me to have left them. Oh God, what was I thinking? I only got us a little money and didn't even find the person Yi Ling said would help. Marshall was a shit. The trip was a waste, and I nearly got caught because I took a fucking *shower,* for God's sake. How *could* I?"

Ruth put her arm around Allison's waist and gave her a squeeze. "Don't be foolish," she said. "If you'd been here, if we'd all been asleep on the boat, they'd have caught us for sure. They'll be all right. They only have to make it through the day. Tyler can do that. He's a good kid. Ren Kai can go after them tonight, when it's dark."

Allison couldn't help herself. "We're coming apart," she said, beginning to sob. "Tai is sick and they're all alone out there. Yi Ling is missing and we don't have a plan and what the hell are we going to *do,* anyway?"

Two lengthy faxes arrived for Major Ma Lin from the Suzhou PSB. He received them just after his session with Yi Ling, which had left him drained and once again unable to sleep. He poured himself a cup of tea and sat at a desk in the Jiujiang PSB. The first was a thirty-eight-page single-spaced log compiled by the officers he'd left working at the orphanage. Their handwritten notes listed babies' names, dates of birth, dates of entry into the orphanage, and date of exit, with disposition. The second fax was a similar list compiled by the officer he'd sent to the Ministry of Civil Affairs in Nanjing, listing children the ministry had either sent to the orphanage or transferred out.

He began with the list from the orphanage. He made a mark next to the names of those children whose files showed no disposition, meaning they were presumably still residents of the orphanage. To the right-hand side of the column he made a rough calculation of their age in years. The officers' handwriting was cramped and often sloppy. It took him several hours to work through the list. When he finished he went back to the beginning and counted the results. There were 617 files in all—175 infants, 168 toddlers, and 274 children between the ages of six and sixteen. He took out his notes from his visit to the orphanage and flipped through the pages until he found the entry from the senior auntie. She'd said there were 155 infants in all—20 fewer than he had files for. He knew there could be age discrepancies; that children he'd marked as infants might actually be living in another ward. He added up the entries he'd made from all the wards. There were 561 children in the orphanage the date of his visit. He hadn't counted noses himself but was reasonably certain the aunties knew their counts. Most likely files were incomplete, with the files of children who'd been transferred away not yet updated by the director, who did the paperwork himself. Short of matching the physical body of each child with its file, there was no way to know. And given the state of the records, he was certain that some children would have no files, while some files would have no children.

He turned his attention to the Civil Affairs log. It showed 1,255 children sent to the orphanage during the last twelve months, with 871 out through adoption, death, release to the streets, transfer to foster care, or transfer to other orphanages. There was no way to compare those numbers with the orphanage's files, because the orphanage made no consistent reference as to whether the children were referred through the ministry, the police, or a hospital.

Ma Lin sighed. Even if all the paperwork was there, it was so poorly organized that there was no way to know whether all the children were accounted for. Even the names were of no use, as names used by Civil Affairs weren't always the same as those used at the orphanage. Some were those given by birth mothers and left on notes pinned to the babies' clothing. Others were arbitrarily assigned by Civil Affairs or by the orphanage. He found some for whom the only name was Mei Ming and a number: No Name 6; No Name 14.

He poured another cup of tea and ran his fingers through his hair, thinking. He began making marks beside the names of children the ministry showed as current residents of the orphanage, then counted them. Seven hundred and twenty-two—over a hundred more than in the orphanage records. Because the orphanage also received children through other sources, he knew the discrepancy in numbers was even greater. Using a different color ink, he went down the list and marked the names of those children who had been adopted, another color for those who had died, and a third for those who'd been transferred to foster care or other orphanages. Each time, a comparison of records showed variances that would be impossible to explain without weeks or months of investigative work. There wasn't time for that.

His eye kept coming back to the green marks, the color he'd used for the dead. It shocked him to realize just how much green there was: on all the papers now strewn over his desk, there was a green sea of death. He tapped his pen on the pile. It occurred to him that Civil Affairs could quickly provide one more list that might help him sort through the mess. In addition to running the orphanages, the ministry also ran the country's crematoria. He made a few phone calls, rousted bureaucrats from their beds, and within two hours was copying down their answers to his questions.

He studied the new information and leafed back through his notes. He felt a chill as he realized he was at last asking the right questions.

Six hundred and nine, the Civil Affairs crematorium records said.

Eight hundred and thirty-two, the orphanage records reported.

Five hundred and twenty-seven, according to the Civil Affairs orphanage bureau records.

One way or another, one thing was clear to Major Ma Lin, as the sun rose over Jiujiang. He was seeing more than paperwork confusion.

Something was happening to the children at the Number Three Children's Welfare Institute in Suzhou. Hundreds of them.

And he couldn't explain what or how.

"The fisherman Ren Kai is not in his home, Colonel Quan," the officer said on the radio. "His boat did arrive last night and he was seen in the village. The neighborhood captain says that no *lao wai* were seen with him. He borrowed a cart and has not returned."

"Did anyone see him leave in the cart?"

"No, Colonel. It was after dark. It was raining."

Quan cursed his timing. So close, yet he'd missed them. By now they were undoubtedly racing south toward Guangzhou. From Nanchang they had a clear shot, over the Dongnan Qiuling mountains to the south. Yet he must not ignore the possibility they were still hiding under his nose, as they had done for a day after the sinking of the *432 Springtime Flower*. "Keep your men there," he said to the officer, just in case. "Ren Kai may return."

Quan reviewed the placement of the roadblocks he'd ordered the night before. The roads to the south and southwest, through Linchuan, Ganzhou, and Chenzhou, were each blocked in five different spots. For good measure he had covered the road west, to Changsha, in case they went there first. As usual, the airport and train and bus stations were blanketed with police, photographs distributed, passenger manifests examined. As usual, there was nothing. He ordered the roadblocks increased on the roads to the south, saturating even the back roads, until the PSBs in the counties complained they had no manpower left for other duties. Quan manipulated the provincial forces like pieces on a chess board.

A clerk told him the deputy minister was on the telephone. In all his years with the ministry, Quan had never dreaded a call from a superior. He knew a call at this hour would not be a cordial one. As he lifted the receiver and listened, the voice of his old mentor was cold and hard. It was the same voice Quan himself used on subordinates when his patience had run out.

"You make me look a fool, old friend Quan," the deputy minister said. "What am I to tell the minister? He wishes to speak with me later this morning, and I find myself ill prepared. What must I say? That the security forces of the People's Republic are inadequate to the task? That we cannot run these foreign rabbits—these *women*—to ground?"

Quan's humiliation at the rebuke was so great that for a moment he was speechless. His long career was an unbroken road of success. No one knew that better than the deputy minister. Yet Quan would not make excuses for this bump in that road. "Our forces are quite adequate to the task, Deputy Minister," he said.

"Then perhaps I should send you some assistance. Possibly you are overburdened."

"I have no need of assistance. It is only that the foreigners have been both lucky and resourceful. Their luck will run out presently."

"I see," the deputy minister replied. "Evidently you are unaware the premier himself was embarrassed at a news conference with the Australian prime minister. They were announcing important trade agreements, and all the press wished to ask about was these . . . *babies*. Now perhaps you are suggesting I tell him he should credit the luck of the *lao wai* for such impertinence?"

"Of course not, Deputy Minister. I am suggesting—"

"I need no suggestions, Quan Yi," the deputy minister interrupted acidly. "I need only arrests."

"I understand, and you shall have them." As much as he wished to hang up, Quan knew he must inform the deputy minister about other developments in the case. He quickly briefed him about the clerk at Civil Affairs who reported an error in the identity of the babies, and about the missing files, and the murder of Director Lin. He had not finished talking before the deputy minister interrupted again.

"You are wasting valuable time and precious resources on a *paperwork* problem?" he snapped. "Your assignment is to catch these fugitives!"

"I have diverted no local resources, Deputy Minister. I am using all available manpower and equipment in my search for the foreigners. But there is evidence to believe—"

"*I am not interested!* I don't care about the orphanage, or about missing files. Others can pursue such things. I will assign them to do so myself! You are to drop this at once!" The deputy minister's voice was a hiss now. His virulence surprised Quan, whose customary thoroughness was well-known to the deputy minister. More than one crime had been uncovered in pursuit of another. He was doing nothing more or less than he always did. Yet Quan knew there was a difference this time. The deputy minister was quite right: he should have caught the Americans long before now. The failure left him disinclined to argue his point.

"Very well," he said, the rebuke still stinging.

He hung up and immediately received another call, this one from Ma Lin. The major told him what he'd discovered in comparing the files of the orphanage, the ministry, and the crematorium. Quan decided immediately to ignore the deputy minister's instructions.

"It's time you returned to Suzhou," he said.

Tyler didn't know which was worse, being stuck with the pigs or being stuck with Wen Li. Both were unfamiliar, unpleasant, and a little intimidating. They were smelly and messy and in his way. All things considered, he supposed, the pigs had the edge.

At first, when Mei Ling had left, he had been frightened. But as the sun rose higher in the sky and he could take stock of his situation he felt better. He'd understood that she was coming back. All he had to do was wait there, shut up, and hide out. The police were poking around the house and boat. He'd heard their voices and the crackle of their radios, but so far they hadn't come near the pens. He'd thought to give his Mao cap some seasoning by rubbing it in the mud, trying to darken it for better camouflage. He hoped Ren Kai wouldn't mind. He kept it on when he peered over the top of the low brick wall to watch. He took them seriously, and he got a tingle in his gut every time he saw them, but from a distance they actually didn't seem so terrible. Certainly not as bad as old Mr. McDonald, who used to chase him and his friend Will out of the strawberry patch behind his house on Fairfax Street. Mr. McDonald had a shotgun. Tyler had seen it through a window, in a glass case on the kitchen wall. The old man was cranky enough that Tyler guessed he'd use it if he had to. He didn't have a wife or any children; Tyler figured he'd probably shot them and buried them in the backyard, which was why he didn't want neighborhood boys poking around the strawberry patch. Tyler had perfected his legendary skills of stealth behind that house. In a way it was like a dare. The more it seemed to bother the man, the more the kids liked to do it, and nobody was better at getting the old man's goat—and then getting away—than Tyler.

The Chinese police, on the other hand, didn't have any weapons that he could see, and they weren't nearly as nosy. Mostly they sat around smoking. By now old man McDonald would have poked around the pens and probably filled them with buckshot, just to be sure.

Of far greater concern was Wen Li. He hoped she'd sleep all the time, the way she did sometimes, but she'd awakened with the sun and had been nothing but trouble ever since. She didn't like being held by him. She squirmed like a worm. The harder he tried to make her stop, the more she did it. He scrounged a bottle out of the bag and spooned in some rice cereal the way he'd seen Allison do, and once he got the nipple in her mouth it seemed to shut her up okay. But then she'd started complaining again. He shushed her, worried that she'd do it loud enough the cops would hear, but the pigs were making plenty of noise themselves, and with some satisfaction he doubted the cops would be able to tell the difference between Wen Li and a pig. Finally he discovered what her trouble was—the nipple had gotten clogged with dry bits of rice formula. He wiped it out with his little finger and blew through it, and after that it seemed to go better. At least she didn't fuss as much. He fed her on his lap while he sat with his back to the inside wall of the pen and munched on cheese crackers for his own breakfast.

It hadn't been another fifteen minutes before she started up again. This time, he was afraid he knew exactly what the trouble was. For the first half hour or so after they'd arrived, the smell in the pigpen had been hideous. Then he'd kind of gotten used to it. It was still strong, though not so overpowering. But now a new fragrance joined the others, and he was pretty sure the source was similar. Wen Li was wearing a sleeper, and he unzipped it enough so that he could get one leg out. He could tell the diaper was soaked with urine; in front it was bulky and squishy. That was bad enough. But then he held up her leg and pulled the diaper away from her skin just enough to see inside.

It was warm and gooey and everywhere.

"Jeez," he said, disgusted. "You make me want to puke. You're a stupid baby." And then it occurred to him that he was the oldest person there, the person in charge. That gave him some new rights. "You're just a stupid *shitty* baby," he said, relishing the sound of the word. "Shit. Shit! Sheeitt!"

Wen Li watched him talking and grinned. Her arm waved wildly and she whacked him on the nose. Tyler winced. "So is that all you do, shit all day and then wait for somebody to clean it up? Well, I'm not that stupid. You made the mess. You fix it." He stuffed her leg back into the sleeper and got the zipper partway up. He set her on her stomach and she scooted forward on the blanket, heading for the mud. He caught her by the leg and dragged her back. She giggled and scooted again. He caught her again, and they played that game for a while. He decided she didn't need changing all that badly after all.

A bit later a pig wandered in from the other side of the pen, curious about the intruders. It was pink and bristly and covered with mud on one side, and it scared Tyler to death. He grabbed Wen Li and pulled her up onto his lap, while he tried to shoo the thing away like he'd seen Mei Ling do. He didn't know anything about pigs and wasn't altogether sure they wouldn't eat him if they got hungry enough, or just bite if they got plain ornery enough. "Get out of here!" he hissed. "Go on, dammit!" The cussing made him feel stronger but didn't impress the pig. It just kept getting closer, its snout exploring the edges of the blanket. When it stepped on the blanket and showed interest in the bag, Tyler lashed out with his shoe. He didn't intend to hit it but connected sharply. The pig squealed and the sound brought Tyler's heart to his throat. He clutched Wen Li more tightly, but the kick produced the desired effect. The interloper returned to its friends on the other side of the mud-brick dividing wall.

When he was certain the pig wasn't coming back, he set Wen Li down on the blanket again. She wormed all the way to the wall and to his surprise began to pull herself up, trying to stand. "Go on!" he said, cheering her softly. "You can do it! Yeah, that's right!" She got partway up and then her legs collapsed. She fell hard, banging her head. She started crying. Quickly he hushed her, worried about the level of noise, trying to quiet her and shield her from the outside with his body. She carried on for a bit, tears streaming. He wiped her face with his sleeve. Her nose started to bubble. "God, babies are gross," he muttered, wincing. He wiped it with a corner of the blanket, smearing nose goo all over her cheek.

As he tended her she seemed to relax, and soon she was happy again. As Tyler held her, he felt guilt nibbling away at the edges of his disgust. He hated the idea of changing her, hated it more than anything he could remember in his whole life. It made him angry. He'd told Allison a hundred times he wasn't going to do diapers if they got a baby, and she'd laughed and said of course not, and now here he had this shitty kid and nobody to do anything about it. He'd have left her like that all day, only when she'd snuggled in his arms a little and—for the first time since they'd met—found comfort in his company, this odd feeling had descended on him. It was her own damned fault she'd filled her pants, but she couldn't do anything about it. She needed help.

She needed *him.*

Dreading the task, Tyler got the things out of the bag—the plastic box of wipes, the new diaper, the piece of plastic Allison kept to change her on. The five minutes that followed were by far the worst of his life. He felt himself nearly barf four different times, once tasting the vile stuff all the way up in his mouth while he worked. He was astounded at how big a mess such a little person could make. At first he daubed lightly, as if the stuff were going to *get* him, then more vigorously as he realized how big the job was. He got some on his hand and wiped it absently on his jeans. Then, realizing that wasn't such a good idea, he used a clean wipe on his jeans. By the time he'd done the worst of it, he'd gone through fifteen wipes, all of which he stuck in a pile in the corner, topped off by the ripe old diaper. He used more wipes to clean the plastic and pretty soon got a new diaper on Wen Li, who sucked two fingers while she watched him. She seemed satisfied with his efforts.

Afterward he surveyed the pile of used wipes. With what he had left in the box, he calculated she could go once more, twice tops. After that he didn't know what he'd use. "But I'm not saying I'm ever going to do that again," he warned her. "You shit again and you're on your own. I *mean* it this time." Wen Li grinned. She liked to hear him cuss, and by midday, when the heat and humidity had combined with full diapers and wet pigs to fill the pen with an oppressive wall of stench, she was grinning a lot, because Tyler was cussing like a sailor.

*　　*　　*

I have betrayed my wife and my son.

Marshall awoke in the Hong Kong hospital with a blinding hangover of drugs, fear, and pain. Bright flashes of light strobed inside his head in a steady rhythm of torment. His ears ached and his throat tasted vile. Even his skull hurt; for the first time he felt bone pain, radiating outward from the area behind his ear. He tried to sit up, but the headache became excruciating. Dizzy, weak, and nauseated, he sank back into the pillow. He rubbed his temples and tried to find relief.

Even with the drugs, the nightmares had never left him, nightmares of flight and capture and death. And he knew that what was fueling the nightmares was his own guilt. It was he who had spawned them, he who had become the monster within them.

God help me, I am no better than Judas.

He had turned his back on them, telling himself that it was all for them, for Allison and Tyler, and—when he could allow her in—for Wen Li. He had told himself it was not a selfish thing he did. Yet now, in the morning, after his fog had cleared a little, when he could allow himself to look for the truth, he realized how ugly it was. It had all been for his own peace of mind, for his own sense of order, for his own conviction that only he knew the right course. From the beginning he had dismissed Allison's judgment. She was bright and levelheaded and he loved her beyond measure. And now in the cold light of truth, his stomach turned in horror at his own actions. It was a vile thing he'd done.

She trusts me and needs me, and I have abandoned her.

Yes, it was all ugly, starting with the truth. He didn't care about Wen Li. Certainly not now, maybe not ever. If anything, he hated her for this trouble. If he could somehow sacrifice the child in order to get his wife and son back, he knew he would do it in a heartbeat. But in fact he simply didn't have that kind of power. In sacrificing Wen Li, he was sacrificing Allison and Tyler as well.

What had he been thinking? He had allowed some perversion of logic to convince himself that from a junction from which all roads led to peril, he should take the one that required him to betray his wife and to trust the government of the People's Republic.

If it had seemed all right in his haze, it seemed all right no longer. Even if all roads were awful, he had to choose a different one.

Somehow he had let himself believe that he had to choose between Allison and the law. The law had always been his life. He had relied on the law to save the baby Mary. He had lost, and in that he would always believe he had failed Allison. Yet *that* had been in the United States, where law mattered more than people, where the courts were not run by politics and whimsy. Now, with this baby, he had already failed Allison again—and this time without a fight at all. The only advice he had given her was to give in, to give up. And in so doing, he was consigning her to the laws of China, where neither law nor people seemed to matter very much. The rules by which he had lived his life seemed no longer quite so clear-cut.

But if the law was his life, Allison was his passion, and she was risking everything for this child. As angry as he was at her for doing so, he knew she hadn't done it lightly. He could only imagine her anguish. Yet his only answer had been to abandon and betray her. If that was the best he could do, to rob Allison of her dream and her faith in him, then he didn't know how he could ever face her again. He didn't know what he would say when she discovered it was he who had betrayed her.

I love her too much to fail her again.

He started to call Victor Li and then changed his mind. Victor Li was not the way, not anymore. He rummaged through the papers on his bedside table and found the one Victor's son, Kan, had left him. Half an hour later his friend breezed through the door.

"You've got a little color back, for a big nose," Kan said. "You feeling better?"

"Still shitty."

Kan helped him sit up and they talked for a while, catching up. "My father is angry with me for quitting the firm," Kan said.

"So you are playing the horses? It wasn't a rumor?"

"Rumor? Hell, no! Two months ago my horse won the Queen's Cup. I made more from that one race than my father did all last year. He doesn't talk to me much, anymore. Says I've wasted my education and disgraced our name. He's probably right on both counts. Anyway, he's convinced I'm in league with the devil."

"Are you?"

"Only a little." Kan smiled. "And I have to tell you, the devil is more fun than the law. The handover of Hong Kong to China is creating opportunities I'd only ever dreamed about before. Real estate, joint ventures—

everything requiring a connection, countless connections waiting to be made. I'm pretty good at it, but some of it's pretty fuzzy around the edges."

" 'Fuzzy?' Isn't that Cantonese for illegal?"

"Just English for opportunity, that's all. But close enought to the line that I knew it wasn't right to do it and stay with the firm. So I got out. And I'm glad I did. I'm having a lot more fun."

"I need your help, Kan. And it's fuzzy, too."

"I wondered when you'd ask."

"I've got to help Allison—to get her to Canton or out of the mainland altogether."

Li Kan didn't laugh, as Marshall feared he might. Instead he grew thoughtful, pacing the room. "Do you know where she is?"

"Somewhere near Nanchang."

"Are you in touch with her?"

"Only when she calls. I don't know when she'll call next." Marshall told him what he'd said to his father, Victor Li. He didn't want to tell him, or anyone else for that matter, but knew Kan might need the information.

Li Kan was astounded. "What were you thinking? I was kidding about the drugs earlier—but they must have had you on some kind of hallucinogen. You can't trust the government to make a deal. They only deal from strength, and they only keep deals as long as they think they're in their best interest."

"I don't need a lecture, Kan. I just want to get them out."

"People get smuggled out of the mainland all the time, but of course those are Chinese. I've heard talk—it's only that."

"I'm listening."

"You've heard of Operation Yellow Bird?"

"No."

"I don't know much about it myself, except for the legends that have built up around it. Yellow Bird began in the aftermath of Tiananmen. It was an underground railroad set up to smuggle dissidents out of the country. There were lots of rumors about it. Some said it was a CIA operation, and that the triads—the old Chinese mafia—had a big hand in it. I think they played a role, but I think it was mostly done by people who were taking a huge personal risk to help the students. Anyway, some of the biggest names got out that way—Liu Gan, Wuer Kaixi. There's someone at the Jockey Club who owes me big-time. If anyone knows whether Yellow

Bird is real, or if any of its people are still operating, he would." The Jockey Club was the oldest, most British of Hong Kong institutions. It was said, not without truth, that the colony was run by the Jockey Club, the Hong Kong Bank, and the governor, in that order.

"It will cost a lot, Marshall, even just to get names. And then there's no guarantee."

"The money doesn't matter. I've got to try."

"All right," Li Kan said. "You'd better take this." He gave his cell phone to Marshall. "It's got a scrambler. A fuzzy phone, if you will. I've got another one like it. Don't use your old phone anymore. I don't want anyone listening in to our calls."

"Mine ought to be good enough. It's from the States. Clarence gave it to me."

"Hell, I don't trust the firm any more than I trust the ghost of Mao. If Clarence gave you that phone, it's probably bugged."

"Bullshit. I don't believe it."

"Maybe not of Clarence, but you don't know my father like I do. Just don't take any chances, that's all. Can you forward your number to this one?"

"Yes."

"Then do it. And get some money."

Twenty minutes later, Li Kan was on the phone with Liu Weigang, his friend from the Jockey Club. Liu was a womanizer, a gambler, and an accomplished forger, whose ties to the triads were well-known. He owed his freedom to Li Kan's legal efforts on his behalf. He listened as Li Kan described what Marshall wanted.

"Of course it's possible," Liu Weigang said. "I'll make the arrangements myself. I'll call you back within the hour."

Listening to the conversation over the tapped line, Li Kan's father, Victor, smiled. He knew his son well and had long since defeated his efforts at keeping his telephone conversations private. Victor Li made a phone call to Beijing. A few moments later, Liu Weigang received another call, this one from a source that made his blood run cold. He had never met him but knew very well who he was. He owed Li Kan everything, and this man nothing, but there was no question whose interests he would serve.

"When you call Li Kan back to advise him," the one-eyed man said, "you will tell him that the only man he can trust to get Mrs. Turk to safety is Tong Gangzi."

*   *   *

Tai lay on a cot, naked but for a light cotton sheet that covered her to the waist. Ruth sat in the chair next to her, looking at the tiny face and tending the skinny little body so red with sickness and fever. Allison stood in the entryway at the only window with a view across the water. When patients came to the house, as they did frequently, Jin Shan's husband shooed her in with Ruth, where the two women sat quietly with Tai, separated from Jin Shan and her patients by only a sheet draped from the ceiling, listening as the old country doctor tended to various illnesses, dispensing medicines and placing needles. And when the door closed and the patient was gone, Allison would rush back out to look through the window, helplessly, at the low brick walls around the distant pens, the walls that never changed and never revealed anything that was taking place behind them. She didn't even know for sure that the children were still there. She just had to trust that they were. No matter how hard she tried to keep the terrible thoughts out of her mind, they crowded in: Tyler had tried to run, or they were hurt, or hungry, or the pigs were terrorizing them, or they'd been captured and no one had seen it, and now they were alone with the police and she didn't even know it. Oh God—she couldn't help the thoughts, couldn't help the children, couldn't tell them how close she was, that she was there, watching. She had failed them and knew that Tyler, at least, would be feeling abandoned. She didn't know what to do. Each time a new patient came and she had to hide with Ruth, Ruth managed to put aside her own agony to comfort her. Allison didn't know where Ruth found the strength.

In the early afternoon, Jin Shan saw that Tai's finger line was longer than before. She got an oxygen pillow from a cabinet and taped a rubber air hose to Tai's cheek, the end of the hose near Tai's nose, and showed Ruth how to pump the bag. "She breathe better with this," Jin Shan said, and after that the noise of the bag was all that could be heard in the little room, a *whoosh* and a *whiff*, over and over. Ruth did it without tiring, hour after hour, refusing Allison's offers of relief. Whenever it was safe Ruth sang softly to Tai, touching her cheek with the back of her hand or caressing her hair. Tai regularly accepted fluid from a bottle that Jin Shan had filled with a sweet solution of electrolytes, but there was little else encouraging about her condition. She slept most of the time, but always fitfully, and when she cried her voice was hoarse and sometimes she rasped like a broken bellows. Ruth kept looking at her finger, trying to read its signs.

Jin Shan told her not to worry, that she thought the antibiotics would begin showing some effect very soon.

As the afternoon sun turned the house into a broiler, Jin Shan worked through a busy schedule, treating lacerations and allergies and a broken arm, and a woman whose baby was overdue by a week. Her pace was crushing and her energy never flagged.

Her husband brought fruit and hard-boiled eggs, but no one wanted to eat. They sipped at cold tea and waited and worried. There was no room for Mei Ling and Ren Kai in the treatment room, so they waited in Jin Shan's kitchen, hiding like Allison and Ruth whenever patients came into the house.

Between patients, Jin Shan tried to formulate a plan. After dark, or sooner if the police left, Ren Kai would sneak back across the water with the little raft and get Tyler and Wen Li. If Tai was well enough to travel, Jin Shan would get them passage south, to Guangzhou. She had known immediately who would—who *could*—do that. Two years earlier, the local population control officer had appeared at Jin Shan's door with a woman she suspected of being pregnant. She imperiously demanded that Jin Shan examine the woman and perform an abortion if her suspicions were true. Jin Shan not only knew the villager in question, but had delivered the woman herself, twenty-four years earlier, during a time when Mao himself had proclaimed that families should have more children, not less.

It was not the first time Jin Shan had lied about such an examination. She found doing them the most loathsome part of her job yet had no choice in the matter. If she refused, her permission to practice medicine would be revoked. So she performed the examination and pronounced her diagnosis: The woman had missed her period because of a tumor. At first the population control officer didn't believe her, but she backed down before Jin Shan, who had treated her own children's illnesses for years. Jin Shan continued the charade for seven months and then secretly delivered the "tumor," which was a healthy three-kilogram boy. Jin Shan's crimes were not yet completed. After the delivery, she forged papers about the boy's birth, using permission documents from another patient who had died. After that she helped the parents find a place to live in the city, beyond the scrutiny of the rural population control officer, who no longer cared as long as her quotas were met. Jin Shan had helped the husband, Ming Jiquan, find a job as a driver for a ceramics company in Nanchang. And now, she knew, Driver Ming made regular deliveries to Guangzhou.

Jin Shan sent her husband into the city, to call in the debt. He returned in the early afternoon. Driver Ming had been terribly angry about the situation, arguing that it could cost him everything he and his wife had sought to protect. What did it matter if Jin Shan had found him his job in the first place, if by helping he lost that job and ended in prison? But his wife had been adamant: Jin Shan's kindness had brought them the boy they had both prayed for, and she had done so at great personal risk.

Driver Ming finally relented. He would be there by nightfall and take them to Guangzhou.

Ma Lin couldn't shake the feeling he was chasing ghosts.

On his return to Suzhou, he had reinterviewed the aunties at the Number Three Children's Welfare Institute, trying to determine exactly how children might slip through the cracks. The women were eager to help but had little sense of anything more than the daily needs of their charges.

He started with the children who had initiated this case. Their files, of course, were missing. Of the six infants originally handed over to the Americans, three had been kidnapped Saturday morning. The remaining three had been returned to the orphanage that same morning, but no sooner had they arrived, the aunties reported, than they were taken away again in a different van. That wasn't unusual, they said. Babies were often taken away in vans, sometimes half a dozen at a time. They didn't know to where. It was not their business to know, any more than it was their business to know where the babies came from when they arrived in vans, again sometimes half a dozen at a time. This was an orphanage, they reminded him. Children came, needing care. Some lived, and some left, and some died.

He found the chauffeur, who said he and the director had taken the children to the train station, where they were met by a man and a woman. The driver didn't know the couple, who had taken the babies inside. The driver had returned the director to the orphanage. No one at the train station could remember seeing the children. They'd vanished.

Ma Lin interviewed other drivers, learning their routine. They reported taking children to and from hospitals, airports, train stations, hotels, and police stations. They kept no logs. None of them sensed anything unusual in the affairs of the orphanage.

The clerk at Civil Affairs had said the six children had been adopted some weeks earlier by Canadian families. On his first visit to the orphanage, Ma Lin had made a request of the Canadian embassy in Beijing for copies of the photographs in the children's visa applications. He requested similar photographs, taken several months earlier, from the children's passport files at the Foreign Ministry in Beijing. He intended to compare the two sets of photos, to determine whether they showed the same children. He wondered what it would tell him if they didn't.

A courier delivered the packet from the Canadian embassy, but there was nothing from the Foreign Ministry. He made another call to Beijing, where he encountered a heavy curtain of confusion and red tape, but he extracted a promise that the photos would soon be on the way. He started to put the Canadian set aside, when it occurred to him that one of the three children, the one known as Xiao Bo, adopted by Claire and Nash Cameron, was at the orphanage in Hukou, where she'd been taken after Claire Cameron's capture. Ma Lin faxed the photograph to the orphanage, asking that they compare it to the child in their care.

He turned his attention to Director Lin. The aunties knew precious little about the man, who was aloof and rarely spoke to them. Their lives revolved around the children, his around the paperwork. He rarely consulted them, except in matters of food and supplies. He took little notice of the children, rarely visiting the wards.

Director Lin's *dáng án,* the state's dossier of his life, was fat but not illuminating. He had no criminal record or unfavorable contact with the state. Ma Lin assigned officers to talk with the director's relatives scattered around the province. He obtained copies of the director's travel permits, which showed numerous trips to Bangkok and Macao. Businessmen from the mainland often went to Thailand for prostitution, and to Macao for gambling. According to family and friends, Director Lin pursued neither vice.

There was no easy way to check on the director's trips to Guangdong. Restrictions had been eased for in-country travel for Chinese citizens, a fact that made police work considerably more difficult. And, like most Chinese, the director carried no credit cards, paying cash for his expenses. His travels left no trail.

Ma Lin found no unusual activity in the bank records, which didn't surprise him. Few Chinese, even the most modern and enlightened, trusted banks at all, preferring mattresses and cookie jars. Any illicit monies the director had acquired most likely had burned with him in the fire. His one major possession was an automobile, a new Chinese-made Audi, which, on his orphanage salary, was certainly an extravagance. It hadn't been found.

For all his efforts, Ma Lin knew he was grasping at wisps of smoke. He had only vague suspicions based on imprecise records concerning a population that was ever-changing. He still had no solid evidence that a crime involving the children had even been committed. But he was a seasoned investigator. The more he couldn't find anything, the more he was certain something was there.

His eyes were beginning to burn from fatigue when he noticed something in the files. He was reviewing the logs he'd been faxed, thumbing through some of the files that accompanied the log entries, files now neatly arranged on the worktables by date of disposition. He noticed that whenever he saw the distinctive and depressing pink slip of the crematoria, he kept coming across the same attending physician's signature.

Dr. Cai Tang.

He opened more files, and then still more, going back nearly two years. They were always the same. Thinking this might simply be due to the limited number of physicians upon whom the orphanage relied for services, he looked at physicians' names in cases where the child had been treated for an illness. In those instances numerous doctors were involved. He made a tick in the log for every file he found with the doctor's name and pretty soon realized that Dr. Cai's name always appeared with the green marks that meant dead children. It was odd but might perhaps mean nothing at all. Dr. Cai might well be the only physician who would trouble himself for the most severely ill of the orphans. Some doctors, he knew, didn't want to bother with children who had no future.

He looked in the files for the doctor's telephone number or address but found none. He asked the senior auntie, who knew the doctor by sight and name but didn't know where he worked. Ma Lin picked up the telephone. It took nearly an hour, but then he had it. The only Dr. Cai Tang he could find lived in Shanghai. That made no sense. What kind of doctor would travel all the way from Shanghai to sign death certificates for babies in a Suzhou orphanage? And why?

He called the doctor's home telephone. There was no answer. He didn't know where the doctor worked; it could be at any hospital or clinic in Shanghai, or elsewhere, for that matter. The major called the local PSB.

He ordered the doctor's *dàng àn* sent to him. The thought crossed his mind that Dr. Cai, like Director Lin, might be dead inside his home. He dispatched officers to the doctor's apartment to check. An hour later one of the officers called.

"It's a very expensive building, Major. The attendant says the doctor has not been in since Monday, which is unlike him. He leaves word when he'll be away for any extended period of time."

Ma Lin knew this was no coincidence, not any longer.

One man was dead, another missing.

And it all had to do with the babies.

Tai's condition changed at last, very quickly and very dramatically. It was late in the afternoon, and Allison, standing at her post by the window, heard her gasping. She rushed in to find Jin Shan bent over the child with her stethoscope and Ruth hunched forward in her seat, still pumping the oxygen pillow. Tai's color had gone pale and her breath was becoming punctuated with sudden, sharp gasps. Jin Shan saw that the skin at the base of the child's throat was beginning to draw in with each inhalation, as was the skin over her ribs and below her sternum. She was laboring to breathe.

"We must take to hospital now," Jin Shan said. "Antibiotics not working."

"Yes," Ruth whispered, aware the situation was becoming critical.

"Our son will drive us. Husband get him now." She set her husband to the task and found a hat for Ruth to wear.

"You shouldn't come—you'll only be in trouble," Ruth protested.

"What they do to an old woman?" Jin Shan scoffed, fearless. "You came to me for help. I gave it. Where is the crime? Now we must go, quickly. We must walk to the road through the back fields so you will not be seen." Jin Shan turned to Allison. "My husband stay here with you. If the police come, he know place to hide you."

Allison looked at Ruth. The enormity of the development was beginning to dawn on them both. "I wish I could come," Allison said. "You know I would if—"

"Don't be ridiculous," Ruth said. "Of course you've got to stay here."

"I'll wait for you."

Ruth sat in her chair, still working the oxygen pillow, *whoosh, whiff,* and she held Allison's eyes and did her best not to cry. She shook her head. "Of course you can't. This is the end of my line, and we both know it. I'm not leaving Tai's side, and I can't get her treatment without them finding out who we are. You've got to go on. When it gets dark, you get Tyler and Wen Li and get the hell out of here. I'll buy you time." Her eyes were brimming. "Get home with your children, Allison. I'll stay here with mine. I'm not giving her up without one helluva fight. They'll have their hands full with the two of us. Do what you can for me from Guangzhou."

Heartsick, Allison couldn't imagine going on without Ruth, but were their situations reversed, she knew she would be staying with Wen Li. She held Ruth close and they wept. Jin Shan's son arrived.

"You'd better hurry," Allison whispered. "Good luck. Thank you for everything, for giving me hope. Don't lose your own."

"Never. We'll see you in Colorado."

Tyler was nodding off when he heard it—or maybe he saw it, or dreamed it, he wasn't sure, but his eyes opened and there it was: a rat, a huge ugly thing as big as any cat he'd ever seen. It was just behind where Wen Li was sleeping, emerging from behind her head, where the covers were bunched up. Its eyes were narrow and black, and it stared right at him, a cold malevolent glare of menace. He stared back, at the quivering whiskers and long sharp teeth, and when he finally realized what he was seeing he squeaked in fright and sat straight up, kicking at it with his shoe. The rat was trapped between him and the open part of the pen and had nowhere to go. It hesitated, and then it ran right over his legs. It was heavier than he'd expected and he felt its claws through his jeans, and then it was gone in a flash of fur, behind the brick wall that separated them from the pigs.

Tyler sat still for a moment, shaking. He realized he'd started to pee in his pants. There was a dark spot, a hot wet stain spreading through the dried mud and pigshit that had already caked there. He had stopped himself, but not before it was too late. On his thighs he saw little pinpricks of blood seeping through his jeans where the rat's claws had been. He started to sob, and that surprised him almost as much as the rat had. *I'm not afraid of a stupid rat,* he told himself, but still the tears came no matter how he willed them not to.

He wiped angrily at his cheek and scooted over to where Wen Li was napping. He pulled back the light cover, terrified the rat had eaten her or something. She looked all right, but she startled awake as he lifted her and responded to his crying by starting up herself. Desperately he tried to shush her, but the more he tried, the louder she seemed to get. He found the bottle and got it to her mouth, but she pushed it away. He shoved Pooh at her, but that didn't work, either.

"*Shhhhh,*" he whispered, fumbling through the pack. He found the little picture book, the one that had children's songs in it, songs that played when the little buttons on the margin were pressed. She liked to chew on the thick cardboard pages while she listened to the music. It seemed to mollify her for a moment, but then Tyler inadvertently pressed one of the buttons and the music started up.

One of the officers stationed on Ren Kai's boat turned his head and listened. He, too, had been nearly asleep; the cove was quiet and their duty was lazy. Doze and wait, wait and doze. But he'd heard something. He thought it was a baby crying. "What's that?" he asked one of the others.

The man listened and shook his head. "Nothing."

The first officer got to his feet and looked out the windows of the cabin. The spit of land was deserted. And then he heard it again. A tinkling or a cry? He walked outside and down the ramp, straightening first his trousers and then his cap. He walked to his right, along the path that led past the two houses to the pens beyond. He stopped near the water and waited, listening. A fishing boat putted slowly by a hundred meters offshore. Gulls cried and wheeled through the air. He heard the chirrup of crickets and the low distant rumble of thunder. The clouds were charcoal and heavy. An afternoon storm was brewing, the fifth one that week. The monsoons were coming, a season he detested. He moved along the path.

From his vantage point behind the mud wall, Tyler watched him coming. The officer would take a few steps and then stop and wait, then take a few more. He didn't seem to be doing anything or going anywhere on purpose, but he was getting uncomfortably close. Once he stopped to pee, and he watched the lake with his back to the pens. Tyler crouched down and whispered to Wen Li, who was chewing now on the blanket. He leaned over her and put his face close to hers and tried some rhymes, half making them up, sensing that the very sound of his voice was keeping her entertained.

"Piss porridge hot," he whispered, "piss porridge cold. Please mix it with the snot, nine days old." He heard the officer's footsteps and felt the hair tingling on the back of his neck and a knot twisting in his belly. If Wen Li made any sound, any sound at all, they would be caught. He got his mouth right down by her ear. "Down by the station, early in the morning, see the little puffer billies all in a row . . ."

Across the cove, from her window at Jin Shan's, Allison saw the officer approach the sty. She bit her knuckles until they bled and watched helplessly, ready to dash out, to start shouting, to distract him.

He was three paces from the pens when a flurry of motion and noise made him jump. Pigs squealed and the rat came blazing out of the pen, running directly at the man. Both rat and officer were startled. The man picked up a stone and threw it at the rodent, which changed course and dashed madly across the paddies toward the village. From the boat there was the sound of laughter from the other officer, who was watching.

The first officer chuckled, too, and turned back for the boat.

The journey to Nanchang was all a blur to Ruth, who saw nothing but the Wee Duck in her arms as Jin Shan and her son somehow led her through the fields near Youlan. There had been a short ride in a hay cart. Tai had sneezed once from the dust, and then, just as the rain started, they slid into the cramped backseat of a car. Jin Shan's son drove like a maniac, over the bumps and around the omnipresent carts and cycles and trucks and livestock, cursing and waving his fists and leaning on the horn, but as fast as he drove, it was the longest trip of Ruth's life.

With Jin Shan's help Ruth worked the oxygen pillow and did the best she could with the song that always made Tai's eyes light so brightly.

> *The itsy bitsy spider went up the water spout.*
> *Down came the rain and washed the spider out.*
> *Out came the sun and dried up all the rain.*
> *And the itsy bitsy spider went up the spout again*

As she tried to sing, her voice cracked and her tears fell onto Tai's bare skin and ran into the folds of cloth beneath her. There had been nothing in Ruth's life to equal the helpless, sick feeling she had as she looked at the frail child on her lap, struggling to breathe.

Ruth was not a religious woman, but during the ride she bargained with God and threatened the devil. She said prayers to Buddha and Jesus and Mohammed. She pumped the pillow and closed her eyes and imagined once more the life they were going to have together, the life she had conjured countless times, the life that grew richer and longer with each imagining. Tai was going to learn to walk, and wear a dress, and smear lipstick and rouge on her little-girl's face, and play the violin, or the piano—yes, the piano was better, she'd have a scholarship—and she'd have dates, all the pimply-faced boys standing nervously in the entry, waiting for Ruth's approval, which would never be given lightly. The Wee Duck was going to have a chance to burn a tray of cookies and ride a horse and pick a favorite color and decide whether to be left- or right-handed. She was going to go to a prom and a football game, and eat a pizza, and have children of her own, and she was going to do all that before Ruth died herself, going to make Ruth a grandmother and maybe even a great-grandmother. No, that was too much. Grandmother was enough; it was as much as anyone as old as she could hope for.

Ruth was certain it was all to be. It had been so in every dream, in every thought, in every reach of her soul, the dark, neglected corners of which had already been so brightened by the mere existence of this child. This was only the end of their flight from China; theirs was a journey only beginning.

She held her arm over Tai's face to shield her, worried the breeze from the car's open window might bother her. She brushed the damp hair from her forehead and willed the child to health, talking to her lungs, her heart, ordering them to work, to thrive.

But it wasn't working. Ruth felt Tai's situation growing more desperate. All during the day when she wasn't sleeping, Tai had opened her eyes every few moments and looked up at Ruth, but now she stopped doing even that. She wouldn't respond when Ruth shook her, or whispered, or sang. Tai closed her eyes and wouldn't open them again, and Ruth felt her battle in every breath. One time she shook like a leaf, and Ruth realized it was a seizure, and she cried out in fear and prayed through salt tears. "It's all right, Wee Duck, Mama's here, Mama's here, Mama loves you, it'll be all right."

They drove for what seemed an eternity, and in that time Ruth saw nothing outside, not the fields or the trees or the crush of humanity on the sidewalks and in the streets. She saw only Tai. "How much longer?" she asked for the hundredth time.

"Ten minutes, twenty," Jin Shan said. The old doctor took Tai's hand in her own. The line was fiery red and had crept all the way past the third joint. There was no warmth in it, and Jin Shan set it down gently. She said nothing to Ruth. She stared out the window, blurred by the rain that fell now in sheets, and thought of all the death she had seen in fifty years of practice. It was always hardest when it was a child. Absently she noticed the flashing lights of a roadblock, but her son didn't stop or slow. The police were halting only the traffic going in the other direction, away from Nanchang.

Finally they drew near the hospital, but the car was stuck in traffic, delayed by the pouring rain. Jin Shan pointed down the street. "There," she said, indicating a grimy tile building. "Hospital." They waited while horns blared. Ruth fumbled for the door. Jin Shan saw she intended to get out and started to open her own door.

Ruth was frantic to be moving, but she knew that was not right. She caught Jin Shan by the arm. "I'll do the rest of this alone," she said. "You have done enough already, and they will know what to do inside. You will only bring trouble upon yourself, and police to your door."

"No. I must come with you."

"And deprive your patients of their doctor? You are a gift from heaven if ever I met one, Jin Shan. You must leave. Thank you for everything." And with that Ruth stepped out into the rain and closed the car door, leaving the old woman in the backseat. Ruth threaded her way through the stalled traffic, wading through deep puddles as she made her way to the sidewalk. She hunched forward as she walked to keep the rain from Tai's body. In the poor light Ruth thought Tai looked gray. It was an awful color for a baby, and she ran then, stumbling once but not falling.

She got through the courtyard and the front door of the hospital. There was no reception desk, and the halls were dark. She rushed up to the first person she saw, a skinny peasant woman with a cane and a white surgical patch over one eye. "Please," she pleaded. "Help me." Through her good eye the startled woman peered at the baby and the foreign woman, and then she hobbled resolutely outside into the rain. Frantic, Ruth looked around for someone else. There were signs, but she couldn't read them. She started down a corridor and began yelling, "Help me! Please, someone!" A few curious faces peered out of doorways, and moments later Ruth and Tai were hustled into an examination room by a nurse, who took one look at Tai and then disappeared back into the hall. The walls of the room were tiled but dirty, and paint was peeling from the ceiling. A metal examination cart stood along one wall. Next to it was a stand lined with drawers in front and bottles and boxes of medicine on the top.

The nurse returned a moment later with a doctor, a bookish-looking youngster with a stethoscope in the pocket of his white coat. He was the first person who looked vaguely hospital-like to Ruth. He said something to her in Chinese, but she could only shake her head. He gently lifted Tai from her arms and set the child on the steel table. Ruth worried that the table would be cold, but Tai didn't react. The doctor listened to the heart, which was racing and feeble. He didn't need to listen to her lungs; he had heard her breathing from out in the hall. He worked feverishly, and Ruth stood against one wall, trying to stay out of the way. There was great confusion then, a blur of people and carts and Chinese and needles and oxygen. Ruth pumped numbly at the pillow, even after they'd taken the tube off Tai's cheek and replaced it with a mask. She saw everything through a haze of terror and disbelief, and she began to cry, her own breath coming in great labored gasps as she watched what was happening. Tai was not stirring anymore. She had gone limp, and in the bright light of the room Ruth saw her gray color was not a trick of light at all. Ruth called out to her, but if Tai heard, she gave no sign. Her chest heaved sharply once, and then again, her ribs straining against her skin. There was nothing for a moment, and then she drew a deep ragged breath once more, followed by a sigh.

Ruth sobbed and watched the life go out of the little body on the table.

The doctor's shoulders sagged. He turned away, and she knew it was over.

Tai, the Wee Duck, was dead.

CHAPTER 19

THE PHONE RANG and Allison jumped. She hadn't even realized there was a telephone in the house. She was standing at the window, her eyes riveted on the pens, as they had been ever since the policeman had come so near. It was raining hard and beginning to get dark. In another hour Ren Kai would be setting off for the children. Allison didn't know if she could last another hour. The fear had cramped her stomach, and she could taste the bile in the back of her throat. She didn't know how they could be staying dry in such a downpour.

Jin Shan's husband answered the phone, which was half-buried behind some books on Jin Shan's desk. Allison turned and watched as he had a brief conversation and then hung up. "Please," she said to him, indicating the phone. "United States?" He slapped his thigh; he didn't know what she meant. "May I use it?" she said, pointing again, holding an imaginary instrument to her ear.

"Ah hah." He nodded. *"Shi."*

She had no idea whether it would work. It was an old rotary phone. She dialed the numbers with unsteady fingers, hoping she didn't need some special prefix, hoping this phone, unlike some she'd tried, could make international calls. To her surprise, all the sounds seemed right— the echo, the ring.

And then he was there.

"Allison?" Unexpectedly, his voice made her cry, and it took a moment before she could say anything.

"Marshall," she whispered.

"Are you crying? Are you all right?"

"Yes . . . yes, I'm fine. I'm just relieved to hear your voice, that's all."

284

He was quiet for a moment, overwhelmed himself. "I love you, Allison," he said. "Thank God you called. I didn't know if you'd be able to. Where are you?"

"Still near Nanchang."

"Is Tyler all right? And Wen Li?" Instantly he regretted the way he said it. Wen Li sounded like an afterthought.

Allison didn't seem to notice. "They're all right."

"Can I talk to Tyler?"

"Not . . . he's not here right now."

"Where is he?"

"He's . . . safe. He's with Wen Li."

"But they're not with you?"

"I can't explain now. It's just that we're all hiding. They—the police almost caught us, Marshall. It was very close."

That hit him like a blow; he wondered how much his own actions had led to that. "But you're okay," he repeated.

"Yes."

"Listen to me, Allison. I'm in Hong Kong. I've gotten some help from Li Kan. He was my partner on the—"

"I remember him. But I called our house," she said, confused.

"I know. Miracle of technology. You need to write this down. Do you have a paper?"

Allison fumbled in her pockets. "No, just a minute." She found one on Jin Shan's desk, and a pen. "Okay."

"There's a man named Tong Gangzi who's going to help, but he can't do it for five days. Can you get to the south?"

"Yes. In fact, I think we have a ride tonight."

"That's good, because he can't get to Nanchang, not now. We've interrupted him in the middle of something else. But if you can get to a place near Zijin, he'll meet you. It's a monastery in the mountains on the way to Guangzhou. It's called Taoping. I gather it's not very accessible. You can wait for him there. He says he's used it before and that you'll be safe until he gets there. He's good, Allison. The best. Li Kan says we can trust him." She wrote everything down and spelled it back to him to be sure she had it right.

"Where's he going to take us?"

"I don't know yet, exactly. We're still working on that. I called Clarence and he's trying for a promise of help from the State Department.

If that works, then you'll go to the consulate in Guangzhou. Tong can get you in safely, past the police."

"And if Clarence has no luck?"

"I don't know. Then I guess we'll smuggle you out. To Hong Kong. Either way, I'll meet you. I can get into China. My visa is still good."

Allison couldn't say anything for a moment. She stood in the little hallway, the cord stretched from the phone, and looked out the window. She had feared another devastating conversation, in which Marshall would lecture her and tell her once more to do something she wasn't going to do, a conversation in which he would be cold and hard and lawyerly and not at all understanding. Instead, this was *Marshall*. "That's wonderful," she whispered.

"I wish there were some other way, Allison. I'm afraid."

"Me too. But—" And with that the line went dead. She heard a succession of beeps and then a dial tone. She dialed again but got only a fast busy signal.

Jin Shan returned to the clinic in uncharacteristically low spirits, feeling every one of her seventy-seven years. She saw no reason to discourage Allison with the news that Tai would not likely survive. She said only that Ruth had gotten safely to the hospital, and then diverted Allison's attention with preparations for departure. "Driver Ming come soon," she said. "When children are safe you must leave quickly. Maybe only short time before police come."

In Hong Kong, Victor Li listened to the recording of the conversation between Allison and Marshall. He made a call to Beijing.

"It worked," he told his one-eyed client. "The fly comes to your spider."

One of the officers milling outside the hospital room told the colonel the *lao wai* woman had caused a terrible scene when hospital personnel had tried to take the baby. No one had been able to communicate with her and no one had known what to do, so no one had done a thing. Quan brushed past them all and walked in. The nurse who was there took one look at him and slipped quietly out into the hall.

The woman was sitting on a stool with her back to him, hunched over next to the gurney on which a sheet covered the body of an infant. Quan approached quietly from one side until he could make out her features in profile, and then he knew immediately which of the two women it was. He watched her and did not disturb her. Her eyes were closed, but he didn't think she was praying. He knew she had no religion. He had read her file, the application she had submitted to the Civil Affairs Ministry requesting the adoption. It had been translated into Chinese and it was all there, a fat file with financial statements and résumés and questionnaires and a detailed autobiography. He had read it in Chinese, and then again in English, looking for clues to her character in her strong handwriting. She seemed a woman of spirit, of quiet dignity, of great determination.

He knew that her brother was a powerful congressman of the United States and that for some reason she had not included that information in her application. Whatever else it might say about her brother, the omission suggested great inner certainty on her part. He assumed that it had been her strength—and not that of the Turk woman or the Camerons—that had sustained them all in their flight. So he had decided to try a completely civil approach with her, using none of the threats and intimidation that he tried with Claire Cameron, whose dossier had suggested to him that she would bend in such wind. In that he had been wrong. She had said nothing useful, nothing at all. She was still alone in her cell in Jiujiang, where she would remain, out of touch but well cared for, until he decided otherwise.

Quan moved to the gurney. He gently lifted the sheet and looked at the dead child, then lowered it again. He touched Ruth on the shoulder and she looked up at him. Her eyes were red and her face was puffy. He saw her devastation, and he also saw her great dignity. "Miss Pollard," he said, "I am Quan Yi. A chair has been brought for you. Please, take it. You will be more comfortable."

His voice was not hard, and the excellence of his English surprised her. She shook her head.

"Miss Pollard, I understand how you must feel. Please believe that I have no wish to intrude upon your grief at this moment, but I am afraid I have no choice. I know you have done what you thought was right, but your China run is over. Now it is imperative that you tell me where I can find your companion, Mrs. Turk. It is futile to carry on this exercise. People have been hurt enough already."

"I don't know . . . I honestly don't know what to do." She said it so softly, he had to strain to hear.

"The best thing is to bring it to a close now, and to prevent further tragedy." He talked gently, persuasively, revealing something of the methods of the police, why it was so certain escape was ultimately impossible, why no one could ever hide for long in a nation of watchers. Gently, but relentlessly, he kept insisting that Allison could never succeed. Gently, but relentlessly, he kept pressing upon her most vulnerable point, reminding her of the toll to date: the deaths, the imprisonments, yes, even the child just there, on the table. The toll would only grow if she did not help. "Everything you have done to this moment has been about saving lives, not costing them. Yet so many are dead already. What is your crusade worth, Miss Pollard? Is it worth the life of another child? The life of your friend, or her son? If you truly care for her, for the two children with her, you will accept this certainty: Nothing you can do will guarantee their escape, because they can never escape. The only thing within your power is to keep them from harm."

"Can you guarantee that? That they would be safe?"

"Yes. I assure you that I act with the full authority of my government."

"If I help you, will you try to help her keep the baby?"

He thought about that. "I'm afraid that is a matter for hands other than mine."

Ruth's eyes rested upon the sheet on the gurney, and her whole body trembled. She had never guessed what it felt like to lose something so precious. "If that's the best you can do, then I can't help you, Mr. Quan," she said. "Allison has a better chance on her own."

As he had anticipated, she had asked for nothing for herself. And he had known very well how Americans loved to bargain with the law. He appeared to think it over, and then he sighed. "I am a colonel with the Ministry of Public Security," he said. "I am not without influence. I don't know whether it will matter at all, but I will try. I have no personal interest in this, other than to see the matter concluded quickly. So very well, Miss Pollard. If you will help me, I will help her."

"How do I know you will do that? That you are not simply making a promise you have no intention of keeping?"

"I am not a barbarian, Miss Pollard, whatever you may think of my government. I am a man of my word."

Ruth put her head down again. For more than ten minutes she didn't move; she might have been asleep. Quan stood without disturbing her. At last she sat up and wiped her eyes. "There is something else. Something for . . . afterward. I want to come back here. I want to be with her. I want to . . . I need to bury her before you put me in jail."

"Of course."

Ruth stood and was a little unsteady at first. Quan helped her by the arm. She looked at her captor and hoped she was doing the right thing for Allison. She had never faced a more difficult choice.

"All right," she said at last. "I'll help you."

Ten minutes later he helped her into the black government Audi waiting by the front door and slid in after her. The car pulled away from curb and sped into the heavy rain of dusk.

Ren Kai slipped off the raft at water's edge and slithered up the mud embankment on his belly. Despite the dark and the rain, he was taking no chances. The police were still on his boat. Hoping to surprise him, they had not lit lanterns or switched on the battery-powered lights. Earlier he had seen the glow from one of their cigarettes through the cabin window. They were watching, and he knew if they looked directly at him, they might see him, but he told himself they would have no reason to be looking toward the lake. Instead they would be concentrating on the approach from the opposite direction, from the village. Besides that, there were no lights behind him to highlight his silhouette, only the darkness of the lake. He reached the top of a dike and crept along it until he got to the pens. He reached up and slipped the rope latch off the post, opened the gate, and slipped inside.

Tyler heard the intruder but couldn't see clearly. Since dark, every noise had frightened him. The pigs had learned better than to interfere with him, but then earlier in the blackness he'd felt something brush by his cheek. He'd swatted at it in panic, poking himself in the eye in the process. After that he'd crawled around on hands and knees, feeling in the mud for stones to use as weapons, which he'd set in a small pile. Now he tried to brain the intruder with one, but it slipped from his hand and went wide, just glancing off Ren Kai's shoulder.

"*Ēi yòu!*" the fisherman hissed. "*Shì wǒ, Ren Kai! Xū!*"

Tyler was so relieved, he wanted to cry. That's all Wen Li had been doing for the better part of an hour, crying and whimpering, and he knew that only the noise of the rain on the tin roof had kept her squawking from the ears of the police. He had done the best he could, seeing to her bottle and her diapers—*again*—and he'd bounced her in his lap and let her gnaw on his fingers, and he'd read her stories until it was too dark, and then he'd made some up until he'd run out of those as well. And after all that, he didn't know what was wrong with her or what else to do. She just kept crying. He'd eaten four packs of crackers and was sick of them, too.

Mostly, though, he was afraid of the dark.

"I thought you were a . . . pig or something," Tyler said, sniffing.

Ren Kai quickly scooped up the blankets and bags. As he did so, he winced at the smell. The children had been camped squarely in the middle of a soft, damp pile of pigshit, and it had permeated everything. He started to take the baby from Tyler, intending to give him the other things to carry, but the boy shook his head. "I've got her," he said protectively.

For Tyler, what followed was the most fun he'd had in a long time. They sneaked out the gate, peering over the top of the brick wall toward the boat, and then, following behind Ren Kai, he ran as fast as he could with Wen Li, who started to giggle at the wiggling and bouncing motion. Along the way, Tyler tried to shelter her from the rain, but it was hopeless and all he could do was keep her face dry. Soon they were both drenched, but the rain was warm and after the pens it felt wonderful and fresh. They arrived at the lake, and Ren Kai steadied the little craft as Tyler scooted aboard. Ren Kai clambered on behind him and began swiftly paddling toward deeper water before turning to the south. As they passed the mouth of the cove, Tyler looked at Ren Kai's fishing boat moored at the pier and grinned broadly. The cops waiting inside were far too stupid to compete with such clever adversaries. It was all he could do not to whoop in victory. Wen Li had no such reservations and shrieked out loud, but the noise of the rain safely covered her joy.

The fun slowed some when they got to the other shore, down the slope from Jin Shan's house. Allison was waiting there, crouched in the darkness with Mei Ling. She was all teary and gross and made a big deal about everything. She asked him a thousand whispered questions, not giving him time to answer a single one. She seemed somewhat surprised to find Wen Li alive and okay. He shrugged it off as if it were all no big deal, but secretly he was quite proud of himself. It was something of a struggle for him, but through her display he just managed to maintain his dignity. Even when she kissed him on the forehead and he felt like crying, he didn't. He refused to admit it to himself, but when she hugged him it felt wonderful. He hugged back—just a little.

And then when she let him go Mei Ling took a turn, but only a brief one. She wrinkled her nose in disgust and said something sharply to her husband, who dutifully took Tyler back down to the water and waded right in with him, all the way up to the neck. Together they washed away the smells and even some of the fears of Tyler's long day, while Allison cleaned up Wen Li.

Driver Ming cursed at the rain and wiped his windshield, which fogged continually in the high humidity. His wipers were old and left huge gaps in his vision, so he had to arch to his right to see at all. That gave him cramps, and that made his mood worse than ever. He was already unhappy, the way his wife had browbeaten him into helping old Dr. Jin. He was carrying a load of ceramic insulators for high-tension electrical wires. The insulators were to be delivered to Guangzhou, where the Ministry of Transportation needed them for construction of the new rail route on the Beijing–Hong Kong railway. He had all the papers for the trip and knew it should go smoothly, but he hadn't counted on an extra load of trouble such as the one he was on his way to pick up. Already, within twenty kilometers of Nanchang, he had been stopped twice at general roadblocks. Such blocks were always unusual, especially so in the rain, when even the stupid guards had the good sense to find shelter and leave well enough alone. But there had been massive delays in traffic while police studied papers and crawled through cargoes and poked through crowded buses. At the last roadblock the impertinent, farting guard with garlic breath had insisted on inspecting the load—*his* load—and the fool had turned over three heavy crates in the process.

Driver Ming took the turn to Youlan and passed yet another police car, going in the opposite direction. He scowled and chain-smoked and squinted through the rain. He arrived at Jin Shan's house in a mood as foul as the weather. In the entryway he stomped his feet and rudely shook the water from his plastic coat. He coughed loudly. He greeted Jin Shan and her husband politely but regarded Allison with undisguised resentment.

"Sorry, he speak no English," Jin Shan said.

"I'm getting used to it," Allison admitted. She smiled and extended her hand in greeting, but he ignored her. Jin Shan told Allison the driver didn't want money, but she gave him two $100 bills anyway. "Please tell him I want him to have this, to help pay for the journey," she said to Jin Shan, who translated. Driver Ming pocketed the money, but his mood did not improve.

They sat at a table and Jin Shan opened an old, dog-eared map of Guangdong province she had found buried among stacks of paper in her living room cabinets. To Allison's dismay, the map was, of course, written entirely in Chinese, but Jin Shan marked it for her. "This is road to Guangzhou," Jin Shan said. "Anyway, *was* road. Maybe changed now. Old map. Sorry. And here"—she peered over her glasses—"here is Zijin," and she underlined it. With Ming's help Jin Shan then located the monastery of Taoping.

"It is out of my way," Driver Ming said irritably.

"Life often is," Jin Shan said amiably, and she gave him a bag of fruit for the journey.

Jin Shan and her husband insisted on walking with them to the truck to see them off, brushing off Allison's objections about the weather. "Jin Shan walking in rain longer than Allison alive," the doctor reminded her. In the downpour Tyler gravely shook hands with the fisherman and reluctantly permitted Mei Ling another hug before climbing into the back of the truck. Allison choked with emotion. She found herself glad she spoke no Chinese, because she didn't know what to say to these wonderful people who had risked everything to help her. As Allison was handing Wen Li up to Tyler, Jin Shan paused and withdrew a tiny bracelet from her pocket. It was a cotton string threaded through four small stones. She put it on Wen Li's wrist. "Called a *fu*," Jin Shan explained. "Jade, for long life." Then she produced a piece of polished wood, which she presented to Tyler. "Wood of peach," she said. "Keep devil away."

"Really?"

"Promise."

"*Xièxie.*" Tyler rubbed the wood with his finger and slipped it in his pocket.

Driver Ming hurried his passengers into the hiding place he'd made. Then he ran to the front and started the diesel engine, and with a clash of gears the big truck pulled away. Allison waved and thought of Ruth and Tai, and whispered good-byes until the figures on the road were lost in the night.

Ruth led Colonel Quan northwest from Nanchang, peering this way and that, pointing the way as she kept to the bigger roads. Twice she said, "No, sorry, not this way. It's hard to see in the rain. I must have missed the turn back there." Quan's driver backtracked and took a different road. Finally she saw a six-story building with huge red neon letters on the side. It was a landmark that could be seen from a great distance—a landmark that even someone who couldn't read the sign wouldn't miss.

"Here," she said confidently. "This is it. This is where we agreed to meet."

During the drive Ruth had been subdued and often had to pause when the tears came. But as Quan coaxed her, the story gradually emerged. She told him about the boat Yi Ling hired in Hukou, the boat that belonged to some fisherman.

"What was his name?" Quan asked.

"I don't know. I don't remember exactly. Wen or something. We weren't with him long, though. He didn't want to help. He was afraid. He didn't want to get in trouble. He argued with Yi Ling, but she had to go back for Claire. She said she'd meet us later, at some place she agreed on with the fisherman. He was very unhappy when she left. He took us on the lake for an hour or two and then he stopped at a village."

"What village?"

"I don't know."

"East shore, or west?"

"I don't know. I wasn't paying attention."

"What did it look like?"

"Just a village, you know? Brick walls and dirt roads and chickens. That's all we could see. We waited on the boat while he left for a while. He came back later with a man and a truck."

"I don't suppose you remember his name, either?"

"I'm not very good at Chinese sounds. It was Shan or Shen. Something like that. The fisherman left. We waited with the driver for Yi Ling. She never came and we gave up. The driver brought us to Nanchang."

Quan asked her about what she'd seen on the way. She described the northern lake all right, but once they'd gotten into the truck, she said, they'd ridden the rest of the way beneath tarps. They had been permitted out only twice, both times at night, to pee. In Nanchang they had switched to a smaller truck and had been ready to leave for Changsha when Tai had gotten ill. Shan had ridden with her and the baby in a taxi to the center of Nanchang, to within walking distance of the hospital. Along the way they had stopped here, at this big building with the huge neon signs, and he had pointed to where they were to meet.

"Why would he come back for you? Surely he knew we might appre-hend you."

"Maybe he won't. But he wanted more money. I had to give him an extra thousand dollars just to bring me this far. I had to promise him more when he picked me up. He said he'd come back every morning and every evening at six until I met him. He said he wasn't going to come back more than four times. He said there was too much risk, and that if . . . if Tai didn't get better, I'd be on my own."

Quan saw the anger in her eyes. "I still hope Allison gets away," Ruth said, "I truly do. But I don't mind if you catch that sonofabitch Shen, because he's a bloodsucking leech."

Quan asked countless questions, trying to shake her story, to poke holes in some small part of it. What had the fishing boat looked like? What had they carried in the truck? How long had the drive taken? How many times had they been stopped by roadblocks or at toll booths? Had the country been mountainous or flat? The road twisting or straight? How many men had there been? But she was always consistent and firm in the details she could remember, if maddeningly sketchy in others, details that he could not disprove.

Ruth had carefully observed half a dozen trucks during their drive, and when his questions started about that, she described it perfectly, down to the color and the fact that the back had steel ribs and a canvas cover, but she had no idea about brands or weights or exact numbers of wheels, which of course she either couldn't read or hadn't noticed. The cargo was melons, packed in crates. They'd eaten such melons with Ren Kai and Mei Ling on the fishing boat. Ruth described them in detail, down to their taste and texture. "They were like cantaloupe, only tougher. He called them 'hammi gwa,' or something like that."

Quan called Major Ma, asking him what Yi Ling had revealed about Yang Boda's contacts, especially drivers. "Nothing, Colonel," the major told him. "She knew the name of Ren Kai, because she'd met him. And of course she knew the name of her own friend in Nanchang." That person, the one Allison had tried unsuccessfully to call, had already been located by Quan's investigators at a trade fair in Beijing and was not involved. "But the other names were given to her by her uncle," Major Ma contin-ued. "She copied them once, but she couldn't remember. She was telling the truth. I'm certain of it."

Quan turned again to Ruth. "Why Changsha?" he demanded. "That is to the west, well out of your way."

"Yang Boda said it would throw you off," she replied, thankful she had remembered the name of that city on her map. "And he had friends there who were going to get us another truck. I remember he laughed because the truck belonged to the army. He said he was going to get us all the way to Guangzhou without stopping, and that he wouldn't even have to pay the tolls. He thought that was very funny."

Ruth remembered precisely that conversation in Yang Boda's father's living room in Nanjing, although as she recalled, they were going to get the truck in Wuhan. She hoped that such details would matter little, and she was right. As Quan heard that, he knew it could be true. It was unlikely this woman would know enough about corruption in the military and how its trucks freely passed the tolls to have made such a thing up.

And it all had the perfect scent of Yang Boda on it.

Ruth's story was just plausible enough that Quan ordered legions of police rousted from their beds to search through index cards and computer files for truck drivers named Sha, Shan, Shang, Sheng, and three common variants of Shen, who might or might not live in Jiujiang or Nanchang and who might or might not own the truck. Even with a first name, which Ruth didn't know, it would be a massive search. China, with its billion-plus population, still had only a hundred common family names. Extra clerks were summoned, to work through the night.

Quan rang PSB headquarters in Nanchang and ordered them to review all entries from Yang Boda's dossier that might reveal known contacts of the smuggler's whose name or operation might fit. He ordered additional roadblocks erected near Changsha. When provincial officials protested about their manpower being stretched beyond limit, he had no choice but to remove some of the blocks elsewhere.

Near six in the morning, Ruth got out of the car, and walked to the parking lot to wait for the imaginary trucker named Shen. A score of police watched from their hiding places.

Major Ma was at the PSB office in Suzhou when he received a phone call from the Hukou orphanage, the one to which he'd faxed the Canadian embassy's photograph of the child Xiao Bo. On the line was the director, who apologized for the delay in responding. He'd been away for the afternoon, and no one else had seen the fax. "So what does the photograph show?" Ma Lin asked him. "Are the children the same?"

"I'm afraid I can't say," the director said, his voice apologetic. "The child is no longer with us."

"Why not?"

"She was taken away the day after she arrived."

"*Taken away?* Where? On whose order?"

"I assume it was someone at the ministry, Major. Here, let me look. . . . Yes, here it is. Well, I can't make out the signature. Tao someone, I think. It says she was taken to the orphanage in Jiujiang. It was just a transfer, probably. They're not that uncommon. Is there something wrong?"

"Fax me a copy of the order," Ma Lin said. He called the orphanage in Jiujiang. The child Xiao Bo had never arrived.

Someone was trying to remove every trace of the six original children.

Ma called Colonel Quan to brief him and learned from the colonel of the death of the Pollard child earlier that evening. "Get someone over to the hospital in Nanchang," Quan said. "Take photographs of the child. Have them get footprints, too."

Ma Lin called the PSB in Nanchang, to have them carry out the order. Within an hour he received a call from the officer who'd gone to the hospital. "The child's body isn't there," the officer said.

"What do you mean, isn't there?"

"The child has been removed from the hospital."

"Removed? How can that be? Don't they normally cremate the dead, right there in the hospital?"

"Yes, Major," the officer said. "They don't seem to know what happened—just that the child's body isn't there, and they're certain it hadn't been cremated yet. I thought they'd made a mistake. I've had them searching the drawers in the hospital morgue. Her body is gone."

Ma Lin knew there had been no mistake. Even the wisps of smoke he was chasing were beginning to disappear.

The fax machine churned out the paper he'd requested from the orphanage in Hukou. It was the transfer order for the child Xiao Bo. Ma Lin's eyes went straight to the line at the bottom. He recognized the signature immediately.

He'd seen it hundreds of times, on the pink slips of the crematoria.

Dr. Cai Tang.

Ma Lin rose to leave. It was time to visit the doctor's apartment in Shanghai. On his way out of the station, he was hailed by a courier coming in. He carried a steel box that had been unearthed beneath the charred ruins of Director Lin's home. Ma Lin set it carefully onto the table. The box had partially melted from the heat of the fire. It would have been destroyed completely, the officer explained, except that it had been set in an outer metal sleeve built beneath the floor. The sleeve had taken the worst of the heat.

Even heavily damaged, the box was sturdy and resisted efforts to open it. Finally a large crowbar broke the catch.

Ma Lin opened the lid.

He knew at last he was no longer chasing wisps of smoke. Thick wads of American currency were banded together and stacked tightly on one side of the box. He lifted them out. The fire had ruined most of them, charring their edges. He flipped through them. They were hundred-dollar bills, wrapped in bands of fifty. There were thirty bundles in all.

One hundred and fifty thousand U.S. dollars.

The other side contained a ledger book, which had not fared as well as the money. The heat of the fire had singed most of the pages. Water from the fire hoses had made the ink bleed, and the pages were wrinkled and stuck together. Little of the original writing was left; there appeared to be columns of dates and numbers and initials, some legible and some not.

He pried apart one of the pages. *Xiang Banli, 14/1/96.* Part of the entry was blurred, and then, *Beijing, 5.000, 22/3/96.* He thought part of the entry was two names. His heart raced as he looked at other names, other entries. He was almost certain what the ledger would show—that, as he had originally suspected, the director had been selling babies on the private adoption market. But none of that explained Dr. Cai Tang's involvement, or why the director had been murdered, or why, of the six children involved in this case, five had disappeared.

Ma Lin was anxious to begin deciphering the ledger, but its secrets would have to wait until he got to Shanghai, to the doctor's apartment. He placed the ledger into a plastic bag and into his case and raced for the airport.

CHAPTER 20

ALLISON WAS LEARNING what a cooped chicken felt like. Driver Ming had rigged an ingenious hiding place for his passengers. They were inside a long crate, the sides and top of which were covered by other crates, all heavily loaded with ceramic. Driver Ming used wire to lace some of the insulators together so that they made an artificial panel just a little smaller than the end of the wood frame. The panel could be raised into place from inside, so that anyone looking from the outside would see a crate whose contents appeared to be like all the others. In all there were eight rows of crates, stacked four high. A similar hatch covered the crawl space behind the first row, through which they entered their little hiding place. The crates were quite large, and Allison could almost stretch out to her full length, although there was little room to move from side to side, and she couldn't get up onto her hands and knees. But with blankets to lie on, it was quite comfortable, and they had everything they needed in their bags. With the ceramic panel down, they could see through the wooden slats out the back of the truck, so there wasn't any feeling of claustrophobia.

What Allison didn't like was that the only way to get in and out of the spot was with Driver Ming's help. He had to move one of the heavy makeshift panels out of the way and then replace it once they'd crawled inside, so that it would look right during an inspection. That meant they were in a locked cage, completely at his mercy for everything, even bathroom stops. But, she reflected, they were totally at his mercy anyway.

As they started off, she switched on her little penlight and mixed a bottle for Wen Li, who drank ravenously and fell asleep with the bottle still in her mouth. She unwrapped the cake she'd gotten from the hotel in

Nanchang for Tyler. It was mashed by now, but Tyler gobbled it down. She started to ask him a question, but then he, too, was asleep. She propped the ceramic panel into place, and before switching off her little light, she played it on her children's sleeping faces. She felt overwhelmed with tenderness and terror as she relived the past twenty-four hours. The children were in no less danger now than they had been then, but at least she was with them again.

Her own fatigue clawed at her, pulling her down toward sleep. She couldn't stop thinking about Ruth, couldn't stop worrying about Tai, couldn't shake the terrible guilt she felt at still being free. She couldn't imagine holding it all up by herself. She wondered about Claire, and their selfless guide, Yi Ling. Allison's life had become something unreal and abstract, seeming as if it were happening to another person altogether and that she was only an observer. First six families, then three. Now she was alone, perhaps the only one still running. She was traveling in a vacuum, helped by people she'd never met and with most of whom she couldn't even hold a conversation. She was cooped in the back of a truck, traveling an uncertain and dangerous road to a destination she couldn't imagine, hunted every moment by the police. It was too fearful, too much to grasp. She had to force herself to stop thinking about it before it drove her mad. She lost herself in the creaking of the wood and the rattle of ceramic, until at last she slept.

The truck rumbled along through the night. Driver Ming intended to drive straight through. He chewed an herb that he used sometimes when he needed to stay awake. It made him even more high-strung than usual, but with its help he sometimes managed fifty hours at a stretch. That was more than he needed now. He drove straight south from Poyang Hu on good highway, through the flat agricultural countryside, passing through the cities of Linchuan and Nanfeng, where the road forked. The good road branched east into Fujian province, while the secondary road, the one he took, fell apart as it continued south in Jiangxi province toward the mountains.

The rain never abated, and in places Driver Ming had to ease his truck at a crawl through flooded sections of highway. He hated driving in such weather but knew good fortune when he had it. At a roadblock at Nanfeng he was waved through by an officer who was sleepy and dry in his car and wanted to stay that way. And while Ming didn't know it, a second roadblock had been removed fifteen minutes before he arrived, its officers hurriedly moved to the west, toward Changsha, at the order of the same colonel from Beijing who had kept the provincial police on full alert for three days.

Allison slept through it all. She never felt the truck stopping for the roadblock set in the middle of nowhere, never heard the police who didn't care about the rain and dutifully climbed through the rear of the truck, never heard the rustle of papers as they examined the driver's permits and cargo manifest. She never heard the horns outside or the rain or the roar of the Xu Jiang River as they followed its course. She never heard Driver Ming stopping for fuel, never felt the bumps and twists and turns as the road deteriorated and flat farmland became hill country that became mountains.

It was still dark as they began their climb into the Wuyi Shan, the range of mountains that rose abruptly on both sides of the road and disappeared into the high mists, mountains where jungles and steep slopes kept the farmers at bay, mountains thick with bamboo forests in which wild tigers were still believed to roam. They drove all night and all the next day, through Ruijin and Xunwu, their progress slowed at times by traffic, at other times by the rain. Finally it was the horrific condition of the road that stopped them altogether. The highway was an unfinished ribbon of concrete, sometimes one lane, sometimes two. There was no shoulder at all, just an abrupt and treacherous drop-off to the adjacent ground. The roadbed sat so high up that if a wheel were to inadvertently slip off the edge, the whole truck might tip over. Allison had seen more than one vehicle that had done just that as she and Tyler watched the receding countryside through the slats of their crate. In places where only one lane existed, oncoming traffic had to stop and back up to let other traffic through. If there was an obstruction in the road, a goat or a sheep or a cart, all traffic squeezed by single file, although somehow it never seemed to slow. Driver Ming seemed good at it, and when Allison felt him swerve sharply she closed her eyes and cringed, waiting for the inevitable collision. By some miracle he always squeaked through.

Then his luck ran out. It was near dusk again, in rugged mountain country. There were no farms and very little road traffic. He was going too fast and tried to slip by a pile of logs someone had stacked on the side of the road. The right wheel dropped over the edge with a sickening thud. Metal screeched and the truck came to rest on its axle, tipping precariously to one side. Driver Ming got out and Allison could hear him cursing as he surveyed the trouble. He retrieved a jack from behind the cab and began trying to free them.

"Can I help?" she asked. He ignored her and worked alone in the rain. The ground was soft and he needed a platform, so he began hauling some of the smaller logs that had caused his trouble in the first place to build a platform beneath the truck. The pieces were too big, however, and he couldn't get them alone. Reluctantly he let her out. Tyler stayed with Wen Li while Allison helped Ming haul some of the wood. She strained at the weight of the logs. They were setting one into place when they heard the noise of an engine approaching from the front. It was too late for Allison to hide; all she could do was keep her head down and hope that her rattan hat would not allow anyone in the other vehicle to see anything. But the other vehicle couldn't pass at all; Ming's truck was blocking the way. A horn blared and there were shouts. Allison allowed herself a peek and felt the shock as if she'd been hit with one of the logs. Men were pouring out of the back of the other truck.

They wore uniforms. Chinese uniforms.

Terrified, she kept her head down and hurried toward the back of the truck.

"*Lao wai!*"

The shrill bark froze her where she stood. How had he known? Was she so obvious? The officer approached her and she stood unmoving, her head down. He had red bands on his tan sleeves and wore a cap with a star. He studied her intently through glasses that were streaked with rain. Driver Ming stood behind the man, a look of horror on his face. The officer reached out and removed her hat. She looked at him, waiting. Raindrops ran down her face, and she had to blink to see. There was nowhere to run, nowhere to hide.

He looked at her curiously. "America?" he said, the word so heavily accented that she almost didn't understand. She nodded.

"*America!*" he said again, happily this time, almost triumphantly. He reached into his pocket and retrieved his wallet. He found a laminated photograph worn from a thousand viewings. It was a large Chinese family, three or four generations, all lined up at attention and staring formally into the camera. He pointed excitedly at a young man in the second row. "Brudder Zhang Yu," he said. "California! University! Stanford! America! Baseball!" Then he proudly pointed to himself, and to another of the figures in the photograph, a boy. Allison looked at the photograph and nodded, laughing uncertainly with him. She hoped Tyler had the good sense to stay hidden but was afraid to glance toward the rear of the truck.

The officer laughed delightedly, then sharply ordered his troops to action. Within minutes they'd built the platform and worked the jack into place, and soon the rear axle was lifted up until the truck teetered, and all together they heaved and got the double rear wheels back up onto the road. As they worked, the officer stood with Allison, chuckling and repeating all the English he knew, until he'd used it all up again. "Baseball," he said with wonder. "America! Stanford!"

"Yes," Allison said. "Baseball!"

Driver Ming inspected the axle for damage. He thanked the army officer, whose men were climbing back into their truck. The officer helped Allison up into the front seat of Driver Ming's truck.

"*Xièxie,*" Allison said, waving. "Thank you. Bye bye!"

But then he had a thought and ran to his truck. He returned with a gift. Allison looked at it with surprise. It was a deck of playing cards that said "MGM Grand Las Vegas" on the box. He grinned brightly as he handed it to her. "Baseball!" he said.

"Stanford!" she replied.

The army driver backed up until he reached a widening in the road and Driver Ming was able to pull past them. The officer waved once more, and with that the Chinese army was gone. Allison closed her eyes and breathed a sigh of relief.

When the other truck was no longer visible in his mirror, Driver Ming stopped. The encounter had made him more irritable and nervous than ever. He stuffed a wad of leaves into his mouth and snapped at her to get out, to get in back. A moment later his passenger was back inside the little cage.

After that he stopped more rarely than ever. The next time was just before dawn on a quiet stretch of road, where he insisted they relieve themselves while remaining inside the truck. It infuriated Allison, because he stood there watching as she complied unhappily. The second stop was more pleasant. He was able to back his truck down to the river, from which he could see anyone approaching, a prospect that was unlikely owing to a thick, smelly forest of camphor trees that surrounded the clearing where he'd stopped. He watched nervously as Allison and Tyler rinsed off some of their road grime in the river and Wen Li stretched and wobbled and crawled around on the short grass near the water. Driver Ming was jumpy and herded them back inside after only ten minutes. During the stops he never smiled, never looked at Allison directly.

Their progress slowed and the engine strained as they began the climb into the Dongnan Qiuling mountains, a rocky inland spine that swept through south China parallel to the coast. Hour after hour they climbed and descended and climbed yet again. Allison told stories and read to Wen Li, while Tyler buried his nose in his video game until he'd gone through both sets of batteries Allison had brought him from the hotel. They played cards with their new deck, speed and war and fish. Tyler was faster than she was and won nearly every game. Between hands he stirred the cards around on the blanket to mix them up. She taught him how to shuffle properly, and he practiced over and over.

"How do you play strip poker?" he asked her once.

In the cramped space he couldn't see her surprise. "How do you know about that?"

"I dunno. I heard it somewhere, I guess. So what is it?"

"You play for whatever the other person has," she said. "The winner gets the loser's things."

"Like what?"

"Oh, odds and ends. Wallets and combs. Things."

"Oh." He dealt them each a fish hand. "I heard it was for clothes."

She supposed he knew more than he was letting on. He was testing her. "Well, some people play for clothes, too. You play until the other person has nothing left."

"Why would you want to do that? What would you do with their clothes?"

Allison laughed. Sometimes Tyler seemed old for his years, world-wise and as cynical as a grown-up. But then at other times, like now, he just seemed *nine*. "I don't know," she said. "It's just a game."

"A stupid game," he corrected her.

They munched on apples and muffins and tins of salt mackerel. Jin Shan's husband, ever helpful but obviously a poor cook, had given her a wooden bowl filled with rice congee, a boiled paste that was bland but filling. They also had a plastic bag of peanuts and some hard-boiled duck eggs. Allison pulled little bits off the eggs and gave them to Wen Li, who chewed them into paste and then expelled the mess with her tongue.

Their quarters made them stiff and restless, but they were safe and out of the rain. And they were moving; Allison was getting excited about that. Their passage up the Yangtze and down Poyang Hu had been slow. Now she watched south China jolting and flashing by through the rear of the truck as the kilometers melted away. She saw quarries and mine heads, chiseled out of impossible places in the mountains, and brick factories, and cement plants next to great piles of aggregate. Terraced fields were nestled in wherever there was an inch of level ground, the terraces disappearing like glaciers up small valleys.

Like all Chinese drivers, Ming was always in a hurry and never saw anything he didn't want to pass. Everything on the road was overloaded—carts, motorcycles, buses, the shoulders of peasants—and the truck would brush by them with no room to spare. She never saw them coming, only saw them going, and sometimes it took her breath away as she marveled that they'd managed not to splatter someone on the roadbed. She worried for them more than they worried for themselves; trucks and buses would blast by, springs straining as they weaved and leaned and rocked to and fro around the pedestrians and geese and ducks, all equally oblivious to the danger bearing down upon them. She saw a sign above the highway in Chinese and English that said "Happy Driving." They went through a long tunnel, two kilometers or more, and then others, much shorter.

Jin Shan had told her that Driver Ming thought the trip ought to take thirty-six to forty hours. That meant they should arrive sometime late the next morning or early afternoon, three full days before they were to meet Tong Gangzi. It made her nervous being so early. She worried about how difficult it might be to hide for that length of time, but, she supposed, being early was better than being late.

It was just after dawn the next morning when the guard saw Tyler.

They were stopped at a roadside check station, where uniformed officers were inspecting traffic. Tyler and Allison had just awakened and were peering over the top of the ceramic panel, blinking away the sleep and trying to see what was happening. Wen Li was still asleep in the nest of blankets Allison had arranged below Tyler's feet, where there was the most room.

Allison didn't think the guards were police, although she still had trouble telling one uniform from another, and no one searched the truck. They seemed in a hurry, probably because of the rain. She listened as Driver Ming chattered with one of the guards. She felt Wen Li stirring and turned to tend to her.

Then the truck lurched forward and Tyler accidentally let go of the panel. It fell back, pinching his arm. He yelped just as an officer was crossing behind the truck. Startled by the noise, he looked inside and stopped dead in his tracks as he tried to fathom just what it was he was seeing—the white, blue-eyed face of a *lao wai* boy, staring back at him from inside a case of insulators. The guard shouted as the truck pulled away. *"Aiyo!"*

Allison just caught a glimpse of the man. "What happened?" she hissed at Tyler.

"I dunno," he said, frightened. "I think he saw me."

Driver Ming saw the guard's expression in the rearview mirror mounted on the side of his truck. "Blue eye! Blue eye!" he heard the guard yelling.

"Tā mā de!" Fuck! Ming crushed the pedal to the floor, crashing through the gears, trying to will the big, lumbering truck to accelerate, ignoring the guard waving at him to stop. Adrenaline rushing, he cursed the police, cursed all foreign devils, cursed the damned meddling doctor Jin Shan for putting him at risk. There was only one bit of good fortune. The guard station was isolated. Its guards were locals, with no vehicles at their disposal. They would, however, have a radio. He knew he had some time, but not much. They were close to the monastery, maybe thirty or forty kilometers. During the night the roads had gotten progressively worse, partly because of the rain and partly because they were little used and ill maintained. His progress would be slow unless he risked breaking an axle. He had never driven this route, always taking the bigger, better roads to the west. He didn't know the shortcuts, didn't know the side roads, didn't know the places to hide.

There wasn't enough time.

They were going to catch up to him sooner or later. He knew it just as certainly as he knew his own name.

And that led him to another, equal certainty: When they did stop him, wherever that happened, they weren't going to find him carrying a cargo of *lao wai*.

He raced along, swerving to miss the deep craters, smashing through the rest, looking for a deserted place to stop. He roared through a village, nearly hitting a bicyclist braving the rain, and then he did hit a sheep, which bleated and tumbled backward in a bloody broken ball. It rolled so far that Allison and Tyler saw it through the back of the truck, but they couldn't tell what it was. The truck was bouncing and swerving and they held on to each other, propping themselves up and forming a shelter between them for Wen Li, trying to keep her from slamming into the sides of the crate. Finally it got so bad that Allison lay on her side, hold-

ing Wen Li in her arms, one hand protecting the baby's head. The truck
hit a series of holes at high speed and they were tossed about inside the
crate like rag dolls.

Allison tried to watch out the back, expecting to see police cars mate-
rializing, but there was little traffic of any kind. An intervillage bus lumbered by in the other direction, crammed with people and boxes. There
were occasional motorized carts and small trucks, but for the most part
the road was deserted. The country was mountainous, with only isolated
villages and occasional farms, and for a long while she didn't even see any
of those.

A wild few kilometers later, Driver Ming found what he wanted in a
series of hairpin turns carved into the side of a hill. He watched his mirror
and then glanced ahead, and by the time he was midway up the series of
turns he could see there was no traffic coming in either direction. He
stopped at a clearing at one of the turns, where the narrow road had been
widened to permit traffic to pull off. He backed in, angling the truck so
that oncoming traffic couldn't see what he was doing. He slammed on the
brake and jumped out.

He raced around to the back, yelling and banging on the side. *"Chū
lài! Nǐ mén chū lài! Xiàn zài! Chū lài!"* He clambered up inside and ripped
the panel out of the way, his shrill voice jolting his passengers to action.
They scrambled out, their own fear increasing with his obvious agitation.

"What are we doing?" Allison asked as she stood up inside the truck.
He was making her afraid, and she clutched Wen Li tightly.

"Chū lài! Chū lài!" He waved toward the outside and Tyler climbed
down into the rain. Allison passed Wen Li down to him and followed. She
slipped on the wet bumper and fell all the way to the ground. Driver
Ming ignored her.

"Are you okay?" Tyler asked, frightened.

"Yeah," she said, getting to her feet. She took Wen Li and flattened
herself to the truck, to keep her baby out of the rain.

Driver Ming ripped bags and blankets from the crawl space and hurled
them outside to the ground. Then he set about rearranging the truck.
Grunting, he heaved heavy crates around until he could get to the empty
one in which they'd been hiding. He jerked it free, swung it around, and
threw it out. It crashed to the ground, splintering at Tyler's feet. "Hey!"
Allison yelled angrily. "Look out!" He ignored her, working like a mad-
man. Next he tossed out the fake ceramic panels, and then began rear-

ranging the remaining crates. Allison and Tyler busied themselves picking their belongings out of the mud. Neither of them had the presence of mind to open Mei Ling's pink umbrella, which was in one of the bags.

Allison picked her wicker hat out of a puddle and slapped it against her knee to shake off some of the water. It was just dawning on her what he was doing—he was obliterating any evidence of the hiding place, so that he could deny it had ever existed.

So what is he going to do with us?

Ming climbed down, breathing hard and sweating. He glared at Allison, the look on his face bordering on hatred. She looked at him fearfully, uncertainly. "What do you want us to do?" she asked meekly. "Where are we going to ride? Do you want us to get in front?" She pointed toward the cab. "Is that it?"

He shooed her away from the truck. *"Nǐ mén kě yǐ zǒu zhe qù, sì miáo shì nèi tiáo lù!"*

With an awful sick feeling, she understood. "But . . . we can't walk! I don't know where we are!" She shook her head desperately. "Please! You can't just leave us!"

He snapped again, *"Gěi wǒ nǐ de dì tú!"* Confused, she shrugged.

"Nǐ de dì tú! Nǐ de dì tú!" With a look of disgust he snatched her bag away and opened it. He found the map Jin Shan had given her. He opened it beneath the shelter of a fir tree. Raindrops filtered through the branches and splattered onto the paper. Allison just watched stupidly as he pointed and explained.

"Wǒ mén zài zhèr," he said, stabbing at the map. *"Zài zhèr, nǐ kàn?"* She shook her head again, her dread growing. She *didn't* see. Exasperated with her stupidity, he pointed at the ground where they stood and then jabbed at the map. *"Zài zhèr!"* he thundered. *"Zài zher!"*

She nodded. *We're here.* He showed her where Jin Shan had marked the monastery and said "Taoping! Taoping!" He indicated the road, then showed her that same road on the map, a tiny red line, and her head was swirling with it all, she couldn't think that fast, couldn't react, couldn't even argue with him. She stammered and stared and tried to concentrate, tried to follow what he was showing her, all the time denying that what she knew was happening was in fact happening.

He stood then and dug his hand deep into his pocket, extracting the little wad of American bills she'd given him. He said something more and tossed the money down onto the map. He turned and ran back to the front of his truck. The door slammed and the engine started, its exhaust filling the clearing, enveloping them in a noxious black cloud. Allison blinked and stared and coughed. The gears clashed once again. The big truck lumbered off, heading up the hill.

"What's he doing?" Tyler asked as Ming disappeared around the next corner. "Why's he leaving us? Is he going to come back?"

Allison didn't answer. She stared at the deserted road. A moment later even the sound of the truck's engine was swallowed by the trees and the rain.

They were alone.

Her knees felt weak. She needed to calm herself, to think. They were standing in the open, exposed so that anyone passing could see them. "Come on!" she said. "We've got to get everything over there, behind the trees."

"He isn't coming back, is he," Tyler said. His anger flared and he forgot himself. "What a bastard." The instant he said it he winced, realizing what he'd done. Such language was not tolerated in the Turk household, but his recent practice in the pigpen had given him an impetuous tongue.

Allison gave him a sharp look of rebuke, but something about the sight of him standing bravely in the rain made her reconsider. There were better times to worry about a cuss word.

"You shouldn't say that," she said, looking back at the road. "He's a *fucking* bastard."

Tyler giggled in surprise. "Yeah," he said, but that's as far as he went, afraid to repeat it. He was pretty sure that was a one-timer and didn't want to push his luck.

They hauled their things out of sight and sat beneath a tree. It wasn't much shelter, and they were already soaked. Tyler finally noticed the umbrella handle. He opened it up and held it over Allison's head while she studied the map.

She saw an incomprehensible series of lines and place names and pen markings and was seized anew with the hopelessness of it all. The paper shook in her hands, and her insides felt all twisted up into her throat. She was overwhelmed. "I don't know," she whispered to herself, shaking her head. She wanted to be brave for Tyler, for them all, but she couldn't do it. "I just don't know." And she put her head down.

Tyler looked at her and then at the map she was holding. He thought the paper was shaking because Allison was cold. "We just have to walk," he said matter-of-factly, and then, feeling awkward, he turned to the task of entertaining Wen Li, who seemed oblivious to everything and babbled happily, gnawing on her knuckles.

Allison wiped her cheek with the back of her hand, angry at herself for sniveling. *He's right,* she thought. *We just have to walk.*

She knew they were in the Lianhua Shan, the Lotus Mountains, which ran parallel to the coast, the last geographical barrier before the South China Sea. Somewhere, down the muddy road behind them, was the monastery of Taoping. She knew it ought to be close but couldn't tell from the map. She saw where Ming had pointed, and the mark on the map Jin Shan had made, but without a scale it might be ten kilometers or ten thousand. If there was a scale, she couldn't find it, and if she found it, she knew she probably couldn't read it anyway. She tried to remember what she'd seen through the back of the truck. They'd crossed a long bridge just before dusk the previous evening. She tried to find it on the map. There were scores of marks that might be a bridge or might not. It was hopeless. She folded the map and put it in the bag.

They had three days to make it to Taoping. *Three days.* Just a few hours ago she'd thought three days seemed too much time. Now, abandoned, it only seemed impossible. Everything seemed impossible. Her response to the situation made her as angry as the situation itself. She knew she was letting herself be overrun, because she was worried about too much. The same thing happened if she worried about a big design project, a dam or a skyscraper. Taken as a whole, it seemed an insurmountable collection of insoluble problems. Yet taken one piece at a time, it yielded to her will. *You're an engineer,* she thought. *Solve the problem one piece at a time.*

We just have to walk.

She knew which way to go. She'd seen paths throughout these mountains, some that followed the road, others that disappeared to parts unknown. It wasn't like being in the paddies of the flatlands, where there was nowhere to hide. Up here there were trees and rocks and hills, bushes and valleys and caves. A million places to hide, and, unlike almost anywhere else in China, very few people.

The rain had at first seemed an obstacle, but as she thought about it she realized it might actually help. It might keep traffic to a minimum and keep the locals indoors. In any event, there wasn't anything she could do about it. The sky was gray and the mountains were socked in. The rain wasn't going to stop any time soon, so it was pointless to try to wait for that.

We just have to walk.

How far could it be? Thirty miles? Forty? That was nothing. At home she ran five miles every day. She could only hope she wouldn't miss the monastery and that she'd know it when she saw it. But that was a problem for later. For now they just had to begin.

She went through the two bags they had, tossing out everything she thought they might do without, which wasn't much. She spread the remaining contents between the bags to make their weight more equal and looped the strap of one over Tyler's neck and shoulders.

"You doing okay?" she asked as she cinched him up. She nudged the tip of his Mao cap up out of his eyes and smiled at him.

"Sure," he said. "I'm okay."

"Can you carry the other bag?"

"Yeah," he replied, hefting it. She took Wen Li in one arm and held the umbrella in her free hand. She didn't want it for the rain; they were already soaked to the bone. Instead she knew it would help to cover them up when someone went by. She knew their clothes could pass for Chinese. Even in the bush the peasants wore as many Western clothes as Westerners did. The biggest problem was her height. If she stooped over and kept the umbrella tipped low, she thought she might not seem too obvious. Just three simple peasants braving the foul weather.

It was less than a minute before their first test. They had just set out onto the road when a lone bicyclist pedaled past, going downhill fast. He was pulling a wagonlike cart behind him, laden with vegetables. He was concentrating on the road, trying to avoid the potholes, and paid them little attention anyway. Allison and Tyler kept their heads down, feeling secure beneath their hats and umbrella. "Just ignore him," Allison whispered as he approached. "Don't look at him. For sure don't let him see your eyes."

"I *know*," Tyler whispered back, irritated by an amateur's instructions for subterfuge.

The cyclist called out something as he passed but never looked up. Allison sighed in relief. It had worked. Once.

They walked through the morning and the rain never eased. It came steadily, pouring off the front of the umbrella, and they picked their way through the mess it made. In some places the road was macadam in poor repair, in others dirt that had not been graded for months or years. The Lianhua Shan weren't as rugged as the mountains they'd ridden through in the truck, but Allison and Tyler still struggled on steep hills, feeling the strain with each step. Their clothing was soaked and slowed their progress, the wet material chafing and pulling at their skin. After the first hour Tyler could no longer carry two bags. Allison took one and carried it for a while over one shoulder, but her neck began to ache. She put the strap around her shoulder and neck, trying to balance the bag on her back, but the strap kept working its way up and choking her. She shifted it around in front and tried making it into a seat for Wen Li, holding the bag in both arms and balancing the baby on top. But then Wen Li tired of the walk and started to squirm, and it was all Allison could do to keep her from falling. She moved the baby from one arm to the other and then back again. Her shoulders began to ache and her neck cramped painfully. They stopped frequently to rest, and it seemed to Allison as if they were barely moving at all.

After a few hours Tyler was hungry and quite ready to quit for the day, although he didn't say so. Allison found a place in the woods off the road to rest. They sat on a big rock beneath a canopy of trees. She fed Tyler and gave Wen Li bits of apple and made formula for her. She had run out of the formula she'd mixed at Jin Shan's house, and without hot water the formula stayed in clumps, refusing to dissolve. She shook the bottle, but it didn't help. With his pocketknife Tyler cut a small branch from a tree, and she used it to stir the mix. It seemed to work all right, and Wen Li sucked contentedly. The child was a perfect traveler. She hadn't cried or fussed or carried on—the way Allison herself felt like acting.

As she ate an apple herself, Allison noticed Tyler rubbing his leg absently. "Is something wrong there?"

"I hurt it before," he said. "In the pigpen. A rat ran over my leg and poked me with his claws. It itches, that's all."

"A *rat*? You never told me about a rat! Did he bite you?"

"No. I told you, he just ran over me, that's all."

"Let me see!"

Tyler shook his head. "It's okay, really." He didn't want to lower his pants.

"Young man, you show me right this instant!"

Reluctantly he complied, loosening his belt and lowering his jeans. His thigh bore six angry red welts. The rat's claws had barely pricked the skin, but now two of the wounds were swollen, oozing with serum and pus. Wounds festered quickly in the subtropical heat and humidity. Without proper care, simple cuts could become serious in a matter of hours. It was the first time she had imagined how bad the pigpens must have been.

"Why didn't you *say* something?" She was angry with him and furious with herself and tried to keep from losing her self-control altogether as she rummaged through her bag. She found the small bottle of hydrogen peroxide and some cotton balls. She scrubbed furiously at his skin, trying to open the wounds even more, scrubbing and pressing until they bled and he cried out from the pain.

"Ow! Stop it!" He tried to pull away but she held him fast, pouring all her frustration and fear into the work.

He was sobbing when she stopped, his tears pouring like the rain that dripped from his cap. He thrust Wen Li at her angrily and pulled up his pants. When she said she was sorry and tried to touch his cheek, he pulled away and sulked.

They walked all afternoon, and the rain did not stop or even diminish. It seemed to come from some infinite invisible reservoir beyond the clouds, poured out in a steady, measured stream. The day was gloomy, the light barely filtering through the heavy clouds so that they seemed to be walking through a perpetual twilight. Allison tried to think of songs to sing, but Tyler didn't like any of them, so she hummed to Wen Li, telling stories and rhymes she could remember, "Wee Willie Winkie" and "The Cat and the Fiddle." Tyler just grimaced at most of it, but then, when she started "This Old Man," he pitched in, his earlier anger forgotten.

They passed a small lumber mill and saw rough-cut fir beams stacked high outside. They heard the whine of a motor but saw no one. A bus roared past them, emerging through the mists from around a corner. In the noise of the rain they hadn't heard it and realized it was there only when its horn jolted them to their bones and they had to jump back out of the way. The heavy wheels plopped one after the other through a rut, drenching them twice. The bus never slowed. What frightened her most was that she hadn't heard it coming. Had it been a police vehicle looking for them, they'd have been caught. She didn't know why there hadn't been any police cars, but every time they heard an engine they scurried into the brush and hid.

She found what looked like a shortcut. The road they were taking zigzagged down to a small river valley and back up again on the other side. She could see most of the road and both hillsides, and a village that straddled the road on the valley floor. It was a serene place, as pretty as it was isolated. There were a dozen brick houses with tin and tile roofs. Smoke rose lazily from chimneys, mixing with the clouds and mists that floated through the valley. Near the houses were small brick shelters for the water buffalo and other domestic animals, but nothing stirred in the rain. There were a few patches of terraced fields, but most of the hills were rocky, covered with rough scrub and trees.

A path left the road where they were standing and coursed down behind the village through a field, to where it joined the main road once again. They started down, slipping and sliding on the muddy path, when they found their progress halted by a creek that had been hidden from view. From the looks of it, Allison thought it was probably full only during heavy rain; it cut the path right in two. There was no way around. They had to either ford it or turn back. It was narrow but muddy, and she couldn't tell how deep it might be, but she thought they could get across.

"Mind getting wet?" she asked Tyler, who was drenched from head to toe.

He laughed and without waiting for her stepped into the water. "Wait!" she called. "Let me go first!" But he was already in and up to his knees. And then, abruptly, he sank all the way to his chest.

"*Tyler!*" She couldn't help him, not with Wen Li still in her arms. He waved his arms wildly and slipped precariously on the invisible bottom. She thought he would be swept away downstream, but he fought the current and kept his footing. He extended his arms for balance and, when he had his balance back, gingerly made it the rest of the way through. Allison breathed again as he clambered up the other side. He looked over at her triumphantly. "Your turn!"

She crossed a little higher up than he had, probing carefully before each step with her shoes, clutching Wen Li tightly to her chest. She did very well, managing to get wet only to midthigh. On the far side Tyler caught her hand and helped her up.

"That was close," she said.

He flashed a wicked grin. "Not as close as the time you—"

"I remember," she said, thinking of her trout-fishing debut in the Crystal River when she'd gone all the way under.

Before they could continue, they had to sit down and empty the gravel from their shoes. Tyler's white socks were black with grime and had sprouted holes in both heels, where his tough skin was rubbed raw. She found him another pair, his last, and he threw the others away. Her own feet were blistered, her soles deeply wrinkled from the constant wetness. Her right ankle was bleeding where the shoe rubbed against it. She had put a Band-Aid on it, but it lasted only a few steps before it slipped out of place. There was nothing she could do about it.

As they descended the rest of the way down the hill, they noticed a man standing just inside the doorway to one of the houses. He stood quietly, smoking and staring at them. "Keep your head down," Allison reminded Tyler, but they were passing at a distance and she thought the villager couldn't see their features very well anyway. She needn't have worried. It never occurred to him to wonder whether the strangers were Chinese or *lao wai*. He wondered only what kinds of fools would be out in such weather, braving mud and water.

An hour later they did see a police vehicle, a compact white station wagon with lights on the roof. Without a siren but with its lights flashing it raced by, wheels pounding through puddles, and it never slowed. They waited five minutes before emerging from their hiding place and then trudged on. She checked her watch and knew it would be getting dark soon, and she began to wonder where they would stay for the night. At one bend in the road they saw a small town, the main street of which was a marketplace. Despite the inclement weather there were many people about, finding shelter beneath awnings and in store openings as they shopped and gossiped and ate dinner.

"Something smells good," Tyler said, picking up a scent from one of the restaurants.

She wanted nothing more than to walk straight into the town, to find a hotel with a warm bath and a laundry, a place where they could dry out and order a hot meal. Instead she turned them around and retreated, not daring to brave the street, through which it would be impossible to pass unnoticed. They had to go around, although she hadn't the slightest idea how best to do it. The village was nestled in the hills. She led them back to a place where the brush seemed thinnest. They left the road and started climbing. In some places the earth was slippery. In others it was muddy and sucked at their shoes. They had to grab on to branches and roots to pull themselves up some of the steeper slopes, and they constantly ripped the flesh of their hands on the branches, which bore wicked thorns.

Allison's muscles ached from the effort of holding Wen Li, the time long since having passed when she could find relief by changing arms. She had a sharp headache, and every time she turned her head to the right she felt the hot fires of tendinitis flashing through her shoulder and down her arm. She knew Tyler must be suffering similarly from the heavy bag he carried, but although he cried out a few times at the thorns, he never complained. She marveled at his resilience, and his stubborn bravery kept her going.

Soon they stood well above the town, whose lights they could see flickering through the trees in the gathering gloom. They walked along the side of a hill, their ankles bent painfully, until they came to a path that went straight up. They followed it, and the way grew more difficult as the thick hillside vegetation gave way to some rocks, and then to scree that slipped beneath their feet. On fresh legs they could have handled it easily, but exhaustion turned their legs and knees to rubber and they slipped often. Tyler tripped and banged his knee hard. He whimpered and she knelt next to him and rubbed it for him. It was getting too dark to walk safely, and her penlight was quite too weak to light the way. They had to stop. She wanted to get well off the path, worried a farmer would surely see them as he went to or from town.

"Just a little farther," she said, helping him up, and she led them into an area where there were some rocks and small boulders. She had hoped to find a cave, but the best she could do was settle them in a hollow where one of the bigger rocks provided a little shelter. They sat with their backs to the rocks, too exhausted to move for a few moments—except for Wen Li, who squirmed and wiggled and wanted down.

"Pretty crummy place," Tyler said, wiping his wet face with his wetter Mao cap.

"I know," she replied. "I'm sorry I couldn't do better. We ran out of daylight."

It was, Allison knew, much worse than "crummy"—it was a horrible place to stay the night. Even if she'd had matches or a lighter to start a fire, they would never have gotten one going. They were going to stay wet. At least, she reflected, they weren't cold, even after having been soaked all day. She wasn't as sure they'd stay that way all night, and there was nothing dry to change into—the bags weren't waterproof, and their contents were as sodden as their shoes.

"I think I could make us a little shelter," Tyler said. "I could use my knife to get some sticks from the trees, and make a—what do you call it, where you prop it up against the rocks?"

"A lean-to," Allison said, surprised she hadn't thought of it herself, but proud of him. "That's a great idea!" He set to work and before long had a wobbly wooden frame propped up against the rocks. They tied the ends of the poles with their shoelaces, and Allison stretched one of their two blankets over the top. They huddled together on the remaining blanket. It was wet but warm.

That night seemed to last forever. They cooked imaginary marshmal-lows over a make-believe fire, and drank cups of pretend hot chocolate, and listened to the rain drenching the earth and the trees. Allison thought of some ghost stories, and Tyler told one of his own as they finished the last of their peanuts. That was something to worry about tomorrow, Alli-son thought through her exhaustion. Wen Li had plenty of formula and rice cereal, but she and Tyler were running out of food.

Tyler fell asleep with his head on her shoulder, and Wen Li was nestled on her belly. She was cramped and wanted to stretch but dared not move lest she disturb them. She couldn't sleep anyway. She was too uncomfort-able, and too many thoughts swarmed through her head.

She felt encouraged about their day. They were lost and on their own, but another day had passed without their getting caught, and they'd done it all with their wits. She had no idea how they were going to get through the rest of this night, or where they'd find food tomorrow, or how she'd ever find the monastery of Taoping, but she knew one thing for certain. Tonight, for the first time in a long time, something was different.

I'm not afraid. At least not this minutes.

And then she laughed to herself, as she imagined what Ruth would say. *If you're not afraid, it's only because you're insane.*

She told herself they were going to get to Taoping—somehow—and that Tong Gangzi was going to help them. He was going to get them to the safety of the consulate in Guangzhou, where the United States govern-ment was going to help. She had come too far for it to be otherwise.

She knew it in her heart, and later that night, when exhaustion finally overcame her, she dreamed it, too.

CHAPTER 21

QUAN YI had known from the outset that the Pollard woman might be playing him for a fool, but if so, she was damned good at it, and he couldn't be *certain.* When no one showed up to get her, it proved nothing. They might have spotted his men waiting or had some kind of trouble and been delayed. He didn't believe it—he thought it most likely they'd abandoned her.

But he waited, of course, leaving her out in the open as bait. Meanwhile he turned up the heat in the province, leaving nothing for granted, strengthening surveillance on the various routes to Changsha, keeping a noose around Nanchang, staffing as many roadblocks as his manpower permitted.

There was little else Quan could do. *Except torture her,* he thought, but he was not about to do that to an American in his care. He wondered abstractly if a time would come when he would have no choice, and if China had changed sufficiently—if *he* had changed sufficiently—to make such a thing impossible. A part of him said yes. Another part admitted no.

He had been deeply shamed by these women. Three of the four fugitive adults were no longer running, it was true. But he knew that none of it was his own doing, that none of it was from police work. The Cameron man had died, and his wife had been captured, only because of a freak boat accident on the Yangtze. The Pollard woman was in custody only because her child had died—another freak occurrence, without which he knew she would still be free. Granted, freak occurrences often helped the police, but this was twice on the same case, a fact all the more appalling because it was not clever career criminals he sought, but *women—lao wai* women at that. That even one remained free was as humiliating as if they all remained free, a point that had not escaped the deputy minister's scathing

317

notice. The disgrace was the worst—the only—blemish on a spectacular career.

Yes, he thought. *I could torture her, or arrange for her death afterward in the basement of Nanchang prison. No one would know. I have not changed so much from the old days,* neh? *Ma Lin would not do it; he is old and grows soft. But I could do it. Yes, I could do it for China.*

He was becoming desperate, but he was not ready for that.

At least not yet.

The report came in from a remote road station at Hsia-pa: one of the guards reported seeing a blue-eyed boy in the back of a truck, hiding in a case of cargo. The guard hadn't seen anyone else inside the crate.

Quan seethed at the news. *The Lianhua Shan!* The mountains were nowhere near his concentration of forces. He knew there could be a mistake, but so far his other search had turned up nothing. The Turk woman and boy had disappeared. Tyler's eyes were blue. It *had* to be them.

Quan spoke with one of the officers over a scratchy radio connection, patched through to his phone from the guardhouse, and he immediately realized the man was as slow-witted as he had been slow to react. Fully an hour had passed between the sighting and the time he was notified of it. The guard explained that it had taken that long to find him. "We knew immediately to contact you, sir, but in Beijing they made us wait, and then someone put us through to Nanjing, and they said you hadn't been there in—"

"Never mind all that!" Quan said. "Tell me exactly what you saw." He listened as the guard rambled.

"You have the license number of the truck?"

"I'm afraid not, Comrade Colonel," the guard said, using the outdated form of address, unnerved by the highest authority with whom he'd ever spoken. "There was no need. We only checked his papers, which were in order. We do not keep a log. Our regulations no longer—"

"What did the papers *say?*" Quan demanded.

"I don't remember, Comrade Colonel," the guard admitted.

"*Think!* A company name! A cargo! Anything!"

"I'm . . . I'm sorry, Comrade Colonel."

"All right," Quan said. "What of the driver? His name? His home?"

"I . . . I'm afraid . . . ." The man's voice drifted. He had known of the manhunt, and had expected to be congratulated for his vigilance, but now the conversation was going in the wrong direction. He was being made to look like a fool instead of an officer who had done his duty.

"Can you describe the truck? Color, size, anything?"

"Oh, yes, Comrade Colonel." And the man did recall a great deal about the truck, which triggered something more. He and the driver had talked about the new Beijing–Hong Kong railroad. The parts inside were for that. Ceramic or something.

It wasn't much, but Quan immediately ordered a massive search of the area, only to find that he had to fight weather as well as incompetence. It was raining in Nanchang, but pouring in the Lianhua Shan, as it had been for nearly a week. Precipitation was unusually heavy; the monsoons were early and had hit the coast hard. Ceilings were too low for air searches by helicopter, although he ordered four to stand by at the Dongguan military base near Guangzhou in case conditions improved.

Besides problems of weather, he had little to work with in the way of local PSB. The area was sparsely populated. The only police were widely scattered and few in number, most of those now occupied with local weather-related emergencies. They could be diverted from those duties, but that all took time. And worst of all, as with Poyang Hu, there were many, many places to hide. There were a labyrinth of roads in the mountains. The truck might have gone in a score of different directions.

Quan worked methodically, ordering in units from the larger nearby cities of Meizhou and Shaoguan. Before he had finished, he had assembled a heavy array of forces, including a contingent of People's Armed Police, which was being driven in by military truck. New roadblocks went up as the area was cordoned off.

He put officers at the Nanchang PSB onto the task of tracking down ceramic parts that had been ordered for use on the railway, and others to interview officials at every ceramics plant and distributor in the Nanchang area.

Through all his preparations, however, Quan made one serious miscalculation. He mobilized his forces with orders to search all vehicles, and specifically to look for a truck matching the description provided by the guard. But it had not occurred to him that his quarry might be on foot.

As he was leaving the PSB headquarters for the south, Quan stopped to see Ruth Pollard, who was confined in a cell in the basement. The guard opened the door and Quan stepped inside. The windowless room was small and stuffy and smelled faintly of mildew and sewage. A tin bowl of rice stood untouched on the concrete floor next to the steel cot. The prisoner had been crying. She wiped her eyes and looked up at him and held his gaze. He struggled to contain his fury at the woman whom he knew, but could not prove, had outwitted him.

Ruth had always believed she couldn't read a Chinese face, that its expressions and emotions would forever be hidden from her. Quan's face in particular she had found impenetrable. But now she looked at him, and—without needing to be told—she understood; he knew she had completely conned him.

As much as she willed it otherwise, the faintest trace of a smile flickered at the corners of her mouth.

Dr. Cai Tang's penthouse apartment faced China's golden mile, in one of the most expensive districts of Shanghai. The building towered over the Bund. There were four rooms, huge by Chinese standards, each with an expansive view of the city and the Huangpu River. The walls that weren't lined with bookshelves bore an eclectic mix of rare art. There were thick Persian carpets and silk tapestries and a glass case in which stood a perfectly preserved vase from the Tang dynasty.

A Baldwin grand piano stood in the corner of the living room, a Picasso on the wall above it. Ma Lin lifted the keyboard lid and gently fingered a few keys. The sound was richer than he remembered, but the instrument was much finer than the upright he'd played in his father's house. How China had changed, he thought, since he'd last touched a piano. Memories flooded in, and he pushed them quickly away.

He still knew very little about the man in whose apartment he stood. Ma Lin had ordered the doctor's *dàng àn* from the Shanghai PSB and had not been surprised when they informed him the file could not be located. According to the building's superintendent, Dr. Cai lived alone and traveled frequently.

There was no evidence in the apartment about the location of the doctor's practice. Calls to local hospitals failed to turn up one in which he had privileges. A search of the city's private clinics had proven equally fruitless. Calls were now being made to other provinces and to the various Chinese medical registries. Banks were being queried and the passport office checked, but Ma Lin believed little of use would surface.

The officers searching with him gathered the doctor's papers into boxes and brought them into the living room, so that Ma Lin could go through them. He found a photograph the superintendent identified as the doctor. He was in his mid-forties, with a shock of black hair and a broad, engaging smile. Ma Lin gave the photo to one of his officers and told him to broadcast it with a description of the doctor to police and customs stations. He found diplomas hanging on the wall of the doctor's bedroom, from the University of Pennsylvania and the Mayo Clinic in Rochester.

He pored through the doctor's papers, trying to learn something of his expertise, trying to understand why he would have journeyed so often to tend to dying orphans in Suzhou. There were thick files and journals, most with a heavy emphasis on Western medicine, and even research papers written by Dr. Cai himself. Some were in Chinese, while others, published in Hong Kong and the Philippines, were in English. Ma Lin himself relied upon traditional Chinese medicine, so most of the terms he encountered in the papers were foreign to him.

He called a doctor he knew at Shanghai's Zhong Shan hospital. It was one of the most advanced institutions in the country and focused on Western-style medicine. The doctor had treated his wife during her last awful year. He had also studied in America and would understand much that Ma Lin could not.

"How may I help you, Ma Lin?" the doctor asked after they had exchanged greetings.

"I am trying to learn about a doctor, about what kind of medicine he practices. I've found some of his medical papers. Perhaps you could tell me what they mean."

"*Shì*. I'll try."

"There are journals and articles here. They're grouped together by subject. There are quite a few about azathioprine." He stumbled with the word.

"Yes, of course. It's a drug sometimes used to treat leukemia."

"Ah. That's a children's disease, isn't it? This doctor worked with an orphanage."

"It's a disease of the blood. Children often contract it, but adults do as well."

"There are other papers here. A section on histocompatibility, and lymphocyte research. T lymphocytes, B lymphocytes . . ."

"Well, that's outside the area of my expertise, you understand, but I think that would be consistent with leukemia as well. Possibly he's working with bone marrow transplants. If he's a surgeon, that would make sense. What else can you tell me?"

Ma Lin worked down the shelves. "There are more, here. Corticosteroids, and cyclosporine. It appears he's written on monoclonal antibodies—"

"Ah, there you are. He may well be working on leukemia, but all of it taken together—the azathioprine, and especially the cyclosporine—tells me he's dealing with more than that. Cyclosporine is a peptide. It comes from a fungus. It's one of the powerful new immunosuppressants. It's a wonderful drug, although it's not ordinarily used with children."

"You're going to have to help me, Doctor," Ma Lin said. "I haven't any idea what you're talking about."

"Immunosuppressants are drugs used to combat the body's rejection of foreign tissue. If he's a surgeon using cyclosporine," the doctor said, "my best guess is he's doing organ transplants."

BEIJING, JUNE 2. NEW YORK TIMES—The Information Center of Human Rights, a Hong Kong–based rights watchdog group, has announced that a second American fugitive, Ruth Pollard of Los Angeles, has been captured by security police in Nanchang. A city in the south China province of Jiangxi, Nanchang is noted for its military aircraft and Silkworm missile plants.

The Foreign Ministry in Beijing has refused comment, calling it an internal police matter. Police officials in Beijing and Nanchang would not confirm the story. If true, it would mean that only one fugitive, Allison Turk, remains at large. Mrs. Turk, of Denver, is reportedly traveling with her son, Tyler, 9. According to the Information Center, a massive manhunt remains under way for Mrs. Turk.

Mrs. Turk's husband, Marshall, a partner at the prominent Denver law firm of Coulter Grogan, was said to be in Hong Kong and could not be reached for comment.

Pollard is the sister of Rep. Fred Pollard (D-NJ), ranking Democrat on the House Committee on International Relations. Congressman Pollard issued a statement condemning the "bastards of Beijing" and demanded the immediate release of his sister. Pollard is leading the fight in the House against passage of most-favored-nation status for China, which is coming to a vote in Congress later this month.

The White House issued a statement saying the President

deplores "in the strongest possible terms" the Chinese actions, once again calling for the immediate release of any prisoners on humanitarian grounds. The press secretary said high-level amnesty negotiations are under way but declined to elaborate. Asked to comment on reports that Mrs. Turk would be granted shelter in the consulate at Guangzhou, the Press Secretary called the reports unfounded but refused to rule out the possibility. The White House also called for restraint, noting the protests that had turned violent outside the Chinese embassy in Paris. Human rights demonstrators there hurled vegetables at the embassy before being dispersed by French police using tear gas.

In a related development, the news network CNN announced that its reporter Colin Chandler, who had initially broken the story of the American fugitives, had been expelled from China for working without proper clearance. The network protested the action by Chinese government officials as "arbitrary and outrageous."

At fifteen minutes before ten in the morning, in the driving rain, Allison stole a bicycle from a peasant.

It was a three-wheeler, a Flying Pigeon that had been altered to accommodate a platform in the back, on which cargo could be carried. A farmer left it just next to the road. She saw him disappearing up a steep hillside, at the top of which she thought must be a house or a field. He made two trips, lugging burlap sacks down the hill and setting them next to the bicycle, then going back up for more. She didn't know what was in the sacks and didn't care. There was no one else about.

They'd struggled through the rain since dawn. They found the noise was the worst part—steady, unwavering, unchanging, a monsoonal Chinese water torture. They had been sodden for more than twenty-four hours, and although the heat and warm water made it feel like walking through a shower, they both had painful blisters aggravated by the moisture. She used the last of the band-aids, which failed immediately, and then tried to pad their shoes with cloth strips torn from Tyler's spare shirt. Nothing helped. Tyler hobbled along bravely but slowly, until his blisters popped. After that he felt better. She rubbed antibiotic cream on his raw skin, worried about infection. She'd scrubbed his rat claw wounds twice more. They still oozed and looked ugly.

Their trek was made all the more difficult because she tried to stay off the road whenever possible, leading them across hills and along paths wherever she could find them. She tried always to stay in sight of the road, or at least to be certain where it ought to be if it was obscured by the terrain. Such caution occasionally backfired, when they encountered vegetation so thick that they couldn't continue or came to hills or rocks too severe to climb or descend. When that happened they had to retrace their steps, sometimes walking as much as two or three extra kilometers. It was during just such a detour that she saw the peasant and his bicycle. She decided instantly.

She put fifty dollars' worth of yuan on top of one of the sacks. Then, not certain what such a bicycle might cost, she doubled it. She loaded the children on the platform. Tyler sat facing to the rear, sitting on one bag, his back propped against the other. He got Wen Li settled in his lap, and Pooh settled on hers, and hunched over beneath the umbrella. When Allison knew they were reasonably secure, she climbed onto the seat.

The Flying Pigeon set off into the storm. It was tough going. The mud sucked at the tires and the handlebars weren't tightened properly, so that occasionally the wheel didn't do as the handlebars ordered.

Allison's legs were weaker than she'd thought, her running muscles not well suited for pedaling a load up and down mountain roads. She had always thought herself in good shape, but now she realized how weak she really was. Their progress was much better than before, although traffic, while still sparse, was a greater concern now. Twice she was nearly run off the road by crazy truck drivers, who seemed to relish testing how close they could come to her.

She pedaled for three hours without stopping. Tyler called questions from the rear: Who was strongest, Arnold Schwarzenegger or a gorilla? Which was taller, a *T-rex* or an elephant? How big was an atom bomb? He never ran out of questions, to which she made up or guessed most of the answers, talking breathlessly as she pedaled. She tried to divert him toward those things she did know, but usually he wasn't interested. Girl stuff, he called some of it, or grown-up stuff, or just stupid stuff. She marveled at his ability to ignore their circumstances, but because of it the time passed quickly and pleasantly.

Twice she came to villages. On a bicycle there was no way around them—she had to pedal straight through. In this the rain was her ally; she caught only glimpses of people, who were shadows in doorways or stared out into the rain from behind their windows or sat on stoops in the markets beneath the shelter of tin roofs that drummed a deafening steady roar in the storm. Normally the roads were thick with crowds, but now the few who ventured outside were invariably in a hurry, holding their hats close to their heads or bent, as she was, beneath their umbrellas or folded-up papers as they dashed for shelter. She entered the villages convinced she'd be noticed but soon surmised the bicycle was such commonplace transport, and the picture of a woman pedaling with two children on the back so completely ordinary, that as far as she could tell, no one paid any attention at all.

In that belief she was mistaken. Despite the fact that Allison did nothing to draw attention to herself, despite the cloak of rain and the fact she never looked directly at anyone, nearly a dozen people noticed the *lao wai* on the bicycle. While there was nothing overt about her appearance, while her clothes were nondescript and could have been worn by any Chinese, and while here bicycle was obviously local, there was nevertheless something unmistakably foreign about the woman—her bearing or her shape or her size—that marked her as clearly as if she had been wearing a sign.

If the rain kept the usual crowds out of the streets, and if no one therefore greeted her in amazement or delight or stupefaction, as they would have done in better weather, it did not keep these dozen people from seeing her from a distance. Small-community gossip began floating immediately, in restaurants and teahouses and shops.

In China, it was only a matter of time before word of the apparition would reach the ears of the police.

Oblivious to the neon quality of her passage, Allison kept her head down and pedaled.

From a distance Allison saw the white mud-splattered Mitsubishi police cruiser coming toward her, but there was nowhere to hide, not even anywhere to pull over into the bush. They were on a long stretch of gently curving road with steep shoulders that sloped into ditches on both sides. There was barely enough room for the bicycle, much less the oncoming vehicle. She saw the bank of red lights on the roof and the black lettering on the front and choked back her fear. She hissed a warning to Tyler and got to the side as best she could, slowing to a crawl, keeping her head down but trying at the same time to peek up past the big brim. Then the Mitsubishi was upon them, coming at breakneck speed, fishtailing in the mud as the driver fought to hold the road and leaned on his horn to move the stupid peasants out of the way.

In the backseat of the cruiser, Colonel Quan and a local PSB official were reviewing deployments of the few police available in that remote area of the province. Quan barely caught a glimpse of the woman with a rattan hat struggling to get her bicycle out of the way through the mud, her children on the back, sheltered by a pink umbrella. Quan's view was obscured by the cruiser's fogged windows inside and further distorted by the sheets of water cascading down them outside. As the cruiser swerved to pass, Quan turned in his seat and saw the bicycle going off the road. His driver, a green youth from Meizhou, had forced the woman into a ditch.

Quan almost ordered him to stop, to back up and help her, for it was precisely that kind of brute and unnecessary police arrogance that he so detested. But he had no time to spare. A farmer had found the wreckage of the truck they were hunting. Quan harshly reprimanded the driver, who apologized to the colonel but never slowed.

Allison managed to slow the bicycle but still couldn't avoid crashing against the embankment. She rammed the handlebar with her hip and flipped right over the top. Tyler shot to one side, miraculously managing not to let loose of Wen Li as he landed in the ditch on his backside, the blow softened somewhat by the mud. He sat stunned for a moment, then struggled to his feet, holding Wen Li in the crook of his arm like a football. He was shaken but not hurt, while Wen Li thought it was all part of the ride and was fine.

Allison was crying, partly from pain, partly from fury, but mostly from fear for the children. She got painfully to one knee in the muddy ditch, and then to her feet. Once she was certain the children were all right, she lifted her own shirt to see what she'd done to herself. The pain was searing, and an angry purple welt was swelling there. She thought she'd chipped the bone. She wiped her watering eyes with her muddy sleeve.

"Better come look," Tyler called. "I think the bike is broken." The rim was twisted so badly that it would no longer pass through the fork blade or support any weight. There was no way to repair it. The Flying Pigeon was dead.

The umbrella hadn't fared much better. Two of its ribs were bent. She tried to push them back into shape. She did all right with one, but then one of the spreaders snapped and punctured the material. *"Aahhh!"* she cried again. One side of the umbrella flopped down, limp and crippled. Frustrated, she kicked the bike, jamming her toe painfully on the frame. It was all she could do not to scream.

"It's okay, Mom," Tyler said, watching her. "You can cuss if you want."

"Gee, thanks," Allison said, rubbing her toe. "Why don't you do it for me?"

Tyler wasted no time. "Fuck you!" he bellowed after the driver. And she half giggled and half cried at that, but now her tears came not from pain or anger or fear. It was a little thing, perhaps, but she'd heard it instantly and would never forget.

He had never, ever, called her "Mom."

She wanted to say something, to hug and kiss him, but she knew that would ruin it.

The rain stopped in the late afternoon, but the clouds were still heavy and it appeared the weather break would be a short one. Six French-built Gazelle Viviane helicopters lifted off from the Dongguan army base southeast of Canton. Flying a systematic grid pattern laid out by Colonel Quan, they began searching for some trace of the fugitives. Each craft carried a pilot and two observers using high-powered binoculars. Three of the choppers were equipped with infrared heat sensors. The choppers flew just above the treetops, following the roads.

Quan hadn't been able to tell them exactly what they were looking for. His options had clouded like the sky when he'd arrived at the accident scene. His hunt for the truck had turned up nothing because the truck had shot off the side of the road and plowed into a creek bottom. A farmer had found the wreckage while looking for a lost cow.

"Our men emptied out the back, Colonel," the officer on the scene reported. "It took them almost three hours due to the angle of the wreckage. There was no sign of the *lao wai*—no clothing, nothing at all. If there was a hiding place inside, it was destroyed in the wreck. And if they had been inside, they certainly would have died. But no matter. They *weren't* inside. Nothing there but ceramic insulators."

"What of footprints? Were any seen near the wreckage?"

"That's hard to say, Colonel. The rescuers didn't realize what they were dealing with. They trampled the scene pretty badly just getting the driver out. We searched up- and downstream and found no tracks at all, other than those of the farmer who found the truck."

"What of the driver?"

"He was unconscious. He's been taken to the hospital in Wuhua. It will be several days, if ever, before he can be questioned."

Quan cursed. Unquestionably this was the right truck. The guard who reported seeing the Turk boy in the rear had been brought in to identify the wreckage. The guard positively identified Driver Ming from his license photograph. So if this was the right truck, and if no one could have walked away from such a wreck, Quan was forced to wonder if the guard's brain was as feeble as his eyes. Perhaps he'd imagined the boy, but that too was ludicrous, even though the guard hadn't been very specific—it was a *lao wai* boy he'd seen, with Western blue eyes. No, he didn't see the hair color. No, he hadn't seen a woman or a baby. But, he assured the colonel, he knew a foreign devil when he saw one.

So why weren't they inside? There would have been no reason for the Turks to have gotten out, unless . . .

He questioned the guard once more. "You say the driver saw your reaction?"

"Yes, Comrade Colonel. He drove away quickly and I saw his face through his mirror. He saw me all right, and he heard me, too. But he didn't stop."

Perhaps, Quan thought, the driver panicked. Perhaps, knowing he'd been seen, he dumped his cargo somewhere along the road, and then, in his haste to flee the area, he had driven off the road. It wasn't much. Allison Turk might be very nearby, but she might be six hundred kilometers to the west or still in Nanchang. She could be anywhere.

Quan thought the guard was probably mistaken. But he took no chances. He called the helicopter wing commander on the radio, telling him the *lao wai* might now be on foot. Quan pressed the state security apparatus in Guangdong province into high gear, calling every available man and vehicle into service. He ordered an investigation into the background of the driver's company, and the driver's family, and the driver's known associates. He dispatched Major Ma to Nanchang to oversee the investigation, hoping the names provided by Yi Ling might provide a link.

But Quan knew that all he was doing wasn't enough.

He was running out of time, and he was running out of room.

The city of Guangzhou lay less than two hundred kilometers to the west, beyond the impossible terrain of the Lianhua Shan. The South China Sea was even closer than that, only a hundred kilometers south, the coast peppered with smuggling villages. The odds of finding the woman were made worse by the monsoons, the curse of China since the dawn of time. In thirty hours, fifty centimeters of rain had fallen. Flooding was as bad as it had been in half a century. More than a hundred were dead, from collapsed houses or levees or dams. High-voltage electrical cables were down. Telecommunications equipment was malfunctioning or out altogether. Mudslides closed roads and wiped out entire villages. A police vehicle had been buried in one of the slides, killing the driver.

Nothing seemed to be going his way. He felt things slipping away. This Turk woman and her son had made him look a fool. His honor was at stake in this contest, and so far he was losing.

He could no longer trust only the PSB. He needed more eyes, more ears, more help. He needed the triads. They were the seamy underbelly of China, more powerful sometimes than the government itself. They were ancient secret societies, created originally to overthrow the Manchus. Thwarted in their political desires, the triads turned to crime. Many moved to Hong Kong, itself created by pirates and smugglers. The ensuing centuries saw them flourish on both sides of the border as their networks grew worldwide.

No one knew more, saw more, controlled more. Their members were everywhere, their tentacles spread throughout every illegal activity—narcotics, money laundering, gambling, counterfeiting, credit card fraud, rackets, and extortion. In south China they were as numerous and resourceful as they were ruthless. They often cooperated with the PSB, with the army, and with the state intelligence service when it needed overseas Chinese executed for crimes against the motherland. Anyone who could afford it could purchase their services. Quan had used them after Tiananmen, to help him track down the criminal elements fleeing prosecution. It was typical of the triads that they had worked both sides of that street, some helping the dissidents, others helping those who chased them. On other occasions he had used them during crackdowns on corruption in the army, the PLA, when they had turned on former partners in exchange for future favors. Through it all, Quan did not trust the triads any more than they trusted him. They all did what suited their best interests of the moment and no more. He had been betrayed more than once.

At five o'clock his reverie was interrupted by word that the helicopters had been grounded once again by the storm. There were only negative reports from roadblocks.

Allison Turk had vanished, if she had ever been there at all.

Yes it is time for the triads.

He began making calls, working late into the night.

Ma Lin sat alone in the doctor's apartment, going through Director Lin's ledger for perhaps the fifteenth time. He'd been there all night, grabbing a fitful few hours of sleep on the sofa.

The table was strewn with the doctor's papers, emptied from desks and bookshelves, papers that had yielded little except carbons of airline tickets that indicated the doctor flew frequently to Guangzhou, just as Director Lin had done. By itself, that information was useless: Guangzhou was a huge city in a large province. Without maps, diaries, or journals, he had nowhere to turn, and the doctor's papers contained none of those things.

So he had turned back to his study of the director's ledger.

The ledger was filled with entries that were either cryptic or illegible, having been ruined in the fire. Of the legible lines, many contained what he took to be a baby's birth date and name, followed by a surname, then by a place name, and finally by a figure that he assumed were dollars. He guessed these entries were for children the director had placed privately for adoption, the amounts being his fees.

He copied the first few dozen of these that he could clearly make out and put the local police onto the task of finding people with those names that had recently added a child to their family. Without addresses or first names, such a task was nearly impossible and, further, he knew, quite unlikely to succeed anyway. Such adoptions, being illegal, would have long since been covered over with bribes to the very police from whom he was requesting the information.

There were more than a thousand entries in the ledger. Less than 10 percent of them contained this sort of information. He turned his attention to the others, which were more abbreviated. Some, maybe fifty in all, had what he assumed to be an entry date or birth date, then a name, neatly scratched out, followed by a second name and a second date, which he thought might be an exit date. Were these "the wrong children" the clerk at Civil Affairs meant?

Sometimes there were amounts on these lines, followed by initials; other times only initials, other times only amounts. He compared these entries to the logs he'd had made from the orphanage files, but he found nothing that matched. He assumed the corresponding files had been removed from the orphanage. He also assumed that had the six files he had first sought at Civil Affairs not been missing, he'd have found his answers there. It was those files, he believed, that somehow held the key to Director Lin's murder.

He looked at the initials and found that the most frequent of those were L.D. At first he thought it might be another orphanage. He checked lists of orphanages in Guangdong, but none matched the initials. He looked for medical terms, calling back his doctor friend to ask, but came up empty.

He rested his head on his arms on the table and closed his eyes and felt the morning sun warming his back as it streamed through the window. He was exhausted and dejected. Rarely had a case taken so much from him, and he knew fatigue was fueling the depression. His interrogations of the guide Yi Ling and her grandparents had left him haunted and unable to sleep. And now the babies—he knew something was happening to them. It was his job to learn what, and he was failing. Everywhere he turned, he found nothing.

An hour later the telephone rang, startling him awake.

It was the break he needed.

It was the PSB in Xiamen, a busy port in Fujian province near the Taiwan Strait. D. Cai Tang had been apprehended, trying to board a ship for Manila.

Eight hours later, his fatigue forgotten, Ma Lin stood in a small humid cell that stank of sweat and excrement. The doctor had at first been quite arrogant, refusing to answer the questions of the local police.

Ma Lin had wheeled in a cart laden with the most potent tools of persuasion he knew, some of which the doctor recognized from his own profession. The major had been uncharacteristically brutal. The more he learned, the colder he became.

Two hours after the session began, Ma Lin pulled off his latex gloves. He turned off the tape recorder running on a shelf. He was sick to his stomach, but not from the smell.

It was from what he had learned, once the doctor started talking.

CHAPTER 22

ALLISON SAW a junction in the road below where they stood, and what appeared to be a road marker at the intersection. They slipped down the hill through the wet grasses and thick bushes to a better vantage point. They crouched to hide from a young boy who passed by, pushing his bicycle with one hand while leading four huge water buffalo on thin lines with the other. Despite the pouring rain, the boy went out of his way to step in every puddle. The four massive buffalo trailed docilely behind as he tested the waters.

After he disappeared, Allison descended the rest of the way alone. Using her map, she tried to make sense of the symbols on the marker. It was a concrete post on which faded red characters were painted above arrows that pointed left, right, and down. She studied the symbols, then looked for the same characters on the map. She detected some similarities but couldn't be certain. She looked from paper to post and back again in growing despair. The more she looked, the less they seemed alike. What if they used different names, local names, on the marker? Were the destinations on the post quite distant or quite near? Cities or towns or lakes or regions? There were no numbers on the post to indicate distances. She was terrified of making the wrong choice. She knew she wanted to keep heading south, but in the mountains it was impossible to discern the general direction in which the roads headed. The road itself gave her no clue; neither fork looked busier or more promising than the other. One branch of the road disappeared from sight just a hundred meters away, while the other zigzagged uphill until it, too, was lost to view. The map itself was veined with possibilities.

In the end she relied on her gut feeling. They took the right fork, following the road that climbed. They trudged uphill for half an hour, keeping well clear of the road, and arrived on top of a promontory from which they had a panoramic view of the landscape beyond. The clouds were in constant motion, rolling up the valleys, roiling and lifting, then descending again, and through them she caught brief glimpses of the countryside. It was difficult terrain, scarred and rugged. Two different valleys stretched away, one to the southeast, one to the southwest, the two split by a massive mountain. A small river flowed along the valley to the southeast, a ribbon of dirt road running alongside. She thought that must be the road they hadn't taken. Spanning the river four or five kilometers away, she could see the trestlework of a railroad bridge and much closer an old stone pedestrian bridge that arched gracefully over the water. The hills above the river were heavily forested, while along the valley floor small farms were nestled among checkered fields that shone tan and gold in the subdued afternoon light. Wherever the steep terrain didn't prohibit farming, the crops clung to the slopes in long skinny terraces.

The other valley had no road that she could see, but she saw what looked like the edge of a lake. Far beyond it, on the side of a precipitous hill, she saw a single structure jutting from the hillside. She squinted, trying to see it better, but it was too distant to make out details. She could tell only that it wasn't a village and that it was too large and colorful to be someone's home.

Her spirits soared. It had to be the monastery of Taoping.

It was much too far to get there before dark, but they started toward it, first fighting more thick brush, then stumbling across an overgrown road no longer used by vehicles. It was an old logging road carved from the side of the mountain, from the days of the Great Leap Forward when the Lianhua Shan had been stripped nearly barren of trees by workers making charcoal for blast furnaces to melt steel pots and pans and woks— steel with which Mao was going to catch up to the West.

As they walked along the road, Allison lost sight of the monastery. The road meandered with the terrain, sometimes disappearing into impenetrable thickets of bushes and trees. They took detours and crossed streams and hiked up sharp gorges and around rock fields and old abandoned mines, and she could only hope they were still going in the right general direction.

The rain stopped abruptly, as if on some invisible command. The clouds parted and the rays of the late afternoon sun filtered through a canopy of ferns that glistened like diamonds in the light, water droplets reflecting splashes of color from the leaves. The sun brought out the butterflies, and the mountains seemed a fairyland; Allison expected to see gnomes and elves and unicorns. They caught glimpses of distant peaks swathed in clouds and walked through wisps of fog that rose eerily from the rich earth beneath their feet. Tyler played with the fog and said it was the exact same kind they used in America for doing magic tricks.

Twice they heard faint voices, but they never saw anyone. Three times they heard the *whump-whump* of helicopters, their blades whipping through the heavy wet air. They crouched beneath fallen logs or hid among the rocks, but the aircraft never came very close, their sound fading until once again there was only the noise of the crickets and the birds. They found a hillside on which there were wooden boxes full of honey. They stole as much as they could carry, putting the honeycombs in one of Wen Li's diapers.

They found a waterfall. They heard its roar before they saw it, and then it was before them, visible through the forest, water tumbling thirty feet down jagged layers of rock. The sun shot rainbows through the mists that rose from a crystal pool at the base of the falls. There was a cave behind the falls, halfway up, and soon Tyler stood inside it, waving at her from behind the cascade. He stripped to his underwear and stood in the warm shower, then climbed down to swim in the big pool. The water was so clear that he could open his eyes and look for fish beneath the surface. He promised to catch dinner bare-handed, but he didn't see any fish and couldn't test his boast. Allison continually watched the forest, fearful some farmer would surely come upon them, but as darkness approached she relaxed somewhat. It was a good place to spend the night. She rolled up her pants and sat on a rock at pool's edge, dangling her feet in the water. She removed Wen Li's diapers and held her by the wrists as she dipped her little feet into the water, swooping her through so her feet made a wake and she shrieked in delight, and soon Allison was waist-deep in the pool, giving Wen Li lessons in back floating. They splashed together and Tyler threw rocks that plunked in the pool, and although they'd been drenched for days, it felt wonderful and refreshing. She imagined Marshall there with them, the four of them sharing a perfect secret place where time stood still and the world outside didn't matter.

The late afternoon sun was swallowed by dark clouds. Then, as suddenly as it had begun, their respite was over and the celestial showers of the Asian monsoon began once again. They found shelter in one of the caves near the falls and fell asleep to the lullaby of water.

The next morning, not yet fully awake, she heard a soft fluttering, a rustling noise. On the ceiling of the cave she saw dark furry things hanging from the shadows. *Bats!* She got the children outside the cave as if they'd been shot from a cannon. Although she knew better, she checked Tyler and Wen Li in the light for puncture wounds. As she worked she felt something stinging her and had to drop her pants and turn to see.

Tyler had a better angle. "Right on the butt," he commented with thinly disguised glee. "Looks like a spider bite or something."

It itched and burned and quickly swelled. She rubbed it with ointment, wondering whether it was better to sleep heavily and suffer anonymous wounds or lie awake all night listening to bat wings and imagining things. She did not imagine the snake she saw a while later, slithering out of sight on the trail in front of them. She saw only the last two or three feet of the huge serpent as it disappeared into the brush. She squeaked involuntarily. She loathed reptiles and bugs. Tyler laughed at her, but she made him stomp along the path, to warn away the monsters.

After that her skin fairly crawled with her imagination. Every branch dripped with deadly snakes. Every bush hid tarantulas and scorpions and millipedes and every other repulsive thing she could imagine. Whether or not such creatures even existed in south China made no difference. No difference at all.

At midday, torn, blistered, bruised, and exhausted, they stood at last before Taoping. It was a massive ancient place carved out of the mountain, with double-storied roofs and upturned eaves. Undulating green dragons stood sentry atop a gold-and-green temple roof that seemed almost translucent in the subdued light. A stone wall surrounded the compound. Beyond the gate stood an immense banyan tree that sheltered the entrance. A canopy of aerial roots descended from its branches, spreading a tangle of secondary roots and trunks that wove through the compound. Walls followed the contours of the branches, and other branches followed the walls, so that it was impossible to tell which had been there first, the temple or the tree. Behind the main structure stood a five-story octagonal pagoda built of stone and brick.

Built in the sixth century, the monastery had served as hospital, orphanage, and guesthouse. Taoping had been destroyed three times, most recently during the Cultural Revolution by Red Guards who executed the monks and sacked its treasures. But the monastery proved more resilient than such transient passions, and now, by the grace of Beijing, thirty monks once again lived and worshiped there.

Allison crouched in the brush, watching and listening. Tyler hid farther down the hill, with Wen Li. A narrow road led up to the monastery from the opposite side from which they had approached. There were no vehicles that she could see. She heard music and chanting but saw no one.

Summoning her courage, she motioned to Tyler and led them inside. It took a few moments for their eyes to adjust to the relative darkness of the interior. They stood in a cavernous temple, the heights of which were lost in shadows. Three enormous bronze buddhas, representing the past, the present, and the future, sat enthroned upon their long altar, the front of which was decorated with elaborate and colorful filigreed panels representing the auspicious symbols of the religion. Concrete pillars rose to the ceiling, decorated with bright red banners adorned with black calligraphy. Other banners hung from the ceiling, ending in rich tassels of red silk. A forest of incense sticks burned inside wide stone urns of sand. Baskets of fruit offerings sat between banks of candles, and it was all Allison could do, after having stolen a bicycle from a peasant and honey from a farmer, not to steal fruit from the gods.

A group of monks in saffron robes stood chanting at the far end of the altar, their resonant chorus echoing from the high stone walls. One of the monks beat on a deep drum that reverberated like thunder through the temple. Another rang a brass gong, while yet another sounded chimes. Their voices rose and fell in unison in a steady, rhythmic mantra of worship, their shaved heads bowed over hands folded in prayer. Seemingly oblivious to the three visitors who stood dripping in the entryway, the monks never faltered in their mesmerizing incantation.

Too tired to keep standing and not knowing what else to do, Allison led Tyler to a corner as far out of the way as she could, and they sank wearily to the floor. She put her arm around him and closed her eyes and listened, finding the music as enchanting as it was deeply relaxing.

"You sleep in such a place?" The voice startled her. She had been nearly asleep, as she saw that both Tyler and Wen Li already were. She looked up to see an old monk staring down at her. He had a round face and kind eyes and skin that was etched deeply with years.

Awkwardly, Allison got to her feet with Wen Li, nudging Tyler as she rose. "I . . . I'm sorry," she said, embarrassed. "I didn't mean any disrespect. We have been traveling and we were tired. We didn't want to interrupt—"

The monk raised a hand. "A guest is always welcome to sleep here," he said, "but I think you will be more comfortable if you come with me. I am called Zhi Kong. I am *zhù chí* here. The abbot, I think you would say. I am afraid I did not hear your vehicle arrive, or I would have come to greet you sooner. I did not mean to be so impolite."

"We don't have a vehicle."

"No vehicle? But then how have you come to us?"

"We walked."

The abbot's eyes narrowed as he tried to understand. He looked at Tyler, and then at Wen Li, and it was only then he realized the child was Chinese. The baby brought understanding to his face. "So," he said at last. "This is the little one who causes the world such trouble."

Allison looked at him uncertainly, unsettled by the reference. "We have a radio," the abbot explained. "I listen to it every night, after the evening sutras. An old indulgence, I'm afraid. On it I have heard Beijing radio speak of the criminal Turk." She was startled by that, and fearful, but he continued. "We also receive the BBC," he said. "And on that radio we have heard of the heroine Turk. It is most unusual to find two women inhabiting one skin. I am just an ignorant old man, so you must please tell me. Which stands now in the presence of Buddha?"

"I don't know," she said. "I'm just . . . a mother."

The abbot laughed, and she saw his front teeth were capped with gold crowns. "So. A mother indeed. A very wet one at that. You need not explain further. Please, come with me. Quite plainly you are tired after your journey, and I am certain you must be hungry as well."

Allison picked up their bags. "You were expecting us, then?"

"No. Should I have been?"

"Is this the place called Taoping?"

"Yes."

"I . . . I don't know. I guess not." Allison wondered if something had gone wrong. She was too weary to worry about it just then. The abbot led them outside the main building and along a covered passageway that skirted an open courtyard. They stepped around the chickens and ducks and dogs and cats that darted or waddled freely about. They came to a large kitchen, where a big iron cauldron of food cooked on a charcoal stove. The abbot introduced them to an old woman who lived in a nearby village and cooked and cleaned for the monks. "This is Lao Yu Yu," he said. "Old Happy Jade, if my English serves. She will see to your needs. I have asked her to feed you first. I'm afraid we eat no meat here—only vegetables, rice, and fruit. I hope that is not too inconvenient."

Tyler winced. "It sounds wonderful," Allison said.

"Very well. I will leave you in her care for now." He said a few words to her and disappeared back into the temple.

Old Happy Jade melted at the sight of Wen Li. She cooed and laughed at the baby and then tousled Tyler's hair, cackling nonstop through a mouth of missing teeth. She heaped steaming food on tin plates, and despite his preferences even Tyler wolfed it down. Allison sipped cup after cup of tea, nursing the little porcelain cup in her hands, while Tyler drank milk. The cook washed out Wen Li's bottles and with boiling water made fresh formula, the first in days that wasn't lumpy from having been mixed with cold water.

After that Old Happy Jade produced two worn but clean sheets. She left them by a concrete basin behind the kitchen where they could wash themselves off, then indicated they should wrap the sheets around themselves like robes. Afterward she took their clothes, intending to wash and dry them. Finally she showed them to a small room where three cots had been set side by side. The weary travelers had never seen more inviting accommodations.

"Xièxie," Allison said as the woman closed the door. She sat on one of the cots and leaned back against the wall, exhausted but clean and dry, with Wen Li on her lap. Tyler plopped onto the cot.

"Now what?" he asked, yawning.

"Sleep for a while," she said. "Then we'll see." He was already out.

She tried to close her eyes, but Wen Li was wide awake now and had no intention of napping. She squirmed and chattered and carried on, and Allison knew she wouldn't be slowing down for a while. She put her on the floor, and the child started scooting toward the door in the gimpy, lopsided way she always crawled, dragging one leg behind. Allison wanted desperately to close her eyes again but dared not while Wen Li was awake. She got off the cot and sat on the floor herself, hoping the cool concrete might help keep her awake. She held out a set of plastic keys for the baby to play with. Her limbs seemed leaden, and every movement was an effort. Even the keys felt heavy. Allison's eyes closed again.

Outside, down the hill toward the lake, the white Mitsubishi bounced up the road, slipping and sliding in the mud. Once, it slid off the road and got stuck. Two of the uniformed officers inside climbed out and worked it free again with shovels and bits of bark thrown beneath the tires for better traction. The vehicle made its way slowly up the difficult hill, its engine straining, and finally came to a stop outside the monastery gate. The abbot stood in the shelter of the banyan tree, waiting for the officer who stepped from the rear. They greeted each other and spoke quietly for a few moments. With a nod and wave of his hand, the abbot indicated they should follow him. The officer turned and beckoned to his men to come along.

Allison hardly heard the knock at the cubicle door and barely sensed it opening. She heard voices and her eyes came open then. She was still on the floor and saw Wen Li had fallen asleep on her lap. For the second time that day, she looked up from her dreamworld into the eyes of the abbot, only now there was something different in his expression. He stepped past her, into the room. Allison blinked and then choked back a cry. A uniformed officer stood in the doorway, regarding her with unabashed curiosity. His hair was sleek and black and neatly trimmed, flecked with gray at the temples. His eyes were jet black and intense. He had a powerful build and exuded an air of quiet authority. She held Wen Li close, her heart pounding, and pulled herself up onto the cot. Tyler was still asleep. There was nowhere to run, nowhere to hide. Other men stood outside in the hall, blocking the way. She could never get by. She glanced bitterly at her betrayer. The abbot smiled benignly, showing no emotion.

The officer was polite, his voice deep, his English quite polished. "You are a remarkable woman, Mrs. Turk. There are not many who could have made such a journey."

Allison said nothing. She wanted to cry. She held Wen Li so tightly that the child woke up and began to cry for her.

"Now if you will please wake your son and gather your things, we must go. I'm afraid we haven't time to let you rest."

"Where are you taking us?"

"Why, to your husband, naturally," the officer said. "I thought you were expecting this."

"My husband? Has he been arrested, too?"

He finally realized what she was thinking and he laughed then, and when he laughed his face became animated and friendly. "Forgive my costume, Mrs. Turk. I assure you, it fits my body but not my soul. I have only

. . . borrowed it for a time, along with a vehicle. It makes one's passage so much easier in difficult times. My name is Tong Gangzi. I am taking you to freedom."

Near the junction at the bottom of the hill, they met another police vehicle. With Allison and Tyler huddled beneath a blanket in the back, Tong stopped to talk, rolling down his window. The officers inside—real officers, this time—were on their way to the monastery. Reports were filtering in from nearby villages of the *lao wai* woman and her son, riding on a bicycle. "I have just come from Taoping," Tong Gangzi told the officer imperiously. "They are not there. I want you to go straight to Shuizhai and sweep southeast, on the secondary road to P'ing Shan. Do you understand?"

"Of course, Major," the officer said. "At your order." They sped off.

"You are all right, Mrs. Turk?" Tong Gangzi called back after they were gone.

"Yes, thank you," she said.

Tong laughed heartily, joined by his driver. "I have sent them on a fool's parade," he said. "At Shuizhai they'll be swimming in mud for a week. I really must consider a career in law enforcement. I think I would be quite good at it. And now you may sit up again, but when I ask, please keep your heads down."

"Of course." She watched the passing countryside through the smoked windows of the vehicle. Their progress was slow as they fought potholes and mud and washed-out culverts. Several hours passed and gradually the roads improved, and finally they made it onto a major paved highway. Along the way Tong regaled her with stories of China and of his youth in Canton. She found him amusing and entertaining. He asked Tyler about baseball and rattled off old American movies he had seen, revealing that Charles Bronson was his favorite actor. He produced plenty of bottled water for them and once ordered the driver to stop at a roadside stand, where he bought cookies and a real Coke for Tyler.

Along the way he made numerous phone calls from his cell phone, apparently carrying on an extensive business operation. He sat in the front passenger seat, turned halfway around so he could see her, frequently interrupting his chatter to make or take calls. Allison could see his profile and thought he went hard on the phone, that he was tough and combative and curt, but then when he hung up he was gracious to her and solicitous of her comfort and altogether quite charming. She wrote it off to the fact she could not understand Chinese tones. It didn't matter, anyway, she thought. They had breezed by three different roadblocks, never so much as slowing. Marshall had done it! She held Wen Li close and stroked Tyler's hair. They were going home. Tong told her they would be six hours getting to their destination. "It's a small village on the coast," he said, "called Pinghai. There is a boat there."

"A boat?"

"You are a tourist once again, Mrs. Turk. I'm taking you to Hong Kong—well, partway, anyway. I'll be leaving you with some associates of mine halfway there, on the open sea. But you needn't concern yourself about details. It's all quite safe, and everything has been taken care of. You need think only of Hong Kong. It is a beautiful city. Be sure and take the tram up Victoria Peak with your husband before you leave." His words rang with hope, and she revealed in the nearness of it all.

Presently Tong Gangzi made another call, this one routed through a secure line in Beijing, so that there would be no opportunity for anyone to trace it. It took patience but eventually the connection was made to a phone not a hundred kilometers from where Tong was calling.

"Ni hao, lao péng yòu." Tong said cheerily. "Hello, old friend. It has been a long time. I trust you are well."

"Yes, a long time," Colonel Quan said. He was always wary when talking to Tong. Of all his contacts among the triads, he liked Tong the most and trusted him the least. There was never any doubt, with Tong Gangzi, that the knife of betrayal might be turned in one's belly before the deal was done. After Tiananmen, Tong had been instrumental in helping Quan run some of the fleeing dissidents to ground. Only later did Quan discover that Tong had then helped half a dozen of the most hunted dissidents to flee, before inexplicably changing gears and exposing the entire operation to the PSB. Quan had never understood Tong's motives, and what he could not understand he could not trust. And he believed that the more he understood Tong, the less he would trust him anyway. Then there had been a deal, two years earlier, in which Quan was quite certain he had been betrayed by Tong, but the latter had so cleverly concealed his work that Quan could only suspect and brood and bide his time for repayment.

"I am told you tried to reach me last evening," Tong said. "I'm sorry I was otherwise occupied, humiliating your less capable colleagues in Hainan. But now I am fully at your disposal."

Quan started to say something, but Tong interrupted. "I am a perceptive friend, Quan Yi. I know what you want before you even say it."

"Oh?"

"I have what you seek."

"What do you mean?"

"A woman. A boy. A baby. They are with me even now, old friend, sharing a humble American meal of cookies and Coca-Cola." Tong Gangzi glanced to the rear and smiled at Allison, who smiled back. "Or am I mistaken? Have my associates misinformed me? They told me a tale of a great tiger chasing a tiny foreign mouse. The mouse, most interestingly—"

"No, you are not mistaken." Quan knew from Tong's playful tone he was not only telling the truth, but that this would be very expensive. "Where can I pick them up?"

"It is not so easy, old friend. I have already been paid a deposit for her delivery. A handsome one, I might say, but I am still owed a great deal more—which of course I shall expect you to more than make up. And I cannot let down my contacts so easily as that. You understand—they would never trust me again. You and I must work out an accommodation. For my reputation." Tong laughed and passed another cookie back to Tyler.

"Of course, your reputation," Quan said dryly. "What sort of accommodation?"

"I must keep the meeting tonight, as scheduled. I must be seen to be making the effort to deliver her. If the Coast Guard should intercept the other vessel and capture the woman just as I am making my escape, that is most unfortunate—but my good name is preserved and your ends are met. Face is saved for everyone. A convenient solution, wouldn't you say?"

"Where are you meeting?"

"I don't know yet. My associates on the Hong Kong side will decide, once they have the night's postings for the Chinese and Hong Kong coastal patrols. Then, of course, they must be certain the patrols go where they are supposed to go. They are better at that than customs, I might add, old friend. Their equipment is newer. Quite sophisticated, really. You should warn our forces to be more vigilant. There are smugglers everywhere, making them look like fools." Tong laughed; Quan seethed. "There are two possible points of rendezvous. I won't know which one until we've already put to sea, forty-five minutes before we meet. I will be honored to share that information with you over the radio, the moment I have it. After that you will wait until my cargo transfer is complete. I will return to the mainland. You make your arrests and our happy business is concluded."

Quan smiled thinly. *And you will have collected the balance of your blood money from the woman's family.* No matter. It was time to discuss his own payment. "And what do you wish in exchange for this generous assistance to your government?"

"There is trouble with a permit in Shenzhen. A minor matter, really. An annoyance for my associates." Tong outlined the problem, which involved a new hotel that would cater to a wealthy business clientele.

Quan considered it. "What you term an annoyance is worth a great deal," he said.

"To me personally, five million Hong Kong, in round figures," Tong agreed amiably. "A pittance for the mighty tiger. Nothing at all for you to arrange."

Tong was quite right. It was an easy trade for Colonel Quan, a simple act of official corruption worth far less to him than the woman Turk. Such arrangements were made every day, although in this one Quan, as always, would gain nothing personally. But it was outrageous, it was extortion, it was more than he was willing to pay a bloodsucker like Tong. It was too much. The triads were running amok, drunk with power and greed. Tong had betrayed him once too often. Quan knew he would not do it, but neither would he let the Turk woman slip from his grasp. His mind worked furiously. Tong heard his hesitation, while the reception on the cellular telephone crackled and faded.

"Do you hear that static, old friend?" Tong asked. "It will be a shame if we lose our connection before concluding our business. You know how unreliable these telephones are, especially in these storms. Why, the next time I'm able to get through to you, the little mouse might already be nibbling at squid rolls and dim sum with her husband and children in Tsimshatsui," he said, referring to a tourist district in Hong Kong.

"Of course," Quan said, deciding. "I agree to your terms. It will be done."

Tong Gangzi hung up the phone and smiled. It was all coming together very nicely, better than he could have anticipated. His instructions from Beijing had been explicit. "You will see that they do not escape," his master had told him about the Turk woman and her children.

"You wish them dead?" Tong Gangzi had asked.

"I don't care about the woman and the boy, one way or another. But the child is not to leave China," the one-eyed man had replied.

So Tong now saw the way to give everyone what they wanted. He was going to meet the woman's husband on the high seas and collect the other half of his money. And then, during the transfer, shots would be exchanged. Quan would never be able to prove who fired first or that Tong had acted in other than good faith. The good colonel himself would be credited with capturing the fugitives, even though they would be dead fugitives, and the colonel would still be obliged to carry out his promises about the hotel.

And most important of all, Tong's master would have what he wanted. The child would die on the South China Sea, never having left the motherland.

It was all, Tong Gangzi reflected happily, simply brilliant.

"So you have disobeyed me." The voice was level and calm, but Colonel Quan heard it seething.

"Deputy Minister, I felt it necessary to pursue—"

"*Silence!* I have already suffered your insubordination. I will not now suffer your excuses. And it was not enough that you disobeyed. You gave me reports two and three times a day about the progress—or should I say the lack of it—in apprehending the *lao wai,* yet you mentioned nothing—*nothing*—of your diversion of Ma Lin to pursue an element of the investigation I ordered you to abandon. And I, in turn, passed those reports to the minister, and even to the premier himself, to help them in their dealings with the press, all the while assuming that you were following my orders and devoting all possible time and resources to the primary goal."

"You have never questioned my methods or my judgment, Deputy Minister," Quan said.

"I never had cause until now. I assigned you to this case, Quan Yi, because I thought you, of all men, would put an end to it quickly. It should have been easy, yet you have failed dismally to produce results," the deputy minister said acidly. "And now the minister himself is furious with me. With *me,* do you hear? He has run out of patience with this exercise and my excuses on your behalf. Repeated promises of results have been broken, and now the press is blaming us, blaming the PSB and its pursuit of kidnappers, for causing the death of the child in Nanchang. We seem cruel and incompetent, Quan Yi. The world laughs at us. Yet I was prepared to continue your defense, until the minister threatened me with my own job, not five minutes ago. I will protect myself, Quan Yi, before I will protect you. Your insubordination only makes what I must do that much easier. You and Ma Lin are ordered to return at once to Beijing. I have assigned Colonel Che to this matter. He will replace you."

Quan was thunderstruck. He had known his failure to catch the fugitives had embarrassed his superiors and the political hierarchy, but he had misjudged just how much. No matter that the order had less to do with the progress of the investigation than with politics. The negative international publicity had claimed its first casualty. In an instant, his career was in tatters. He had seen this happen before, to other men abandoned by their superiors. A lifetime of service meant nothing; in the fickle world of Chinese politics, a career could disintegrate in humiliation and disgrace in the blink of an eye.

He started to say something, to reveal the arrangement he had made with Tong Gangzi for that very night, but he knew it would do no good, that it would seem yet another empty promise. He couldn't even tell him that Ma Lin's own investigation had resulted in anything other than failure, for Ma Lin still had no answers.

Quan Yi was not one to grovel. He would obey the order, but not until the next morning. By then he would either have the Turk woman in custody or she would have escaped to Hong Kong, and his humiliation and ruin would be complete anyway. "As you order, Deputy Minister," he said.

The call he received an hour later from Ma Lin did not change his plan, but broadened it. "I have learned everything the doctor has to tell," the major said. His voice seemed flat, without triumph, and Quan heard the weariness in it. "There is a compound in Guangdong, in the coastal mountains near Lao Ding. I had suspected only a small part of the truth. The children—at least some of them—are there. More than we realized, Quan Yi, and not simply from Suzhou—there are four other orphanages involved." He explained what he had learned.

Quan's brain raced. It was all coming together, if too late. Briefly he told Ma Lin of the deputy minister's order that they both return to Beijing, and of his arrangement with Tong Gangzi. "If you continue with me now," he said, "it may well be the end of your career."

There was not the slightest hesitation in the major's response. "I'll raid the compound this afternoon. And I'll join you tonight."

The lead police vehicle broke through the front gate, ripping it from its hinges and smashing it into the mud. Within seconds, eight other vehicles roared through the opening in the high wooden fence into the enclosure beyond. Armed police swarmed from the vehicles, fanning out through the compound, Major Ma in the lead. The doctor had assured him there were no armed guards. There had never been a need, he said. The few people who knew of the place assumed, correctly, that it was a private orphanage. Nevertheless, Ma Lin took no chances.

The compound was located in a clearing hacked from the dense jungle a few kilometers outside the town of Lao Ding. Ma Lin never would have found it without the doctor's directions. The road to it was not on any map. Nor was the adjacent airstrip, on which stood two military helicopters and a small jet, idle now in the storm.

There were a dozen buildings in the compound, arranged in two rows on either side of a large central yard. Their cinder-block walls were painted in light colors—white, green, blue, and yellow. Their roofs were made of tin, on which the heavy rain drummed like thunder. The police slogged through the mud of the courtyard and into the buildings. In the noise of the storm, their arrival was a complete surprise. Ma Lin heard muffled shouts as his men barked orders.

Ma Lin dealt first with the staff. He'd given advance orders that they be assembled outside. They were hustled out into the rain, where they stood waiting and fearful. He passed quickly through their ranks, ordering the arrests of several whose names had been provided by the doctor. Most of those arrested worked in the compound's office, but among them were also two doctors and a nurse. They were herded quickly to one of the waiting trucks and locked inside. The others, mostly aunties, laundresses, and cooks, were sent back to their work. Still others, off-duty staff who lived in the town, were being arrested in their homes.

Ma Lin strode toward the administrative offices. He noted how efficiently the place had been designed to accommodate a high volume of humanity. The kitchen and laundry were well equipped, their floors tiled, the equipment as modern as that in a hotel. Through the windows he could see iron vats steaming atop gleaming stoves. There were banks of wall ovens and walk-in refrigerators. He passed large vegetable gardens near the kitchen, and beyond those, near a stream that ran along the rear of the compound, were pigpens and chicken coops. It had to be efficient, he thought grimly. At any given moment, the doctor said, there were more than seven hundred children to feed and clothe. Ma Lin put off seeing the seven hundred. He knew he must see them eventually, but he decided to secure the records first.

The offices were air-conditioned and well equipped, like the rest of the compound. There were fax machines, laminating machines, computers, and copiers. Visa and passport photographs were processed in a cramped darkroom. A sophisticated computer-driven printing press created assorted identity papers that filled several wire baskets. He picked up a maroon passport with gold flecks on the cover and opened it. There, above the computer code strip and the imbedded watermarks, were the photograph and particulars of a ten-year-old girl. He couldn't tell the forgery from a real one. He opened a drawer and realized that the passport *was* real; it came from a deep stack bound with a strap bearing the Foreign Ministry's own seal.

Four of his men helped him search the office. Some records had been destroyed, and for many of the affairs of Lao Ding no records were kept at all, but there was more than enough evidence to piece together what was going on. The papers detailed an endless tide of lives that had flowed in and out of Lao Ding for years, lost lives that had come to have value in only one perverse way. His men stood silently as the major sat at the desk, leafing through the files one page at a time, reading.

He found the name Tong Gangzi. The doctor had told him he would. Ma Lin smiled grimly. At last, the notorious captain of the triad known as Black Bamboo. The man was an elusive cancer whose time had come at last, a man he was going to meet that very night. It would be an honor to end his career. Quan Yi would be pleased.

When he had seen enough, Ma Lin signaled his men. They began boxing the rest of the papers, documents that would lead to a hundred arrests. He stood up. The hour was growing late. The time had come to see the children of Lao Ding.

He spent the next hour in a state of surreal detachment. The doctor had told him what he was going to see, but Ma Lin was ill prepared despite the warning. It was the scale and audacity of it all that took his breath away.

Nothing the triads had ever done had surprised him, before now.

Lao Ding was a giant clearinghouse of human flesh.

What he hadn't expected was that the children of Lao Ding would be so well cared for. He had envisioned something harsh and grimy. But from the first he could see there was no privation in food, dress, surroundings, or care, and it was the very normality of the place that made it so hideous.

The buildings resembled those of a typical orphanage but were better kept. The windows were screened from the insects of the jungle. Ceiling fans kept the air moving. The walls were brightly painted, the furnishings well-worn but clean. The cribs were made of steel or wood, the bedding freshly laundered.

The smells were those of any orphanage: ointments and liniments, dirty diapers and food. The sounds were those of any place where children played: laughs and shrieks, rhymes and cries, sniffles and coughs. The sights, at first, were normal, too, for an orphanage: there was a nursery, its walls brightly decorated, its shelves filled with toys.

The place was overflowing, of course, with children. There were infants in cribs, and toddlers wandering about, and older children, underfoot and in the way. They played together at small plastic tables. A girl skipped rope alone, while behind her, in a cavernous playroom, others played ball. There were books and blocks and more toys by far than Ma Lin had seen at the state-run orphanage in Suzhou. He watched the aunties. They cared for their charges with love and compassion. As in Suzhou, they were overwhelmed. As in Suzhou, they did their best.

It took him a while to understand what was not the same as in Suzhou, and then it struck him. There were not as many blank stares and dull looks as he'd seen at Suzhou. At least in this ward, the children were neither retarded nor disabled nor ill. There were only the curious eyes and bright smiles of the healthy. These were the cream of the orphanages, carefully selected for their looks, personalities, and robust health from among thousands of their cribmates.

They had to be healthy. The ledgers he'd seen put their value at $6,000 U.S. each, for girls. The boys, though far fewer in number, sometimes fetched three to four times that price. As the most highly coveted residents of Lao Ding, the boys generally stayed the shortest period of time. They were adopted quickly, almost always by Chinese couples desperate for a son, couples who could not legally qualify to adopt or who could not find a boy. But even the girls moved quickly; the average stay was only four months. Ma Lin counted 225 children.

This was Ward Green, the private adoption ward, the only ward whose existence Ma Lin had suspected when he'd first realized the children from Suzhou were missing.

But there were two other wards, called Blue and Yellow.

He walked toward Blue. It was the largest of the three, spread through five buildings. Its residents were older girls, aged six to sixteen. They slept in three-tiered bunk beds arranged in rows. There were playrooms with dolls and paper dragons and drawing boards on which they made bright cartoons with pencils and paint. There were books to read, and four television sets, and boom boxes scattered here and there, on which he heard American music.

The commerce of Ward Blue, Ma Lin had learned, was organized in a hierarchy of age and looks. The oldest and most beautiful of the girls, screened not only for their beauty but for their personalities, went through a three-month training period, conducted by a woman who used videocameras and slides in her classes. She was teaching her pupils to become high-priced call girls, for the discerning businessmen who patronized the "iron caves" of Hong Kong and Dongguan, the private nightclubs that belonged to the triads in which gambling and karaoke bars entertained members and their VIP guests.

Also from this ward, good-looking younger girls were taken to the airstrip, and from there to the coast, where fast smuggling boats carried them to the Philippines or Thailand. The youngest were six, the oldest fourteen. The ledgers put their value to the triad at $7,500 each. The sex markets of Manila and Bangkok attracted men from all over the world, men whose appetite for young girls was both lucrative and insatiable. Organized sex tours brought customers in groups from the United States, Britain, and Japan. Virgins were in high demand, particularly among clients fearful of contracting AIDS. When the girls were no longer virgins, they were forced into service as prostitutes, where they sat at night in windowed rooms above bright boulevards and the men chose them by number.

Less beautiful girls, usually over the age of twelve, were taken overland to the remote western regions of Guangdong, where farmers desperate for wives paid as much as $1,200 apiece for them. The value of these girls was growing the most rapidly of all the children of Lao Ding, because all over China the effects of the one-child policy, and the consequent drop in the female birth rate, were beginning to be felt. In another ten years, such girls were going to be earning the triads even more than virgins.

The least attractive girls, those with sturdy frames and low intelligence, were sold to work as forced laborers in Shenzhen, Guangzhou, and Hong Kong. They worked as housemaids or in factories, at carpet looms and sewing machines. Some were kept as housemaids; others even worked in quarries. They were sold not for a lump sum, but on a commission basis, with the triad collecting a fee for each month they worked. A very few escaped; some died. They were quickly replaced.

Ma Lin walked through their quarters as if through a dream, his sense of unreality growing in each room. The older girls whispered and blushed at his passage. One sat in her bunk, giggling, her legs crossed as she held a mirror and applied makeup to her cheeks. Another played a flute, while her friend moved awkwardly through the steps of a ballet; they dissolved in laughter when they saw him. Still another worked on a watercolor. One asked him politely for a pencil.

They all seem so normal. He kept counting, until he passed 320 in Ward Blue. He knew he didn't need to count. It made no difference, really. He did it to occupy his mind.

The doctor had told him the math. He'd known it by heart. At any given time, he said, Green and Blue held merchandise worth over $2.5 million. With normal turnover, they generated annual revenue to Black Bamboo of just over $8 million—more than double what the triad made from opium.

Ma Lin stepped outside. The day was still dark and the rain showed no signs of abating. He tried to light a cigarette, but the rain put it out. He crossed a concrete pad toward the most modern structure in the compound. It was set off from the others, distinguishable by an array of equipment pads that stood to one side. One held twin diesel generators, which, since the storm had knocked out the electrical lines, were now providing power to the building. A large air-conditioning unit stood next to the generators and beside that a series of corrugated baffles containing air filters fed by large tubes that ran to and from the structure.

This was Ward Yellow.

He walked inside and found himself in a modern hospital that smelled heavily of disinfectant and medicine. There were ninety beds in four rooms, he knew, each separated from the others by large expanses of glass, so that one could see from one end to the other. Every bed and crib was full, holding children of all ages, from infants to teens.

Ma Lin could see this was not a clinic for minor cuts and bruises. The patients were desperately ill, their faces yellowed from jaundice, their bodies twisted with birth defects, their systems ravaged by cancer. The most seriously ill were cared for in small cubicles, where they lay beneath oxygen tents or breathed through ventilators. Ma Lin counted eight nurses working the ward, carrying bed pans, adjusting IV drips, and retrieving medicine from a well-stocked pharmacy. Monitors beeped; ventilators puffed and hissed. Catheters and wires sprouted from nearly every bed.

Like the perfect residents of Wards Green and Blue, selected for their good health or looks, these children, too, had been carefully selected from the orphanages. The difference was that these children had been chosen because they were dying.

He walked slowly, trying not to look directly at them. Most were too sick to look back anyway. Any illness made him uncomfortable; in children it took his breath away. His heart was pounding wildly by the time he reached the far end of the room, and he stopped to calm himself before going on.

A corridor stretched away toward the next set of doors, beyond which stood a room the doctor had described in great detail.

As lucrative as the trade in flesh was in the rest of Lao Ding, it was this room that had prompted the triad to hack the compound from the mountainous jungle.

This room, he knew, was the heart of Ward Yellow and the soul of Lao Ding.

This room produced the real money.

He walked through the double doors and stepped through an enclosure containing scrub sinks and shelves that were well stocked with surgical supplies and gowns. He pushed through a final set of doors marked with signs that warned of a sterile environment inside. He stood in a completely modern operating theater, now quiet. Four stainless-steel operating tables were arrayed beneath powerful lights. There were EKG machines, a dialysis machine, blood and plasma refrigeration units, an autoclave, and even a heart-lung machine, all replete with dials and digital displays. Ma Lin had no idea what any of the devices did. There were electrodes and countless tubes and wires. Sterile surgical instruments were wrapped in plastic and packed together on racks that reached the ceiling.

It was here, Dr. Cai Tang had told him, that the sickest of the children were brought, children whose diseases or defects made normal life impossible. It was here, on these tables, that their healthy organs were removed. Carefully and humanely, he said. They never felt pain. Kidneys and corneas, skin and livers. The newly harvested organs were packed in dry ice and carried to the airstrip, from which they made the short flight to the military hospital at Nanfeng.

At first Ma Lin had not believed the doctor. Oh, yes, he knew the ill-kept state secret about what was done with the organs of prisoners executed for their crimes. Ma Lin himself had presided at more than one execution and had known only too well what the shadowy men who wore no uniforms did to the freshly executed, whose bodies were thrown into a truck where their organs were removed. Ma Lin knew, too, of the hospital run by the People's Liberation Army at Nanfeng, where desperately ill foreigners came with hard cash. Thirty thousand U.S., he had heard, would buy a kidney.

But those were prisoners, Ma Lin had said incredulously to Dr. Cai Tang. *You're talking about children.*

And it was the doctor's defense of what happened at Lao Ding that had caused Ma Lin twelve hours earlier to inflict a frenzy of pain on the man as he'd searched for the truth.

"You are a fool, Ma Lin," the doctor had said defiantly through broken teeth. "I have taken the bodies of those who have been discarded, those who have no hope, and extracted something good from them. And along the way I have done important research on anticoagulants and organ rejection. I have written papers! Do you realize how important that is?"

The doctor's screams had filled the basement then, as Ma Lin had lost himself in the horror of it all and applied too much current. The doctor lost consciousness. When Ma Lin revived him and threatened more of the same, Cai Tang denied that healthy children were ever used. It was only the brain dead, he said, or those dying who found their way to the operating tables. The doctor had sworn it while writing in pain, pain Ma Lin himself had administered with all the delicate precision of a surgeon. The major knew the man ought to be well past lying. But Ma Lin was a good judge of such things, and he was certain the doctor was still lying. And then after a while it hadn't mattered anymore to Ma Lin. It had only mattered that he come to Lao Ding, to see for himself, to put a stop to it all. There would be another time, for the doctor.

Ma Lin thought of the ward he had just walked through, filled with children awaiting their turn in this room, and the thought overwhelmed him. He steadied himself on one of the operating tables. He looked down, into a bucket that stood near the table. There was a gory mass at the bottom. He had no idea what it was. He fell to his knees and vomited onto the gleaming tile floor, vomited until there was nothing left inside.

Ashamed at his weakness, he stood and wiped his mouth with his sleeve. His eyes watered from the pungent smell of astringent, and his ears were pounding. He turned and fled from the room, past his own startled officers. He went outdoors and stood in the rain and breathed deeply of the heavy jungle air, trying to push away his nausea.

He knew he was not yet finished. Two concrete walks diverged from where he stood. The first led toward a gate, beyond which lay the airfield. The other led toward the rear of the compound, where massive trees overhung the fence. He could just make out the white brick building there, all but lost in the shadows.

It was a small place, the last of the structures he had come to see.

Efficient, like the rest of Lao Ding.

He knew what it was because the doctor had told him it was there, and because of the smokestack on top, and because he'd seen a bigger one like it in Suzhou—a grim structure run by the Ministry of Civil Affairs, a place tended by outcast men wearing gray pajamas.

He shoved the door open and looked inside. There was a metal cylinder with a large iron door on one end, and a smaller door beneath it, from which ashes were extracted when the burners went off. Shelves held crates into which the ashes were shoveled, before they were spread in the vegetable gardens or dumped in the stream.

It was the building where the truth or falsehood of the doctor's claims about the ultimate castoffs of Lao Ding had been obliterated forever.

Ma Lin stood in front of the little building and felt the rain on his face. He hated this case, hated everything about it, hated what had happened to the children, hated the system that had brought them here. He knew that there would be a few executions for the criminals of Lao Ding. Then it would all be buried. He had helped Beijing do precisely that before, in other cases, and what he hated most of all, standing there in the rain in front of the oven, was the sure knowledge that he was going to help Beijing do it again.

He closed his eyes and turned away.

It was nearing dusk when he finished giving the last of his orders to the police who would remain behind. Wearily he climbed into his vehicle for the trip south, for his meeting with Quan Yi and their rendezvous at sea with Tong Gangzi. It was the only aspect of the case Ma Lin would be glad not to miss.

His car passed through the gate. The driver stopped for a moment, waiting for one of his men to climb in back. Ma Lin looked up at the wooden beam that hung over the gate. Someone had nailed a wooden placard there, upon which had been painted the image of two mandarins. Both wore a goatee, their mustaches long and black and pointed at the ends. Their flowing robes were adorned with dragons and kites. On their backs they carried quivers of arrows.

They were often seen at New Year's. They were the door guardians, Ch'in Ch'iung and Yu-chih Kung. Almost every child in China knew them.

They protected the inhabitants of the house from evil.

CHAPTER 23

IT WAS NEARLY MIDNIGHT when Marshall Turk stepped off the quay onto the old trawler. Across Victoria harbor the lights of Kowloon blinked through the rain clouds. A Japan Air 747 appeared through the mists on final approach to Kai Tak and then was lost again, with only the roar of its engines remaining. Despite the lateness of the hour the harbor was alive, bobbing with lighters and ferries, sampans and garbage scows, all plying the waters between dark freighters slipping to and from the sea. Deep horns blared rights-of-way, and the smell of salt air was strong.

Marshall's ears had improved, but even the gentle motion in the harbor made him instantly woozy. He blanched and felt nauseated. Li Kan reached out to steady him. "Perhaps you should remain here," he said, looking at his friend's face. "You're white as a sheet. It will be worse out there, on the open water. I will handle it for you."

"Not a chance," Marshall said stubbornly. "I'm going." He held a canvas bag stuffed with $125,000 U.S., the balance due for the exchange at sea. Li Kan had told him he'd gotten off easily at a quarter million dollars. "Even the poorest peasants pay thirty thousand or more for single passage to the States. They cross the Pacific in a filthy hold, and these people smuggle hundreds at a time."

Marshall had found it more difficult to raise the money long distance than he'd imagined, but as he was scrambling to do so, Clarence Coulter had stepped in. "The firm will loan you the cash," Clarence had said. "I'll wire it first thing in the morning." Marshall knew the firm never did anything like that for its partners. Clarence was making the offer personally, and Marshall accepted gratefully.

Tong Gangzi had prevailed on Li Kan to convince Marshall they should bring Allison out of China by boat, rather than getting her inside the consulate in Guangzhou. The sea made more sense, Tong had explained. He did it all the time and said it was the easier course. The consulate would be under heavy surveillance, and even if they succeeded in getting her inside, there was no guarantee Allison would be any better off. "She'd still be in China," Tong had pointed out, "giving the diplomats fits. Just get her out of the country. Let the authorities in Hong Kong wrestle with this."

So now Marshall and Li Kan stood in the wheelhouse next to the captain, a hard, rude man who smoked and spat endlessly. Banks of instruments lined the console, bathing the man's face in a dim red glow. Regular weather bureau reports were broadcast in Chinese and English over a transistor radio, while the ship's radio crackled with weather reports from ships at sea. The captain told Li Kan they were lucky. A stationary front had parked along the coast, and although it was raining the seas were low and calm. That could change at any time, he warned, but if it didn't, it made for an easy night's work.

After conversing with the captain, Li Kan had explained the routine to Marshall. "Except in a squall the captain heads out every night at this time to fish, so no one will notice anything unusual. We'll run east until we're out of territorial waters. The captain has contacts both in Hong Kong and on the mainland, contacts who will intercept the nightly orders for coastal patrol boats for both sides. They are creatures of habit. Quite lazy, and they rarely vary their routines. They usually concentrate well to the north of where we'll be. He'll soon know which sectors are being patrolled, and at two-thirty he will radio Tong Gangzi about where to meet us. Tonight he'll work one of two places." They bent over a map and Li Kan showed Marshall the area. "We'll make the pickup here, or here." His finger spanned an area of a hundred kilometers. "We should make the pickup around three. After that we'll fish until midmorning, and be back at our berth by noon."

"What happens if the coastal patrol spots us?"

"Nothing, unless they actually witness the pickup. Otherwise we're just a fishing boat. The captain says don't worry. He's done this for eight years and never had a problem. He says the worst case is that if the PRC gets lucky, he'll just take what's in your bag there"—he indicated Marshall's money—"and give it to the Chinese captain."

Marshall nodded. "What if the Hong Kong side catches us?"

"Unfortunately they're not so easily purchased as their cousins on the mainland. They sure won't turn us over to the Chinese. We'd end up in a Hong Kong jail, I suppose. I can imagine worse things just now."

Marshall tried to stay out of the way, watching as the crew moved about its tasks. Two of the men retrieved arms from a locker. There were semiautomatic pistols and rifles and endless steel clips of ammunition. His queasiness grew as they expertly rammed clips home and checked chambers. The awful thought of his family being on either end of such an arsenal was just beginning to sink in. The night sea, the darkened ship, the electronics, the radio, the guns, and the money—it was all becoming real. He wondered what Allison was doing just then. Tong Gangzi had radioed word that he had the woman and two children and that they ought to be on the water soon. Marshall's head pounded with it all. He felt the engines rumbling to life. Chains rattled and lines were cast off. They pulled slowly away from the dock. The captain pushed his throttles forward and the trawler made for the open sea.

Across the South China Sea, at the harbor of Shanwei on the mainland, Colonel Quan Yi was making his final preparations. He had wished to leave nothing to chance, hoping to utilize helicopters as well as a ship, but the weather showed no sign of lifting and the Eurocopters remained grounded at Dongguan, their crews standing by.

He stood in the bridge of the coastal patrol vessel that he had requisitioned. It was not a customs craft, but a Huchuan class fast attack boat— a military vessel, built in Shanghai. Quan had chosen it over a customs craft for two reasons. The first was that he didn't trust south China customs officials, particularly not where Tong was concerned. Tong would undoubtedly learn of Quan's true orders almost as quickly as Quan himself gave them. But Tong was unlikely to wield such influence over naval authorities. The second reason was speed. With three M-50 diesels and a forward pair of hydrofoils, the navy boat was capable of making fifty knots—not as fast as some of the smuggling vessels, perhaps, but faster than anything customs had. It was equipped with sophisticated surface search radar and carried a sixteen-man crew. The boat was armed with everything from 14.5 mm machine guns to Soviet-built torpedoes. It sat at anchor alongside the brightly lit wharf, its crew making final preparations for departure.

The ship's captain had initially balked at taking orders from a civilian, even a colonel in the PSB. Quan Yi of course had not been able to call the deputy minister, who had ordered him to Beijing, but his other contacts in the capital were more than sufficient. Soon a call was made to the head-quarters of the South Sea fleet at Zhanjiang that quickly erased the captain's objections. A matter of state security, the vice admiral told him. Now the captain listened attentively as Quan, standing over the chart table on the bridge, outlined his orders.

"This is more than a simple case of smuggling," Quan told the captain. "Our quarry is Tong Ganzi, well-known to customs and police. Ordinarily his commerce would not have raised attention in Beijing. But we have learned today that he has added industrial espionage to his list of activities. He has stolen vital computer chips from the Silkworm missile plant in Nanchang. He intends to convey them to Hong Kong for sale on the international market. He will not succeed."

Quan indicated the very same two positions Marshall had been studying earlier. "Our target will be using a fast launch. He will be departing from somewhere near Pinghai, and intends to rendezvous with a Hong Kong–registry trawler in one of two places—either here, or here," he said. "We won't know which for another"—he looked at his watch—"five hours, at precisely two-thirty. We will already be positioned along his route, just here"—he pointed again—"and await the radio signal. When we have the location we will not wait for the rendezvous to occur. Instead, as soon as the boat has been acquired on radar we will intercept it."

The captain studied the nautical charts. "If Tong acts as you predict, it should present us with no special difficulties, Colonel," he said. "It is his speed that concerns me."

"As it does me," Quan replied. "However, Tong will not be expecting us. He'll be running in open water, relying on visual contact for other shipping. His boat carries only a GPS, and no radar, while we will detect him at a range of . . ." He looked at the captain for an answer.

"Depending on the sea and the weather and the composition of his craft, about twenty kilometers," the captain said.

"Quite sufficient. And the range of your guns?"

"Seven thousand meters."

"So. We'll have plenty of time to position ourselves directly in his path. If we're running black, he won't see us until it's quite too late. And that brings me to your orders, Captain. Tong and his men are armed, dangerous, and desperate. He is to have no warning of our presence, and no opportunity to escape. Once we are in a position to be certain of success, your men are to fire upon Tong's vessel, until it is totally disabled. If any resistance is encountered—I repeat, *any*—your men are to shoot to kill all occupants of the boat. Is that clear?"

"Of course, Colonel," the captain said, looking forward to the engagement. His men rarely had a chance to test themselves with live fire.

"Do you have any questions?" Quan asked.

"What about the trawler? If they are positioned as you expect, they will be in Chinese waters."

"I don't care about the trawler," Quan replied. "In fact, it serves our interests if it observes what happens to Tong and is allowed to flee to Hong Kong."

Quan reveled in his perfect position. Tong's involvement in the Turk case had presented him with an unusual opportunity. He knew that of course Tong would fire back with an impressive array of small arms. But his light boat, designed for speed and not battle, would be no match for this vessel.

Quan had long since learned that for the good of the state his methods must vary. There were times when finesse was the best approach and times when deals had to be made with the devil himself. There were times to make an example, to send a message. He knew now, with absolute certainty, it was time to send a message. In the midst of communism's death throes, Tong and his kind were helping to criminalize the state apparatus itself. The cancer of corruption was fast metastasizing to officials at every level. If it weren't halted, all China might follow the Russian road to ruin. If Quan gave Tong what he wanted, it would mean the further debasement of a nation that could ill afford it. Tong must become a casualty of his own greed. What Quan had learned from Ma Lin, about Tong Gangzi's role at Lao Ding, changed nothing. If anything, it strengthened his resolve.

There was, of course, the matter of the Turk woman. If she died in the course of the lesson, it did not trouble him. The People's Republic was not to be trifled with. If she died—yes, if the children died, too—the government would express its regret, while the real message to the world would be quite clear: China was absolute lord of her own domain. Those who sought to test that truth would always pay a heavy price.

There was, Quan knew, a chance the woman would survive. If so, she would be his captive. Whether she lived or died, he would have stopped her. At least some face—his own and the motherland's—would be preserved.

In every scenario, he was rid of two devils.

He debated whether to tell Ma Lin of his orders to the captain, once the major arrived. Ma Lin might object, but he would do so discreetly. What Ma Lin wouldn't know was whether Quan wished to kill Tong or the woman Turk.

And it didn't matter that he not know. Ma Lin was a good officer, a man who had spent a lifetime accepting orders. He would accept these, too.

In the end, Quan decided not to tell him.

The police car moved through the small seaport of Pinghai, a town favored by smugglers for its location on a small peninsula near Hong Kong. Its shops were filled with smuggled consumer goods—televisions, motorcycles, refrigerators, computers, and countless vehicles whose right-hand drive was a sure sign they had been imported illegally from the British Crown colony. No one cared. Bribes bought illegal plates and papers for the vehicles, which were then driven by officials who spent their days hunting smugglers and their nights enjoying the goods they brought in.

Allison was getting nervous again. She and Tyler had entered China with their noses pressed against the window of their jet. Now their noses were pressed against the window of the police car as they prepared to leave. They felt the sea, and then they smelled it, and then they heard it, and at last, they saw it. She squeezed Tyler's hand, and he squeezed back.

An armed guard waved them through a gate. They turned onto a road that ran past the docks. There were small craft in the water, mostly junks and sampans, and a forest of cranes tending freighters they couldn't see. They kept on driving past the docks and down a dirt road to a sandy beach. They arrived at a lone wooden pier, at the end of which there was a white cabin cruiser. At the sound of the approaching vehicle, two men lounging at land side jumped up. The doors opened and the passengers were quickly hustled down the pier.

Allison was carrying Wen Li, and Tong smiled broadly. "You are as good as home now," he said, helping her across the gap between pier and boat. "There, you see? Already you have left the soil of the People's

Republic. Just a short trip now and you'll be with your husband." Tyler hopped in after her, while Tong Gangzi saw to the transfer of their bags. It was done quickly. One of the men remained behind to take the police car to a warehouse where it would be stored for later use or stripped for parts.

With Tong Gangzi and his crew of four, they set out. The boat was a cabin cruiser, its four 250-horsepower inboard engines capable of eighty knots. There were two steering wheels, one on an upper flying bridge, the other in a lower cockpit. The craft had been specially modified for speed. Its bunks, galley, and storage cabinets had all been stripped out. The boat carried no radar but was equipped with a global positioning device, radios, and infrared signalers for silent communication with other vessels. It carried a light arsenal of weapons, including machine pistols and high-powered rifles equipped with nightscopes.

Allison settled with the children on the lower deck, just beneath the shelter top of the flying bridge deck. There were no benches or seats, just low stoops surrounding the four engine compartments that rose boxlike from the deck. Tong found some foam pads and they sat on them between the engines, their backs resting against the compartments. The boat left its mooring. They felt the vibration of the powerful engines all the way to their bones as the prow of the boat lifted from the water and their speed quickly increased.

Tong was cheerful. The clouds were low and the rain was steady but light. A low-pressure system was camped over the area, while the typhoon that had shown signs of developing farther south had lost its energy. There was only a light chop to the seas, and their ride would be smooth. It was a perfect night for business. He made certain his three guests were quite comfortable. He had already informed his crew that they were to be shot during the transfer. He checked to see that all weapons were at the ready, then sat back to enjoy the ride.

The call came at two-thirty in the morning, after the captain of the trawler from Hong Kong made his decision about the meeting point. His message was coded and curt, broadcast over a prearranged frequency. "Kowloon two," he said simply. "Kowloon two." He waited five minutes and repeated the message. Tong's acknowledgment crackled over the radio: "Two Kowloon." It was to be the southernmost point.

Quan Yi and Ma Lin stood behind the captain as the message came through. The captain kept his eyes on the radar screen. All shipboard lights were doused and smoking was forbidden. Weapons ready, his men stood watch, peering out into the blackness.

Fourteen minutes later they saw the blip. "Small vessel approaching forty degrees off the starboard bow, Captain," the radar operator reported. "Speed thirty knots, bearing oh-seven-oh. Range eighteen thousand meters." As Quan had confidently predicted, Tong Gangzi was coming to them, expecting open sea for another twenty nautical miles, where he was to meet the trawler.

"Very well. All engines ahead full, course three-one-three. Extend hydrofoils."

"Three-one-three, aye, Captain," the helmsman said, and the engines roared to life. At the waterline two forward panels slipped open and the hydrofoils slid into position. A moment later the boat was racing through the water on a course to intercept the other craft. It didn't have far to go.

When the cruiser reached position, the captain ordered the engines stopped. On the radar, the blip that was Tong headed directly toward them. "The moth to the flame," the captain muttered, watching the screen.

There was another blip. "The trawler," the captain said to Quan. He called final orders to the crew. Two sailors had removed the canvas shroud covering the double machine guns. Now wearing night goggles, they perched behind their turrets, ready to open fire. Belts of high-caliber ammunition were neatly laid by, ready to feed the hungry guns.

They saw the dim bow light first, like a blinding beacon in their sights, and then, as the eerie red-and-black-and-white image grew closer in their goggles, they could see the face of the pilot sitting atop the flying bridge, oblivious to the disaster that awaited him. The sailors took aim, awaiting the captain's order.

When the boat was a hundred meters away, it came.

To the steady rain of the monsoon, the navy of China added thunder and lightning.

In one terrifying instant, the night caught fire. Tyler was asleep, his head slumped on Allison's shoulder, while Wen Li slept on her lap. Allison was looking up when she saw flashes of light zip by in the night sky. She thought at first of a meteor shower, even though it didn't look right. What else could it be? The streaks were well overhead but dropping rapidly, and then she heard something slapping the hull. Instinctively she cringed and held Wen Li closer.

Tong Gangzi was aft when he saw the tracer bullets. He cursed the treachery of Quan Yi and ran forward, bellowing a stream of orders as his men scrambled for their weapons. The pilot swerved sharply, changing course as he rammed the throttle forward for speed. The prow leapt from the water as the big engines surged, but an instant later the engines slowed to an idle again as the pilot slumped over the wheel, dead. The other sailors opened fire against an enemy they could not see, aiming back down the stream of tracer bullets toward their source, their own bullets falling far short to the sea. Tong Gangzi reached the lower instrument panel and doused the running lights as he prepared to take the wheel. The cabin windows exploded next to him. Wood splintered, and he took two bullets. He crashed sideways to the deck. Electrical instruments behind the helmsman's wheel sputtered and shorted out.

Tyler awoke in confusion. Stupidly he started to stand, to look, but Allison caught him by the shirt. "Lie down!" she screamed. "Get between the engines!" He didn't move fast enough and she yanked him then, so hard that he crashed to the deck beside her. They huddled together in the bottom of the boat, the night on fire with the sound of weapons and the smell of powder and death. In the murderous fire streaming from the unseen vessel, Tong's crew had no chance. Men fell to the deck, screaming or dead. One toppled from the flying bridge, his leg catching in the ladder. He hung upside down, his face stopping just above hers. Allison cried out and tried to push him away.

One of the bullets struck a box of signal flares stored in a forward case, setting several on fire. The flares sizzled and hissed and howled and shrieked. A fountain of sparks poured to the deck. The whole box caught then, and flames began licking at the bow from inside the cabin. Certain that a gas line would rupture and blow them all to hell, Allison started to scoot backward between the big engines, hauling Tyler and Wen Li as she went. But she quickly reached the end of the protective hatches, behind which she realized she and the children would be exposed to the guns.

Fire in front, bullets behind.

There was nowhere to go.

As suddenly as they had begun, the huge machine guns fell silent. The flares burned themselves out. The engines had died along with the crew, and the boat bobbed dead in the water.

Allison clutched Wen Li on one side and kept Tyler pinned on the other. He struggled and cried, but she snapped at him and at last he ceased fighting. His cries fell to a whimper. Above the baby's wail she heard only the hiss of rain against hot metal.

Then their boat was bathed in light coming from the other vessel. She could hear the throaty, burbling sound of its engines growing louder as the craft drew near.

Blood and fuel mixed with seawater and swirled at her knees. She covered her children with her body and waited.

Aboard the trawler, the captain was startled to see the two radar blips where he expected only one. He was just calling a warning to Tong when the firefight erupted. Tracer bullets arced through the sky. He spun the wheel hard to port and gunned his engines. The heavy trawler began to come about. He kept hold of the mike, repeatedly calling Tong's vessel. There was no response.

"What is it?" Marshall demanded. He stared out into the blackness, his mind not immediately grasping what it was seeing. Streams of fire scarred the night horizon. Flashes of light flickered against low clouds.

The captain said something to Li Kan, who explained to Marshall. "There is a fight ahead," he said. "He thinks the Chinese have caught the other boat." In the distance they saw more bursts of light and this time heard the awful roar of gunfire.

"He can't leave!" Marshall said frantically. "Tell him he can't! We have to go there! We have to help!"

Li Kan tried his best, arguing heatedly. The captain ignored him. The firefight was aft now, and Marshall was outraged. They were armed, but they were running! The bastard was intending to abandon Allison and Tyler! Desperately Marshall tried to push the captain aside, to take the wheel himself. The captain turned and clubbed him viciously on his bad ear, knocking him to the deck. Marshall struggled back to his feet, his ear bleeding. Li Kan restrained his friend as a sailor materialized from the bridge deck, his weapon raised threateningly.

Realizing there was nothing he could do by force, Marshall ran outside and stood watching in the rain. He could see flames rising from the water now, and the lights of a boat, but no detail. Helplessly he watched the flames receding as the trawler left the scene behind. He ran back into the wheelhouse and thrust his bag of money at the captain. He pulled out a handful of dollars and shook it in the captain's face. "Here!" he said. "Take it! You can have it all, and more! Take me back! We've got to try! Please!" The captain turned away, his face hard. There wasn't enough money on earth to tempt him to steer his ship into *that*.

Fifteen minutes later the trawler crossed back into the safety of Hong Kong territorial waters. The captain never slowed, his course set straight for Victoria harbor. Marshall slumped outside on the deck, sobbing, his knees drawn up to his chest. On his way out of the wheelhouse he'd dropped the bag, its top still open. A pile of hundred-dollar bills spilled out onto the deck. A few peeled off and flittered to the sea.

Li Kan stood by, wretched and helpless, watching his friend. Then he stooped to gather the bills that were left, stuffing them back into the bag.

The Chinese attack cruiser slowly approached the burning boat, powerful searchlights illuminating its cockpit and flying bridge. A dozen sailors trained their weapons upon the boat, alert for the slightest motion. Three bodies were clearly visible. One slumped over the upper wheel, the other draped over the gunwale, the third caught in the ladder, hanging upside down by one leg. A ribbon of bullet holes perforated the hull, extending from the gunwale to the waterline. Rudderless and adrift, the boat was already taking on water and beginning to list. As the navy boat passed aft of the stern, its lights illuminated the interior. Tong Gangzi lay sprawled across one of the engine hatches, its gleaming white surface running with his blood. They saw him move. He was still alive, but beyond resistance.

Colonel Quan and Major Ma stood on either side of the captain, watching as the scene unfolded. The shadows between compartments were soon bathed in light. They saw the woman crouching near the lower helmsman's seat, nearly obscured by one of the hatches. She was still alive, shielded by the engines between which she had hidden. The crew of the navy boat stared at her in astonishment, having expected only Tong Gangzi's men to be aboard. Behind her, flames licked at the cabin.

Quan Yi stared down at Allison as she looked up into the blinding lights. Her face seemed as familiar to him as if she were an old friend. Her arms were spread over something, and he realized she was shielding the boy and the baby with her own body. *To the end, a remarkable woman. You have been both lucky and unlucky this night neh? You have lived, but you have lost.*

The captain barked orders. Two sailors dragged a bulky fire hose across the deck and trained a stream of seawater on the flames. Two others, clutching machine pistols, made ready to leap aboard the cruiser, to make certain Tong's men were all dead. Behind them others stood watch, weapons at the ready, while others prepared ropes to lash to the sinking craft once the fires were out.

Ma Lin stared, too. Quan had said nothing about his orders for the one-sided firefight, which had lasted only seconds. Ma Lin was not disturbed by the manner in which Quan Yi had dealth with Tong Gangzi, although he would have preferred to have the man on his interrogation table before seeing him shot. Now Tong might well die before he had that chance.

Ma Lin did not understand the recklessness, however, that had prompted Quan to order the naval vessel to open fire while the woman and children were on board.

Now he stared down at the face of Allison Turk, at her outstretched arms, shielding her son and the baby from harm. He saw the fear and the defiance in her eyes as she looked into the lights that blinded her, stared up into the mystery ship that had rained so much sudden death. And he saw her determination, this *lao wai* woman who, for a baby, had led them on a chase across the whole of south China.

Yet another woman who will die rather than yield.

He felt no sense of elation in her capture, no victory, no satisfaction. Instead he felt old and worn out and haunted, just as he had with everyone else involved in this case—the old man and his wife, and Yi Ling, who had all suffered so much for these babies. Yi Ling in particular had eaten at him. The information she had provided after being tortured had come to nothing: worthless leads extracted at horrible cost from a child no older than his own daughter. Not since her death had he felt so vile. And now he was looking down at the latest victim of the case, a woman hunted for trying to kidnap a child the state didn't want anyway—a baby cast off, like the countless thousands of Lao Ding and Suzhou—children with no names and no future.

Just as the boats bumped gently into each other, a nervous sailor saw a movement just behind Allison. Thinking it was one of Tong Gangzi's men, he raised his weapon and fired. The bullet went high, slamming into the deck of the flying bridge. Splinters flew from the deck, and one of them hit Allison. She screamed, one hand going to her neck as she sank from her knees to a sitting position.

The noise galvanized Ma Lin into action. For the first time in his life, he acted on instinct, against order, against authority, against overwhelming odds. In thirty years he had never drawn his weapon except for practice, but now he ripped it from his leather holster and fired twice into the air. "Stop! Hold your fire!" he yelled, brandishing his weapon at the astonished sailors. The man who had shot at Allison stood frozen, his weapon at the ready. No one moved. Breathing heavily, Ma Lin held his gun to the captain's head. "Tell your men to put down their weapons," he ordered. The captain gaped at him, not comprehending.

Quan's face was ashen with disbelief. He stared dumbly at his old friend. "What are you doing, Ma Lin?" he asked quietly.

Ma Lin ignored him. "Tell them!" he said again to the captain.

"Do as he says," the captain ordered. His sailors complied instantly.

"Get your corpsman down there," Ma said, nodding toward the cruiser. "See if she's all right." The captain snapped the order, and the cruiser's medical corpsman slung his bag over his shoulder and climbed down into the boat.

Tyler saw blood on Allison's shirt. He held Wen Li tightly in both arms. His face was white with shock. "Are you all right?" he whispered.

"I'm okay," she said as she looked up at the other boat, trying to understand what was happening. She saw men and guns and heard shouts and wondered if the Chinese were going to murder them all. "Stay behind me," she said. Warily she watched the corpsman approach. She saw he had no firearms. She knew she couldn't fight him anyway and waited. He knelt over her. Expertly, quickly, he tended to her wound. The splinter had torn a gash in her neck, exposing muscle. "It's just a flesh wound," he called up.

Major Ma felt no fear, only purpose. He ignored Quan Yi's repeated entreaties that he come to his senses before it was too late. "There is nothing you can do against all these men," Quan said. "Your situation is quite hopeless."

"Perhaps so, Quan Yi," Ma Lin replied, his voice wavering a little. "But it is *my* situation." He issued more orders to the captain. Soon one of the cruiser's two tenders, a dinghy with an outboard motor, was lowered from the afterdeck into the water. It was brought around next to Tong's boat. Acting on Ma Lin's shouted orders, the medical corpsman helped Allison stand. She was shaking, a little in shock, but she reached back and took Tyler's hand in her own, letting him keep hold of Wen Li. The sailor led them across the deck of the sinking boat. Allison and then Tyler stepped into the dinghy, where another sailor stood to help.

Ma Lin knew the *lao wai* had little chance on the tender, but their alternative was no chance at all. His own options were limited. He couldn't go with the *lao wai*. If he did, the cruiser would follow, of course, and blow them from the water. Besides, he had no desire to flee to Hong Kong. His place was China.

The only chance was to set the tender on the right course, to show the woman and the boy the direction to follow on the compass, and then, keeping Quan and the captain as his hostages, order the cruiser back to the mainland while the *lao wai* tried to make Hong Kong. The currents favored them, but not much else. There was no telling what the storm might do. If it worsened, their little boat would be swamped. But none of that mattered. It was the only possible way. The woman had braved death to come this far. If all he could do was to give her one more chance, then that was what he would do.

As Ma Lin stood issuing orders, he knew what would be facing him when it was all over. He didn't care. The realization gave him the first sense of exhilaration he'd felt since the birth of his daughter so many years before.

As the dinghy pulled away from the cruiser, a desperate Quan Yi leapt toward Ma Lin, trying to knock the gun from his hand.

The major was ready. Barely moving his pistol from the captain's head, he shot his old friend, the colonel from Beijing.

All the next day, in the gloomy gray light of the seemingly permanent rainstorm, every available craft belonging to the Marine Region of the Royal Hong Kong Police Force patrolled the waters near the reported incident. Marshall had been allowed to ride in the command vessel, the *Sea Panther*. He wore a slicker and stood in the rain on the bridge deck, his eyes glued to the high-powered Royal Navy binoculars the captain had lent him. He scanned the horizon, listening dully as, behind him, the captain orchestrated the massive effort. There were twenty-three police craft participating in the search, with helicopters and light planes standing by in the event the ceiling lifted sufficiently for an air search. But it was clear that would not happen for some time yet. The wipers beat furiously on the *Sea Panther*'s windscreen, testament to the storm's dreary determination.

Marshall muttered about the rain, but the captain told him they were lucky even so. Despite light rain there was no wind, and the seas stayed calm. Were it otherwise, any search at all would be impossible.

Every so often Marshall spotted bits of flotsam bobbing on the water, and he'd yell out even before the official watch saw anything. The most promising bits were fished from the sea with gaff hooks and inspected carefully. It was always nothing, just trash cast off from passing ships or washed down the Pearl River from the mainland. Each time, Marshall breathed a sigh of relief. He didn't know whether he was more afraid to find something than to not find something.

He saw numerous private boats, motorized junks and small yachts and fishing boats, an entire fleet chartered by a score of different news agencies, whose reporters were anxious to catch the first glimpse of wreckage, or bodies floating on the water, or any other sign of the skirmish. The news had flashed all over the colony once Marshall had gone to the authorities for help. From the colony it had flashed all over the world.

In Beijing the Foreign Ministry denied that any armed confrontation involving the fugitives had taken place. From Kowloon the BBC reported that Allison Turk, her son, Tyler, and the baby, Wen Li, were missing at sea and presumed captured or dead.

The two fleets crisscrossed the vast expanse of water, the Hong Kong police methodically, the reporters haphazardly.

The hours passed with wretched empty slowness. Day became dusk. Half an hour after dark, the captain of the *Sea Panther* regretfully informed Marshall Turk that the search was being abandoned for the day.

That night, with Li Kan's help, Marshall hired another boat, to continue the search himself. A private helicopter stood by in Kowloon, its pilot waiting in case the weather lifted.

Marshall stayed out all night on the boat.

The sea gave him nothing.

Three hours after the *lao wai* parted from the Chinese naval vessel, the propeller of their little outboard got hopelessly fouled on kelp. They yanked at the slimy stuff but were unable to free it. Tyler volunteered to get into the water, where he'd have a better angle, but Allison wouldn't hear of it. They took up oars, propping them in the oarlocks and straining against the sea. They both had trouble. Allison's shoulder and neck throbbed painfully. It was hard for her to apply the same force to both oars. Tyler took turns with her, grunting as he worked the heavy blades. They kept at it for hours, stopping frequently to rest and tend their blisters.

The rain was steady and they had to bail every so often with an empty tin can they found in an emergency stores compartment. They found matches, too, but had nothing to light. There was tinned food, but nothing to open it with. Tyler had his knife, and they dined on mackerel and stale biscuits. There was fresh water in small plastic jerricans.

At first Allison watched the compass to keep their course, the way the sailor had showed her. But then it seemed pointless. They were half rowing, half drifting, with no way to tell whether they were keeping to their bearing or not. They scanned the horizon constantly. Once they saw a ship, a big container vessel. Allison scrambled for the flare gun the sailor had given her. She checked the chamber to be sure there was a cartridge. She aimed high, closed her eyes, and pulled the trigger. Nothing happened. She pulled the trigger again. Nothing. Tyler stood and whooped, waving his shirt wildly while she ripped at the chamber, putting in a second round. It, too, was a dud. The ship disappeared into a gray wall of rain.

Tyler took naturally to the sea, but late in the afternoon Allison got sick. The corpsman had given her some pills. Allison was certain they were the problem, even though the little boat bobbed endlessly up and down on the gentle seas. She spent much of the time leaning over the gunwale, retching, or on her back in the bottom of the boat, too nauseated to sit up. When that happened no one rowed, because then Tyler had to keep an eye on Wen Li, who was not feeling well herself and fussed endlessly. Allison did her best to help but was too sick and weak to do much. Tyler fed Wen Li and changed her, and Allison smiled gratefully through her misery. She heard him cussing—"You little shit, you're going overboard!"—but he took good care of her. His attention lagged once, and Wen Li slipped away from him into the foul water in the keel. He bent to get her and lost one of the oars. The blade knifed down into the water and jumped from its oarlock. He lunged for it, but it was gone. Madly he paddled with the other oar, but the boat turned circles while the oar disappeared. Frustrated, exhausted, he gave up, angrily tossing the other oar into the bottom of the boat. It was getting dark. Tyler nestled up against Allison and took Wen Li in his lap. They drifted and slept fitfully.

Allison woke once and it was night. The storm had eased. She felt a little better and drank some water, and stroked Tyler's forehead. He was fast asleep, Wen Li still in his lap. Overhead she saw fields of stars between rolling banks of clouds. She saw the big dipper once but couldn't remember whether the North Star poured out the dipper or dropped from the tail. And then clouds swallowed the dipper again, and it didn't matter anyway.

When she opened her eyes again, she had to blink away the sun. Startled, she realized the storm had lifted. She looked up over the gunwale and her face lit with excitement. "Tyler! Wake up!"

They saw rocks on a ragged coast that jutted up from the sea, and the long, low walls of a prison or jail. Observation posts stood at the corners, and wicked curls of concertina wire looped along the walls.

"Is it China?" he asked when he saw it. The question chilled her. She couldn't tell. Houses were perched on hillsides. Traffic snaked along wooded roads, car windows glinting in the sun. Wherever it was, it was beautiful. She had never been so relieved to see anything in her life.

They heard breakers then, pounding on the rocks. The waves were beginning to pitch them toward the shore. She thought the little craft would be smashed to bits. She thought about trying to row again, to fight it. But she knew it was useless. She just wasn't strong enough, not against the waves.

She told Tyler to lie down on their bag. She got down next to him. They sheltered Wen Li between them. She wondered if she could somehow carry both children and swim at the same time and knew she could not. The boat surged and eased, the waves lifting and settling and lifting again. She tensed and closed her eyes, waiting.

And then over the waves she heard voices. Chinese voices. She really didn't care if they were caught, because she was so afraid of the rocks. She *wanted* to be caught. Then there were hands on the side of the boat, strong hands and a rope. The tender slowed and then came to rest, crunching on a bed of sand. She felt it being dragged a little way up onto the shore. The next moment a cop was standing over them. A second cop appeared at his side. The two men stared down at the apparition from the sea.

"You must be Mrs. Turk," said one in clear English.

Allison nodded weakly in wary surprise. "Is this China?" she asked.

"It's always been China, Mrs. Turk," the guard replied. "But not officially again until next year. For now, welcome to the Crown colony of Hong Kong. The whole world has been looking for you."

Allison tried to stand but couldn't. She was weak and nauseated, and they helped her back down. Tyler stood up, holding Wen Li. One of the guards steadied him by the elbow, but Tyler's legs were rubbery and he grew dizzy and nearly fell. He was so relieved at the feel of land beneath his legs, and that he didn't have to try anymore, that he started to shake all over. Then he began to cry. One of the guards tried to take Wen Li from him, intending only to help the obviously exhausted boy, but he wouldn't let go of her. When the officer gently but firmly insisted, Tyler kicked him viciously in the shin. The man prudently backed off, content to wait until someone in higher authority could get there to deal with the ill-mannered little bugger. Tyler sat down again in the boat next to Allison and waited. He rocked back and forth with the baby.

The guards had seen the boat coming from a distance, had seen its occupants through their binoculars, and had reported their discovery over the radio. Within minutes the roads near the Stanley prison on the south side of Hong Kong island swarmed with police and reporters and curious onlookers. Allison heard them and watched through a haze of relief and emotion and disbelief. Someone brought her a blanket. An ambulance slowly made its way down the hill and through the crowd, lights flashing.

Then, above the noise and the confusion, she heard the *whump-whump* of a helicopter. She'd heard the sound before, when they were hunting her, and the deafening noise made her cringe. The sunlight gleamed off the copter's nose. Allison watched the craft come down. It landed in a clearing behind the prison, the surrounding trees whipping in the wind.

She saw the door open and a dark-haired man get out, crouching as he ran to clear the blades of the helicopter. He straightened up and she saw him running across the parking lot, pushing and shoving at the tourists and reporters who blocked his way. She struggled to stand then, casting off her blanket and pushing away the gentle hands that encouraged her to stay where she was. She began to cry, and even from the distance she saw that he was crying, too.

Tyler saw her and looked around, to see what she was seeing, and his eyes lit up like the sunrise.

"Dad!" he shouted. "Dad!" And he was up then, much faster than Allison. Still holding on to Wen Li, he ran toward his father, his Mao cap falling down around his eyes. He snatched it off and they banged together in a whirlwind of laughter and tears. Marshall lifted them both easily from the ground, kissing and hugging them, and even as he did, he was still half running toward Allison.

A moment later they were all together, oblivious to the commotion around them. Flashbulbs strobed and reporters yelled and they heard none of it. Allison touched his cheeks and melted in his arms. "Thank God," he whispered. "I thought I'd never see you again."

She looked up at him, tears streaming down her face. "There's someone I'd like you to meet," she said. She lifted Wen Li from Tyler's arms. The baby was screaming, and Allison held her up. She remembered something Marshall said sometimes, when he went fishing. "I had some trouble hauling her in," Allison said, "but she's a keeper."

Marshall choked up and couldn't say anything. He just nodded and smiled and wiped the tears from Allison's cheeks. She said something else, but he couldn't hear over the noise, and then he caught her as she dissolved into his arms, totally spent. "It's all right," he murmured. "It's all right. You're safe now. We're all safe now."

He picked her up and climbed with her into the waiting ambulance. Tyler, holding Wen Li once again, climbed in behind. The doors slammed shut. Klaxon blaring, the ambulance made its way through the gathering throng.

CHAPTER 24

"ARE THE REPORTS TRUE that the CIA was instrumental in helping Mrs. Turk to escape?"

The White House press secretary betrayed none of the pleasure he felt at having such a rumor floating at all. Sometimes, he thought, no matter how badly things got bolluxed up, they somehow worked out for the best. "I can neither confirm nor deny that," he said gravely with his best "yes, that's true" inflection. "It would be counterproductive to discuss our methods or any specifics about this case. I can only say that this administration has been deeply involved every step of the way in ensuring the safety and well-being of all the families involved in this unfortunate affair. We continue to press the Chinese government for word about the status and whereabouts of the remaining two women, Ms. Pollard and Mrs. Cameron."

Later that afternoon the Justice Department announced that the child Wen Li Turk was being formally admitted to the United State under a regulation granting broad authority to the attorney general to permit a person to enter the country for emergency reasons or for the public interest. The government of the People's Republic of China had no public comment on the decision.

NANCHANG PRISON
Jiangxi Province

A steel door clanked open loudly and then closed again. Distant footsteps echoed in the hallway. Major Ma Lin felt his pulse quicken. The footsteps were for him. They grew louder, closer, and then stopped outside the door of his cell. He heard low voices. Someone fumbled for keys. Outside the prison walls, a rooster crowed faintly. A key clattered in the lock and the door swung open.

Three officers filed into the cell. One carried a sheaf of papers on a clipboard. "You are Ma Lin?" he inquired formally.

"I am."

"You know of the crimes of which you have been convicted?"

"I do."

"If you wish, I will read them for you."

"There is no need."

"Very well. You are aware of your sentence?"

"I am."

"It is my duty to inform you that your petition to overturn that sentence has been denied." No such petition had been made, but the words were read anyway.

"I understand."

"It is my further duty to carry out the court's sentence." He sounded almost apologetic, Ma Lin thought. The man had worked for the major more than once.

"Yes."

His ankle chains were unlocked and he was allowed to stand. He wanted to rub his feet. They were numb and he felt clumsy. But they held him by the arms and moved him to the wall and stood him there with his back to it. A guard raised a camera and tried to take his photograph. The flash didn't work. Muttering, the guard tried again. The second time it worked and Ma Lin blinked with the bright light.

Another man approached him. It was the prison's doctor. He carried a battered tin tray on which rested two syringes. With the first, an empty one, he drew a sample of Ma Lin's blood from the vein of his arm. With the next he injected an anticoagulant. He worked quickly, expertly, and when he was done he put a small ball of cotton on Ma Lin's arm and covered it with a bandage. If he noticed irony in the gesture, he gave no sign of it.

Ma Lin's captors remained polite and correct. One of his jailers asked him to please turn and face the wall. Steel handcuffs were clamped around his wrists, less tightly than usual. Certain accommodations were made for prisoners of rank. He was not gagged, as they all knew he would not try to incite other prisoners as he was being led outside. Then one of them used a roll of tape to bind the bottoms of his pant legs. Ma Lin knew it was so that when he soiled himself, the guards would not have to bother with it. It was the only time he felt himself falter, when he thought of that.

They led him from the cell and down the hallway, one guard in front, the other two close behind. Some prisoners had to be dragged down these corridors, but Ma Lin's nerve betrayed no sign of failure. His step was steady.

The condemned were often taken to sports arenas, their sentences carried out in public. But in this instance there was to be no public display. No sign around his neck; no placard bearing his name with a crude X drawn through. Ma Lin and the two others who would die today would do so anonymously, so his own journey was therefore blessedly brief.

At the end of the hall there was another steel door with a metal bar. The lead guard pushed it open and stepped aside as Ma Lin walked through. Outside he paused and looked up. What he could see of the sky was blue and clear. It was the first time he had been outdoors since being brought to the prison. The air was heavy, hellish hot and humid, and he smelled the acid fumes of traffic. Nanchang was a hellhole. He preferred the air of the north, dirtier but always cooler and drier, but after the air in his cell it smelled wonderful anyway. He saw the first rays of sun just striking one of the high masonry walls. He was marched quickly to the other side of the dirt enclosure, where he was forced to kneel. His guards stood behind him, waiting. No one spoke.

Another steel door banged open. Two other men were brought through it into the courtyard, several minutes apart. He was surprised to see them. His own efforts had helped bring them here, but he had not known they would die beside him this day.

Dr. Cai Tang struggled fiercely at first, yelling and crying like a child. They gagged him tightly. Then he collapsed, and they dragged him the last few feet, his shoes leaving a gash in the dirt. Ma Lin was embarrassed for the doctor's loss of dignity. He had seen it many times: the doctor was a man who would not die well. His pants, too, had been tied at the ankles, and his arm bore the same patch of cotton that his own did, from where they'd taken his blood and administered the anticoagulants. In his case, the injection had not been voluntary.

The last prisoner was brought in then. He was the overlord of Lao Ding, the man who had conceived of the monstrous scheme. There was no longer any fight in him, though his body bore evidence that there had been not long before. The guards had to support him as he walked. His cheeks were puffed black and blue, his fingers covered in bloody gauze, his right foot crippled. His interrogation had been efficient, his trial swift and secret. An hour from now, his tragic and untimely death from a massive cerebral hemorrhage would be announced to the press.

He had been caught only because Tong Gangzi, captain of the Black Bamboo, had regained consciousness briefly after being shot at sea, just long enough to reveal his identity to Ma Lin, still in control of the naval vessel. Now the once powerful man was pushed roughly onto his knees, to die.

When arrested, he had refused to say anything at all, but under the vigorous interrogation of his subordinates he finally talked, until there was nothing left to be told. Arrests had been made in three provinces on the basis of his statements. More were expected.

Ma Lin knew all of this because the previous evening, as an act of courtesy, he had been allowed to read a copy of the man's full written statement. From that confession Ma Lin learned that they had all come to this courtyard because of the petty greed of Director Lin, the man who ran the Number Three Children's Welfare Institute outside Suzhou. Director Lin's orphanage was one of five working the same scheme, under the supervision of Tong Gangzi.

Babies normally came to the orphanage through official channels, after having been orphaned or, more commonly, abandoned by their parents. Those children became wards of the state, which contributed to their support. Some were adopted, many died, and the rest were released onto the streets. Every day more poured through the front doors—a flood of them, too many to track. They were children in whom the state had little interest, and it was in that reality that the scheme flourished. Healthy children were declared dead by Dr. Cai and sent to the jungle. Other children, near death, were supposedly transferred to hospitals, when in fact their true destination was Ward Yellow of Lao Ding. This much, Ma Lin had learned from the doctor.

Director Lin was also buying babies privately, paying destitute mothers for children they had to abandon anyway. In this manner he obtained children off the books of the state, babies who could also be substituted for those funneled off illegally. Four other orphanages were doing the same thing, to feed the insatiable hunger of Lao Ding.

It would have continued that way, but for the avarice of Director Lin.

He and his cousin, a clerk at Civil Affairs, had seen a way to make money twice—money that could be hidden from the triad. By shuffling papers, they collected funds from the province for children officially in their care, by substituting children bought privately. They needed only to be able to account for a certain number of live bodies. Even after the children had been diverted to Lao Ding, there were enough other babies that Director Lin could continue receiving money from the province for their care, even after the triad had collected the profits from their sale. It was a huge shell game, with children beneath the shells.

What the ministry paid for the care of children who otherwise would have been removed from the books as dead—children who in reality had been spirited away to be sold at Lao Ding—was a trifling amount. Yet it was that very pittance that had unraveled the entire enterprise. Director Lin had been in Bangkok when his cousin, his accomplice at Civil Affairs, contracted pneumonia and died. The paperwork for the six babies of Suzhou hadn't been switched yet, meaning the documents on their way to the Americans were for children who had already been adopted, while the children the Americans actually received had been bought off the black market. Their files contained the wrong physical descriptions, and, most damning, even the wrong footprints. If discovered, the files would have exposed the whole scheme.

By the time Director Lin returned from Thailand, his cousin was dead and the Americans already had the babies. Unable to fix the paperwork itself, he realized the only way to salvage the situation was to get the babies themselves back from the Americans and to substitute others. He seized upon the technicality of special needs, a legitimate requirement generally ignored by the Ministries of Justice and Civil Affairs.

His plan would have worked, except that three of the American families did not do as ordered. Their flight placed him in great danger, potentially exposing his crimes. He had no good choices. For help he had to turn either to the police or to his own triad, the Black Bamboo. He *had* to choose the police, knowing that if the truth was discovered, that he had been stealing from the triad, it would mean his own death sentence. But Tong Gangzi had already suspected the truth and obtained the files himself. A day later Director Lin and his family were dead.

Tong Gangzi knew it was important to remove all traces of the six children, in the event that records he did not possess or even know about—records from hospitals or police stations—might come to light.

Director Lin had seen to the first three babies himself, sending them to Lao Ding. When Claire Cameron was captured, Dr. Cai had been sent to remove her child from the orphanage at Hukou. Upon Tai's death, it was Dr. Cai once again who removed her body from the hospital.

Only the child Wen Li had remained free. Thanks to the efforts of Marshall Turk's law partner, who was feeding information about Allison Turk's movements to the Ministry of Public Security, Tong Gangzi had that child taken care of as well. He could have ended everything at the monastery of Taoping but saw a way to collect a great deal of money for himself, from Marshall Turk. His greed, and his misjudgment of Colonel Quan Yi, proved fatal.

The colonel himself had been used all along, assigned to the case because it was believed he would apprehend the Americans quickly. Their babies would simply disappear, with no one the wiser. But Quan had failed to catch the fugitives as fast as everyone expected, in addition to which he had followed more than just their trail. Against the direct orders of his superiors, he had investigated the death of Director Lin. Then, again disobeying orders, he had refused to return to Beijing when relieved of duty by the man who now knelt next to Ma Lin in the courtyard.

The one-eyed prisoner looked over at him, blinking through a crust of blood and serum that had formed around his good eye. He was no longer fearsome to behold. Instead he looked pathetic. He seemed at first not to recognize the major, whom he had known for years.

"Is that you, Ma Lin?" he asked at last. His voice was weak and raspy.

"*Shì*, Deputy Minister," the major replied.

"So. You die for this, too. It seems . . ." He coughed. "Do you have a cigarette?"

Before Ma Lin could answer, a steel door banged open behind them. The deputy minister craned his neck, trying to see. The doctor began to moan.

Quan Yi emerged into the courtyard, his arm still in a sling. He was in no mood to prolong the morning's business. He strode briskly forward to the kneeling line of prisoners. He began with the deputy minister. In imperial China, the executioner never faced his victim, for fear the soul of the dead man might return to haunt him. Quan Yi, however, was a man of modern China. He looked into the deputy minister's good eye, to be certain the prisoner knew his executioner. Then he drew his pistol from its holster and stepped around behind him.

Ma Lin flinched as the roar of the shot reverberated from the prison walls.

Quan Yi next stood before the doctor, who was weeping and sobbing through his gag. The doctor would not look up. Quan Yi placed the barrel of his pistol under the man's chin and made him look up. He let go, then stepped around behind him. A new sound of muffled terror arose from the doctor's throat. His eyes bulged and he lurched forward, trying to escape the bullet.

The gun roared again.

Finally, carrying with him now the smell of powder and blood, Quan Yi stood before Ma Lin.

The major looked up at his old mentor and friend. They each understood what was in the eyes of the other. In one, contentment. In the other, resolve.

"I am glad it is you, Quan Yi," Ma Lin said at last. "I had hoped it would not be a stranger."

"I am sorry it is you, Ma Lin," the colonel replied. For the last time, Quan stepped around behind the prisoner. Ma Lin bowed his head. He felt the gun barrel, now hot, against the base of his skull.

An odd thought occurred to him just then.

He had no close family left alive. The state would have to pay for the bullet.

The three bodies were dragged away to ambulances waiting just inside the prison gate. Forty-five minutes later, insulated coolers holding kidneys, livers, corneas, and one pancreas—for which an advance order had been received from Taipei—were placed aboard a jet, en route to the PLA's hospital at Nanfeng.

Seven years was not so bad, Yi Ling thought. She could manage seven years. She was only thankful it hadn't been more. The procurator had threatened her with fifteen. There was no trial, just the sentence. One day they put her in the back of a wagon and brought her to the Shenda Hand Tool Works in Linping town. Shenda made wrenches, hardware, and wire and was more commonly known to its workforce as the Provincial Number Two prison camp.

Yi Ling made galvanized iron wire for export to the United States. She

worked seventy hours a week running a spooling machine that fed the
wire onto heavy wooden bolts. It was difficult at first because she was not
used to heavy physical labor. Her ears ached from the whine of the
machinery, and at night her muscles cramped painfully. She nursed constant cuts from the wire. The gloves they'd given her were worn through,
and the metal strands sliced her hands to shreds. The foreman told her
that if she slept with him, she could move to the plumbing wrench area,
where the machines were quieter and the work was easier. He even promised a new pair of gloves. She stayed at the spooling machine.

She slept on a floor mat in a barracks with thirty other women. They
ate from a communal pot, and at night they shared pictures and stories.
The women who had been there for a while told her the worst part was the
winters, when there was no heat. Collect clothing, they said, but there was
no way to collect it.

Her life settled into a routine, and the weeks passed into months, and
she knew she could do it. The worst part was not knowing about the others. First in jail and now at the tool works, no one would tell her anything.
Maybe no one knew whether Yang Boda had survived or what had become
of his father and mother, her own grandparents. Someone—the major, she
thought—had said once her uncle was in a hospital, asking for her. Or had
they? Her memory of that was vague, and she wasn't at all certain she
hadn't dreamed it. She dreamed a lot. Most often the dreams were about
the babies. She could summon them up in her imagination as clearly as if
she'd seen them the day before.

They brought the only joy to her life, those babies. It was harder with
the three women and the boy Tyler. She couldn't see their faces as clearly.
She hoped she wouldn't lose them altogether.

In Denver, Allison and Marshall gave no interviews to the press. The
State Department had warned them they would only jeopardize Ruth and
Claire. Allison was beside herself with worry and couldn't sit by. She and
Marshall mounted a massive campaign of letters and phone calls, while
the world press kept up the heat. Human rights groups took up the case of
Yi Ling, whose whereabouts were unknown.

Allison sent money to the fisherman Ren Kai and his wife, Mei Ling,
with photographs of Wen Li but no letter, in case the mail might be
opened by the authorities. The authorities, however, had already picked
him up. Ren Kai denied ever seeing the *lao wai*. He was able to prove his

boat had been searched by officers and that nothing had been found. The guide Yi Ling was asked to identify him, in exchange for two years off her sentence. She studied his face carefully and said they had the wrong man. The Pollard woman said the same thing. After two weeks of detention, Ren Kai was released.

Just after their return, Marshall summoned the courage to confess what he'd done while Allison was running, that he'd tried to have her captured for her own safety and that of Tyler. She was stunned, and she choked with rage. "How *could* you?" she cried, reliving her terror. "You have no *idea* what you almost did." And she slapped him so hard that her hand hurt and she collapsed in sobs. In the first few moments her fury and hurt were so great that she was certain their marriage was over.

But the weeks passed, and as she healed and China became more remote in her memory, the pain dimmed somewhat. They lay awake together at night and talked, and she slowly came to a bittersweet understanding of what he had done. She began to forgive. Her task was made easier by the fact that—as she had known all along that he would—Marshall clearly adored Wen Li, as the child adored him. She rode everywhere on his shoulders, legs wrapped around his neck as his hands steadied hers. She hunched over like a hawk, surveying the world at her feet. Once she threw up on him from her perch. He didn't flinch as it cascaded down over his head. He didn't mind at all. Only real fathers didn't mind that sort of thing.

It took Tyler about a month to become less protective and more like a big brother, by turns tormenting and tender. His friends came over and played with the curious little baby with almond eyes and luminescent personality.

Tyler puffed up at that, and told them big stories about China.

BEIJING, JULY 22—(REUTERS WORLD SERVICE): The south China province of Guangdong executed 33 people yesterday for involvement in a prostitution and kidnapping ring near the town of Lao Ding, the official Xinhua news agency reported. More than 70 others were convicted of lesser unspecified offenses involving corruption and bribery and sentenced to varying terms in labor camps.

The Ministry of Foreign Affairs denied widespread reports,

including allegations by the HongKong–based Human Rights Watch/Asia organization, that the cases involved the abuse of children in a privately run orphanage. "No such orphanage even exists," the statement said. "These are nothing but the slanderous fabrications of a discredited organization, aimed at damaging the international image of China. The People's Republic has always shown the greatest compassion for its children and their rights."

One late summer evening they were returning to their home on Forest Parkway after a long walk. Tyler rode his bicycle and Wen Li perched atop Marshall's shoulders. Down the street they saw a taxi round the corner and pull up in front of their house. The door opened and a woman got out. Allison squinted, but it was Tyler who knew instantly. "Ruth!" he called, and he pedaled furiously to greet her. His bicycle pitched to the grass and he ran to hug her.

She tousled his hair. "Last time I saw you, you were consorting with pigs," she said. "I see you're keeping better company now."

A moment later the two women were hugging, crying, and laughing at the same time. Ruth looked thinner, but her spirit was strong and her face was shining.

"They told me you made it," Ruth said through her tears, when she could say anything at all. "I had to come see for myself."

"I didn't know you were out," Allison said. "We'd have come to meet you. God, we've been crazy with worry."

"They didn't publicize it. They put me on a plane in Shanghai in the middle of the night. When I got to L.A. I just kept coming."

"I'm so sorry about Tai," Allison said. She brushed the hair from Ruth's forehead. "When they finally acknowledged they had arrested you, they . . . well, they said that she had died."

Marshall arrived then, and Allison introduced them. Ruth looked up at Wen Li on his shoulders. Her eyes glistened and Marshall leaned down so she could take the child. Wen Li was tentative at first, but she remembered, and soon she and Ruth were fast friends once again.

"What about Claire?"

"We were on the same plane. They told her they'd let her out if she signed a confession."

"Did she?"

"Yes. She just wanted out. They told me that, too, but I wouldn't sign. I think they let me go because I cost too much to feed and they got tired of my lip."

"What are you going to do now?"

A look of excitement crossed Ruth's face. She handed Wen Li to Allison and pulled a fat envelope from her purse. She extracted a batch of papers. "There was a man from the State Department who met me in L.A. and he gave these to me. Six of them, from all over the world. He said there were more back in Washington. Vietnam, Korea, Bolivia, Romania. Look here—even Kansas." There were photographs of babies and letters from orphanages and parents. "I guess I'm pretty famous for a nonmom. Suddenly I've got a choice. And I think it might have already been made for me."

"How so?"

"Look at this one, from Vietnam." Ruth pulled out a photo of a scrawny, frizzy-haired, wide-eyed waif. "See there? Only eight months old and already her hair looks as wild as mine, like she got it done in an electrical socket. Can you believe it?"

"God, she's beautiful. What's her name?"

Ruth smiled. "That's the best part; it's how I know. The name on her birth certificate is Wi Duc Tu."